WISDOM

She is ageless, boundless…ruthless.

W I S D O M

a novel by Patrick Tylee

CAMEL
NEEDLE &
ASSOCIATES

Copyright © 2015 Patrick Tylee

Published in 2015 by Camel Needle & Associates ®.

Camel Needle & Associates

PO BOX 57101

Tucson, AZ 85732-7101

www.patricktylee.com

Library of Congress Cataloging-in-Publication Data

Tylee, Patrick

Wisdom / Patrick Tylee – 1st American Edition

Library of Congress Control Number: 2014944792

ISBN Paperback   978-0-9905498-0-2

ISBN-10   990549801

LCCN   2014944792

Cover: Crimson River Productions

Manufactured in the United States of America

To my son Moses,
who reminds me that it's okay to play with things that don't exist.

Acknowledgments

There are many great stories, though most will lie undiscovered. Those found must then be written. Does the story hide itself from the lesser mind, so that the greater may do justice to the depths of a world previously unimagined? Or does the story find the humble one who is willing to risk all, to give life to the unreal, words to thought, and ink to paper?

From that first day when I typed out page one of Wisdom, it was my sincere hope that the characters who'd revealed themselves and their story to me would find satisfaction in being brought to life through my efforts.

A huge debt of gratitude goes out to my editors, Erin M. Hall and Anne Marie Markowitz, and to my Beta-Read Group: Janet, Philip, Patrick, Julie and Louise.

You guys are awesome!

To Deb Bates of Bates & Hook Press: thanks for your friendship, honesty and courage.

A special thank you goes to my dear wife, Chris, who endures the lights being on until way past bedtime, and having to hear every single detail…again. I love you more.

Chapters

Obedient Sand
2470 CE
Polaris Ab4 *(Alruccabah)*

I've existed for centuries, but never as a child. Yet within me is this childlike awe of things that sometimes seem so insignificant. In my travels across the Orion Arm, I've witnessed events to cheer or to abhor, along with the science, nature and the glory of a thousand worlds. But I stand transfixed by this delicate sensation. Here's this one thing: to see and feel these tiny grains of Earth's Cooperative Sand as they trickle between my toes.

Balanced back on the heels of my blue silicone feet, I lift up another little pile of fine, brown silica on the tops of my toes. The lens of my eyes zoom my field of view down to only a few millimeters, right where the crest of a micro-dune is supported by one or two grains at the bottom edge. If I had lungs, I'd hold my breath. The breeze cooperates so as to prevent any slight disturbance to my silly game. I watch the microscopic grains press together. They strain against each other as the weight of the ones higher up presses down. The miniature slope has settled to a state of perfect equilibrium. I feel anxious, like a real human. I wait for the moment of release when chance brings just one crystal of silica to the brink. There's nothing but the whirring hum from my moto-vascular servos deep within my chest.

Any moment now…

"Daddy!"

Instinctively, I blink. The crest heaves as hundreds of grains topple over the edge. The avalanche rushes down the slope, to accelerate across the vertical centimeter. It jumps into space and away in freefall. The shadow of my big toe swallows the crash of the crystals within my tiny personal cataclysm.

She did that on purpose. She's always done things like that on purpose. It's a human trait. I saw it on Earth many times.

"Catch me, Daddy!"

Her symphonic voice goes right through me. I can't stay mad.

She bounds up the dune with a grace and speed as only cybernetic legs will do.

"Hello, my darling," I say. From four meters away she launches herself into the air, straight at me. Oh, this is going to hurt. I can hear her metallic laughter even before she slams into my outstretched arms. We fall backward together down the windward slope of the dune; tumbling, tumbling, tumbling. This is the best. I hear more laughter and realize it's my own. Finally, we reach the bottom. Somehow I've managed to hold onto her, and all of our appendages are still attached as they're meant to be. I stand up from my seated landing and hoist her higher to a more comfortable position in my arms. "Oh, my, you're getting heavier every day! Do you ever stop growing?"

"Now, Daddy," she scolds, "you know very well my weight hasn't changed a single bit in ever. I'm exactly the same as when they grew me again."

True, of course. Except for the new polygold hair, she's still my perfect little Elmyrah, my…adopted daughter from Earth. Even after five reconstructions, with much of her biological self replaced, she's so beautiful, so exquisite. I'll have her forever, my forever child.

"I know," I say, "but on your planet, daddies say that to their little girls quite often."

"Carry me back," she says.

"That's a long way, Em—"

"Do it," she whispers, her warm face against my cold cheek. "Do it or…you know."

We begin to slog up the face of the dune, indeed remittance for the previous amusement. On the hike to the landing site, she doesn't say a word, her face, stony. I worry sometimes how she has taken to worrying. Another example of how she's become more like me. Or more like her, like Wisdom.

Programs aren't supposed to act like that. They're designed to help you. Elmyrah has gone through enough already. I see now how I should've kept them apart.

Perhaps it was an error in judgment on my part to involve Elmyrah in certain distasteful errands, so long ago. And having her bodily mass reanimated, along with some much needed improvements, of course. I'm not convinced that she would've chosen this path for herself. She's lost many of her friends to age and time, an unfortunate consequence of immortality. The guilt of this impossible situation can have a terrible stranglehold upon a person, even an artificial person like me. My own guilt is burden enough, for the things I've done, for the things I've failed to do. You can make a lot of mistakes in the course of four hundred years.

I envy Elmyrah when I catch her crying. At least she can. The part of my programming that causes me to learn and discern truth from my surroundings, from the emotions and thoughts of others, also brought to my mind the realities of love and hate, joy and pain. I'd hoped that my inner turmoil would be vented in that one moment when I pressed the Fire button and sent that immeasurable nuclear wrath upon my enemy. We watched their ships melt in my conjured furnace of hell, hanging weightless in the heavens. The churning surface of their home world brought to a boil, dissolving; a cindered mist blowing away in a puff of stellar wind. *If it was me that did that*.

I was there. But we were all there, the three of us.

There was no satisfactory feeling to the recompense. No feeling. Just…observation. They needed to die, all of them. And now, that's done.

Well, perhaps my darling Elmyrah can cry enough for both of us.

My weight pressing on the ship's first step, it groans and creaks loudly, in a pouty kind of way. Elmyrah and I look at each other with matching smirks.

"Are you ever going to have that fixed?" she asks.

"That's not a problem. That's a feature!" I give her a gentle, tickly poke in the rib cage before we climb aboard our opulent land-able star-craft, Abandon. I admire how the knurled titanium railing transitions to interior platinum and zebra-wood. Aloe-snail upholstery flows in streams over the bama cushions and piles of pillows in several shades of purple. Not just transportation, this is living in luxury while you have to be on the way to someplace else.

When I took delivery of the new TransWave vessel from the Deneb system, the shipwright's representative asked what name they should engrave on the cockpit placard. I looked at my First Officer, Gemmeck, who'd accompanied me.

"What do you think, Gemmie? What shall we call her?" He

shrugged, to avoid my potential displeasure. "C'mon," I pressed, "use your imagination. What's the last word you'd ever want to see next to the word 'ship'?" We all roared with laughter at his well-timed punch line, and it stuck. Abandon Ship, it shall be.

Elmyrah jumps out of my arms and trots down the aisle to paw through her stowage; likely to pick out a couple of Flight Buddies: cozy, stuffed characters to keep her company during the long trip to Lupus' KeKouan. If she falls asleep, I'll busy myself writing in my journal titled, 'Note to Self'. An ink pen on actual paper is my expensive indulgence, much like my printed photo scrapbook.

Lift thrusters begin to raise their howl against the ground below. Elmyrah leans close to rest her head on my shoulder. I figure she'll be asleep by the time we climb out of Alruccabah's pink sky and into the deep blue of space. I'll just pass the time performing a mental edit of my newest sales pitch that I've reserved for the Twin Princes of KeKouan. But who can resist? The marble-sized crystals of Obedient Sand are like magic to most, but merely a natural geologic jovian phenomenon. I mean, really, doesn't everyone have sand that comes alive and responds to your every command? Not yet anyway.

Anomalous, it exists in one star system, Sol. And who has the monopoly on the Obedient Sand of Jupiter? Who has the exclusive rights to the Cooperative Sand of Earth? Yours truly….just forward your nics to—

"Daddy? Tell me the story again about how you saved Earth, how you were made and found me for us to be together forever. And about the Prawl-Tang monster that would've destroyed everyone. Tell me the story, please?"

"My perfect girl," I say, "you don't want to hear that all over again, do you?" I can feel her head nod with enthusiasm against my shoulder. When she behaves childish this way, it almost seems like acting, pretense. Though, in what do we not pretend? She is no child. I am no father. I know that deep within her lurks a reality. She hides it well.

"How many times is it that I've told you the story…hmmm? Ten or twenty, I bet, no?"

"Five hundred, thirty-seven," she whispers into the furry face of Omni-Pooh, the polyester filled Flight Buddy.

Yes, I'm sure that's correct. Of course it's correct. With a brain like hers, mass-optimized and converted into the oxyserum chamber above her pelvis, could she ever be incorrect? I can only imagine how much more intelligent and process capable she is than I will ever be, no matter how many upgrades I get. It's a good thing I bought all those spares. There should be enough extra me and me parts to last…a lifetime. Well, another millennia anyway, if I don't get killed too often like in the early days. Oh, yes, speaking of…

"Okay, my daughter, I'll tell you the story. But nobody was going to destroy us, now, don't be silly. You know better. They just wanted to harvest the Earth."

How can I even say that without stammering?

Memories of those awful days push their way from the archive to my visual cortex, a very human thing to happen, it seems. I am the only patron of a haunted theater, watching the most gruesome, gut wrenching history projected inside my head.

Just harvest the Earth…of everyone…of everything…animal, vegetable and mineral. Doesn't sound so bad if you're billions of miles away and going fast in the opposite direction, Brothers! But I *was* there. I should have been long gone, but I stayed behind, wanting everything to be just so. What if this happened instead? Maybe I will do this and not that. Maybe I will screw everything up.

Boy, did I screw everything up. All I was supposed to do was deliver the message. It shouldn't have been anything fancy or unplanned. Just go there and deliver The Great Deception to the people of Earth. Heck, I could've told them I was Jesus or something and half of them would've volunteered to drop dead for Heaven. Well, the transparent skin over bluish-chrome meat was a sure giveaway. I don't think Jesus had transparent skin.

I hear her snort a little snore - perfect. Well, I really didn't want to tell it again anyway. Who am I kidding? I would tell the story twice to a mirror. Here goes number five hundred, thirty-seven.

"In the beginning...wait...not *my* beginning, and not even *the* beginning. But you know, as far as the Sand is concerned...it all started one day when the sensors on a lost Prawl-Tang ship detected a high probability of a large concentration of hydrogen on a planet in a star system not too terribly far away."

Note to Self

They said they were sending me off alone. Of course that wasn't entirely true. Seemed a bit scary at first. Still, it was good to have someone to talk to. But now, between Elmyrah's constant need for…everything…and Wisdom. What I wouldn't give to be alone in my head, just once.

Jove

Monsters
812 CE
Alnitak High Orbit

"Commander, the screen." The voice over the intercom was controlled, but for the slight quiver and choked consonant. "Here they come now."

Commander Defflan's words were a reflex. "Kill all systems now." His crew knew what orders were coming, but they end up said anyway. "Okay. Go over them again. Make sure everything's off."

Seated two by two in the four-seat reconnaissance starship of the Legion of Worlds Intelligence Corps, they could lean over to cross-check each other's panels for any circuit left active. All good - four gloved thumbs pointed up towards the clear canopy overhead.

Now that all potential electrical and plasma noise was secured so as not to broadcast their presence, the only two methods of communication between crew members was by sign language and good old fashioned gas tubes to yell through. Seals pressed tight and clicked into place, the hiss of gaseous nitrogen-oxygen could be heard filling their rudimentary, X-shaped talk-a-phone.

"Okay, clear on comms?" Defflan asked, again following The Book.

"Affirmative, Sir," the rookie, Priminat, said. He was not quite humanoid, being from Rigel's seventh planet.

"Yaht," said the pilot, Irrique. Not human, he was Crazor, from outer Deneb.

From Lieutenant Schizmar in the right-rear navigator seat, could be heard the imitated sound of a chicken clucking. Like Priminat, Schizmar was a Eutherid, not mammalian.

"Excellent, three officers and some poultry checked in and talk-tubes operating." The humor couldn't pierce the tension of the moment. Lack of laughter told Defflan what he already suspected. They were so far from their base on Rigel Seven, and so deep into Prawl-Tang space; parked on the edge of an asteroid belt in the Alnitak system. The blue giant star seemed to fill half of their field of view out the starboard side of the canopy. The intense light washed out their faces, now grayish yellow instead of natural, sandy gold tones for the three Rigelians. For Irrique, bright sparkles glimmered across his silvery scales and black cheek horns.

"Would the Rookie please operate the foot-pump heater? I think my butt has frosted over," Schizmar said. The tradition continued, referring to any newly assigned officer by the designation 'Rookie', as opposed to their name, and always in the third person.

The squish-squish-squish sounds of the leg driven pedals produced vibrations in the frame of the ship and through the talk-box tubes. Soon, the warmth could be felt in the seats and other interior surfaces. There was no air to heat in the cabin. Head-to-toe suits sealed tight and pressurized was a requirement for a mission like this. Just in case things got complicated, like a tracking spear through the hull.

Defflan shook an index finger at a large lever near the top of the left-front operator's panel in front of Irrique. Performing a series of well-rehearsed manipulations of the manual controls, they transformed the ship's nose into the best telescope you could carry aloft.

With adjustments to the mirrors and screens, the view coming in from the huge lens began to take shape and gain focus.

"There you are, greedy monsters," Defflan said. On the edge of the view screen, just to the left of the star's horizon, a string of objects began to arc across. Irrique went back to his primary task of keeping the ship stable enough for the telescope to stay centered on the subject, while maintaining the semblance of just another bunch of useless rocks huddled together, adrift in space. Tiny puffs of compressed gas from the station-keeping thrusters activated every few minutes.

This particular LoWic ship was designed to reflect light in random patterns and shades. From a distance, the fuselage looked like a jumble of boulders. Though a long and narrow rectangle, it was just random geometric shapes stuck together. Even if the ship was scanned by laser spectrometer, the result would be low-grade basalt, rubble, presumably spewed from some volcano on a long dead moon. It was nothing of interest that might entice a closer look.

Schizmar spoke up while he viewed the image before him. "Let's zoom in. I want to know if these are just the new Super Scoops we've heard about, or is there a big something with cannons on it hiding in the pack." The Commander adjusted the telescope controls to increase magnification by fifty.

"What does the Rookie see?" Commander Defflan asked. He hoped this first training mission for Sergeant Priminat wouldn't also be his last.

"I see—I mean…the Rookie sees twenty-five long range gas condenser ships, grouped in five sets of five, typical formation. They're the usual walnut shape with the humpback prominence aft. Density is more like rock, less like metal. But, according to…the…

Rookies calculations…" Priminat hastily scribbled notes on a pad. "Each of these ships measures out to three times the size of a standard Scoop. They are roughly the size of—"

"If you parked it on my street," Schizmar said, "just one would fill up Millorian Valley, from the east ridge to the river."

After several hours of recording video of the fleet of giant ships, Commander Defflan decided to break the silence. He remembered a speech he gave many years ago to a room full of his peers, just prior to launching a bloody campaign against this brutal enemy of the Legion of Worlds.

As he took the podium in the hangar bay then, standing before a hundred other senior officers, he admonished them about defeatist attitude in the ranks.

"Do not allow yourselves to be in awe of the enemy. Do not admire them. Regardless of their size, or their strength, their determination to conquer or their previous victories against us and others in this struggle, do not allow yourself to, even for a second, imagine that they might ultimately win. You are to visualize yourself succeeding at your task at hand. Imagine your squad will win the skirmish you're in at *that* moment. Imagine your platoon won that engagement, that day, in that battle."

Words to live by, words to die by; half of the people in that room were killed in the following weeks.

"Sergeant Priminat," Defflan said.

"Sir?" His mouth dry, even the one syllable required an effort.

"Would the Rookie please tell his crew, the Rookie's knowledge of the enemy?"

Behind a deep breath, the Sergeant quoted a previous academy assignment he had written.

"The Prawl-Tang: a symbiotic race of one intelligent species conjoined to a much larger, brutish version. Both species are shaped—"

"Wrong!" Schizmar said. "What makes you think they're intelligent?"

"Well, somehow, under the sea of their blood red planet exists a form of technology that fostered space travel. That led to interstellar capability and the beginning of the Pillage of Orion."

"Oh, the Pillage of Orion," Schizmar said. "You were there?"

"You know I…the Rookie just graduated from the academy," Priminat said. "The Rookie wasn't there."

"Go on, Sergeant," Defflan said.

"Uh…they're shaped like a starfish, with five identical sections, each section consists of a flexible arm with sensory organs at the clawed tip and digestive organs in the heavier base where it meets the other four arms. The Prawl are the exosymbiote, the smaller, but mentally calculating half of the pair. The Tang are six times the size of their thinking counterparts. Sluggish but strong, they provide the muscle and motility as the host for the smaller ones. Once the Prawl has attached itself to the top of the Tang, they become permanently fused together through phenomorphic process, subsequently acting as one being."

"And you've seen them?" Schizmar said, "Seen them yourself, these 'conjoined starfish'?"

"No. I'm just—"

"Who is?" Irrique asked.

"The *Rookie* wishes to explain what the Rookie was taught in the classroom, Sir!"

"Ignore Schizmar," Irrique said, his forked tongue making a whistle and a lisp.

"They um…the Prawl-Tang," Priminat said, "are not necessarily hostile or warlike. They methodically hunt down and gather resources for the good of their kind. If you have something that they decide they want, and you are maimed or killed in the process, don't take it personally. It's just the Prawl-Tang version of survival of the fittest."

During a brief pause to collect his thoughts, Priminat is interrupted again by Schizmar, bent on delivering a good beat-down of the newb.

"…not necessarily hostile…?! What the fr—"

"Zip it!" Defflan cut off the Lieutenant midway through the expletive.

But Schizmar refused to be silenced. "You gonna tell me this is the hooey they spout at the Academy nowadays? Not warlike? Well, what'll it take for a species to be labeled 'warlike'? Do they have to murder billions instead of millions? What? What!" Schizmar's ears burned hot from a spike in blood pressure.

"Lieutenant!" Defflan said. "You'll make my point for me, but about ten minutes too soon. Please shut up."

Priminat had retreated to staring out of the window. The view outside began to fade as the fog from his mouth breathing worked its way up the inner bubble of his headpiece. He couldn't understand why they were making it so hard. He was first in his class. He passed every test. That's why he was picked from the hundred others who'd hoped for the assignment.

Priminat thought back to a day at the Academy, in a struggle to overcome his stage fright. He stood in the front of the other cadets, nervous, a sour acid taste leftover from his recent run to the head.

"The Prawl-Tang home world: a large, mostly liquid planet, the fourth of twelve in the Alnitak system. The sentient inhabitants have apparently not spent any time considering a name for their red sphere. During any first contact, when asked, 'Where do you come from?' their only response is, 'The place we are sending your body to.' The conversation will often take a downturn from there. They use one of their five massive, scissor-like claws to snip the argumentative end off of every other being they encounter and take all the good stuff for themselves. Regardless of where you travel within the Sagittarius intersection of the Orion-Cygnus Arm, the language of every species interprets the Legion of Worlds chosen name for this planet with the same brutal clarity: 'The Blood of Many'.

"Not much is known about the geology of their planet, as no one ever gets away from it still breathing. Under the shallow argon-nitrogen atmosphere is a deep red fluid. Liquid sulfur and carbon disulfide oceans cover the entire surface. Beneath the waves are forests of giant coral that extend down for miles to the crust.

"As of last count, there are at least two million four hundred sixty-two thousand two hundred and seventeen persons reported killed or missing due to activities of the Prawl-Tang. There are likely many more casualties, yet unreported. Were it not for the combined defenses of the Legion of Worlds to curb the onslaught, no one would be safe to do more than hide in caves on the dark side of whatever ball they find themselves on."

It was a good presentation then. But that was just a room in school, in a small town, safe and warm, so very far from here. Here was space. He had never really thought about it before, why they call it that: space. It made sense now, stuck here in this tired old ship, so distant, so cold on one side, blistering hot on the other side. Only a few centimeters to his right, the most aggravating person he's ever met. On his left, billions and billions of kilometers of empty, nothing, space. Which was worse?

"Sergeant," Defflan said. His comforting voice drew the young man out from his memories, his depression. "Now tell us what the enemy has for a strategy. What's their plan?"

"Based on their actions, the enemy is primarily concerned with gathering all high-energy resources that they've recognized as potentially useful. For instance, they spend what seems like a ridiculous amount of time, materials and energy to suck up any hydrogen within a radius of about eighteen parsecs from Alnitak, hence their Scoop ships. At last report, there were no fewer than eleven hundred Scoops in the Flame Nebula. They spiral through in close formation; their intake ports wide open, and harvest about eighty percent of the gas they cut across. Now, what they plan to do with three hundred fifty trillion tons of hydrogen is a mystery. It's presumed they're using it to fuel power plants under the surface of the Prawl-Tang home planet and in their ships. They've been known to send the Scoops into the atmosphere of a gas giant planet to skim hydrogen."

Schizmar asked the question nobody wanted to hear the answer to. "And what explanation do your enlightened professors at the Academy give for what the monsters do with the people they drag under the surface of that bloody planet?"

Priminat turned back to stare at the rocks floating outside his portal window. "The Prawl-Tang corpses that we've taken back for dissection and study have only algae in their digestive organ. However, we've detected traces of some partial humanoid DNA, along with other species, within the cells of the algae. From what we can surmise, they use us for fertilizer."

The pilot, Irrique, turned to look squarely at the Commander. "I suppose that would explain our poor performance in diplomatic efforts."

This time, Schizmar's foul word was fully delivered.

Defflan turned away. He didn't want any of them to see the pallor, the truth. The view out his own port only reinforced the facts. Strong blue starlight highlighted the string of enemy vessels, now headed in the opposite direction, on towards their goal. There was no inspiration here. As had been his experience, words of heartfelt encouragement before an engagement were as valuable as the eulogy afterwards.

Clearing his throat, Defflan urged Priminat to continue. "Please… um…would the Rookie please explain for his crew what this particular fleet of enemy vessels is doing?"

"Yes, Commander," Priminat said. He angled the console to get a fresh look into the telescope viewer, focused on the lead Super Scoop. "During this time of year for the Prawl-Tang, their planet is almost exactly opposite the position of the Flame Nebula, with regards to their star, Alnitak. They use the star's gravitational pull to increase their velocity as they swing around, just outside the horizon of the corona. In fact, they are now part way into the exit maneuver; firing thrusters to push themselves away from the star with the velocity needed to expedite their trip to the nebula."

Priminat reached forward in front of Irrique and spun a forefinger counterclockwise to indicate he wanted to zoom out the viewer for a better image of the entire fleet.

"Well, that's interesting…" Priminat said.

"What is?" Leaning to get a better look into the viewer, Defflan bumped helmets with Irrique, who snorted a chuckle in retreat.

Priminat dialed in a tangent calculator lens to overlay the image, filling a need to measure something important with greater accuracy.

Defflan drummed his fingers where the Rookie could see.

"Okay, the Rookie has determined that the Scoop in the trailing position of the formation may have experienced a failure of the auto-pilot navigation system. It's obvious they are not on manual flight mode, as their trajectory is almost perfect. However, the last ship is stuck in the acceleration orbit. The rest have pulled out and away from the star, but he is continuing around, still building speed and way off course."

Defflan sat straight. "Irrique, swing us around so I can get the scope back to center. Schizmar, keep an eye out for enemy scout ships or interceptors. Priminat, you get photos of this, could give us some insight into their shielding. If he can swing halfway around a blue giant and not go up in smoke, they have not only tripled their size, they've made significant improvements in their shield technology."

Priminat caught the use of first-person directive. He wondered if it was just the excitement of the moment or if he was beginning to be accepted as an equal. No sense piling disappointment upon disillusion.

"The Rookie is photographing, Sir."

The next few hours seemed to drag for the crew while they took measurements and tracked the path of now twenty-four monstrous ships intent on their exquisite destination. The errant vessel had almost moved out of range for visual observation, and the corona of the massive star was more than a match for even the best filters. It was time to either move the ship or lose sight of the wayward Scoop.

Defflan had already spent a few minutes listening with the passive SCAN-Ear, focused on any electromagnetic crackle that could be a Prawl-Tang sensor sweep. "Lieutenant, we're going to maneuver around behind. Can you give me an all-clear for other enemy vessels within scanning range?" This close to the giant, fast spinning Alnitak, it was difficult to discern the natural noise of the star from the almost organic manipulations of the alien scanners. Schizmar had better ears for that. Another minute went by, then a big silver thumbs up appeared in the Commander's peripheral vision.

"Alright, gentlemen, we're moving the ship," Defflan said. All four men began their respective pre-start-up checklists. "I want to keep us lined up so the asteroid belt is directly aft, as seen from the main fleet. Orient the nose so we have a good look at the ship stuck in orbit. On my mark: three – two – one – mark."

Glowing orange and green against the flat-black composite panels, the navigation and attitude control screens came to life, to present a much improved perception of the star system and other objects within its three parsec range.

Schizmar was the first to take advantage of the renewed onboard electronic voice amplification. "The Lieutenant would like to thank the Rookie for his previous attention to the manually operated heater. However, I for one do prefer the luxury of direct electrical current over your intermittent stompings."

As much as you can nod your head within the confines of a spacesuit helmet, the others did so with alacrity. "Amen," the chorus.

Using his right hand, Irrique gave a sharp twist and a yank to his left hand to disengage his prosthetic fingers from the attachment point at the wrist. No matter how many times Defflan witnessed that, it always made his eyebrows go up. Irrique angled his left arm down and into the socket of the VYNIC – Virtual Yoke Neural Interface Control. He tucked his artificial hand into a small drawer under his seat. It soon ceased wiggling around. With no moving parts, the

VYNIC's pilot could control nearly every aspect of flight using five imaginary joysticks. A voluntary program for the Legion of Worlds military pilots, seventy qualified individuals had agreed to have their left forearms removed; replaced with the hardware necessary to connect their nervous system to their ship.

With a few short blasts of the thrusters, they were clear of the asteroid belt. When the plasma convector engine opened up, a shudder ran through the ship. Creating an artificial stellar wind with decompressed cold plasma expanding through a de-Laval nozzle, the stealthy reconnaissance ships could propel themselves across a star system at moderate sub-light speeds, but leaving virtually no trace of exhaust behind them.

Irrique moved a virtual thumb forward against a throttle lever in his mind. The shudder matured into an intense press of the seatbacks into the torso of each crewmember. Well trained, they all knew to just relax their limbs against the force, and to practice breath constriction. The ship's automatic functions added pressure to the respirators of their helmets to help keep their lungs from going flat during the profound acceleration.

One of the major benefits to the VYNIC is that the forces of flight do not act upon the controls of flight. Even subjected to sustained centripetal force, the pilot does not become fatigued just trying to keep the yoke steady. Only a picture in his mind, the 'joystick' has no weight.

The nose of the ship settling down from a minor wobble, Irrique eased his 'thumb' forward two mental notches. If anyone hadn't emptied their bladders yet, this would take care of it. With eyeballs temporarily misshapen and the moon sitting on your chest, fourteen seconds is enough to make even the most seasoned Legionnaire say uncle.

Throttle eased to half, Irrique said, "That should be enough crush for a bit."

On course, with acceleration steady at twenty-four Newton-meters, the time to reach maximum velocity was three hundred twenty seconds. After that they could cruise along at a fourth of light-speed; only a fraction of what the doomed Scoop had attained, but at least they could flare out to where they could get a better look at him when he went 'poof'. As the LoWic ship rolled on its horizontal axis, the colossal star now blazed from above and behind them.

"Can we get our non-conformist on the multiRad sensor screen yet?" Defflan asked. "I've lost him in the glare."

"Oh, he's right where we left him - now at three degrees, two seven two," Schizmar said. Able to alternate between redundant navigation screens, he kept one tracking system locked on the craft mired in gravity; the other antenna still keeping tabs on the main group that performed their slingshot exit on schedule.

Priminat jolted. "He's firing his thrusters! He's starting his escape maneuver."

Irrique had successfully rotated the ship to give them the best view of the event, while in expert control of their fast slide away from the star.

Priminat leaned closer to his own screen, and then rotated around to catch Schizmar's attention. Both men nodded in agreement. "The Rookie has confirmed, enemy vessel speed holding steady at zero point six five light. He's going nowhere fast, but at least he saved it."

Someone or something was piloting the giant spacecraft – a lucky someone.

"Would the Rookie care to take a guess," asked Defflan, "as to where the far flung Scoop might end up?" Priminat borrowed one of Schizmar's screens to plot the projected course.

The Prawl-Tang used a form of stasis or hibernation during extended voyages. This ship was scheduled to wake up when they *would have* reached the Flame Nebula, but they would never arrive there. On a heading for Vega or Aldebaran, they could come out of stasis anywhere along the well-populated route to Deneb or beyond.

Priminat let slip a civilian thought. "They'll be on their own. No backup if they piss off the wrong aliens."

"If…?" Schizmar punched a button on his panel to get the tracking screen back, but too late. "Incoming!" he yelled.

The incredible force of the projectile striking the rear underside of the ship was brutal enough to snap neck vertebrae. The ship tumbled out of control, end over end, leaking cold plasma from a ruptured engine casing; the de-Laval nozzle shorn off at the venturi and rolling freely in space. The first to regain consciousness was the younger and stronger Priminat. His eyes opened for a brief moment, the sight of the millions of stars wheeling about overhead told him they were flipping end over end.

"Second Lieutenant!" Priminat yelled over the intercom. "Irrique! You're the only one who can get us out of this. If you can hear me, fire the front landing thrusters for two seconds - front *only!*"

The pilot was conscious, but disoriented. The VYNIC system was made for a situation exactly like this. Aware that he had lost his wrist connection, Irrique pushed down as hard as he could, to reset the interface into the flight controls.

Rear landing thrusters – disable. Ventral landing thrusters – disable. Activate landing sequence – thrusters to maximum. Stability thrusters ready – manual. Two second burst – Fire.

With mighty blasts usually reserved for high gravity landings, two bright yellow cones of fire erupted under the nose of the ship, putting the brakes on the wild tumble. The ship now just in a circus show loop-d-loop, Irrique gathered himself and found his bearings. A few seconds later, he'd managed to accomplish no worse than one large outside loop, plasma still shooting from a hole in the belly of the accurately targeted engine.

Irrique's racing thoughts took him back to his first day at the Legion Flight Academy, with the young officer anxious to get his first Prawl-Tang lined up in the gun-sights. The instructor, seasoned and experienced in battle, displayed his prosthetic legs. "You want to battle the Beasties, eh? Well, here's the reward they'll give ya, boy!" The tracking spear having just grazed the teacher's hardened warship, now he could only teach survivability tactics.

Desires of glory now vanished, Irrique said, "Sergeant! Pop that engine loose now!"

"Already working on it," Priminat said, his gloved fingertips not quite as deft on the palpable controls as Irrique's were with his imaginary version. A series of small vibrations rattled the hull as the explosive emergency release disengaged the rearmost section of the ship from the central fuselage. Engine status lamps on the panel in front of Priminat all changed from yellow to red. Their sub-light engine was gone, oddly, an improvement.

Irrique stole a quick glance over his right shoulder. "Schizmar!" Controlled flight was top priority, but locating the enemy vessel was a close second. They needed the First Lieutenant for that. Defflan was still unconscious or dead. "Schizmar, if you're up for it, there's a Prawl-Tang Interceptor out here that just shot the ass end off our cruiser! A little help would be awesome!"

Slumped over in his seat, Schizmar was not moving. Priminat could see what appeared to be spinal fluid that had drained out of the First Lieutenant's nose, to float around inside the helmet. Reaching over and patting him hard on the shoulder was rewarded with a muffled response, barely heard on the intercom over the pilots random cursing and yelling at the Commander to wake up.

"Irrique, get us out of here! The Commander is dead. Schizmar is done. We can't do anything else."

Priminat's helmet slammed hard against the portal window as Irrique executed a one hundred eighty degree snap roll to the right, to get a quick look at what could be coming up from below. Sure enough, there was the Interceptor, black and bristling with spines for some ungodly purpose, using the glare of the nearby star for another ambush. It was prepared to fire another spear, and then would follow it in for the kill.

As modern weapons go, the Prawl-Tang tracking spear was simple. It could follow prey that it had locked onto across ten parsecs, but it couldn't track more than one at a time. Driven by a powerful sub-space transpresser, it had twin leading-edge V-blades that glowed green with excited plasma, ready to melt anything within two meters. No shield could stop them.

Priminat had an idea. "I'm opening the nose cover for the telescope. We'll extend it out a little. Then you fire the braking thrusters and I'll eject the scope. That will give the spear two targets to track. We get a fifty-fifty chance."

"I'll initiate a full up maneuver to dive directly at them," Irrique said. "We can close the gap so they won't get another shot off until they circle back around."

"Now!" Priminat engaged the circuit for the explosive bolts

securing the huge scope. It lurched outward, with a slam into the arched covers that had not quite moved out of the way. Irrique fired all six landing thrusters and the attitude thrusters under the nose cone. The ship pitched violently, up in attitude but back down towards the star. Priminat could feel his body being squeezed into the seat bottom. His feet and hands felt like they weighed a ton. Formerly pointed out to Irrique, he knew there was nothing else they could do, just hope for a miracle.

The telescope, now cut loose, kept the same course the cruiser had held moments before. A miracle needed was answered. The spear blazed past the side of the cockpit, to drive itself through the telescope and shear the massive cylinder into four crumpled wads.

The black interceptor veered to avoid a collision with the crippled cruiser diving straight at it. True to universal dog-fight tactics, it would begin a hard turn to gain the advantage by coming around behind the retreating recon vessel. For Irrique, the trick would be to pull out of the dive in the right direction to put as much of a gap as possible between them. Distance equaled time. And time is what they needed to survive the encounter.

Again, Priminat's helmet swung hard to the left to smack into the window.

"Sorry!" Irrique said.

With fuel reserves down to half, they had to get lined up for the run home and they were using all of their maneuvering thrusters just to wallow around. Without the main engine pushing from behind, this was some real ugly flying.

"I have…oooowwch… some good news." Priminat winced a bit as the safety harness dug into his groin.

Irrique smiled big. "There's a fleet of Legion War-Cruisers moving between us and the monsters from hell?"

"No, but you will find the TransWave Drive to be online and functional. It has green lights across the board."

"Freakin' awesome - and the bad news?"

"The TransWave aperture for Rigel is busy pulling another client. It won't give us a lock to the Drive. However, the beacons for the apertures of Alnilam and Mintaka are currently showing us the welcome mat. You pick. But either way, you're gonna want to hang a left to line us up."

The ship yawed in abrupt counterclockwise rotation. This time, Priminat's helmet swung to the right to bounce off of Schizmar's dome. The now deceased First Lieutenant didn't complain.

Through his virtual controls, Irrique activated the start-up for the TransWave Drive. The computer's automated checklist pinged in the pilot's earpiece, followed by an electronic verbal scolding. "Insufficient forward sub-light velocity for activation of TransWave. Accelerate to the minimum zero point five and retry." He pressed the Override button on his virtual console – still nothing.

"Oh for the love o'...Sergeant!"

Priminat was deep into a controls menu. "I seriously can-*not* believe we are *not* dead right now. Come on! Okay, try this!"

Irrique pressed start-up - green light. "What did you do exactly?"

"In maintenance mode you can recalibrate the velocity zero. The computer sees us doing about point-seven. Can we go now?"

The four TransWave pods extended out from each quadrant of the central fuselage, with immediate projection of their subspace signal across the mere one hundred light years to the TransWave aperture in orbit around the nearest inhabited star system, Mintaka. Just outside of Prawl-Tang space, it was populated with plenty of friendly humanoid species and a dozen well-armed Legion of Worlds outposts.

Upon reception of the return signal and Wave tip from the distant aperture, the ship felt like it was on steel rails, solid and secure. With a requirement of only modest thrust from an onboard engine, the Wave acts more like a galactic tow cable, which draws the craft across the void of space.

The energy required to move a starship at hundreds of times the speed of light did not require a huge engine. Ninety-nine percent of the power was generated at the destination. Critics decried the use, postulating that it's really deferred-effect time travel; that the universe would implode one day when all the 'borrowed time' was called to account.

Often described as you being the fish in the lake, with a bite of the hook, your tug is felt by the fisherman in the faraway boat. He pulls hard and you're reeled in to land in the waiting net. A starship so equipped can travel to any TransWave aperture in what feels like only minutes. Afterwards, you do have to reset your wristwatch.

"Mister Priminat," Irrique said, "we are locked in and should be—"

The tracking spear penetrated head on, the top half of the recon cruiser's cockpit carved away, canopy obliterated, the seatbacks and the upper torso of the four occupants vaporized. In another miracle, the auto-pilot and interstellar drive continued operation despite the collision.

The last reflected light from the blue sun faded in the shape of the LoWic cruiser, already part way to Mintaka. The second interceptor, hiding black against the dark of open space, dispersed any lazy photons of the Legion vessel as it plowed through where the cruiser had just been.

Caught with loving care in the net of the Mintaka fisherman, four Legionnaires will be graciously laid to rest in soil, not sulfur.

Note to Self

Elmyrah had that look on her face again today. I honestly thought that the longer we were together, the easier it would be to make her happy. It would seem the opposite is true. This whole immortality thing could turn out to be one royal bitch.

Jove

Lost
2042 CE
Edge of the Sol System

Within the confines of the control pod at the tapered aft portion of the lost Prawl-Tang gas condenser ship, the hard, rocky organ of the vessel's Navigation Onus was sick.

Able to reach out from its allocated chamber by use of long, worm-like tendrils, it was obligated to divulge the current status to the Mission Steward. Delegated as the principal mode of communication between the ship and the singular crew, the translucent follicles felt their way through the seething liquid sulfur atmosphere inside the hollow space, to locate and caress the nearby arm of the giant starfish.

Awakened from decades of slumber, the alien draws in a great inhale-swallow of the blood red carbon-disulfide soup, opens its psyche for intramental contact with the ship's navigation thoughts. Reasoning and intellection of the vessel and the occupant merge. The mountainous ship, grown in the depths of the alien world, initiates terse dialogue with the Mission Steward.

"Auto-pilot malfunction detected," Navigation Onus said.

"Reinitialize navigation function," replied Mission Steward.

"Navigation function failing to operate at acceptable levels," the organ reported.

"Reinitialize navigation function to root level."

"Navigation function operational at root level."

"Locate prescribed waypoint."

"Waypoint not within range," the ship said.

"Locate ship $\Omega 94\lambda 24\theta$."

The Mission Steward sought the ship that the Navigation Onus had been directed to follow in the mission to the Flame Nebula, where it was to harvest the accumulation of thick hydrogen gas floating within.

"Ship $\Omega 94\lambda 24\theta$ not within range."

Perhaps they are lost, too. "Locate fleet $\Omega 94\lambda$."

"Fleet $\Omega 94\lambda$ not within range."

The Omega Species, Ninety-Fourth Fleet, Twenty-Fourth Ship, should be less than a parsec ahead of Ship Twenty-Five, but it was gone. They were all gone.

"Perform subspace ping with distress suffix," Mission Steward said, alone and lost.

"Subspace ping performed."

"Estimate time for response."

"Unknown."

"Estimate location of $\Omega 94\lambda 25\theta$," Mission Steward directed, wondering where he was.

"Unknown."

"Reconfigure all ship systems to hunter-scout mode."

"Reconfiguration complete."

"Configure harvest scanner for long range detection of hydrogen."

"Harvest scanner configured."

"Scan all nebulae within range." There must be something out there.

"No nebulae detected."

The sensors would detect any hydrogen gas nebulae within five hundred light-years. The Helix Nebula, at six hundred fifty, was the nearest, but the Prawl-Tang was not where he expected to be when he fell asleep so long ago.

"Scan all astral and sub-astral bodies within range."

"One astral body, eight major planetary bodies detected," Navigation Onus declared. "Assigning temporary designations."

"Perform focused scan for atmospheric hydrogen on planetary bodies."

"Positive identification of hydrogen detected."

"Report estimated percentage of atmospheric hydrogen by designation."

The ship's ultra-high-frequency mass spectrometer could taste for the presence of any element or compound in milliseconds; now sated only by that lone atom with the single electron.

"PB1 = 22%, PB2 = Intermediate compounds < 1%, PB3 = Indeterminate compounds, PB4 = < 1%, PB5 = 90%, PB6 = 97%, PB7 = 83%, PB8 = 74%, end report."

"Scan astral system for evidence of TransWave operation." The Mission Steward wondered if he was even in the Legion of Worlds anymore.

"Result negative."

Wondering if there were any other ships at all, he said, "Scan astral system for interplanetary navigation beacons."

"Result negative."

"Scan PB5 for inorganic orbital devices."

"One detected in polar orbit."

That is of interest - a satellite? a ship? "Activate magneto-reflective shield."

"Shield activated," said Navigation Onus.

"Adjust course for orbital intercept of PB5," Mission Steward said. He could at least find a worthy reason to be wherever he was.

"Course adjusted."

"Estimate time to intercept PB5 orbit."

"0.0042 Life."

Not too long, he concluded. "Prepare suborbital atmospheric hyper-speed probe."

"Probe ready."

"Configure probe for automated navigation of PB5."

"Configuration complete," Navigation Onus said.

"Launch probe."

"Probe launched," Navigation Onus confirmed. The large ball of calcified sensory organs broke free of the ship's hull and sped away, towards its rendezvous with Jupiter.

"Prepare spear," Mission Steward said.

"Spear ready," replied the ship's mind, "Awaiting target."

Note to Self

Humans are infectious. No, they're addictive. Not only do I find that it's preferable to be near them, there's an ache within me when I'm not. I have no component for that: longing. It is not of Union manufacture. We do not long for anything. Either we're supposed to be involved or we aren't. It is my conclusion that I have a defect. If I was with my Brothers, it would be repaired. Among the humans, I am broken in just the right place.

Jove

Moon
2043 CE
Saudi Arabia, Earth

At least this time they got to ride on the inside of the bus. With a look down at the blisters on the palm of her hand, Elmyrah al-Otaibi thought of the same trip she took with her older brother just two days prior. They had to hang onto the rusty pipe rail on the roof. The wind, the dust getting into her nose and mouth, and the awful bouncing against the corrugated metal arch made the trip practically unbearable.

"Now you hold on to that rail for your life M'rah," Abdallah, her older brother had warned her early that Wednesday morning. "If you let go, you will surely fall off. They will not stop or turn back for us. You would be left here in between. Bad things would surely happen then."

Then bad things would happen? For an eight year old kid, what could be worse than falling off the roof of a huge bus?

Today, with the jagged tip of a dirty fingernail she poked gingerly against the soft dome of reddish skin that covered the clear protective puss underneath. It felt really weird. She'd never had a blister that huge. The abrasions on her knees smarted no matter how she stood.

Yes, today was far better. Abdallah had been able to sell a nice lamp he'd found Wednesday. He made enough money to buy food for two days and the bus ride today. Having to stand or sit on the floor for the two hundred sixty kilometers from her hometown of Al-Zulfi all the way to the KKMC really wasn't so terrible.

The rear tires abused by a large pothole, the bus rocked strongly sideways. That sent the pretty little Arab girl face first into the back of another passenger.

"Oh! Please forgive me," Elmyrah spoke upwards to the tall stranger. She felt humiliated. Oh that's just great, she thought, I get a face-full of his stinky butt and I have to apologize to him?

In slow motion, the man swiveled around. Dressed in a brown wool suit that was clean but worn out along the seams and cuffs, he towered over the much smaller girl who coveted the space between them in the groaning, overcrowded vehicle. His hair was oily and streaked with gray, as was his wild and bushy eyebrows and mustache, both in serious need of grooming.

Elmyrah was quick to avert her eyes, to stare at the floor, as she always did in the immediate presence of any man other than her brother. She noticed that he was wearing shoes, not sandals. He's not from Al-Zulfi, she said to herself. I've never seen him before. He's probably traveling from Riyadh to Kuwait City on business. Nobody would dress like that to go to the KKMC.

King Khalid Military City, in eastern Saudi Arabia, was once home to tens of thousands of Saudi soldiers and their families. Elmyrah could not remember anyone living there during her lifetime. It was deserted now, a derelict of another time, another age.

Abdallah had come home one day telling her that there were inspectors inside the gates to see what was left and if there was anything worthwhile left behind. They were to form crews that would dismantle the interior of the base and load the materials and furnishings into trucks. Abdallah could get an actual job to go to almost every day and even get paid, like they say it used to be.

Elmyrah stole a brief glance up from the man's dusty loafers to see if he was still looking at her. He was. With a dodge of her head to the left, she buried her face in the tail of Abdallah's dusty shirt. Her sore, blistery little hand reached up to grab her brother's tightly. Her body was tense and now feeling very cold, even though crowded by the other fifty-some people on the bus. Her pink hijab and khaki abaya were suddenly inadequate to hide within.

The youthful but hardened al-Otaibi family leader looked down to offer a smile of reassurance to his little sister. He had raised her for the past two years, since their parents went missing in Riyadh. There were few reasons why she would hide her face like this.

With a curtive clearing of his throat, Abdallah caught the attention of the man in the suit. His gaze locked with the much older man, Abdallah lifted the front of his shirt and slid his other hand to the handle of a large knife that was tucked down into his trousers. He pulled it halfway out of the worn leather sheath, just enough for the morning sunlight to glint off the crusty, chromed blade.

Message delivered. Message received.

The bus lurched to a stop outside the perimeter, southeast of the main entrance gate. Weary passengers filed out towards the front door of the vehicle. With a blind reach to the step on the rutted dirt road, they flung their arms over their foreheads to shade the bright sunlight from their tender eyes. Wandering about in the glare, they resembled a scene from a bad zombie movie. Elmyrah and Abdallah broke away. A purposeful stride took them down King Fahad Road to the security guard at the main gate.

"I need to see your work permits," he said.

His Arabic didn't sound right. It was…dreary. Not the beautiful and poetic flow so typical of the ancient language. Elmyrah considered that he wasn't really Saudi, Turkish maybe. Perhaps one of those mercenaries stranded here after the American's war with Iran. Maybe he was a Texan. Everyone says Texans sound funny when they speak Arabic.

"The boss said it should be the one to the south of the mosque," Abdallah said.

She pointed ahead, holding the permit sheet up to block the hot sun. "Is that the mosque there with the many blue domes on top?"

At the structure's entrance, Elmyrah was struck by the old, musty smell of the interior. Only just unsealed after many years vacant, the air inside had grown stale and lifeless. Another odor, one or two molecules fitting into a rarely used olfactory receptor, stopped her feet cold, death. She had smelled that once before. Something had died back here, or someone. In the front of her mind, she didn't want to know. In the back of her mind, she was always curious. Did death look as bad as it smelled?

One other time, her brother had met her at the entrance to a neighbor's house, grabbing her by the arm, spinning her around and back out into the street. Maggots, he had said. Maggots, she wondered. The poor person must have died from maggots, she figured, whatever they were.

In the afternoon, they were successful in finding a separate section of the office building to work in that had neither death nor maggots, as far as she could tell. One of the rooms, when opened, made her think that they had discovered treasure. There were many closets filled with clean boxes with amazing pictures on the outside. She'd never before seen so many wonderful things.

"Brother," she said, "is it alright with you if I look at these beautiful boxes while you load your cart?"

"Yes, of course," he said, poking her in the ribs with a finger, "But you don't have to whisper," he whispered. She couldn't help but giggle, admiring his humor.

Opening the next closet, she found another pile of beautifully colored boxes. Most had the same pattern, some had others. They all reminded her of the best tapestries, of the lavish rugs and curtains that could once be found for sale in the marketplace in Al-Zulfi. Some of the smaller boxes had ribbons and bows on one side.

"Brother!" she whispered, "I mean..." laughing, "Look at these! Have you ever seen anything like this? What do you suppose that they are?"

Abdallah patted his hands together to get some of the dust off and straightened his hunched back with a grimace. Over on her side of the room, he hefted one of the larger boxes, spinning it around, wondering what made these boxes so special.

"Oh, wait a minute! I think I have heard of things like this... about the Americans... spending their money on...Christmas presents."

"Christmas presents." Frowning, Elmyrah listened to herself using the new English words. "That sounds funny to say," she said. "What does that mean?"

"The Americans go to the big stores in Riyadh, Kuwait City and Bahrain, taking all of their money. They buy the most expensive things. They cover them with golden paper and silver bows, giving them to their friends and family and sometimes the poor."

"Are all Americans so rich?" inquired the slight Arab girl with two sets of clothes and a single pair of mismatched sandals.

"Yes, all of them are. Rich beyond what we can even imagine," replied brother, who had never actually spoken to an American.

"Why do they do that? Are they crazy, too?" she asked. The few Americans she had met certainly seemed to be.

"Actually, they are not crazy." Abdallah said. "They are obeying the Prophet Yeshua." He paused to let that sink in. "The Prophet Yeshua commands them to give Christmas presents to everyone on their birthdays."

Little sister's eyes were as big as a camel spider.

Half joking, Abdallah completed her Yuletide education. "If the Americans do not obey the Prophet Yeshua in this way, he will send a jinni, wearing a red tunic and red turban, into their homes to eat all of their sweet food, leaving them to starve."

Aghast at the imagined sights, she could barely breathe. "Oh, no wonder they all give Christmas presents!"

Abdallah returned to the pile of office supplies he was boxing. Alice returned to Wonderland to pick through the assorted boxes, hoping for one like he had told her about. Finding something high on a shelf, she reached to the tip of her toes, digging her fingernails into the corner. She teased it to the edge to get a better grip. It was very heavy for a little girl, certainly too heavy for a little girl who averaged five meals per week. As tough as kids get in the desert, she wielded her determination and lowered the spectacular prize to the floor.

"My brother," Elmyrah said softly, "I want to give you something."

Abdallah was focused on his task, balancing two dozen office staplers and a typewriter under his chin. Finally, when he had filled the wheelbarrow well past its flat-tire capacity, he turned to see what she wanted. Her eyes were beyond full. Tears streamed down her cheeks, to leave tiny trails of clean.

In her trembling arms was a huge box, hiding most of her from view. It had the purest of gold paper with a wide silver ribbon wrapped all the way around every side and finished in a double-size bow on the top. It looked like treasure.

"I love you, my brother, and I think the Prophet Yeshua wants me to give this to you."

What passed in the space between their souls at that moment was beyond words, more than speech, free of earthly description. In silence, Abdallah stepped forward and carefully eased the weight from her jittery arms. The two of them knelt down together on the green carpet of the forgotten office. Their first Christmas present sat between them.

After a few minutes of silent contemplation, Elmyrah spoke. "Now what?"

"I have absolutely no idea," Abdallah said. The small paper tag partially hidden under the bow looked like a good place to start. He flipped it over and back trying to make sense of the English block lettering. With a proud smirk, he held up the words so she could see where he pointed with his other hand. "This? This says 'Daddy'. I know it does."

You don't know anything of the sort, she thought. You can barely read Arabic.

A few minutes later, they had delicately removed all of the wrapping and ribbon. The conundrum: which was more valuable, the gold wrapping or the…this…whatever it was?

"And how are we going to get it into the bus without getting caught?" Elmyrah would keep up the family tradition of smuggling necessities without getting your throat slit for the trouble.

Abdallah had once stolen a ride in the undercarriage of the bus, on a day when he had more courage than cash. The heavy steel basket for the spare tire could accommodate extra items, even a lanky boy. He could hide it there.

"I hope your plan works, Abdallah, and they don't catch you." She gently caressed his cheek in her tiny hand. "If it doesn't, I will have run out of brothers."

The following Saturday, Elmyrah awoke to the familiar voices of her girlfriend and her brothers. They had come over to see the incredible device that Abdallah had coaxed from within the box. One of the girl's oldest brothers recognized it right away.

"That, my friends, is a telescope. I would say that it is a large one, too. See how big around this tube is here?" Hatim Sayed ibn Khoury certainly sounded confident as he held the massive white cylinder up in front of him. His teenage biceps bulged from the weight. "Yes, it is. This is a very good telescope. It is much better than others I have seen. And look, it even comes with instruction manuals and a DVD. It's very nice, very impressive." He looked across at Abdallah, who stood there with arms crossed over his puffed out chest and jaw set strongly, how Elmyrah remembered her father doing. "So, tell us Abdallah. Where did you get this? Who did you steal it from?"

"My sister gave it to me as a Christmas present," he said, with a glance her way. Everyone else burst into loud and derisive laughter at the thought of what was just said - everyone except the al-Otaibi siblings, anyway. Somehow, in this dreadful life both shared, they had managed for this one fantastic thing to be true.

Elmyrah decided that if she knew any foul words or curses,

she would've said them then. At least that's how her insides felt at hearing the others laugh. Foul words and curses be upon you, she thought.

"You know what," Hatim said, "my uncle Hatim Hassan ibn Khoury knows something about these. He owned one once. He could help you assemble it, maybe. Maybe even show you how to see the planets and the stars." Abdallah nodded silently in agreement. "Tomorrow night, we will take it over and set it up on his roof. He has a place for this exact thing."

The next evening, Elmyrah went to bed early. Colluding with dreams of her lost family, the rumbling cramps from a big meal worked their way through to her subconscious. It was a relief to be awakened and rescued from the awful pain, her unbridled longing.

People had said her parents had been executed. But she could feel them…out there, alive.

"M'rah, wake up." It was Abdallah, his hand on her shoulder, drawing her from the night's inner world. "You've got to come see this, M'rah. Wake up, sister." She looked up at him through puffy eyelids. "M'rah, come on. You've got to come see this."

Groggy from fitful sleep, Elmyrah sat up. "What is the matter? Do we need to move again? Are the soldiers coming?" A sudden feeling of strong pressure within trying to make its way out chased away the sleepiness.

"No, M'rah, we're fine. Look, it is very early in the morning. Get up and come with me to Hatim's uncle's house. I have been there all night with his family, using our telescope. There are wondrous things in the heavens!" Abdallah was so excited. "Come on, M'rah!"

"Yes, brother, I am coming. But please, I need to go. Please watch for me while I use the box, and no laughing at the sounds this time!"

At the front gate of the walled residence, Abdallah pushed it open and guided her across the patio right up to the front door of the house, giving a few quick raps on the thick carved wood panel.

"Abdallah," she asked, "should we use the front door like this? Shouldn't we go through the laundry door?"

"It's okay, I tell you. They will be fine with it." Abdallah gave her a brisk rub on the shoulders to help warm her up.

When the door opened, she was astounded to see all the lights on in the house and there were quite a few people milling about, some in their pajamas, adults still in their office clothes. Even the children were up and about, allowed to run and laugh, taking advantage of the rare freedom.

Her feet felt heavy, almost stuck to the mat as she tried to fathom the reality of actually being invited to such a beautiful home. To be welcomed through the foyer like this was unimagined. She remembered being chased away from the rear gate of this same estate once about a year ago, while poking through the garbage to find something edible.

She cringed at a woman's loud voice behind her. "Oh, look at this! Can you imagine? It's little Elmyrah al-Otaibi!" The harsh light from the room behind the person presented only a silhouette to the sheepish visitor. "Just look at you, little child!" Elmyrah fought the urge to flinch. Usually, an adult standing so close with their hands on their hips was portent of a slap across the face.

Another loud voice was a man seated to her right. "She looks like a half-burned stick that rolled from the fireplace!"

"Oh, you shush, you!" the loud woman snapped sideways at the loud man.

Thankfully, Abdallah grabbed a handful of blanket and guided the half-burnt stick away. He led her down the hallway, up a utilitarian staircase in the rear of the expansive home, which took them to the rooftop veranda. Back in the dark, moonless night, she steadied herself against the weight of her brother while her eyes adjusted. There were at least ten other people up on the roof with them.

"M'rah, follow me up here. Can you see me? Hey! Follow me up here." Even Abdallah was using his quiet voice; the one he used when they would be hiding and someone's footsteps were crunching slowly close by.

There in front of her were more steps, wood, once painted white, now peeling and rickety. It didn't seem to go anywhere; no more house to go up to, only sky. Step by step she climbed up the small platform constructed so long ago. It was all very strange. In fact, this was a completely amazing day. First, Abdallah bounded in showing off the wad of money they would use to buy armloads of fresh food. Then the feast! She had never feasted before. Then, he would wake her so early before the sun was up. Yes, this was the most completely amazing day she could remember.

"Sit down, M'rah," Abdallah said. "Yes, right there. Sit. It is alright. You won't fall off. I've got you."

With something firm under her behind, the odd dizziness melted away. She tested the operation of her neck at so great a height. Okay, my head won't fall off, even way up here, she thought.

Turning all the way around to the left, she saw an object which she recognized as their telescope. She rotated back around to flash a broad smile at Abdallah. She could see the whiteness of his teeth in the darkness ahead of her, which made her grin all the more.

"We've spent the whole evening up here, M'rah," Abdallah explained, "myself and Hatim and his brothers and his uncle's whole family looking at the stars and the planets and the many moons through our telescope."

Over the next couple of hours, Hatim's uncle Hatim assisted the al-Otaibi siblings with locating the more majestic views of the solar system and beyond. The eight inch diameter refractor could bring incredible images down to the near forgotten town. Even better, being in the middle of the vast Arabian Desert, there was practically no light to obscure the performance of the device.

At first, the tall, kindly gentleman allowed her inquisitive personality to guide them across the span of the Milky Way. The obviously brighter stars chosen first, they swung the hefty lens back and forth: Capella, Sirius, Procyon, Rigel, Aldebaran and the Pleiades. Once she got the knack of focusing the eyepiece herself, Uncle Hatim brought the astoundingly clear face of Jupiter into view.

"So, that place – Jupiter – is another planet like Earth," Elmyrah said, her mind reaching now beyond the necessities of her normally threadbare subsistence. "How long would it take to fly there?"

"Oh my young one," his fingers twirling a corner of his full gray beard, "that, I am afraid, would take…forever."

"Uncle Hatim? My brother Abdallah says that other planets can have moons, too. Is that true? Or was he just making fun of me because I wasn't a telescope-user yet?"

"Oh, yes, yes, that is quite true! Your brother was telling you… yes!" Hatim said in a sudden fit of exuberance. "Now, I will need a minute to locate one of them. But you know, there are sixty-seven natural Jovian satellites!" As his parental experience overtook the flood of adrenaline, he paused to look her nose to nose. "That means, Jupiter has many moons." Finding himself in close proximity to the darling, filthy one, he made a mental note: there was something he might suggest after completing their shared rendezvous with the cosmos. In short order, Hatim focused the viewfinder on one of the larger Jovian moons.

After he helped her locate the small orange sphere, he said, "Our moon, the big white and gray one that you see, is named Luna. This one is about the same size as ours and is named 'Io', though it's very far away."

"Eye-Ohhh," she repeated. Two vowels without a consonant sound silly in Arabic. That's not even a real word, she thought. How can there even be a word like that? After quite a few minutes she asked, "So then, if eye-oh is a moon of Jupiter, what is the name of the eye-oh's moon?"

"Well now, Io doesn't actually have a moon itself. It *is* a moon."

She seemed intent, though likely mistaken. "If a little planet flies around a bigger planet and is called a moon, then what's the tiny planet that flies around the moon? Is that a moon, too, or is it called something else?"

"My dear, perhaps it would be best if I took a look at what you are seeing. I think you may be seeing…perhaps Io caught up to Europa just now." Not impossible, if he had missed the larger moon hidden in the colorful backdrop of the Jovian surface.

"Uncle Hatim," she affirmed, "there is a very tiny something going in circles around eye-oh. I am sure it is a moon. You can see it yourself if you want to."

"Oh, well, only at…umm…your convenience, my daughter," he

said, choosing the most polite way to say 'Move your scrawny butt,' to his guest of honor.

Bent low to get under the refractor, Hatim squinted to bring the speck of light into focus.

"You have younger eyes than I do, my girl," he said, replacing the eyepiece lens with another of stronger magnification. "But… umm…let's see what we can see now." Improved multiplication brought the image to the forefront of the expert stargazer's scrutiny.

Elmyrah could tell that something was troubling him. For the first time in two hours he wasn't talking. Perhaps she had done or said something wrong? Should she have not seen the extra moon? Maybe that was against the rules of telescoping; only see what's already out there, not what you think you see. That must be it. She should have kept her mouth shut.

Still apparently mute with telescope rule indignance, Mr. ibn Khoury stood up very straight and glared down at the bedraggled angel, who was feeling less welcome by the minute. In a rush toward the door that led down into the house, he nearly stomped his way across the roof and disappeared. After several tense minutes, he returned from his brief errand to his office, ascending the last few stairs and walking directly at her. Holding a cell phone to his ear, his gaze was fixed on Elmyrah. The two children froze in place, discerning the serious tone of his phone conversation.

"Yes, I am aware that it is four thirty-two in the morning." His unwavering stare was zeroed on his guests, but his round, hairy face began to soften a bit; a few wrinkles could be seen behind his glasses. "Well, now that he is up and inquiring, put him on the telephone, please." Finally, his smile broke the tension of the moment. "Good morning to you, Yosef. This is Hatim Hassan ibn Khoury. Oh, yes indeed, it has been too long my dear Professor Shalhoub."

Hatim still had fond memories of sitting on the stone steps of the lecture hall, fortunate to have money to spend on astronomy classes. He missed the sound of the old man's cane tip grinding the sand against the colorful tile floor as he expounded on faraway places.

"First, let me apologize for any interruption I may have caused your family. However, as you know, my friend, astronomers keep odd hours." Just then, a little light turned on in his grandfatherly component, remembering the earlier suggestion for his starry pupil. The microphone end of the cell-phone covered, he leaned closer to Elmyrah with a message.

"My little joy, I have arranged for you to take a nice hot bath."

In what was once the quarters allocated to servants, Mrs. ibn Khoury had changed the bath water once, but now it was already cloudy again as Elmyrah soaked in the steamy, soapy heaven.

"Ugh! Once we get all the dirt washed away, there won't be any girl left!"

Elmyrah couldn't remember having been pampered like this. To be mothered again was beyond what she could've ever hoped for. Surrendering herself to the care of this plump and rosy neighborhood matriarch, she figured that it would last about another hour or so before they would escort her to the rear exit and into the dismal alleyway. She had no idea that this day would be the turning point in her life.

Mrs. ibn Khoury asked, "So, Elmyrah, tell me about school. Do you like your classes? Which one is your favorite?"

"Oh, Mistress, I am not permitted to attend school anymore. The headmaster wanted my father's signature on a paper about something. I do not know what it means. Abdallah signed my father's name on the paper. The headmaster said my brother had done a bad thing by signing it. My brother went to the school to ask them to let me return, because he knows I should go. The headmaster said Abdallah is not welcome there anymore, since he had to stab that older boy. So....now..."

"Yes, I had heard about the stabbing, Elmyrah. That is why I do not care for your brother. He is a violent boy."

"Oh, no, Mistress!" Elmyrah cried, "Please do not think badly of Abdallah! He only did that to protect me from the boys who were going to rape me!"

Slowly, the grim reality of this pauper's life began to pervade the woman's preconceptions. Some suds wiped away from the tiny face, she asked Elmyrah to tell her what had happened.

"About six months ago, I was on the way to school. Someone from behind picked me right off my feet and carried me through the doorway of an old shop. There were three older boys. I had never seen them before."

As the memory of the dread and powerlessness crept back into her soul, her eyes welled up with tears. Spilling over to roll down her cheeks, they corralled some lather down to her chin, where a frothy goatee dripped sorrow.

"They pushed me very roughly into the back room where it was dark. I fell down hard and got splinters in my hands. One boy grabbed my hijab and yanked it from my hair, tearing some out. I started crying. Then two boys grabbed my arms and held them out. The other took my pants off and threw them away, my underpants, too." Now sobbing, she hid her face in her hands as she confessed to the woman the part she'd tried to forget.

"I closed my eyes. I could not bear the thought of what was going to happen to me. I fell to the ground and prayed for Allah to save me, and he did. May his name be praised! When I opened my eyes, there was Abdallah standing in front of me, holding the knife. The boy who took my pants was crawling. He was coughing and crying. The other two boys were gone." At that, Elmyrah leaned over nearly into the surface of the bath water, sobbing. Releasing control, she was at last able to let go of the pain and the embarrassment, to pour it all out on her mother-for-a-day.

With tears of her own, Mrs. ibn Khoury reached down, lifted the girl from the tub, wrapped a large towel around her and sat her up on her lap. Just at that moment, the morning sun cast a bright golden beam through the window of the bathroom, to alight on the girl's face.

Her tired head turned to lie on Mrs. ibn Khoury's shoulder, Elmyrah said, "Look, Mistress, at the Sun. Did you know that up in the sky, you can see forever?"

Upstairs, in Uncle Hatim's library, he was still in conversation with his past professor from King Saud University in Riyadh. "It is confirmed then. You saw it as well; absolutely amazing, yes? Of course we have to name it. Oh, no, Yosef, not me, one of my.... students discovered it. Her name? Uh....her name is Miss Elmyrah al-Otaibi. Address? I do not know her address. It's somewhere here in Al-Zulfi, of course. Hold on, let me ask my son.

"Sabih! Come up here! Sabih, you know Abdallah al-Otaibi and his young sister, Elmyrah. I need their address."

Sabih laughed, fingertips tapping his smart-phone, as he pretended to look it up.

"Oh, sure, their address is two-oh-two-five, Mercedes Benz, three hundred, Dee."

His father was not amused. "Sabih, shut up now and tell me. What kind of ridiculous address is that?"

"It's not a street address, Father. It's the broken down car they live in. They are homeless, you know!"

After a lengthy silence, his forehead at rest in the palm of his hand, Uncle Hatim provided the information to the Senior Director of Astro-Sciences, to name the newfound sub-moon after its young discoverer.

"Yosef…yes…her address, it would seem….um….she lives here….with me and my family."

Note to Self

Armed with my telepathic function and the Diplomatic App, I should be able to convince anyone of the truth, even if it is contrary to what they believed a minute ago. The challenge with humans though, is that some of them are more comfortable with a good lie. Still others prefer to not know the truth. 'Ignorance is Bliss' as one of them described it. And then they 'change their minds'. No, no, no! You can have any number of brains, but only one mind! These people have it backwards.

Jove

Innocence
2043 CE
Jupiter cloudscape

"Double dare you," said the super-giant squid, the one with a flash of purple bands that rippled across his skin. His recent hormonal surges were flaunted in marching color.

Three juveniles, panting from their ill-advised climb into the Drane Zone, swam in circles around the smaller, yellowish one. He boasted mere mild brown stripes, none of the flickers of red pigment beneath.

"ScaredySquid," they teased, "MakeSpit for DraneSparks!"

Bullied to perform for the slightly older males, the younger cephalopod gathered his courage and pressed higher into the atmosphere, a bolus of saliva readied in his beak. The crackle of the electric air-snakes felt near his tentacles, he spun around to face upwards, spewing a stream of spittle in their path. In an aggressive dive toward the target, the Drane seared the cloud-tops with sparkling urgency, instinctively drawn to any movement.

His four enormous eyes opened wide at the rare sight, the adolescent Jovian completed his fraternal rite of passage. So engrossed was he in the experience of being higher than anyone else on the giant world, he never noticed the invasive Prawl-Tang probe, likewise determined to investigate any solid mass. It used destructive methods.

Deep below the massive planet's gaseous atmosphere, concealed beneath the visible curtain, the creatures and created beings of Jupiter, both indigenous and alien, thrive and multiply as they have done since long before the first earthly enzyme passionately embraced a protein and slithered matrimonially into the happily ever-after.

In the upper boundary of the clouds, the single most common organism is the Drane. Wispy, ribbon-like animals, they have little color, but sparkle along their flat surface. These great glittering streamers trail through the sky as they frolic among the clouds. Schooled together in great masses, they feed on static electricity and free ions. On occasion, with their magnetic fields interwoven, they blast across as one brilliant lightning bolt, covering vast distances in mere seconds. Separated at will, they dance and coil, flit and fly about without much of a care.

Below the clouds, where vapors combine into constant mist, the three-dimensional latticed cubes known as OverSingers bob and roll about as they float in foggy space. From a distance, they are perceived as a soft silvery box, evenly constructed, three kilometers wide on each side and slightly more dense than the air in which they exist. To observe one of these lazily drifting along, it would appear to do absolutely nothing. Not originally formed on the planet, they are a transplant, known to exist on a handful of gas giants throughout the Orion-Cygnus Arm. Alive, but not truly aware, they are tended and cared for by the primary sentients maintaining the lower depths, where the air is heavier and cooler.

The Knowers, the sentient beings of Jupiter, were prompted by evolution to share thoughts and feelings among individuals of their kind. They progressed to moving their whole psyches across the physical plane, able to jump from one to another. Bodily travel became secondary. Their mind's thoughts were sent branching into the multitude or bounding across, the last willing consciousness to share the space in their mind. Making good use of the joined awareness, they educated themselves to the concept of 'beyond us'. Over many generations, they continued to practice reaching into the heavens with the combined strength of millions of minds in a simultaneous "Hello?"

With a close resemblance to the giant squid in the oceans of the Earth, and perhaps even related to them, the Knowers populate the southern polar regions of Jupiter, their 'habitable zone'.

In shape, they're cuttlefish. In size, they're as big as an aircraft carrier. Their bodies boast very low mass, like a jellyfish. Just one of their four eyes measures over twenty meters in diameter on an adult. Their bulbous mantle is divided horizontally by an external fin that separates the upper and lower portions of the main body. The head and adjoining seven tentacles make up the remaining one-third. Motion is, like most cephalids, from jet propulsion. Dense air sucked into their cavernous mantle, they shoot it out through twin nozzles, aimed to the front. When at speed, they always travel backwards. With no natural enemies, they use their ability to change the colors and textures of their thin outer tissues to communicate visually, impress potential mates and to conceal their approach while on the hunt.

Diving deeper to the levels at which a foamy atmosphere boils atop the wind-tossed sea below, the Knowers feed on the 'fish' that migrate up from where the liquid surface is found. Like Jovian salmon, the smaller animals leap up out of the liquid helium to spray their eggs and milt into the foamy bubbles above, out of the reach of other, lesser creatures that would seek to devour the fertilized embryos. Some will spring right into the waiting maw of the hungry Knower, hidden above.

Far below lays the true solid surface of Jupiter. A rocky, encrusted ocean floor, the liquid metallic hydrogen and helium sea filters down through a loose layer of crystals. The four-sided quartz compounds emerge from the outer core. Like a fetal star that died in the womb, the giant planet's inner core burns cold, its birth as a brother to Sol never delivered. The continual bombardment of pre-stellar nuclear radiation is absorbed by the ancient crystals, now imbued with a favor, elsewhere unavailable.

The circle of life finds Jupiter's depths no exception. The massive beings far above come to their end. Nutritious particles fall to build a layer of detritus at the bottom. Those creatures which inhabit the realm of darkness and decay often swallow crystals along with their meal. Layers of predation above act out their instincts, causing the grains to be transported higher, until they are deposited in the gall bladder of the highest order of carnivorous life, the Knowers.

In a further display of grand design, the autonomic functions of the Knowers' bodies find a willing partner in the active silicates that comprise the grains of Jovian sand. Constant and controlled buoyancy is required in an atmosphere where the major elements are the lightest of molecules. Their brain broadcasts a message along the nerve net around the unique organ that surrounds their singular boney structure, "Lift up." The sand complies.

Noble creatures, they lack ego and consider any single thought to be incomplete without at least momentary rumination by others in the vicinity. Like ripples on the still surface of water, each projected thought goes outward from the initiator to other Knowers nearby. Their one fault, most notably as individuals but to a lesser degree as a governed community, is a childlike naiveté.

Without question, the most profound and beneficial experience in the history of the Jovians was their covenant with the altruistic Manufactured Flesh and SynThinker Union. When these artificial beings first responded to the welcoming call from the Sol System, the Knowers gave them the name 'TinyMakers'.

Patterned after the generic, bipedal humanoid design so prevalent throughout the Orion Spur, these voyaging clone makers (and clones themselves) are the wandering missionaries of creationary science. They show up on your planetary doorstep, as it were, and ask exactly what or who they could make for you. In return, they ask only for the opportunity to study the local sciences: ecology, physiology, nature, psychology, mortality, etc. Using their base in orbit around a planet in Sirius to launch out from, their substantial fleets are fully equipped to aid these master-craftsmen of the cloning arts.

With an established friendship and enthusiastic cooperation among the telepathic Knowers, the Union, or TinyMakers (everyone is tiny to a four hundred fifty meter long squid), set about the task of growing an incredible living telescope that the Knowers could use to see beyond the clouded skies above into the depths of space.

One of the proudest achievements for the Manufactured Flesh and SynThinker Union, the two hundred eighty kilometer tall Ocuquad was two and a half jovian years in growth before being ushered into place in the South-Southern Temperate Belt. In the Knowers' nomenclature, LookingFar transformed their societal awareness, and allowed for expansion of their imaginations and intellects. Their favorite subject, Earth, was named LittleBluePearl.

Never to let a philanthropic opportunity pass them by, the Union found the many immense OverSingers to be freezing to death on their own planet. It was losing mass and cooling rapidly. In a plan devised to rescue them, the clones confirmed that the very similar and much warmer planet in the Sol system would make a near perfect habitat. The Knowers could keep an eye on them (or four) and would give them a chance to participate in the greater good.

To everyone's surprise, once adapted to the somewhat lighter atmosphere of Jupiter, the immense glass cubes could be heard to sing. Helium, not present on the dying planet, modulated the voices to reach a higher pitch that the Knowers and the Union clones could hear. Further, it was discovered that when OverSingers gathered into a large conical group of at least a few thousand or more, and coaxed up into higher levels, their combined electromagnetic magnification allowed the Knowers that hovered below to hear sounds from beyond the surface of Jupiter.

With much practice, the Jovians perfected the art of herding the OverSingers into gigantic swirls, as large as three thousand kilometers in diameter, which were timed to coincide with alignment of other planets in the Solar System. Once the enormous white circles were spun close to the surface of the cloud tops, the Knowers huddled together below by the millions, intent to listen for the miraculous vibrations of the distant planetary neighbors.

A great wave of excitement pulsed across the planet as the news of an unbroken multi-mental link between the users of the space known as HearingOthersBeyond and the LookingFar operators. Working together, and much to the amusement and cheers of the Manufactured Flesh and SynThinker Union scientists, the Knowers exemplified their own creative flair by forging an alignment, the same point in space seen and heard in simultaneous phase. It seemed for a whole day, the fish below found that they could spawn, uneaten.

On the following day, the first ever revision to the historical records of SeeingFarPlace was documented: the LittleBluePearl should now be referred to as LittleNoisyBluePearl.

Over the two hundred seventy-two jovian years that followed, about a lifetime for the Knowers, they were the rapt witnesses to the industrial age of Earth. Twice, they were certain that the LittleNoisyBluePearl had sent flaming fish on course for Jupiter. Soon after, there was a report of a burning fish falling from the Drane Zone, leaving a smoky trail down into the TurbulentPlaces. Ink, presumably.

The Union themselves would one day be alerted to the presence of another ship in the vicinity. But this would not bring joy to anyone, nor would it be cause for celebration.

To deliver news of the unwelcome visitor's arrival, whose ship had settled into orbit around FastMoon, the TinyMakers came down in their vessel to communicate directly with the Knowers in telepathic exchange.

With thrusters at one hundred and two percent of rated capacity, and interior pressures maximized to withstand the crushing clouds, the shuttle of the Ambassador from the Manufactured Flesh and SynThinker Union slowed its hover near the first group of Knowers that was encountered in the upper limits of the sky. Always recognized as a friendly 'face', the ship's arrival encouraged the enthusiastic approach of a handful of the giants.

The bluish chrome biped, Ambassador Moyab-4, unfurled his artificial mind into the thought-laden, semi-fluid world.

"Ambassador TinyMaker welcomes the Knower," Moyab-4 said, "I bear news DangerNear."

"Knowers welcome Ambassador TinyMaker," they said. "Say

DangerNear?"

"In PlaceFarAbove, DangerComes to Knowers. TinyMakers see and know," Moyab-4 said. "TinyMakers watch DangerNear in PlaceFarAbove. TinyMakers know DangerNear in other PlaceFar-Far. Now DangerNear is DangerComes to Knowers."

The Knower at the front of the group flicked his long, striped arms and tentacles, curling a few back over his eyes, like a shield from the bad news.

"Knowers hear TinyMaker knows of DangerNear," the Knower said. "DangerFar comes to DangerNear. DangerNear is Danger-Comes. Knowers say no to DangerNear. Ambassador TinyMaker say go to DangerNear. Yes, make DangerNear go to PlaceFarFar."

"Ambassador TinyMaker cannot say go to DangerNear," Moyab-4 said. "DangerNear ListenNot to TinyMakers. DangerNear ListenNot to Knowers. DangerComes is DeathMaker to all. Knowers MakeHidden. TinyMakers MakeHidden. TinyMakers must Make-Hidden be HiddenFast. TinyMakers GoFar."

Moyab-4, one of the leading administrative clones of the Union, had been assigned the Jovian Project. His goal was to give the sentient cephalids a window beyond their murky depths, and like a caring father, to introduce them to basic science, like a telescope. Today though, he worried that should the Union constructs on the planet be discovered, it would lead to the capture or annihilation of the Knowers.

"Knowers hear TinyMakers," they said. "GoFar and be Hidden-Fast. Knowers MakeHidden be HiddenFast. DangerComes not see Knowers. TinyMakers say MakeStop to DangerComes."

If only it were that easy. Every previous encounter with this unrelenting evil resulted in the destruction of the Union vessel and all the clones aboard. In the vocabulary of this particular enemy, the words for 'truce' or 'peace' were nowhere to be found.

"TinyMakers cannot MakeStop DangerComes. TinyMakers Go-Far now. Prawl-Tang comes," Moyab said.

"Knowers be HiddenFast. Prawl-Tang be DangerComes?"

"Yes, Prawl-Tang be DeathMakers," he said.

With only a handful of ships in the Union fleet docked together in orbit around Jupiter, it was possible to maintain orbital counter-point, opposite from the lone Prawl-Tang Super Scoop. The Union could effectively remain out of sensor range, but only if the predators kept their close orbit of Jupiter. The Union did not and would not possess weaponry to fight back. They were sworn to manifest creation.

His shuttle docked at the underside of the lead Union cruiser, Ambassador Moyab-4 called for an urgent conference of the Union Council. Gathered together in the circular Court, each of the fifteen members took their place along the concave outer wall. Hands grasped with the mostly identical clones to either side, their metallic robes rustled and rang as they brushed against one another.

Although the physiologic process of their creation produced a duplicate of the prime pattern, the subsequent moments began to define them as separate and identifiable beings. Equipped with their own engineered DNA, they were free to become unique persons. Even among synthesized replicants, prolific debate was fueled by combined millennia of subjective experiences.

His title relinquished for the moment as he strode into the Court of Council, the Ambassador opened the proceedings. "I, Moyab-4, bid you welcome in this Court. You are all aware that a Prawl-Tang gas condenser vessel has been detected in orbit around one of Jupiter's moons. For the brief time that we had to scan their ship without our own presence revealed, it is determined that the craft itself, previously known by the Legion of Worlds as a Super Scoop, was designed to draw in free hydrogen or other similar gasses and liquids from a nebula or a suitable planet. Micro-condensing that resource into a proto-solid, they would transport it back to their star system, which of course is Alnitak."

With a telepathic gesture, another Council member requested the opportunity to inquire.

"Is it known why the Prawl-Tang would send a ship so far?"

"Acknowledged, Doshl-2," Moyab said, nodding. "It appears to be accidental. Our scan detail shows that the outer hull has endured excessive wear from sustained sub-light travel with minimal or no shielding. Our Chief Navigator believes that this ship lost course, finally reactivated here, in the Sol system. It is highly doubtful that they are able to raise a communications link with others of their kind. Even if they are aware of the passage of time, it is evident by the activity of their sub-orbital probe and the approach vector of their craft toward the thermosphere of the planet that they intend to carry out harvesting missions."

"I, Choyt-72, wish to speak," the eldest of the members said. Among the founders of the Manufactured Flesh and SynThinker Union, Seventy-Two was a soul of enduring age. His blue flesh more closely resembled the humanoid original; the features softer, less chiseled as in the later designs.

"If we do not act with utmost vigilance, we stand to risk catastrophe for the Knowers, perhaps the entire jovian ecological matrix. We have seen with our own eyes what the Prawl-Tang are capable of, even to an advanced race equipped with modern defenses and military expertise. These childlike, innocent creatures below cannot begin to fathom the gruesome ends to which they may befall in the coming days. Make no mistake, when – not if – but *when* the Prawl-Tang discover LookingFar or any of the lesser constructs we have developed for the Knowers, they will rightly surmise that these are of Union manufacture for use by indigenous life forms. We will have led them to their hapless prey and stole away as cowards."

Serving as the proverbial pin-drop, a small crystal that had strayed from the planet's rings struck the outside of the clear floor, leaving a small frosty spatter, not unlike a snowflake.

"I, Cairn-14, wish to address the Council." Head of Security for this Mission Fleet, his supernumerary eyes had born witness to many encounters with aggressor species. His memories stretched far back in time, undoubtedly involving interactions with the blood-thirsty Prawl-Tang. His core strategy to turn and run had kept this fleet free of loss or damage for centuries. Indeed, a long-lived, successful coward.

"If we remain with them," Cairn said, "what good will it do, our perishing alongside the Knowers? It would be suicide to stay within ten parsecs of this system."

"Who can truly argue with that?" Doshl-2 said.

"I can argue that," said Trayd-7.

"I can argue that *and I will!*" Moyab-4 said. "In the archives of Only Brother Xut-Xon, it reads, 'Thou shall not overlook the lives of the lesser ones, nor ignore their plight.' Tell me brothers, how does that not apply—"

Cutting of Moyab, the indignant Cairn nearly steps out of the circle. "If we are quoting history instead of policy, let's not forget the Commandment of Hoyjet. 'Thou shall not permit a brother to perish!'"

"We're wasting valuable time!" Doshl-2 said, looking to the ceiling. "Should we debate religion or vote on how soon we leave orbit? And does it really matter?"

"It does matter." Choyt said. Again, all present turned toward his place in the circle – all but Doshl. "As Choyt-1, Assistant to Only Brother Hoyjet, I copied his words as he recited them while in meditation. Not only was I there to immortalize the spoken words of the Only, I continue to exist as his word."

Barely a handful of the entire populace was of the original five Ones; the Choyt succession being the single constituent of those rare lines in this particular fleet. Derived from the Onlys - the actual mortal patterns at the Beginning - the Ones were the original clones of their humanoid source. Of the tens of thousands of clones belonging to the Manufactured Flesh and SynThinker Union, if they were not of the five Ones, they were secondarily contrived beings, imagined and designed by other clones; the artificial species exercising their right to procreate.

Moyab-4 was the only one in the Court with the courage to break the silence. "You have lived our history, Brother Choyt. Please tell us, what is the right course of action today?"

"We have chosen to never again participate in violence, nor will we now," Choyt said. "It is because of our unique ability to create ourselves as we deem appropriate, there can be no exceptions to our oath to maintain the Union as strict pacifists. Otherwise, it would not be the Prawl-Tang known as the Scourge of Orion, but us.

"I believe our duty is to aid the Knowers, now more than ever; to move beyond construction of mere corporeal playthings and be-

neficent monstrosities. Today is our moment to create something....
someone, who can rise above the totality of our combined sciences.
Let us build a Savior Class being. We shall send him into the mist
of Jupiter, armed not with weapons, but with the mind, skills and
capacities necessary to save lives. This is for the sake of peace, the
opposite of that which we have enjoined from ourselves, the capacity of destruction for the sake of war. We once did build ourselves
into war machines, though it was forced upon us. It was far too easy
to excuse the greater violence to prevent the lesser."

Cairn was curious. "And this new creature, this....Savior....will
be left alone to fend off—?"

"*Not* alone!" Moyab-4 said. He understood the visionary Choyt.
Here before them was the responsibility to establish an entire series
devoted to the realization of a destiny.

"Never alone." Choyt raised his arms in triumph; the ring of
clasped hands soaring in mirrored waves around the Court. With
Cairn the last, he had no choice but to join the two abreast. Such
was the nature of the Court. "We should design a new series, with
enhanced telepathy, empowering them to communicate directly
with the Knowers *and* the Prawl-Tang, without the need of a ship-
board intramental carrier. He will possess the Knowledgebase of all
our experience with both races... of all races within the Legion of
Worlds....as well as this star system. A small starship should be refitted a full hypertrophic cloning lab, endowed with the latest autogenic functionality. The ship and the clone should have reinforced
structures to withstand the temperatures and pressures of sustained
operation below the thermosphere."

"I, Chrayt-4, would like to address the Council," said the Director of the PolyGenetic Research and Science vessel. His break-

through in the area of autonomous experiential transfer allowed for real-time multiplexing download of sensory and synaptic history from the active clone to all subsequent numbers simultaneously, a spectacular achievement. It was feared as a potential aberration, as any failure in one clone could pass to the entire series.

"Please, Chrayt-4," Moyab said, "Your input is most welcome. Speak freely."

"Thank you, my brothers. While I listen to the discussion about the grave situation and especially to the fervor brought forth when reciting the words of the Onlys, I am reminded of one of my favorites: quoting our Only Brother Jon-Jan, 'Always follow your instincts, but not over a cliff.'"

The abrupt laughter yielded faint echoes in the well-insulated chamber.

"As some of you may have heard," he said, "our prolonged visit to the Sol system has prompted scientific inquiry into the hypothetical adaptation of a Tactical SynThinker to a robust dynathoracic module, which could be permanently assigned to continuous exploration of these planets. I won't pretend that our focus would be other than that marvelous cacophony, the LittleNoisyBluePearl, otherwise known as Earth. However, and wisely so, this Council long ago ruled that the alpha sentients of that small world are far too aggressive and unpredictable. Hence the great lengths at which we go to disguise ourselves from their probes and orbiting arrays."

"Hypothetical adaptation?" Doshl-2 asked. "With all due respect, Chrayt-4, as I monitor resources of all departments within the fleet, your 'hypothesis' has taken on a decidedly cogent dimension. Perhaps your scientific inquiry has blossomed into more than prototypes?"

"In truth, we have a series of thirty individuals. He has been specifically designed to interact with the Terrans, to befriend them. All that is left to perform is configuration of the upgraded Wisdom interface, awakening the first of an entirely new level of our species."

Chrayt's confession stirred the members, who looked around the room at each other in near disbelief.

Moyab-4 would have liked to rub his brow, but for the tight grip of his two brothers.

"This new series…do they possess autonomous experiential transfer capability?"

"Yes, they have installed component," Chrayt admitted. "However, the standard sequential sub-space crossloader is enabled as the primary means of transfer. The real-time device is optional, disabled."

The massive intelligence of Choyt-72 calculated the weight of this decision. His contemplative process so extreme, the Brothers close by could hear the breathy sounds of the polysynaptic river inside his head.

"And if this secondary crossloader protocol did somehow become enabled," Choyt said, "then, all remaining individuals in the series would…."

Chrayt was hiding his own deeply conflicted sensibilities. "….would automatically activate at the required dual pre-cognitive levels of the SynThinker." As a scientist, this could be the hallmark of his existence. But this was to be no controlled laboratory experiment. This was hoping that the dominoes would fall one into the other, starting at one end and toppling gracefully across to the other, without you being present to witness if something jars the whole table. "All true and perceived experiences of the active clone, as well as previous beings, would be copied into all remaining pre-beings, alive but not awake, unaware of their surroundings, neither self-aware. When the active subject terminates, the series consecutive awakes to everything his predecessors were, to continue the mission."

"My brothers," Moyab-4 said, "we have the means to do the right thing. When the Onlys constructed the Ones, did they wait for every conceivable failure to be realized and overcome? If they had, none of us would exist, I assure you. It is my belief that the time is right to close the floor for open debate and move forward with a vote."

Surveying the room for any obvious disagreement, Moyab-4 asked Choyt-72 to define the ballot measure.

"Yes, of course, Brother Moyab-4. Council shall vote that the Union will immediately execute on a plan to complete a new series Brother to remain behind to aid the Jovians at risk from the Prawl-Tang, as long as it takes and to whatever end. The fleet shall extract from the Nexus Base and prepare to leave orbit. The Sol system is off limits until further notice."

Choyt stared through the windowed floor just as the massive moon, Callisto, completed its ecliptic course past the conjoined starships. The brilliant beam of yellow sunlight filled the room from the distant star.

With broad smiles at the portentous illumination of the Court, Moyab, Chrayt, Choyt and all between them raised their joined hands above their heads. Cairn and Doshl, with only two others between them, kept their hands down at their sides.

"Let the record show the count is twenty hands in favor, ten opposed. The motion is passed," Moyab said.

There was much murmur and discussion as the members filed out of the room and into the main corridor of the Union Ministry vessel. Moyab and Choyt embraced Chrayt as he strode past the group.

"I am curious about this starship you mentioned, Choyt-72," Moyab said. "Exactly where is this craft coming from?"

"Well," Choyt replied, purposely loud enough to be heard by the Brother exiting the Court just then, "I have no doubt that one of the fleet Captains will graciously donate his personal TransWave cutter for such a noble cause."

Captain Raytk-31 of the Command vessel, Endurance, stopped up short of his exit between the two clones.

"What about my cutter?" Raytk was sure that he had missed a punch-line.

"Thank you, Captain! That is so generous of you!" Moyab said, giving him a hearty pat on the shoulder.

Choyt-72 called down the length of the deep, oval corridor to the fast-stepping Chrayt rounding the corner on his way to the airlock and his docked science vessel.

"Hey! So, what's his name?"

Chrayt, nearly out of earshot, leaned back to listen.

"The Savior Class series…what's his name?"

Chrayt's wide grin filled the space of the robe's hood.

"He is to be the god of Jupiter, right? So, what else could it be - Jove!"

Note to Self

There's something inherently strange about being a clone. First of all, it feels like déjà vu all the time. You get used to that. Knowledgebase tells me that since I was made to be around humans, I should be comfortable with the term 'artificial person'. I'm only artificial compared to creatures that grow from a sperm and an egg into hairy, smelly, jiggly, deteriorating mammals. It's just a matter of perspective.

My body is gelled silicone over a hardened poly-silicate frame. Electrical tensors make my parts move. The SynThinker is the best brain ever poured out of a jar. If I experience a failure, I will cross-load into the next me. This is not abnormal at all.

In fact, I'd say it's perfectly natural when you think about it.

Jove

Jove
2043 CE
Nexus Base, Jupiter High Orbit

I awake, for the first time, as Number One. There is a cold sensation against my back. It is firm, hard. I do not like it. In fact, I find myself becoming annoyed at the feeling. Pushing it away here makes it all the more uncomfortable there.

As I prepare myself to try a secondary tactic against this relentless adversary, I hear and feel a tick-tick-tick up where I am, with me, in my…wherever I am.

Then I hear something, out there, that jars me from my defensible, irritable place.

"Look at that," says….something. "His autonomic initiator keeps rejecting the new Wisdom download, like they're out of phase, or maybe a fault in the core program?"

I decide that I will ignore the cold evil behind me, and attempt to embrace the curious sounds above.

"You're correct," says a second voice, somewhere to my left. Yes, that is not just a sound, it is a voice; someone speaking.

"His precognitive relay is firing, but to no effect. He just doesn't want to wake up to the download."

It certainly sounds as though they are talking about me. The voices sooth me and seem to bring a familiarity that I need, here in the dark, cold, hard place.

"This project is too important to allow any potential defect to be released," the first voice says. "We should abort this one and check the interface in all the rest. What if it was to fail later in the field?"

Somehow, that is about me, too.

A strong pressure, up where I am, penetrates in toward me. Maybe I can reach out to meet it and make contact. Solid. Something. Definitely a solid something. I will let it meet with me. The cold firmness behind me subsides. Still darkness, though. No coldness.

I awake as Number Two. There is that terrible, hard coldness again. Tick. Only one tick this time. More sounds. But these are coming from very near to my place of being.

It opens wide, revealing a…hallway? No, it is a vast hall with infinite walls with countless doors. Doors fading. Walls disappearing. Openness. Light.

A new sensation now, I feel a recurring pressure against my arm. I seem to be aware of far more than my previous place of being. There is much more to me on the inside as well as the…outside?

"Open your eyes. You should be awake now," said the familiar voice above. "Open your eyes. Right here."

Now I can feel a pressure poking me in the….eyes. That's rude.

I squint to keep the fingers from jabbing into my eyeballs.

"Thank you. I'm awake. Please stop poking me, whoever you are." I cover my face to prevent further assault. There's an overwhelming urge to go…where…Earth? What is an Earth…oh. I should be there, doing…something. I belong there, with the humans. Am I a human? That's it, I must be a human, and I should be—

The second voice interrupts my attempt to remember anything.

"Listen! Hold still for now. You're not unplugged yet. Be still while the diagnostic routine completes."

I feel pressure against my chest, pushing me backward. Daring to open my eyelids for the first time, the rush of visual data startles me. I look down to see hands pressed against me, preventing me from further forward motion. I follow the shape up with my gaze, to recognize an arm, a shoulder, a face, a hooded face. On the right, another one with a similar face, though this one is gaunt and wrinkled. I allow the hands to push me back against the….hey! There is that cold evil again! Turning around to face my adversary, I find a white ceramic tabletop. Not quite the horror it was a few minutes ago.

"Welcome to life," says the one with a crooked smile. "I am Chrayt-4. This is my associate, Thayl-2."

Nodding, I hope to manage better than my initial outburst. "Hello, I am….I have no idea who I am. I'm Number Two?"

Chrayt-4 offers help. "You are Jove-2."

"Jove-2," I say. "What happened to Jove-1? Hope it wasn't anything I did."

Thayl-2 looks over at Chrayt-4. "Was that humor? Sarcasm?"

"The Terran specifications," Chrayt-4 said, "exerting themselves already."

"But he's going to Jupiter."

"Yes, of course, but he still has the core load in his SynThinker for operations on Earth, as that was to be his primary function. Knowledgebase provides the vocabulary and grammar for conversation on Earth of the present day. It would seem the blooders there all speak to each other with an irreverent tone, at best."

I notice there is a flat cable running from somewhere to a crease in my abdomen. I cannot tell where it goes from there. Maybe it's better not to ask my Brothers…Brothers? Yes, these are my Brothers. I understand now. I am one of them, or Two of them to be precise.

Thoughts of who I am and who everyone is fall upon me. The truth of my own existence among a society of tens of thousands of manufactured beings is brought to light within my mind.

In the beginning, there were the Onlys: Hoynom, Jon-Jan, Hoy-jet, Xut-Xon, Fonmet. One million eight hundred forty-one thousand twenty-four days ago the Onlys created their first clone of Fonmet: Payl-1. Soon after came Muyyg-1, Merch-1, Shairn-1 and Choyt-1. The Onlys taught the Ones to replicate themselves, to imagine and create more original Ones. After the Onlys no longer breathed, they were preserved by the Ones so that their essence and patterns would always be available in the future.

Chrayt-4 glances at me over his tabletop interface. "How do you feel?"

I have to think about that one for a bit. How do I feel? Good question.

"I....feel...plastic," I say. A more accurate word unavailable in my vocabulary, it's pretty close to the sensation coming from my extremities.

"That's actually a good thing," Chrayt-4 responds, "because, in a sense, you are. In time, that artificial, disconnected feeling will fade and you won't really notice it anymore. It happens to all of us at first. We call it Transient Mortal Cognizance."

"So," I say, "I do not yet realize that I am not really real?"

"Okay."

Chrayt-4 has an air of urgency about him.

"As soon as Brother Thayl-2 disconnects your diagnostic link," he says, "we'll get you dressed and head to the briefing room where you'll be prepped for the mission."

After some help to fit me into the metalized, gray tunic and cloak, Chrayt takes hold of my hand to guide me along the corridors. "All of us Brothers possess some level of telepathic bond with our kind. You, however, have....an upgrade. Here in this place, you're like a mental megaphone. Everyone on this ship can hear your thoughts, I'd guess."

"Why am I different?" I ask, the question of every child.

"Because you are created for a specific purpose, not to stay here among us. You are meant for direct interaction with very different beings – corporeal beings – to communicate through telepathy or bi-directional transference of intent through their organic devices. With one of the species, there has only been sparse opportunity for dialogue, and it's not always been positive."

I catch him looking across behind me at Thayl.

"Each of us is designed with various abilities," Chrayt continues, "but as distinct individuals we have a singular function that guides our primary objective. Mine is scientific research. Yours is diplomacy. As you begin to take action in any given situation, you may notice that your feelings draw you toward finding the best resolution for others. However, unlike anyone before you, this core process has been interwoven with a highly tactical operations protocol. This will help you....well, not to be too blunt about it, it may keep you alive longer."

"Shall I expect that there will be potentially hazardous situations?" I ask.

"Jove-2, I programmed you myself, so I know that you have brave and courageous properties. That gives me the confidence to send you on this mission. You have been given a comprehensive download of all available data pertaining to this star system, its inhabitants, their histories, societies, languages, relationships. You will need all of that."

Just as it sank in that the plan includes me getting murdered more than a few times, we enter a tactical bay with many displays, monitors and interfaces. Arriving ahead of us are several clones that I have not met in person, but seem to know anyway: Ambassador Moyab-4, Captain Raytk-31, Security Director Cairn-14, Elder Choyt-72 and Trayd-7. Over the past hour, the fogginess of my mind has cleared. It feels like I have direction and a reason to exist.

Moyab-4 welcomes me on behalf of the group. "This is a historic moment for the Union and our Brothers. As the Onlys look down on us from Elysium, they send their blessings to you, Jove-2."

Choyt-72 reaches forward, taking my hand. "Brother Jove, I have waited a very long time to witness this day. You represent the Union and your Brothers, as the mediator in a conflict of potentially genocidal proportions. By now you have received all of our available information about the irenic inhabitants of planet Jupiter and of the Prawl-Tang, the marauders that launch countless attacks from their home system of Alnitak, to ravage many peaceful societies, taking no prisoners alive. And even as we speak, they have a ship on course to enter the middle atmosphere where the Knowers exist. This work that you have been designed, constructed and commissioned for will be exceptionally difficult."

Choyt lets go of my hand and rests his on my shoulders, turning me to look squarely in the eye.

"You should anticipate insurmountable resistance. If the Prawl-Tang are agreeable at the outset, weigh their words against the history of their actions. They are not above falsehood. They are single-minded in their quest to consume, seeing all life as mere plunder, spoils of another planet overtaken by force. You must, above all things, act to preserve the well-being of the Knowers. We will provide you with some resources, and you are free to take advantage of opportunities to consign others that will aid your mission. You will have no weapons of any kind, as the Union cannot promote violence. The Prawl-Tang on the ship, or any others that you encounter on the planet below – their lives are not to be considered worthless or sacrificed to spare the Jovians. That would be far too easy; for us to merely take one life to balance the potential loss of another. Revenge is not ours to wield. That belongs to another. I trust that you will choose the correct course of action, as required by the circumstances you encounter."

"Let me introduce you to Trayd-7," Moyab-4 says, "His function is to provide you with data, materials and constructs that will be of use to you."

Not the typical silvery blue most common on our people, this one is a soft, translucent orange with bright yellow musculature that shows through the clear dermal layers. Two pairs of eyes on his forehead - gold orbs with cruciform pupils - adds to the rarity of this individual. Even more so what I could not see, he has four arms and a third set of eyes in the back of his head.

"Welcome Brother Jove," Trayd says. "As your Tactical Advisor, I will be in constant communication with you during your flight to and within Jupiter."

"I'm sure you'll be of great help," I say. It occurs to me that he didn't add *from* Jupiter.

Trayd-7 shows me several devices on the countertop, some mechanical, others of biologic manufacture.

"Every Prawl-Tang vessel has a communications organ that serves to scan and locate other ships in the area, their own as well as others. It also releases a powerful subspace beacon, detected at great distances. These two devices on the left will simulate that 'ping' for you. It is very important that your ship sound like another Prawl-Tang vessel. Otherwise, Captain Raytk's fancy cutter will make for easy target practice."

Trayd points to the flat, circular device on the far left, with an array of glowing fins that stand straight off one side, a small plasma duct and mounting webs on the other.

"This model is on loan from the Legion of Worlds military group. It came off an outpost orbiting Rigel. Although it mimics them well, if you get too close they might distinguish the sound from their own, hence our own version grown for use in the fleet vessels." Next to the metal disk is a long tube in a tight v-shape about as long as I am tall, leathery with bright white speckles all over. "Now, this one doesn't scan. It only emits the subspace call when it hears one or if you prompt it to. These never fail to fool the Prawl-Tang into thinking we are one of them, but it is a smaller construct, so it tires easily."

I have to ask.

"….or if I prompt it to?"

Stepping closer to me, Trayd leans his chin next to mine.

"Yes, you just tell it…" he says, almost imperceptibly, "*Aw-hoot.*"

"Awhoot?" I say.

Trayd has already made a dive for the floor; the others bend over or hastily cover their ears. I am left mouth agape when the thing inhales at least half the room's air, swelling to thirty times its ambient size, then blasts out a ferocious, deafening crash. If a thousand cymbals slammed together, that might compare. The tube shoots in a fast arc through the room, hitting someone hard in the behind.

I trip backwards over Captain Raytk, to land on my back. A large window between this space and the office next door collapses. Pieces of disintegrated laminate fly across to slam into the far wall over there. My own auditory impulse filaments overloaded, I can at least read the Security Director's lips. It's something rude, from his list of expletives.

My lesson in high-performance cosmotympanics at a juncture, most of the group retreats to the docking port of the much smaller craft nestled into the Fleet Command cruiser. Cairn-14 has had enough, it seems, and Choyt-72 wobbled away.

Captain Raytk manipulates the controls that operate the dock doors in the ceiling above. Usually there are beeps associated with the pressing of buttons for the pass code. However, it would seem that my ears are still in auto-diagnostic mode. Wiggling a fingertip in the hole on the side of my head seems to help, just in time to catch the Captain's discourse.

"….in the rear of the vessel, which we access from the next deck up of the Command Ship. At present, that's being used to install the hypertrophic cloning equipment and autogenic systems. Your entire series will be placed there as well, each pre-linked to the core loader while still inside their delivery cassettes."

"…which, by the way," Chrayt-4 adds, "has undergone considerable modification for you. For the first time, a clone can be surgically refitted and upgraded while the cassette is gravid, prepartum."

Sounds disgusting, maybe I will turn my ears off again.

Captain Raytk waves me to the bridge, to the pilot and navigation functions. With a look across at Trayd-7, he inquires about my
abilities to operate the vessel.

"I would imagine that his Tactical Download includes Advanced
Pilotage?"

"I have complete knowledge of shuttlecraft operations and flight
controls," I say.

By the look on Raytk's face, I should have just stepped on his
foot.

"This is no shuttle. It is a cutter. There are significant differenc-
es," Raytk says. "This vehicle is four times the size of the largest
shuttle. Not only does it possess the latest TransWave Drive capability, its sub-light performance is on par with any robotic military
vessel. The moment we begin to interface with the controls, our Pilotage subroutine activates within us. Visual acuity, syncardic pressures, dexterity, fibrous pretension, as well as many other autonomic functions will increase to far higher levels than normal. This is
required to survive the improved flight characteristics of this ship.
Should you encounter a corporeal being, a mortal, use extreme cau-
tion during maneuvers while they're on board. What you might experience as a bump will flatten them against a bulkhead, potentially
injuring or killing them. Do you understand?"

"Yes, I do. Thank you for the clarification."

My training continues while Trayd leaves to supervise the final
configuration of the automated cloning hardware in the....cutter's
aft compartment. I had asked if I was to receive instruction for operation and service of that equipment. Trayd points out that it should
only activate if I am dead, so, no.

All too soon, I am left alone on the bridge, intrigued by the many switches and gauges across the wide panel of the cockpit. I can actually hear the hiss of microplasma surging in my head. The unrelenting flood of the sub-space crossloader is my continued education. Regardless of how much intelligence is conveyed from Knowledgebase into my SynThinker, I haven't done it until I actually do it, and even then, what am I going to do? According to my mission parameters, it's safe to say that I fly down into the clouds to hunt for the Prawl-Tang, to stop them from doing whatever mayhem they do. I don't think anyone expects me to actually make it out in one piece.

Stepping up onto the pilot's bama, I try the fit of the padded braces that support my head and torso during flight. It seems a bit tight. Trayd-7 mentioned that my series had a 'heavily gusseted dynathoracic module'. I wonder if that makes my butt look big.

My presence detected at the controls, the ship-board computer projects a three dimensional hologram of the craft's exterior before me. Reaching out to touch the photons, I inadvertently change the scene to an exploded view of all critical ship systems. Pulling my hand back returns it to a slowly rotating view of the outside. I can plainly see the shape, when viewed from above, as a slice of pie, about thirty degrees wide at the tail, narrowing down evenly to the bridge at the front, at only about one-tenth the width. Viewed from the side, the front is nearly half again as tall as the rear, sloping down and back, the edges a little more so, a gentle arch on both the top and bottom. The bridge windows at the uppermost point lean out about forty degrees from its base. Across the aft surface, the four flared openings for the engines are easy to spot, with the rear-central port for the aft cargo area between them. For some reason, the shape of the cutter brings to mind a stringed musical instrument. Without any further input from me, the image times out and disappears.

A colorful brightness in my peripheral vision catches my attention. I lean a bit to see around the window frame of the bridge's left - Jupiter. In a flash, a myriad of similar images cross my mind, a light-speed slide show of the planet. None are anywhere close to the incredible depth and beauty of this magnificent sphere right here in front of me.

"Command Control Bridge to Jove - please acknowledge," the fleet supervisor says, calling over the audio system.

"Um…yep?"

"Yep? It is time to bring your systems online and initiate the startup sequence on those four lovely Yenyks," he says, paying homage to the creator-clone of the cutter's high-powered engines. "Would you like to try or shall we take care of that from here?"

"Why don't you? I'm busy," I say.

Deep within my consciousness, I hear crowds of laughter. Chrayt-4 had said, 'Here in this place, you are like a mental megaphone. Everyone on this ship can hear your thoughts.'

The cheers from within give way to the hum and whine of the ship's operational devices as they gain breath, spin up, burp, gasp or whatever the case may be on a para-bio-craft with a defined caloric requirement. A dozen sharp bangs around the perimeter of the hull are the release of clamps that hold the cutter during fleet ops. On an indicator in the panel ahead: Bridge Port Door – green - Dock Port Door – green; almost like I knew where to look. An orange lamp near the upper center edge begins to flash – auto launch imminent. Here we go.

At the instant of my decision to cooperate with this action, my body feels quite different, very solid. Every movement exceptionally precise and swift. The number of stars I can see triples, quadruples.

Row upon row of mental bullet-points pass through my Pilotage Program checklist. I must admit, in the life of serial clones, there's a certain thrill to being the first to experience something like this.

"Command Control bridge to Equus bridge – prepare for launch," sounds over the intercom. I do believe I can hear them clapping. And not just in telepathy, but in the background of the audio monitor.

"Thank you, my Brothers. I wish you well, and….uh….sorry about the window thing!"

More cheering.

The low frequency boom of the cutter launching from atop the Command ship is followed by a most unnerving sensation (of which I have had many on this my first day). I see the nose of the ship below promptly disappearing. This does not match with the lack of acceleration data from my tactile and balance sensors. That must be what Captain Raytk had mentioned.

The ship yaws around one hundred sixty degrees, to line up Jupiter's horizon, previously behind us. Four triangular indicators on my right change from yellow to green. The organic engines are well fed, pressurized and eager to honk out their ominous tones as they push against sub-space.

Signaled by the darkening of the auto-launch lamp, I glance at the forward flight auto-guidance controls. I feel good about their configuration, so I mustn't have anything to worry about there. Reaching down with my left hand, I grasp the outer sleeve of the throttle rake, giving a gentle downward push through a quarter of its travel. With four massive tubas roaring far behind me, I perceive that Jupiter is getting bigger.

"Equus, we have you on target for entry into stratosphere in seven hours, forty-two minutes. The auto-nav will lead you to the last projected coordinates of the Prawl-Tang vessel, along the rim of the South-Southern Temperate Zone."

"Understood," I say. "That's good to know, and thanks."

Another two hours pass before I hear from the Union again. As it turns out, this may be the very last time I do.

"Equus, this is Command."

"Yes, I hear you."

"Brother Jove, this is Choyt-72."

"I had hoped to say goodbye to you," I say, "and thank you for this opportunity....for the chance....for my life, however long it lasts, anyway."

"I consider myself fortunate to have seen all that I have over the many centuries of my existence. I can tell you that my bearing witness to this day is the highlight of all my memories."

For the first time in my entire life of fourteen hours, I am speechless.

"Jove, you have more to rely on than vast knowledge and diplomatic protocols. You also have Wisdom. You have the voices of the Onlys, and the archived experiences of the Ones. The many sentient species of the blood are born, and are given time to grow and learn all that they need. We are different. We awaken as the complete form. Yet each of us requires the opportunity to absorb and accept the accumulated experiences of our ancestors. Might I suggest that, as you travel down to the fate that awaits you, you pass the time by interacting with all of them. Then, when you need them the most, in the trying times, your mind will join with your ancestors, to bring you peace. As Only Brother Fonmet reminds us, 'Wisdom calls out from within ourselves and leads us along the right path.' Avail yourself of her, Jove. Listen with the innermost parts of your being. There is so much more to you than artfully arranged organo-silicates. Every clone possesses a design, an imprint of the original. It is your true self. You may have been born just today, my Brother, but you were conceived five thousand years ago by the Onlys. They knew you then. Know them now."

"I believe you, Brother Choyt," I say. "I will do as you suggest."

I waited for a farewell from the elder, but he was gone. He had said all there was to say.

"Equus, the fleet is prepared to leave the system. We await our turn to link to the TransWave Aperture at Tau Ceti. We've left a beacon behind that you can use to contact us if for whatever reason your long-range communications should fail. With your secure administrative encryption, you can modify it to emit a signal that it is safe for us to return to Sol. Take care."

Take care - what exactly does that mean? After mulling that for a few milliseconds, I come to the conclusion that 'take care' is less uncomfortable to say than 'try not to get yourself killed more than twenty-nine times.'

In the primary sensor array, with my galloping steed represented in the center of the oval screen, the greenish crescent filling the right side is Jupiter. A stream of TW's march down from the top to a point near the symbol for the moon, Callisto. That's the Wave from the Tau Ceti aperture, twelve light years away, reaching to draw the fleet through interstellar space. Like an ocean beach on any planet, the wave comes in on top, and the undertow pulls in the other direction.

"Goodbye, my Brothers."

Although my SynThinker receives a continuous download of information from the Knowledgebase, the data traffic is far in the background. I make a query of the crossloader to help me locate Wisdom, as Choyt had recommended. She is there, pointing the way. I move past her to the virtual doorway. My mind opens to the whole of the history of the Brothers before me.

Archive Vision: 2989 BCE, Anchorsut Township, Sirius A3

I find myself in a daydream. I'm not me in the dream, but essentially the same. I'm a clone, a Synthetic, but it feels different. That artificial, plastic sensation has returned. It's even worse than before.

There is another person with me. It is the Man, Fonmet. We lay next to each other on our backs, on the bare ground. We are on a vast plain of some remote place. All I can see in any direction is more dusty ground, dry and barren. With raised head, I can see the curvature of the planet all around. He tells me to stop fussing, to just look at the clouds in the sky above us. I change from my faraway focus on the desolate horizon to look at him more closely. His face seems familiar. His skin is a pale blue, soft, with a lightly grained texture. On most of his scalp are golden filaments that are loose. They fall down to curl about his neck and below him on the dirt.

His mouth is moving, as engaged in speech, but I cannot hear any sounds. I hear wind. But the wind is….out there. We are here and there is only quiet. It is not an unfavorable circumstance, this quiet. Though the lack of sensation is….causes me to….it feels like something is missing that should be there….here.

I feel his hand touch mine. His fingers wrap around my palm.

What are you missing? What am I missing? What are you missing? I sense this question but I cannot hear anything. I look back to the Man. He is staring directly at me.

"What're you missing?" Well, I heard him *that* time.

"I do not understand the question," I say.

"Payl, this is the third time we've come out here together to look at the clouds. Every time, you cannot hold still. You lay there and fidget. You look around and around like you're missing something and you think you'll find it out there somewhere."

The Man has made four statements and all are correct. He has made one supposition that is—

"Don't analyze. Just answer my question," he says, "What're you missing?"

"I...am missing...input."

The Man rolls back to look up at the pink sky and yellow clouds.

"Thank you," he says. "Was that so hard?" I hear air come from his nose. He once called that a 'sigh'. He does it often. "Lay your head back and look at the clouds."

I do.

I have previously asked this next question of the Man fifteen times and not received a suitable answer. However, he recommends that I overlook failures and continue further attempts.

"Explain for this One. What are we supposed to see in the clouds?"

"No, Payl," he says. "What do you see in the clouds?"

Sixteen.

"I see water vapor."

"Of course you see water vapor, Dummy," he says. "I've told you, what *shapes* do you see?"

He called me Dummy again. He has apologized for that before. I will ignore the error.

Again, I look at each cloud within my peripheral range. There

are one hundred and four individually recognizable patterns....
no....one hundred sev....no....now there are only eighty....there is
a problem.

"I see a problem," I tell the Man.

"So, he *can* see something other than water vapor."

"The various atmospheric pressures at the higher altitudes are
causing a potentially infinite number of obtuse formations to adapt
at irregular intervals," I say. "It is not possible to distinguish any
given shape."

The Man rolls his head to the side to look at me again. I choose
to continue in the vertical.

"So your processing capability is too slow to imagine the shape
of something – anything – in a cloud structure, and not verbalize that
before the shape changes?"

That is one of those statements that could either be a question
or a factual oration. He wants me to learn something specific. My
process capabilities far exceed that of the Man. Yet, he is apparently
aware of an obvious fact that I cannot perceive. That must be why
he repeatedly expends an inordinate amount of effort to bring us to
this place of...nothing.

Nothing. That is it. I get it. I finally understand. He wants me to
visualize 'nothing'. This is allegory. He has been bringing me here
to a place that comes as close to nothing as he can find, to teach
me to see something where there is nothing. There is nothing 'out
there'. He wants me to find it inside of me.

Now I know what he wants. I look over at him. I feel my face
smile and look back up into the nothingness of the sky and random
clouds.

"I see a star-nosed cat."

The Man is very excited. With his hand on my shoulder, he shakes me harder and harder. I'm moving and rocking under the strain. He looks concerned. He yells again but I cannot hear him. Shaking me, now violently. There's something terribly wrong. Why can't I hear him?

End Archive Vision

Jolted from the dream, I see the control panel of the Equus before me. Many of the indicator lamps that should be green are red or yellow. The ship pitches and vibrates with harsh vertical accelerations. I gather that I have arrived at the upper limits of the atmosphere with excessive velocity. With a slight pull up on the throttle slide and manipulations of the attitude controls, I bring the ship out of the cloud tops and back above the ceiling of the giant world.

With my Pilotage Program using the lion's share of my cognitive throughput, not to mention my out of body experience to the desert adventure with one of the Onlys, my enhanced telepathic ability had taken a back seat on the journey.

Now in the planet, I feel a strong sense of dread, out there, panic. I allow myself to ignore the path of the ship for a few moments, to focus on a distant cry. Unprepared for the onslaught of emotion that accompanies that decision, my body flinches and tries to twist its way free of the pads and railing of the pilot's bama, subconsciously reacting to being buried alive, drowning or strangled by some inescapable horror. As quick as the flood of terror washes over me, my Tactical application comes to my rescue, to manage the instinctual urge of fight or flight.

With an intramental cough and sputter, I find the clarity needed to survey the telepathic landscape. Somewhere down and to my right is a place of hatred and doom. Down I go, and just in time. Directly ahead in the mist is the edge of the OverSinger field.

By the narrowest of margins I avoid a fatal crash into the upside down mountain of living crystals. The Equus dives along the lower rim of the shallow cone, toward the space between the underside of the OverSingers and the tops of the next layer of heavier, foaming hydrogen. Throttle to one percent and braking thrusters on full, I need not rush to my death and the premature end of my twenty-eight selves stacked in the rear cargo hold. According to the Union Knowledgebase, there could be at least half a million of the indigenous cephalids below me. So far, none have appeared on the ship's bio-scanner, only the large mass of giant glass cubes above.

Just then, the proximity alarm lets out a strong whoop. Not something that would show up on the bio-scanner, which is tuned to detect the faint electrical impulses of living beings, is the enormous body of a deceased Knower hanging limp in the sky directly ahead. With the crystals encased in the bladder around his cuttlebone no longer receiving autonomic messages from its nervous system, they have buoyed him up higher near the base of the thermosphere, to bounce and bob along, like a lost ghost, adrift in a shadowy cumulous maze.

With a stiff correction in the course of the ship, I manage to avoid contact with the floating corpse, passing it on the right by just twenty meters. My Pilotage app prompts me to press a small purple button on the far left of the control panel. A tiny subspace marker beacon shoots out of a barrel located in the stern of the Equus, to park itself in the foggy air near the Knower's body.

Was this a natural death or will I find evidence of violence against these gentle warless creatures? The starboard fly-brake extended to its maximum angle, the ship executes a solid turn to the right. Thickened air raises a howl through the perforations in the plate. The auto-nav recognizes the signal of the marker and maneuvers to bring me alongside. Braking thrusters and lift jets on the belly of the ship spit and roar to keep the ship steady against the determined gravitational pull of Jupiter.

A barely perceptible ding comes from a gauge before me, to alert that the rate of fuel consumption used to hover on a gas giant planet exceeds manufacturer recommendations.

The Equus shows all stop, station-keeping mode active, and the sensor screen places the marker beacon just a dozen meters ahead. I hear a thud against the far right cockpit window. Turning, I see four large suckers, each a meter in diameter, and one stuck to the outside glass. They appear to be the tip of a more extensive pattern on a cephalopod arm. I step out of my tubular framed booth atop the pilot's bama and walk over to get a better view out the window. Crouching low, I can see the massive and muscular arm, with many more, even larger suckers, shrouded by the mist above the bridge. At least two of the suckers are adhered to the pane, but there's nobody home up there to flex the appropriate valve to release the vacuum.

"Hell's Bells," I say, from my List of Mild Expletives. Stomping back to the flight controls, I try a hard yaw to the left to get the poor dead beast to break free. Not going to happen, it just sways and pivots up there above me.

"Well, Mister Jove the Second," I say to myself, "the most foolish thing you could do is go up on top of the ship, in the terribly hazardous conditions of the upper atmosphere."

I climb the ladder leading up to the top deck over the bridge. The lighting is dim, but I can see where some hasty modifications had been performed. Many girders and braces are attached from the outer hull to the secondary bulkheads, installed throughout the fuselage to prevent the exterior pressures from crushing the vessel during idiotic maneuvers like this.

Ding.

Yes, my dear, I am aware that we are burning too much fuel right now.

I climb up the ladder within the inner port hatch and close it behind me. Next, I should equalize the pressures before opening the outer hatch. The valve was intended for use under more reasonable circumstances. No sooner have I cracked it open to about ten degrees and the enormous pressure of fifty kilopascals slam it the rest of the way, taking most of my thumb with it. Okay, this is where I thought the Tactical app should come in handy! Why did I let myself do that? The hurricane force wind lasts only a brief two and half seconds, but it is enough to shove me back against the interior hatch fairly hard. I hear a crack in my inner somethings. Now I've only got one opposable thumb to do other dumb things with outside. Not severed, but it is flopping around at the joint.

After a one handed crawl up onto the roof of the Equus, I look up to see that I'm in the shadow of the deceased Knower. His, hers, its, arms and tentacles are draping down like a veil over the right side of the ship. The scaled body is hanging loose from the single boney plate along the top of the mantle. Like a deflated balloon, the translucent skin sags and flaps in the strong wind. I push my way through the gelatinous fibers and toneless musculature to search for the one arm stuck to the window.

Oh, it's a him. One for the record books, I'd guess.

Finding the arm that won't give way when I tug, I see that it falls down towards the front of the bridge. That's the one. With my arms wrapped around the narrower section near the tip, I squish the mass together with great effort and drag it up almost to where I can see the end.

Thankfully, my Tactical Notifier gives me a rap on the forehead. Hey, Dummy! Now where have I heard that before? If it does come loose from the ship, I will be hanging onto a three hundred meter long, lighter than air, corpus dirigibulus. Not so smart. I resign myself to logic and release my hold on the poor thing.

Ding – Ding!

Maybe if I can anchor the body to the deck, it won't float away while I get the arm unstuck. With a stretch up, I grab one of the smaller tentacles near the twelve meter wide, razor sharp beak. I pull down hard; it lifts me off my feet. I see a metal loop behind me that I bet would be right to get my foot through. I pull harder. It won't budge.

"Oh, come down, already!" I yell.

The Obedient Sand within the gall bladder of the Knower heeds my ill-tempered instruction, and drops the weight of the entire creature onto the Equus, with me under the huge pile of flaccid flesh. Seventy-five tons of active silicates doing exactly as they were told by my genius has only made a bad situation worse.

Okay, think, Jove. Below me I hear a muffled Ding – Ding – Ding!

Forget logic, talk to the rocks.

"Get off of me!" The Sand complies. The weight on top of me eases up and drifts sideways. As the body of the Knower swings around to move off, I see the wound across the head. Right through the center of an upper eye is the tell-tale X-shape of a Prawl-Tang tracking spear.

With the weight of the beast in a slide down the side of the ship, the thrusters struggle to maintain level. They fail. The ship rolls hard to the side and over I go. Even two thumbs would be of no benefit. There's just nothing to grab hold of. Well, that's that.

The fluttering of my robe and hood becomes an odd irritant as I plummet into the depths of my planetary namesake. It doesn't take too long. That's good. I'm sure that stupid fuel gauge is dinging its little self silly.

I awake as Number Three. The far panel of my cassette drops down and I am deposited feet first into the make-shift cloning lab. Standing, I do a cursory review of my important systems.

"Two thumbs? Check."

My SynThinker whirs to catch up with all of the data from my previous me. The ship is upright, thank goodness and yes, there's that lovely alarm bell now pretty much constant. I run forward into the bridge cockpit and get settled into place to get the ship moving again. The roof hatch closed, I get two green lights there. Fuel reserves are down to eighty percent. Okay, so I have used a month's supply in the past twenty minutes.

All six of the sky brakes set out to full, I back down the lift thrusters to minimum to let the craft slide its way down further under the OverSingers. Peering up through the roof portals, I can barely make out the rotation of the many layers of them. I glance over at the now quiet fuel gauge.

"Happy now?"

In no time, I feel some oscillations from the brake plates as I continue the dive down to where the Knowers should be.

The feeling of dread begins to creep in again. Through my hypersensitive eyes, I make a gruesome count: two, three....six....ten, twelve, twenty dead Knowers pass by in the first minute. Then, no more, just sky.

A writhing consciousness slams into my psyche, just like before. I am under attack? No, not me, but someone out there feels this overwhelming terror. My enhanced telepathic reception transfers those paralyzing sensations to me. Although the Manufactured Flesh and SynThinker Union did not find it necessary to include goose-bumps in their clones' design, I would find them appropriate about now.

The bio-scanner display lights up with a large signal down and to the right. Far larger than any Knower, this blip on the meat radar is more like a small moon. With a momentary bounce of the starboard sky brakes, the ship leans around to line up the signal with the top center of the monitor - dead ahead. Gee, there's got to be a better word for *that*. The altitude indicator of the scanner advises me to pull up level and get on the braking thrusters. I lean the ship over and aim the nose to just pass whatever it is on my right, so I can get a better look.

What I see is completely unexpected. In a slow spiral, around and around in the gray sky is a mass of Knowers, at least a few hundred of them, all gripped tightly onto the front of the Prawl-Tang Super Scoop, of which I can barely make out underneath. There are another dozen or so Knowers wrapping their arms and tentacles over the crusty lump astern where the Mission Steward should be encapsulated. These harmless doves of the jovian cloudscape have turned from their retreat and attacked the enemy, and are not about to let it go.

Terror, like a rising wave, startles me. It's the Prawl-Tang I am feeling! It's scared to the bone, which is on the outside, I think. Their species may have never before encountered a prey that brings a pugilistic method to the battle. More often than not, the Prawl-Tang would enact their brutal carnage and then skulk away to rejuvenate their weapons and fuel. This time, however, the Scourge of Orion has lost the advantage and the opportunity to mete out death at its pleasure. The giant cephalids of Jupiter have proven that they have what it takes to put up a fight, without guns, laser-cannons, bombs, or subspace dislocators. They're going to wrestle the devil to…to…. what? I have no idea what they're going to do next.

Just then, my Diplomatic Protocol app steps up to take front and center in my mind, while Pilotage goes back to agitating the fuel monitor with a slow hover. The words of Choyt-72 ring clear. "You must, above all things, act to preserve the well-being of the Knowers…. the Prawl-Tang….their lives are not to be considered worthless or sacrificed to spare the Jovians."

Okay, Jove, it's time to jump in there and negotiate. The first thing will be to make contact with the Prawl-Tang, so they can see me as a neutral party and not as taking sides with the Jovians. If I can convince them to cease hostilities, it should be an easy next step to get the Knowers to release their grip. The hard part is to avoid a collision with this colossal dogpile that's spinning around in the sky. The Equus is a high performance craft, but it doesn't exactly dart around with every flick of the stick. One good bump from that Super Scoop would make a little smoky poof where my ship used to be. I back away to a reasonable distance and program the auto-nav to take inputs from the proximity detector. That should give me some elbow room outside as well as in my head.

Led down the intramental path to the source, I reach out to the Prawl-Tang's mind, with hopes to make heads or tails of ten arms glued together. Certainly not the cheering and well-wishing that I'd heard in my head during departure from the Command ship, this experience is akin to a face-first dive into mosh pit anarchy. With historical Union Knowledgebase detail for how this has worked with the Knowers, I looked – or felt for – a mental pillar out there; an anchor in the churning waters, in a sea of turbulent thoughts. I find it in the most unlikely of entities: the Prawl-Tang vessel's para-sentient Navigation Onus. Doggedly executing its last directive from the Mission Steward - to yaw abruptly right - the nerve-laden tree of living calcite is eager to converse with someone not engaged in a brawl.

"External input detected," it says. I'm guessing that's for 'hello'.

"My name is Jove. I wish to help you."

"External input not recognized," it says.

"I am a new input."

"External input is not Mission Steward," it says.

"Correct, Jove is not Mission Steward."

"Navigation Onus is secure-linked to Mission Steward," it states, "external input recognized as potential subversion."

"Jove is not the enemy of the Prawl-Tang."

"Incorrect key," it says, "Two attempts remaining."

"Jove wishes to make contact with the Mission Steward."

"Incorrect key," it says, "One attempt remaining."

My available List of Moderate Expletives at the ready, it finally occurs to me that although the Navigation Onus is willing to chat on an intramental level, it's looking to satisfy some obvious security protocol through an internal channel.

With a wince, I use up my last chance to make friends with a bloody rock.

"Awhoot."

The Union grown Prawl-Tang communications organ is mounted remotely in the belly of the Equus, so the staccato cymbal crash was just slightly deafening this time. Hey, and no windows broken, that I can see anyway.

"Key accepted," Navigation Onus replies. "Secure-link with external input registered."

"Jove wishes to make contact with the Mission Steward."

"Mission Steward not responding," it says.

"Understood, Mission Steward is…um, unable to effectively control the vessel," I say.

"Mission Steward not responding," it says, confused.

Too many words, Jove, simplify.

"Mission Steward failure," I state.

Silence - not good - it's going to figure me out….

"Mission Steward failure not recognized," it says, "External bioplastic organisms are interrupting internal communications."

Wow, that qualified as a complete sentence. Not bad for a lump of coral.

"Jove to repair internal communications," I say.

"Proceed."

"Navigation Onus disregard last Mission Steward directive," I say.

"Rate of yaw stabilized."

"Station keeping," I say, seeing that the swirling mass had slowed rotation.

"Rate of yaw zero," it says, "Horizontal velocity zero; vertical velocity zero; all accelerations zero."

Um, yeah, I think that's what I said in two words. Looking out the starboard bridge windows, I can see that the Scoop is no longer in a wild, off-balance spiral, but is indeed executing a steady hover. I wonder if his fuel gauge is nagging, too. Quite a few of the Knowers have let go and are scattering around it, as if re-analyzing the situation. Maybe they think they've won the battle. That could be a fatal mistake on their part.

One of the cephalids on the outer edge of the mob spots the Equus soaring nearby and begins to head this way to investigate. It should see the ship as typical for a Union vessel and not attack; however, I *did* just broadcast a Prawl-Tang identifier ping. No doubt that was heard by everything sporting ears on this side of the planet. If this gets ugly, Jove-4 is going to have his hands full with the back half of a chomped Equus.

Goose bumps - I distinctly feel goose bumps. And here comes the Knower, now halfway between the Equus and the mass of flustered cuttlefish. I exert gentle pressure on the control stick, to let the craft slip to the side, opening the gap slightly.

Surprising me, Navigation Onus speaks up.

"Mission Steward responding."

"Navigation Onus connect Jove to Mission Steward."

"Connection accepted. Mission Steward standing by," it says.

"External input Jove - external input registered." I say, using my new credentials.

"Mission Steward is hearing external input Jove," the Prawl-Tang says.

Its mind sounds stressed, worse than the irritable Navigation Onus.

"Jove wishes to help Mission Steward," I tell it…him?

"Ship Ω94λ250 is under attack by external bioplastic organisms," he says.

"Jove will ask bioplastic organisms to cease attack of Ship Ω94λ250."

"You will launch all spear at bioplastic organisms now," he says.

"Jove has no spear. Jove has ambassadorial privilege." I expect starfish laughter.

"Jove is Omega or other?" he asks.

"Jove is other," I say, "Jove wishes to intercede."

No goose bumps this time, but I am so tense, I have white-knuckled the round railing into a gentle oval shape. And it's wiggling.

Wait, not the railing – the whole ship! The giant cephalid Knower has reached out and given the Equus a friendly nudge; not a good time for a squid visit. Or is it? I need an idea and fast.

Ding – Ding – Ding – Ding.

Is that an idea or the fuel gauge?

I gently stretch my thoughts to the Knower with a tentacle curled against the nose of the ship. "TinyMaker welcomes Knower."

"Knower welcomes TinyMaker," it says. "DangerComes be DangerNear. DangerNear be DeathMaker. TinyMaker stop DeathMaker!"

"Yes, TinyMaker want stop DeathMaker," I say. "TinyMaker say help to DeathMaker. DeathMaker stop."

"TinyMaker no help DeathMaker!"

C'mon, Jove, think before you think louder!

"TinyMaker say DeathMaker stop," I say. "Knowers stop. DeathMaker stop. Knowers let go DeathMaker. DeathMaker go."

"TinyMaker help Knowers!" it says, my loyalty expected.

"Knower confer with Knowers on DeathMaker?" I ask. "If DeathMaker say DeathMaker go, will Knowers let go of DeathMaker?"

Oh, please tell me you can understand that. It is so rare to have a conversation with only one of them at a time, according to the Knowledgebase, anyway. This is my first go at a life-or-death discussion with a squid.

The Knower releases his grip on the nose of the Equus and in a display of immense power sucks in a great inhale of air and blasts it out his nozzles, rocking the ship and in just two seconds casting himself halfway back to where the others are. Accidentally leaving a little trail of ink behind him to darken the sky between us, I figure the poor fellow must be nervous. In no time he begins to return with a half dozen others. Thankfully, the Prawl-Tang are known for their patience as well as brutality. I keep waiting for the Mission Steward to take exception to my admission of being 'other'. If I were him…. it….I would ask how I managed to come by a Prawl-Tang ping organ.

In my head I can hear the discussion among the Knowers that are on their way back to me. With the Scoop holding steady about eight kilometers away, I let the Equus drift a little closer. The fuel rate alarm has given up on me. Perhaps it has resigned itself to the fact that I don't care if we burn through the entire tank on the first day out.

"Knowers say go to DeathMaker," they say. "DeathMaker stop! DeathMaker go Far! TinyMaker say go to DeathMaker. Knowers go. TinyMaker say go Far to DeathMaker."

Okay, I believe they're willing to break up the fight. Makes sense for the victim to agree to that; now I have to convince the bully. For all I know, the Mission Steward was content to wait them out for as long as it took to regain the advantage. So, am I really just giving it time to prepare for a second attack? Is this what I was warned about; that it shouldn't be easy; that easy was a trick? The Union Knowledgebase has many recorded instances of attempts to open peaceful negotiations with the Prawl-Tang and none have ever made it this far. This is what I was created for; to do exactly this. So, why shouldn't it work?

I mentally pull myself back from the noisy, schoolyard experience of contact with the childlike Knowers, and project my thoughts back out to the cold anxiety of the Mission Steward.

"Jove wishes to help. Jove made agreement with bioplastic organisms to release Mission Steward."

More silence - perhaps if I....ugh....just wait, Jove.

"How does Jove help Mission Steward?" it asks.

"Jove will mediate between Mission Steward and bioplastic organisms."

"Mediation unnecessary," he says. "Bioplastic organisms are inconsequential."

"Bioplastic organisms are sentient and choose life over death. They will continue to fight."

"Bioplastic organisms are inconsequential. They will continue to die," he says.

"Jove has calculated that sufficient numbers of bioplastic organisms exist to overcome Mission Steward. Jove will mediate." I presume that even an echinoderm wants to save its own skin. If I can convince it that enough Knowers might drag it down into the boiling depths to a painful death, perhaps now is a good time for it to back off.

Then, just like that, the argument is over.

"Jove may mediate," he says.

"Jove will tell bioplastic organisms to release Mission Steward. Mission Steward will cease attack of organisms."

"Mission Steward will cease attack," he agrees, all too easily.

So, now I am wondering if that was difficult enough to be real. I decide to take it anyway. Elated, the Knowers accept the terms. I think they're just mentally tired and physically exhausted from hanging onto the giant ship and each other. One by one, they release their hold, the last few disappearing into the mist.

Nudging the Equus a little closer, I get a much better look at the Super Scoop. The entire front third of the hull shows obvious signs of damage, as well as the aft control hump. The massive beaks of the cephalids have gouged deep crevasses in the shell.

As I stare closely at the mottled rusty red and bone-white surface, I get that weird feeling that I am falling. But it isn't me moving down, or the Equus, it is the vast wall of the Super Scoop accelerating up. The ship lifts up past me, creating a vacuum beneath in the dense atmosphere. It draws the Equus in and up along with it. I cut throttle and ride the wave coming up from below to fill the void under the giant ship.

Once the cutter's flight controls are reconfigured for sub-orbital travel and free space, I crack open the two outboard Yenyks, blasting my way up and out of the cloud tops. The Scoop is far ahead and climbing out of the atmosphere, just visible through the upper window.

I keep waiting for the Prawl-Tang to swing out and away from the planet, but it maintains a steady course across the southern face, in the direction of the pole, or at least to a point in space high above it. I program the auto-nav to match speed and heading of the tracked vessel.

My marker beacon still transmits from the location where I found the twenty-some cephalid corpses adrift near the tropopause layer. After the Prawl-Tang leaves orbit, it would be a good idea to circle back to check on the Knowers; to see if I can offer any assistance, or maybe just be there while they grieve the loss of their members. I query the Union Knowledgebase: Funerary Practices of the Jovian Knowers?

The voice I hear inside is familiar, though melancholy.

"Entry four hundred ninety-six, by Ambassador Moyab-4. My visit to the Knowers had an unexpected flavor today. Instead of their typical cheer and inquisitive demeanor, the Knowers all but ignored me. I thought perhaps I had done or said something to offend them; made some alien faux-pas.

"After several hours of careful observation, I understood that they were purposely involved in some solemn ceremony. They had gathered themselves en mass, many thousands of them. Their giant bodies linked together to form a tower or tube of sorts, the bottom of which I could not visualize. The upper formation was very high up for where they normally travel within the boundaries of the thermosphere. Upon closer inspection, I found that they had made an incredibly tall spiral, about six or seven individuals per circumference, interlocking their arms; they all seemed to be pushing the whole assembly upwards, nearer and nearer the base of the cirrus clouds, into the lower stratosphere. Piloting my shuttlecraft higher, where the air is almost clear, I could view them as they broke through. What I witnessed left me astounded.

"There had been a death of a soul of the Knowers. This is a

wholly separate instance from the failure of the cephalopod corporeal body, routinely shed, and discarded like a cloak. In this case, the mind of the entity within had succumbed to whatever brings an end to these amazing beings, the others nearby realizing that the ForeverSleep had fallen upon her. (I found out later it was in fact, an elderly female, a matriarch.)

"A few held her gently in place, so as not to be tossed about by the fierce winds, while many others began to construct this immense tower above her. Some silent call had gone out. They came from great distances to join this vertical procession.

"Now, most delicately, they passed her body up through the center of this living tower, this tube to the furthest reaches of their aerial domain. I could make out her progress as she was lifted to greater heights through the center, even as the tower itself climbed up into the feathery cloud tops.

"I could see no more individuals adding to the rim of the structure, and it swayed and wobbled a bit at its uppermost. With considerable effort they were managing to keep it steady and aloft. When the deceased reached the top, the most awesome act unfolded before me. The Knowers at the pinnacle grabbed her violently and tore her corpse asunder, right through the middle, spilling the vast quantity of Obedient Sand into the air.

"As is always necessary for us to achieve telepathic contact with them, the ship itself translated their thoughts for me. In a fantastic rush of expressive thought and delirious hopes, I heard the sound of all of them cry out together, "Spirit, go!" With their arms and tentacles and faith, they flung the Obedient Sand upwards to space. And it went, as commanded. I could see her shredded body falling down the way it came, through the center of the tower of beloved friends and family. I could not see the end, but I believe they just let the empty shell fall down to the fluidic zone.

"While I watched the individuals fall away from the top of the tower, a blazing streamer of Drane swooped in to fly through where the Sand had just been. I couldn't tell if they were making contact with it or somehow consuming it or otherwise interacting with the process, though it was clear their presence was an integral part of escorting this soul on to the next level of existence. This concludes my report."

What an amazing experience that must have been for him. I wonder if I will be fortunate enough to be present for such an occasion. Given the recent tragic circumstances, there should be ample opportunity to attend.

Something in the back of my 'Thinker tells me that the encounter with the Mission Steward was not thoroughly successful; that somehow, all I did was buy time for the Knowers. Could it really have been as simple as breaking up a fight? There are numerous entries in the Knowledgebase of how the Prawl-Tang prefer to advance and retreat, all the while planning their next attack. There are no records of them willing to abandon a viable resource for very long. I feel very alone out here and with too much at stake for just one person to wrestle with.

I decide to take Choyt-72's advice. I'll make the most of my travel time in review of Knowledgebase and Wisdom. What was it that he said? Oh yes, a quote from Fonmet, 'Wisdom calls out from within ourselves and leads us along the right path.' Well, if there is any wisdom within me, I sure wish it would surface.

"Knowledgebase query: Wisdom."

After a few seconds of the whir of the ship's datapath cooling fans, it occurs to me that I didn't narrow it down to just the Wisdom program within me. This query might be searching through the archives of a hundred known worlds.

"Peace cannot be kept by force," Knowledgebase says, "It can only be achieved through understanding. Knowing is not enough; we must apply. Willing is not enough; we must do. If the fourth hand is empty, three knives remain behind the back. Today I shall behave as if this is the day I will be remembered. Three may keep a secret, if two of them are dead. Incline your ear to wisdom, and apply your heart to understanding. The first Brother of a clone series thinks often about his life; the last Brother of the series thinks often about his death."

Stop. This is too random. There must be countless proverbs available from across the galaxy. I can't digest them all into a single right course of action. Really what I need is to have the best guidance come to me as I need it, like from some all-knowing, all-seeing partner that understands my situation. I shake my head at my own delusion. I'm no different than any other creature that ever existed. I want it all and I want it when I want it. Like this is supposed to be easy. Maybe that's why I was given that dream of lying in the desert with the Only. It was me, as Payl-1 looking up at the clouds. He could've just told me what he wanted me to learn, but it's more important for me to learn it myself. Knowledge can be given but wisdom must be born out of oneself. It must come from within.

"Wisdom, are you there?"

"I am here," she says.

The auto-nav computer interrupts with an audible bong. Programmed to fly a course based on the movements of the giant Super Scoop in the distance, it now indicates that the Prawl-Tang vessel has slowed its pace and is in fact, setting itself into a polar orbit. I manage to place the Equus into the same pattern, about four-hundred kilometers behind. Dialing up the controls for the focused sensor beam, I aim directly ahead toward that big....what shape is that anyway? When the Manufactured Flesh and SynThinker Union grow something, at least we have some sort of molds or framework to guide the cells as they mature and reproduce, you know - symmetry. These Prawl-Tang don't seem to care much about aesthetics.

"Form follows function," says Wisdom. Okay, thanks. Then if the function is to fly through a dense cloud of gas vapor pooled in a nebula, then you need a moon-sized strawberry?

I realize that I've been leaning out of the secure padded railing, stretching my neck toward the glass, as if moving my eyes a foot closer will somehow improve my vision. When I lean back, another hologram alights before me. This time, it's the Super Scoop modeled in three-dimensional glow. The sensors have detected something worthy of scrutiny; motion or activity on the rearmost surface of the ship. Zoomed in, I can make out that one of the nodules or prominences along the aft taper has broken loose. Some debris floating around; chips and shards of the ship's hull that flaked off as the node cleaved from the edge; not very efficient, and certainly difficult to repair. Who knows what goes on in the mind of a starfish? Come to think of it, the Knowers have more in common with the Prawl-Tang than just about any other catalogued sentient species. If they could reach a telepathic connection with each other, I'd bet much of their respective silliness would make perfect sense to both.

Speaking of...I get the distinct impression that the Mission Steward has a very good reason for being down here. Some sort of device has extended from within the ship, out through the newly hatched hatch. It would seem to be at least as long as the massive Scoop, and about two hundred meters square on the ends. Now loose from the main ship, it is clearly an arc-section of about ninety radii with a virtual circumference of almost four kilometers, the partial framework of a much larger circle.

The hologram disappears as the auto-nav displays a projected course for the Scoop. He is moving away from the satellite placed in orbit, to head back up in the direction of the southern bands. I cancel the restart of the main engines and consider giving him some room while I move in closer to inspect the satellite. The Equus' sensor beam realigned to the arch, I run a spectral analysis of the materials used. Expecting rocky coral, I am surprised to find various metals and what could be elements common to plasma control. It's awfully big for a beacon. But then, they do things big. A quick check of the Scoop's position and I can tell that he's already far off, doubling back the way we came down. When done snooping around here I may need to take the whip to my horse, getting back to the Knowers before he does.

Knowledgebase provides no less than sixty potential methods of testing the functions of an unknown satellite. Tried all of them; all I have left is no clue. I need to see this thing with my own eyes, mechanisms though they may be. The Equus makes short work of the four hundred kilometers. In fact, I end up having to lean a little heavy on the braking thrusters to keep from overshooting my parking spot. It's enough to elicit a tiny squeak from the fuel rate dinger.

I can make out rows of high-energy emitters running the entire length of the concave side; various antennas that stick out, but no ports or hatches. Well, a hatch to anyone not a complete freak like the Prawl-Tang. There's something familiar about the layout, but

I'm almost afraid to ask. Time is getting away from me, as is the Scoop. I need to know and there is only one test to find out the truth.

With the four throttles slammed open, the Equus rockets away from the satellite at maximum acceleration. The roar from behind is matched only by the extreme forces that have squeezed me back into my pilot's booth. I let it run for a few minutes, then ease off to swing the cutter around, lining up perpendicular to the arch. More than fifteen thousand kilometers away, I am on course to fly through the arch. I get hard into the throttle again, and then switch on the TransWave Drive. The pods rotate out from their positions in the hull and bring four green lamps and four yellow lamps to life on the panel. Checking the velocity indicator, the rate for sub-light scrolls up briskly: point three – point three five – point four – point four five.

A new metallic voice chatters at me from the control panel. "TransWave Drive activated, threshold achieved." At ten-thousand kilometers distant and moving along at half-light speed, I press the button that signals any apertures within range. Hopefully, I won't end up in distant Aldebaran.

The emitters on the satellite energize, and project a huge bright blue chromodynamic disk in space. All eight indicator lamps are now green. The Wave reaches out from the arch and grabs the Equus easily, like a banner in a stiff breeze swatting at a bug. The cutter crosses the remaining nine thousand five hundred kilometers in just two one-thousandths of a second. Almost sixteen times the speed of light. That was cool.

This is terrible.

Not only does the greater mass of Prawl-Tang fleets have access to this system in a matter of minutes, but if this Super Scoop can deploy a TransWave aperture, they all can.

I wonder what Wisdom has to say about this.

"The good fighters of old first put themselves beyond the possibility of defeat, and then waited for an opportunity of defeating the enemy," Wisdom says.

Gee, I must have left that running. "Well, thanks anyway," I reply. "Who was it that blessed us with that cheery news?"

"The previous quote was taken from The Art of War, as written in the original by Sun Tzu, a successful military general of ancient Earth history," Knowledgebase says.

Oh, yes, Earth - those characters enjoy a good fight, massacring each other ever since Cain found a rock that fit into his brother's skull. At least that's how the story goes, anyway.

"Okay, Wisdom, I need to come up with a way for Mister Sun Tzu and me to defeat the operation of this aperture. Tell me everything you know about TransWave aperture construction and sabotage."

Having fine-tuned the cutter's tracking sensor to more reliably sniff out the trail of a Super Scoop, the auto-nav has guided the Equus well and caught me up to only a few thousand kilometers behind it. In fact, I need to back down these four eager steeds of my chariot so as not to go sailing past.

Wisdom had offered up a most ingenious suggestion about the arch and I was pleased to follow the instructions to the letter. Now, the prudent action was to re-engage the Mission Steward in negotiations that would hopefully lead to his agreement to go back to his end of The Spur.

The words of Choyt-72 reverberate through my 'Thinker. "You

must, above all things, act to preserve the well-being of the Know-ers." That concept: 'above all things', weighs on my soul. That cold feeling of being alone creeps back in. I feel so small here. It doesn't help that everything around me is....well....Jupiter sized. While talking with the Knower about convincing the others to let go of the Scoop, I'd noticed my reflection in his eye. I could tell that he was squinting to see this miniature figurine in the window of a toy ship. How must it feel to be them, to rely on something or someone so puny to save them from anything? I had gained their trust; not even I, but the Brothers before me, the TinyMakers, and to be more ac-curate, Ambassador Moyab-4. Throughout the centuries spent with these gentle beings, he had always been so careful to not so much as startle them. I wonder what he's thinking now. Perhaps he wishes he had never discovered them, and that the Union should've just flown right past this little out of the way star system.

The Equus hurtles along, miles above the cloudy surface below. It occurs to me that if you didn't know better, this would appear to be just a really big ball of steam, in a wild spin in empty space, with nothing remotely interesting inside. Possibly, that's what Moyab-4 thought as he peered out through the window of his shuttle on that first day.

Auto-nav hums a little ditty to let me know that the Scoop has slowed and has dropped back into the clouds, very near to the loca-tion I had encountered it before. I will meet it there, but we're going to do things a little different this time.

With the air brakes out, the Yenyks resting, and the auto-nav pre-programmed to handle things for a while, I ease the cutter down into the clouds. Nose high and steady, the ship plows through the mist as I make my way to the belly of the craft to get myself into place.

I reach out with my mind to make contact with the Knowers in the vicinity.

"I am the TinyMaker. I have returned. I am your new Ambassador, Jove. Can you hear me?"

"Knowers hear TinyMaker. TinyMaker Ambassador Jove. TinyMaker has returned."

"Yes, can you sense my ship above you in the sky? I have come to you."

"Knowers feel TinyMaker ship pushing air," they say. "TinyMaker in Drane Zone. TinyMaker come down to Knower place. Knowers meet with Ambassador Jove."

As I reach the hatch in the outer hull of the underside of the ship, I'm as nervous as a synthetic quadruped in a room full of unstable organic seating surfaces.

"Equus auto-nav: execute program Function Six."

The inner hatch that I've just lowered myself through slides shut and seals itself. The yellow strobes and claxon announce the pending purge of the port and the opening of the outer hatch. I brace myself against the blast that I anticipate will follow, staying clear of the valve handle this time. Hurricane force wind and extreme pressures test my grip on the support rail, the duranium tubing bows out where I hang on. I don't want to fall to my death on the way to my funeral.

My thoughts extended into the billowy tufts that speed past, I put my complete trust in those who are so trusting in me.

"Catch me," I say.

I let myself fall out of the port, and momentarily pass right through the flames of one of the rear stabilizer thrusters; hadn't thought that through, I suppose. Wrapping what's left of my cloak around me, I turn to face up, hoping to catch a glimpse of the Equus.

I'm only just able to see its shape as it climbs up through the cloud tops and back into space as planned.

The dense atmosphere is pressing hard against my back as I drop into the planet. Violent flapping of the fabric in my tunic and cloak changes to an annoying buzz, then to a shrill whistle. The noise attracts three Drane that are adventurous enough to accompany me on my gravity assisted visit of their world. One of them accelerates down and seems to make a game of almost touching my feet. Darting back and forth, the other two crackle and sear the air with their high voltage excitement.

For no apparent reason, they cease their fun and zip off into the open space between the thick clouds. The pressure against my body noticeably increases and corresponds to the reduced frequency of the singing tatters that were my garment. Passing through the tropopause, my fall slows some. The temperature has dropped, too, thank goodness, as my design specifications include a melting point which was nearing. More than that, my grave concern is that I could severely injure the Knowers whom I am dependent upon to save me.

I struggle to calm myself against the memory of my previous self falling to my death. I'm about one fifth of the distance I'd been when I finally terminated. But I'm not alone. The Knowers are here. In fact, I can feel them nearby. Yes, they are below, waiting. This is their world, their realm. They can do this and I will believe in them. Closing my eyes to hope, I end up dreaming again, this time deeper into memories of another past not my own.

"Fly high, baby! Fly high!"

Whose voice is that? It sounds familiar.

"Oh! Baby flying high?"

There it is again.

"Oh, Daddy's got you!"

I open my eyes. There's a face. It seems to fit the voice. It is a good face. It comes closer, goes down. The face is smiling at me. The face is Daddy. Daddy is good. His face is blue. His hair is long and golden. His hands are strong. He smiles when I fly. I make Daddy laugh.

"Oh, big boy! Big boy flies so high!"

His voice makes tingles. This is good. Fly me again, Daddy. I wish my voice was good like Daddy's. I can only laugh. Daddy tosses me higher. I can't stop laughing.

"Got you!"

Now, that is not Daddy.

Okay, that was a weird dream…of an Only…an infant? But then, a voluntary free-fall into a gas giant planet qualifies as weird, so—

Somebody's got me, anyway. I'm not falling anymore, and…. something smells fishy.

I refocus my vision, white - whitish gray - whitish gray with dark bands and swirls of browns and blues. I know what that is. I'm buried in a tangle of cephalopod arms and tentacles. They did it. They caught me.

"Thank you. Thank you. Thank you."

"Knowers say TinyMaker welcome," it says.

I wait patiently for them to sort out who's got who's what around my various limbs. Just need one somebody to hang on to me, then things can only get better. Well, not if everything goes according to plan, actually.

At last, I'm extricated from the slithery rescue and find myself sitting cross-legged in a single massive sucker that is at least as big around as I am tall. I can detect what could be a few dozen sharp hooks clenched through my tunic, a few have pierced my skin slightly, ow, and a little more than slightly there. There're more muscles in this one sucker than most humanoids have in their whole body. I'm not going anywhere.

I look up and realize that in my entire periphery is one big eyeball. Wow, I can even see the pulse of the blood flow through the arterioles of the iris, amazing. If I peer past my warped reflection on the glossy surface, I recognize my wavy upside-down image on the back wall of the retina, about ten meters away. Okay, this was worth the near death experience.

"Knower fascinated," it says.

"Yes, that makes two of us."

The tall piles of damp leathery flesh drop away, or I am lifted up, I'm not sure. Turning to look back and forth over my shoulders, I count more colorful eyes, all crowded in to see the itsy-bitsy blue guy. I quit at forty-four. There are many more behind the mist, I know. Their vision permits them to see through the darkest fog.

Though I'd prefer to enjoy this capacious cuttlefish camaraderie, there're more urgent matters to be addressed. We need to get a move on and the Knowers need to be made to understand the plan. With me in the saddle, this one will have to travel the old fashioned way, swim.

"Knowers take TinyMaker," I say, "Ambassador Jove speak to DeathMaker. DeathMaker has returned to DangerNear. Ambassador Jove help DeathMaker understand Knower's friend."

"Knowers not friend of DeathMaker! DeathMaker go to FarPlace! Ambassador Jove not make DeathMaker friend!"

These poor beings are still mourning their murdered family members and I'm blundering. I've got to help them to understand that things could get a whole lot worse, to get them to cooperate in a peace deal with the Prawl-Tang. Do I tell them the truth? Do I treat them like the naive innocents they are? Do I lie to them; trick them into performing actions that will fit the greater cause that only I can fathom? They trust me. Can I betray that trust by coercion; lead them into an agreement with the most evil force they've ever encountered? Okay, Wisdom – give me something here.

"If the father wakes to find his house on fire," Wisdom asks, "does he first run outside and then call to his family to come out? Of course not, the father wakes the children in their beds and carries them to the flames. With courage in the face of danger, he pushes them through. There is no guarantee of safety. Living is what happens up to the moment of death."

Thank you. That's just what I needed.

"Knowers, listen and understand," I tell them, "Ambassador Jove sees more than the place of Knowers. Ambassador Jove understands thoughts of DeathMaker. Carry Ambassador Jove to Death-Maker now."

"Knowers listen and understand Ambassador Jove," they say. "TinyMakers understand much. TinyMakers see FarPlace. Tiny-Makers come FarPlace to Near and make Knowers friends. Tiny-Makers true. Knowers take Ambassador Jove to DeathMaker now."

As the others out in the mist around us begin to disperse, the Knower that carries me turns himself around and inhales a great quantity of air. Just prior to the exhale through his jets, he rolls me up in the folds of his arm. Maybe he has done this before, with one of their infants. I can feel the muscular tension in him as he jets across the sky.

I need to either convince a member of the most viscous, oppressive race that he would be better off not to mess with these help-less fish anymore or – and here comes the crazy part – I need this Knower, who attends to my safe passage, to pull my head off at a moment's notice.

It seems like we gain some altitude. I shove a big flap of brown and blue striped flesh off of my head so I can peek at the goings on. We're not alone. I'm not alone. What a wonderful sight. There're many hundreds of Knowers all accompanying me on my ride up to find the Mission Steward. A smaller green-tinged one just to the right seems to swerve closer and look directly at me. I could swear that she winks. How could I not be astounded by this opportunity; just to be in the presence of these magnificent creatures? Perhaps in one of my future selves, I will grow some tentacles.

The Knower discontinues the rhythm of his jets and allows him-self to float straight up for a few minutes. The Knowledgebase men-tions of how when they are rising, you can make out the Obedient Sand in the upper portion of their bladder, as it presses out against their flesh, the scales puckered like countless little mounds. I envi-sion that to happen now as he thinks, "Higher".

A ripple of nervous energy runs through him, which causes a flexation of my private cushion, so a few more talons end up driven into my buttocks. He rotates himself around and I see all of the oth-ers gathered into a vast circle. In the midst of the circle, surrounded, is the Prawl-Tang. High above are more of us. If I could see through these thick arms, no doubt I would see many more below him.

"Rats."

I did not mean for us to move into attack formation. This was supposed to be a conversation. Wisdom, where art thou?

"Speak softly and carry a big stick," she says.

What? Who the heck is Teddy and where am I going to find a stick on Jupiter? There isn't a single tree on this entire planet. What I really need to do is to leverage the fact that we have the enemy at a tactical disadvantage, but not threaten him to the point of violent action. Then maybe he'll concede without…a…fight. Oh, duh. Okay, I get it.

"Knowers, hold places," I say. "No attack DeathMaker. Ambassador Jove to speak."

My thoughts cast out into the sky ahead, I sense that distinct tremble. He is there. He waits, and he doesn't like what he sees outside.

"Jove calls to Mission Steward. I wish to talk of peace for you and the biologics."

He replies, "You say peace. But I see the makings of war."

"There are many biologics present, asking you to leave their planet in peace."

"Does Jove speak for the biologics?" Mission Steward asks.

"Jove does speak for them."

"Is not Jove of the Synthetic's Union?" he asks.

"Jove is of the….Synthetic's Union. I am here to negotiate peace for the biologics."

"The Synthetic Union is internally prohibited from war," he states. "You speak of peace because you are incapable of anything other. You do not speak for the biologics. Their actions say war."

"What actions would show peace?"

"The eradication of the biologics would bring peace."

"The eradication of the biologics is unacceptable."

"The eradication of the biologics is inevitable," he says.

"It is not inevitable. We will prevent that from occurring."

"…by actions of war," he says.

"If the Mission Steward would agree to leave the planet and not return—"

"We lay claim to the resources of PB5. There is no advantage to relinquish the resources to the biologics. We shall overcome and prevail. You may affect the destruction of $\Omega 94\lambda 25\theta$, but you will not overcome the advancing fleet $\Omega 204\lambda$. We are the Omega species. The lives of the biologics are inconsequential."

He is convinced that he has a bigger stick than I do. He's called my bluff. He wants war. I can do war. I just cannot promote violence.

I break contact with the ever obstinate Mission Steward and turn my thoughts toward the Knower in whose palm I sit. Palm? Hand? At this point it doesn't matter.

"Knower, listen to Ambassador Jove. I need you to do that which we discussed on the way. Remember? I need you to do it right now. Knower! Trust Ambassador Jove. MakeDeath to Jove now!"

"Knower listens. Knower trusts Ambassador Jove. Knower scared," it says.

Do it. Come on. You can do it. Just grab on and break or bite or whatever.

It seems ridiculous to sit there with my butt stuck to his sucker, to await the taste of death again. Before long though, he gets the job done. It happens with a snap. I have the sensation of air rushing up my nose. I open my eyes to see the sky tumble around my head. I seem to be missing everything else.

I awake as Number Four. It is dark, and exceptionally quiet. I am aware of myself, but I detect a problem with my initialization routine. Foundation Download: Fail. Crossloader Download: Fail.

Maintenance Diagnostic: Execute…redirect…Tactical Patch One: Execute.

There is an odd sensation of being disconnected from a larger self, but there is purpose. I open my eyes to see only starlight. There is no sound. There is no weight, no gravity. Correction, I am in orbit, in space, high above a large colorful planet. I must act. There is a purpose.

I twist around in an attempt to visualize my predicament. After some investigation, I find that my waist has been tethered by a length of cargo webbing, which is pressed into a crack in a rock wall at the other end, about twenty meters to my left. The other end of the webbed belt is tied to the remains of the lower third of a clone cassette frame which floats nearby. The umbilical from the frame is still embedded in my abdominal port.

With a gentle tug on the tether, I pull myself closer to the wall and grab on. The end of the web belt has been deliberately crammed into the crack, and there is an object forced in to maintain pressure against the material so that it does not come out easily. Upon closer inspection, I recognize the object as a finger. I inspect my hands – two thumbs, seven fingers. That would be mine. I have a memory. It is brief. It repeats. It would seem to be a directive.

"Tactical Patch One: Climb onto the arch, locate emitters on convex side, remove two emitters. Discard emitters and step into one empty emitter socket with both feet. Reach into other empty emitter socket, take hold of plasma contactors, and maintain positive contact with plasma contactors in both empty emitter sockets. Do not permit any sensations to override this function. Do not permit any outside influence to override this function. If Tactical Patch Two is executed, you may comply."

I find that to perform these tasks in zero gravity is difficult, but manageable. I brace myself against one emitter casing to provide the required torque to dislodge the other two. My interpretation of 'discard emitters' is to let them float away in space. I hope that is acceptable. There is no more webbing and I may require the rest of my fingers. As I prepare myself to step down into the socket, I detect an energetic vibration in the arch. I will ignore it.

The emitters toward the center of the arch ignite, which projects a significant amount of energy outward. From the middle, progressing outward, each row of emitters does likewise in their sequence. The ones to my immediate right and left are activated, with a slight gap in the light-field where the two missing ones should have been. I will ignore it. I step down into the socket. There is a tingling sensation in the soles of my feet. There is considerable heat. It is beyond the capacity of my epidermis to sustain. I will ignore it. The tall, vertical light-field amplifies into a contained plasma aperture. A thin, flat sheet of plasma, as wide as the arch, shoots from the center of the circular light-field and out into distant space. The bright white sheet begins to ripple as the waves extend out along the path.

Bent at the waist, I lean over, with some difficulty, to reach down into the other empty emitter socket. The plasma contactors are glowing red. I estimate their temperatures as beyond the capacity of my epidermis to sustain. I will ignore it. My fingers wrapped around the flat metal contactors, I detect an immediate failure in several of my critical systems. The flow of plasma through my thorax has begun to liquefy certain critical organs and neural conduits. The reflection of the light-field on the surface of the arch fades. The plasma sheet fails and disperses. I continue to maintain positive contact with plasma contactors in both empty emitter sockets, though it is challenging to verify. I smell smoke.

I awake as Number Five. Sorry about that, Number Four. Lowered out of my cassette, I take a few steps into the dimly lit bay and trip over the remains of the mess made when Three removed my predecessor from the stack and took what was needed out the hatch.

With a jump up the staircase to the bridge, I find the Equus' auto-nav has performed its duties admirably; climbed out of the clouds and entered a lazy orbit around the moon, Io, which I had... er, Three had correctly calculated as passing by while he would be in the midst of negotiations.

Back to manual flight mode, I bring the engines to life and swing the ship up and over the moon, in a dive back to Jupiter. My little beacon is still an active marker on my screen; that's where I head back to. My hope that the Mission Steward will have stayed put and the Knowers will have waited for me, and not devoured him and his ship. I check the clock. My Number Three terminated just eighteen minutes ago. All in all, it's been a busy day.

Air brakes hoot and whistle in the thinner air of the upper stratosphere, I level out my decent into the planet. Velocity indicator shows me on target to reach the beacon in less than five minutes. The blip that should correspond to the Scoop is not where I thought it would be, but rather, deeper into the thermosphere and eight hundred kilometers to the north. He is moving, too, so I will need to accelerate to catch up. I drop the nose and the Equus quickly builds speed as it plummets into the thickening cumulus hydrogen vapor.

I see motion in the breaks of the clouds below - a large group of Knowers at top speed. It could be the same group that had accompanied me earlier. I bring the nose of the ship level so as not to frighten them or scorch any that might get caught by my bow shock. The intense heat at the tip of the vessel has traced black streaks on the glass and the vibrations are severe. If I ever do run into Captain Raytk again, he'll be more than a little miffed at how his beautiful cutter has been mistreated while on loan to the new Ambassador.

The auto-nav bings an alert that the Scoop has come to a stop. Nose high, the Equus plows through the sky with a thunderous roar. My Pilotage app executes a very nice chandelle, if I do say so myself.

Settled into a gentle rolling hover around the backside of the Scoop, I am careful to keep my trajectory well outside his personal space. His sensors should make it obvious that I am not on an intercept course. I just want to get in his same neighborhood. We've had enough threats today.

And this time, I don't even have to ring him up.

"Are you the replacement for the Synthetic or are you Jove's clone?" he asks.

"I am Jove, the same entity as the previous one you have encountered."

"You are a clone," he says. "You continue to exist within another Synthetic body."

"My offer remains the same," I say, "on behalf of the biologics, the rightful caretakers of this planet. Their lives are not inconsequential. It is in your best interest to depart this system immediately. You have put your ship and your life in danger by risking another confrontation with the Knowers. They have the force of will to destroy you."

"You underestimate the resolve of the Omega Species."

"How can this one planet be worth your destruction? Or a battle on any scale? It's just hydrogen. There are other planets in this system with similar concentrations that have no biologics to interfere. Why not just focus your harvest operations there and forget about Jupiter—PB5?"

"We are the Omega Species. All that comes to our knowledge belongs to us. The fate of $\Omega 94\lambda 25\theta$ is of little consequence. Just like you, Jove, if I terminate, another will take my place to resume efforts until the goal is achieved. Tell me that I am incorrect and I will leave."

He's right. How can it come to this? I'm failing.

"Knowers speak to DeathMaker – to Prawl Tang," the Knowers nearby say.

I didn't even notice the cephalids encircle us. There must be thousands out there – tens of thousands. I'm bewildered. Why've I been so unsuccessful at avoiding this escalation? Aren't I supposed to be a diplomat at my core? My Tactical 'Thinker seems to get me into plenty of trouble. Surely, the stronger, more disciplined self can get me out of it.

"Knowers say Ambassador listen," they say, "Knowers speak to DeathMaker – to Prawl Tang. Ambassador Jove to MakeThoughts through."

"If I can help you connect to him—wait. If Knowers speak to Prawl-Tang, what say?"

"Knowers speak to Prawl-Tang. Knowers say GoFar to Death-Maker. Prawl-Tang no Near. Knowers say Prawl-Tang find Make-Death Near. Knowers MakeDeath for Prawl-Tang."

I can't believe what I'm hearing. What've I done? By having the Knower tear my head off so that Number Four could sabotage the TransWave aperture, I've taught them to kill. They were scared to do it, but they got over it. They don't comprehend the difference between what I had them do and the awful truth of taking a life that cannot be replaced so easily. Where they had previously revered the TinyMakers, now they're aware that we're barely one step up from the fish they devour. TinyMakers can die. Knowers can kill them. It's not so bad. And if they can kill a friend, how much more can they envision themselves tearing an enemy to shreds. I'm not their savior. I have ushered in the demons of hell.

"The biologics speak to you, don't they?" Mission Steward says.

"They do. I can communicate to them as I do to you. They are telepathic."

"Tell them that many of the Omega Species will arrive soon. Tell them that they have no choice but to flee or die."

"Mission Steward, you're mistaken about your fleet's pending arrival. I have disabled your aperture - your FTL conduit from Alnitak. Your ships aren't coming as you think. Further, your fleet is stranded somewhere in-between worlds. They're lost, at least a hundred light-years from here. They'll be lucky to make it home alive. Again, my offer stands. Leave now, or the biologics will surely destroy you."

Maybe I can put this big stick to work, after all.

"Knower," I call to the cephalid, "Ambassador Jove MakeThoughts through for Knowers and Prawl-Tang now."

My Diplomatic protocortex asserts itself within my SynThinker, just as I was told it would. I can feel my thoughts branch out into space. Each mind out there becomes clear to me, opens up and flows like water. This is easier than I thought. Just divert my stream into these two streams to make one body, pooled together. The challenge will be to keep the many thousands of Knowers from flooding in as they tend to do when they get excited. It took much trial and error for Ambassador Moyab-4 to develop the language necessary for dialogue.

"Knowers call to Prawl-Tang. Be not DeathMaker," they say, "Be not DangerNear. Prawl-Tang listen."

"I do not understand 'Prawl-Tang," Mission Steward replies. "But I hear you. You call yourself Knower?"

"Mission Steward, this is Jove. The biologics call themselves Knowers. You are known as Prawl-Tang. I am known as TinyMaker or Ambassador. Knower could be one or a hundred. They think in groups. Simple language is better understood."

Mission Steward responds to them. "Prawl-Tang is Mission Steward of the Omega Species. I am here to remove the air from your world. I will finish my work. Do not try to stop us."

"Knowers live in air! Knowers MakeLife in air! Air cannot remove! Prawl-Tang go! Prawl-Tang be DeathMaker! Prawl-Tang MakeDeath for Knowers. Mission Steward GoFar!"

"Mission Steward will not go. Knowers will die," he says.

"Prawl-Tang be DeathMaker. Mission Steward say DeathMaker! Knowers say stop DeathMaker. Knowers have MakeDeath. Knowers bring MakeDeath to Prawl-Tang. Mission Steward lose Spirit to LowerPlaces," they say, the threat of death and hell's damnation coming from the once pacifistic Knowers.

"Mission Steward dies - more Prawl-Tang come," he says, "More Prawl-Tang bring more death. You cannot stop us. If Knowers prevent us from removing air, you will all die. Your air is Prawl-Tang now."

I sense a deep intelligence in the Mission Steward, though there is a natural tendency toward egomaniacal behavior. He reasons well, and by all accounts, he dove right into the conversation with the cephalids - that's never easy. Whether you're chitin or hollow scales or polysilicates, a brain is a brain. There's someone who thinks in that flying lump of coral, and I'm going to find a way to compromise with it.

"Mission Steward," I interject, "does the word 'bargain' exist with the Omega Species? Do you understand what I ask?"

"I understand what a bargain is. As the Mission Steward, I made a bargain to trade $\Omega 94\lambda 25\theta$ for a half life of service to the gathering of resources. For one half of my existence, I am tasked with continued provision of resources for the Omega Species. The ship and all of the implements which comprise $\Omega 94\lambda 25\theta$ are my responsibility to operate. If I do not complete my mission, then my life is forfeit. Yes, Jove, the Omega Species are honorable. We understand bargain."

It begins to make sense why they're so methodically homicidal. I'm sure the Knowers heard that statement from the Mission Steward. I wonder how much of it they understood. We may be on to something though.

"Thank you, Mission Steward," I say, "for your words. It helps to know that there exists the possibility for common ground between us – between you and the Knowers. I believe that you, as well as all of the Omega Species, value life above resources."

"The resources are the life. The life of the Omega Species is above all," he says.

"Are you willing to consider a bargain with the Knowers?" I ask.

"I have already claimed the atmosphere of their planet for the Omega Species. The transport of the resource is all that is required. This conversation is irrelevant."

"This conversation *is* relevant because it is about the preservation of life. You believe that the value of the life of the Omega Species is above all. Likewise, any species believes the same. You must understand that to be true. There is no profit in death. You will die. Some Knowers will die. More Missions Stewards will come. They will die. More Knowers will die. There will be no resources transported."

"I will listen to the Knower's bargain," Mission Steward says, "I cannot agree to ignore the value of resources I have acquired for the Omega Species."

"Knowers," I call, "Mission Steward listens to Knowers. Mission Steward not GoFar without…um…GoodThing from Knowers. Knowers give GoodThing to Mission Steward. Knowers MakeTrade."

"Knowers MakeTrade with Mission Steward," they say. "Knowers give GoodThing. Mission Steward GoFar. Prawl-Tang stop MakeDeath. Knowers stop MakeDeath."

"What is good thing Knowers bargain with? Air is worth much," he states.

"Knowers have many EatFish. Knowers bring EatFish to Mission Steward. Mission Steward have many EatFish, then GoFar."

"I do not want your fish. No bargain," he says.

"Knowers MakeTrade with Mission Steward. Knowers give LookingFar. LookingFar is MostGoodThing. Mission Steward MakeTrade with LookingFar."

"I am aware of your LookingFar. The Prawl-Tang do not require your telescope."

Knowers MakeTrade with OverSingers. Knowers give all – OverSingers, LookingFar, and all EatFish. Knowers give all for

MakeTrade with Mission Steward. Prawl-Tang accept MakeTrade. Mission Steward take all and GoFar!"

"As I expected," he tells me, "the Knowers do not comprehend the value of their resources. The Omega Species has what it needs: the atmosphere of PB5. There is nothing to bargain with here."

"Mission Steward, wait, please," I say. "Do not disregard what they are offering you. There is nothing else. They are offering everything they—"

"Knowers give BestGoodThing for MakeTrade," they say.

"I grow weary of this nonsense," he says. "What is your best thing to bargain with?"

"Knowers MakeTrade with LittleNoisyBluePearl."

"I do not understand 'little noisy blue pearl'. How is that of value?" asks Mission Steward.

"Knowers have LittleNoisyBluePearl," they say. "The Pearl flies in FarPlaceNear. Knowers watch and listen to Pearl. Pearl has many sounds. Pearl is beautiful. Pearl is best treasure. Knowers give Pearl to Prawl-Tang. Prawl-Tang stop MakeDeath. Prawl-Tang GoFar."

"Jove," he asks me, "I do not understand. What is this pearl? Where is FarPlaceNear?"

Before Mission Steward can ask the question, Knowledgebase fills me in. Where I had the slightest hope that the Jovians did, in actuality, possess something the Prawl-Tang would consider, was now despair that they believed the Earth was theirs at all, much less something they could give away.

"Mission Steward, the Jovians – the Knowers – are alluding to the third planet of this star system. You would call it PB3. The Knowers - for them to have that planet to observe and to monitor with electro-optic magnification is one of the greatest achievements of their society. They have believed the Earth, as it is known, as belonging to them. After many centuries of observation and in-depth study, they have a valid affinity for their LittleNoisyBluePearl. They obviously consider it to be of high value."

"And are they incorrect in their assumption that it could be valuable to the Omega Species?" he asks.

"Yes," I say, "but, only in how the value is measured. So, no, they are not incorrect about its true value as a resource." No sooner are the words out of my mouth, and those butterflies I felt earlier become burning coals. This is the tipping point I'd hoped for. My diplomatic self and my directive to protect the Knowers could align behind this idea, but my Tactical 'Thinker was extrapolating consequences, all dire.

"PB3 has only trace amounts of metallic hydrogen," he says. "It is far below the threshold."

"Earth – PB3 – is made up of heavier elements," I say, "The atmosphere and surface does have a large amount of hydrogen that is bound with oxygen. Perhaps—" The coals in my stomach are now a firestorm. Perhaps the best thing right now would be for a giant squid to rip my head off.

"Previous scans of PB3 were focused on metallic hydrogen," Mission Steward says, "as the primary configuration of $\Omega 94\lambda 25\theta$ is to gather and condense that molecule. Heavier elements require far less energy to process prior to transport. Certain cold planets can be harvested with high efficiency. I will execute a wide-spectrum, high-powered scan of PB3 to determine its resource threshold."

All of a sudden, I find myself in a positive conversation with a Prawl-Tang. So, if this could work towards a bargain, why do I feel like I am about to make a huge mistake? My directive, from

Choyt-72 himself was to, 'above all things, act to preserve the well-being of the Knowers'. This course of action must be aligned to that end. So what if the Mission Steward fills up his ship with sea water and hauls it back to Alnitak a time or two? It wasn't my idea, anyway. What's this odd feeling - guilt? According to Knowledge-base, the humans of Earth are always engaged in trade. They'll have something far more valuable than helio-fish and hydrogen gas. This could work out.

"Jove, I have completed phase one of the scan," he says. "PB3 does indeed possess numerous elements in such abundance and free of compound, that the resource threshold can be met. I am willing to consider that $\Omega 94\lambda 25\theta$ could be reconfigured for harvest of those elements."

"You're willing to enter into a bargain with the Jovians?" I ask.

"I am not opposed to redirecting $\Omega 94\lambda 25\theta$ operations from PB5 to PB3."

"Mission Steward, I'm pleased that you've been willing to consider the bargain."

"Knowers MakeTrade with Prawl-Tang," they say.

"Yes!" I say, "Knowers! Prawl-Tang MakeTrade for Little-NoisyBluePearl. This GoodThing."

"Prawl-Tang stop MakeDeath. Prawl-Tang go," they say.

"Agreed," the Prawl-Tang says.

Agreed…he agreed, it, he…whatever. This is fantastic. The Prawl-Tang will leave Jupiter. The Knowers are safe. I did it. I didn't fail. It wasn't too easy. It wasn't too hard. It only cost me my life a time or two. I can do this. I did do this—

"Now, we will consider the terms," Mission Steward says.

"Mission Steward, the terms are that you will leave this planet, and move your harvesting operations to Earth, to PB3."

"There are always terms to any agreement," he says. "There is no guarantee of complete success. There may be resistance to operations on PB3. Cold planets are known to harbor indigenous life, biologics that may require extermination, eradication. That may affect the point of threshold."

Back to reality, the Prawl-Tang will default to 'eradication'. This whole exercise of a bargain with the Knowers is a fluke, a singular event. They don't look for ways to find a peaceful resolution. As he said before, 'peace is the death of the biologics'. Agreeing to any bargain is the last resort for the Omega Species. It probably takes too much effort to even consider not killing.

"If the resources are polluted or are of low grade or are contaminated or non-compliant in extrication, so as to negatively affect harvest threshold to less than three hundred percent, the agreement is null and void."

"Mission Steward, the Jovians have no leverage over those outcomes. It's not possible for them to improve upon that which they cannot control. This is beyond—"

"These are standard terms. There is no agreement without them. If there exists extraneous objects that interfere with operational efficiency, the cost of eradication is deducted from the harvest balance."

"By extraneous objects, you mean the people of Earth."

"'People?' I do not understand 'people'."

"The Earth, PB3 is largely populated by carbon-based humanoids, very similar to those encountered throughout the region of space known to the Praw—the Omega Species. Those are people."

"People, I understand," he replies. "This will not pose a significant challenge. People...are a threshold resource for the Omega

Species. Their containers are well suited to caloric transport, their microflora of considerable value. I will arrange for the processing and delivery of the...people."

"Mission Steward, may I make an inquiry not related to the agreement?"

"You may make inquiry."

"Does the Omega Species consider the, um, Synthetic's Union to be a threshold resource?"

"It does not. The Synthetic's Union is at best, a curiosity, occasionally a nuisance."

Good to know. At least if I end up with my head on a pole in Planet Bloodville, it'll be for something I said, rather than the value of my plastic.

"I have an inquiry of my own, Jove," he says.

"Go ahead." If he asks me what the Union thinks of the Prawl-Tang, should I lie to him?

"What profit is there for the Synthetic's Union to interfere with the harvest of PB5?"

Oh, please! He doesn't care about what anybody thinks of them! What a bunch of—no, no, no...now is not the time for the List of Extreme Expletives; although that one there certainly fits. Okay, need to respond carefully here, Wisdom. What do we want him to think we think? Uh, okay, this sounds good.

"The Synthetic's Union values information resources above all," I say, "We seek knowledge about unstudied planetary bodies, ecologies, biologics, and societal interactions. The combined resource meets threshold when the sum can be used to improve the state of the Synthetic's existence."

"That is beneficial," he replies, "But, you did not answer my question."

No, I guess I really didn't. And he's a good listener.

"The proposed harvest of PB5 by the Omega Species qualifies as an extraneous object which would interfere with our operations to extract information about the biologics and their capacity to thrive in a hostile atmosphere."

"I understand," he says. "When I first entered this star system, I scanned for other operations and found none. Detailed scans of PB5 revealed only one artificial object in orbit, and that was not involved in acquiring the known resource."

"So you'd say that were we to be found harvesting metallic hydrogen, you would've moved on to another planet, like PB6?"

"Of course, the risk of conflict between us would have posed a risk to the threshold. It would be wrong."

It would be wrong. It's not wrong to annihilate every sentient being on a planet, but it's wrong to horn in on another guy's dig. "I understand, Mission Steward. Thank you for your candor."

"I do not understand 'thank you'," he says.

Why does that not surprise me? During this conversation, my Tactical app was running on high in the background. There're serious issues to work out. Not the least of which is my own revulsion at the thought of sending the Prawl-Tang to ravage the humans of Earth. But, I cannot afford to allow that to be my concern. I must follow my directive. The Elder said he trusted me to find the right course of action. I must follow this path. A plan formulates in my 'Thinker. It's a good one, but I don't like it. It's outside my moral perimeter. This uses evil to thwart another evil.

"Mission Steward," I say, "there is some valuable information that the Synthetic's Union is aware of about PB3, that you should know. There's significant risk to the operation that I may be able to mitigate."

"I am listening," he replies. "What is the information?"

"The biologics of PB3 are a warlike and violent race, more so than others the Omega Species has encountered. Their perpetual state of intraspecies war and their prolific technological advancements has led them to develop weapons of such capacity, they themselves are at a loss to control them."

"Intelligence does not preclude foolishness," he says.

Wow. The wisdom of a murderous echinoderm could be framed on a wall.

"The humans possess the capability of defending themselves against the... $\Omega 94\lambda 25\theta$. They can strike anywhere within their atmosphere and a short distance outside of it. Their weapons are more powerful than your tracking spear. Just one of them could destroy the Mission Steward. They have many. I will assist with the sabotage of those weapons, to reduce the risk to the harvest operations."

"What weapon is powerful enough to destroy $\Omega 94\lambda 25\theta$?" he asks.

"A nuclear weapon."

"I do not understand 'nuclear'."

"The humans have perfected atomic fission. They compress unstable elements so that the substructure converts to energy, to cascade through the surrounding elements. This event can be delivered with great accuracy. They are well practiced."

"I understand atomic fission," he tells me. "That technology was deemed unacceptable by the Omega Species. It is not permitted."

"I believe that I can prevent them from using those weapons against the Mission Steward," I say.

"How many of these weapons do they possess?"

"Difficult to know exactly, as they hide them from each other. We've counted over a thousand that are either detectable by scans or as documented by the humans themselves."

"How could one Synthetic possibly stop a thousand atomic fission detonations? You have no weapons, no shielding that could be deployed. You have no experience in such matters. I doubt your informa—"

"I will use the one thing that the Synthetic Union has employed since the beginning. It is a force so strong that no war machine can survive its overpowering presence. I will go to the Earth and meet with the humans. They are looking for me. They have been hoping for me. Most of their wars are fought over religion. Their religions seek the messiah. They hope for their messiah to end all wars. They will no longer need their weapons. I am going to fight them with... peace."

"I understand 'messiah'," Mission Steward says. "I can foresee your plan. This is an evil thing, Jove."

Note to Self

Every action has an equal and opposite reaction…except telling lies. Lying doesn't do that. Lies leave out the front of you, building momentum as they circle around your world. Then they hit you in the back, with far greater effect than when they left.

Jove

Humans
2043 CE
UN Headquarters, Earth

From the forty-second floor of the United Nations Plaza, you can see the East River between Manhattan and Long Island, Roosevelt Island and adjoining park, the Queensboro Bridge, as well as many important international headquarters. The southeast offers a grim view of the remains of the previous United Nations Headquarters buildings. Since their completion in nineteen fifty-two, they have served as the global center for the administration of international peace and humanitarian aid. Now just an empty hulk, blasted and burned, ruined by a dirty bomb.

Here at 327 East Forty-Eighth Street, on the corner of First Avenue, the tall, black-glass tower looms over the desolate intersection. Once a haven of high-dollar condominiums for the wealthy, it seemed to make a reasonable location for the temporary UN offices. When the news broke of radiation down the street, all but a few residents made for anyplace else. Tests were performed to see if it was safe. According to the experts, working up to eight hours a day here was the same as a job as an X-ray or fluoroscopy technician. The homeowners responded with enthusiasm when the UN asked to rent their spaces until more permanent arrangements could be made. Of the five thousand staff employed in the original buildings, the surviving twelve hundred now crammed into sixty-two condos on nine floors.

Marisol Tonuay, the Chief Executive Assistant to the Secretary-General, could even now, five months later, remember the
smell of the smoke and dust, the screams, the frantic scene that day.
Her step-daughter had woken up with a high fever. Staying home
to await the nanny, she had missed her ride in the secure, hardened
limousine. She'd called a cab instead. Had she made it to work on
time, she would've been there – right where the bomb detonated,
murdering her boss, the previous Secretary-General, and the many
others who were in the office.

"Marisol…Marisol…" her assistant said. "Please, what do you
stare at out there? I'm sorry, but…it's just that you do that every day.
I don't…"

Turning towards her desk, Marisol nodded at the slender girl.

"Miss Tonuay, please. The phone lines are backed up. I can't put
anyone else on hold."

Ah, yes, the news, everyone is freaking out today.

"Alright, Dina, don't stress out."

With the overnight announcement of the breakup of the United
States, half the planet would be calling today for a comment. Marisol thought, "Um…how about, 'Oh crap!'?"

With a catch of the phone dropped from the younger blonde's
hand, Marisol used her soft Catalonian accent to cover her irritation.

"Dina, go get four coffees, one for me, two for the SG, and one
for yourself."

That should keep her busy for a while, Marisol thought. Fifteen
lines flashing and one on solid. He's on with the Canadian Prime
Minister. Yes, that was a good one to put through.

She bent over to jot down a quick list of the important people on hold and how long they've been waiting, and a brief report prepared for the Secretary General. Her long black hair now clipped back and her blouse buttoned to the collar, she stepped to his office door and quietly slipped in.

"Right, Mac, right," the S-G was saying. "Yes, that sounds like the best course of action."

He was almost giddy with excitement and nervous energy, belying his typically stern, high-born British accent. "Now, that one, I am afraid, will require a bit of...oh, I know, yes, and the bloke does tend to chunter on as well..." rolling his eyes as if to say 'like this guy on the phone doesn't!' Marisol used her digiPad to cover a smile. "Alright then, say, I know I'm keeping you, so I'll leave you be, then. Okay, then. Cheers." The handset left to rest on his shoulder, Sir Dwight Ward-Howard plopped himself down into the thickly padded office chair.

"The Queen's got MacDonald all wadded up." Dwight said, "She actually told him to '...get down to the States and straighten things out.' As if he's her dogsbody and would have a chance in hell with those Reds and Blues..."

Marisol spoke up at Dwight's inhale. "Sir Ward-Howard, there is a meeting of the Intelligence Committee at nine-fifteen, and it is now nine twenty-two. After that is, or was, as I am sure you will now cancel, a conference call with the Editor in Chief of the Xinhua News Agency and the Associated Press—"

"Yes, cancel that."

"...you still need to return a call to Moscow about their request for Peace Keepers—"

"Yes, I will take that call," he said.

"No, you are returning their call, third call, Sir," she said.

"Right, you let me know." He kept nodding. Somehow he expected to remember all this. Of course, it would be Marisol who remembered for him.

"Lunch in the car to meet with the Force Commander and the Special Representative for East Asian Refugees. Topic: reported mass movements of the Chinese Army along their northern border."

Ward-Howard's mind was catching up, and as he leaned back into the chair, the seriousness of the violence around the world seemed to all meld together, evil everywhere.

"We can't wait our turn to start a bloody war," he thought out loud.

She pretended not to hear. "Excuse me, Sir?" Marisol said.

Dwight's depression was a warm blanket, a shield from reality. His brooding often ate away at his daily schedule. Another day wasted, another sleepless night.

"Sir, the time is now nine twenty-five," she said. "Shall I continue?" He managed a nod while he pressed his palms around his face. "The interim President of the Palestinian Authority has asked for a conference call at two p.m. I will arrange the connection. The agenda is, of course, to discuss last week's detonation of an alleged stolen Israeli nuclear bomb aboard the ship that entered the Port of Gaza. At three o'clock will be a follow-up call with the Security Council."

"Is that the whole of the schedule for the day?"

"Those are the items on your schedule at present. I would expect that to change, given the news about the United States." With that, Marisol stood and headed to the door.

"Right, of course, of course," he said. It was sinking in, with the loss of a strong American administration, he alone was left to make the hard choices. The long, slow slide finally reached the precipice. No more USA. Their internal divisions had split them down the middle. And now, without the West as big brother to the Israelis, the many terrorist organizations are taking advantage of the situation. Even some of the larger Arab governments have seized the moment; prepared to launch monumental tirades against their longtime Middle East enemy; rallying for an alliance to stand up to the smaller but stronger Semitic group. And this bomb – this damnable bomb; where did it come from? If Israel had really allowed one to fall into the hands of Islamic extremists, so they'd be caught with it, to discredit UNIPAL, would they have let it be detonated so close to their coast, to their own countrymen? It was insanity, no matter how it came about. Half of the Gaza Strip was flattened. The cities of Sderot and Ashkelon have been evacuated. The Palestinian people are huddled along the Sinai border to escape into Egypt. What a bloody mess.

Marisol's voice came over the intercom from her room. "Sir Ward-Howard? There's a call on line fourteen for you. It's the President of the Constitutional Republic of North America. I believe his name is Dean Trombley. You have about five minutes before your car will be ready." Dwight stared a long while at the lcd's metered animation before he could bring himself to press the button.

"Mister President, this is Dwight Ward-Howard. I have been looking forward to your call."

"Yes, Mister Secretary. Thank you for taking my call," Trombley said. "As you're aware, sir, it was necessary for the Republic of the United States to separate itself from factions that'd been suiciding this great nation for far too long. We'd been in deliberations with several camps and decided that it was time to act. I was previously the Governor of Nebraska, for the past eleven years. Recently, just two days ago in fact, elected to the position by the Congress of the Constitutional Republic of North America."

"You have my congratulations, Mister President," Dwight said. "How can the UN be of service to you?"

"As you know, Mister Secretary, our country has been a member of the UN since nineteen forty-five. I just wanted to reassure you that we'll continue to maintain a strong relationship with all the member States of the United Nations."

Dwight started to respond, but had no words. The most powerful nation of the UN divided itself due to their incapacity for resolute dialogue and their boundless arrogance. They then expect to 'maintain' anything about their relationship to the global family.

"Mister President," Dwight said, "It is my sincere hope that we can build upon the strengths of the former American Republic, while welcoming the fresh ideals of the new governments that will have charge."

Dean Trombley realized that he would need to do more than pick up where the USA left off. "I get you," he said, "and well, again, I hope that we can work together to build a safe and secure world for our people and our children. Thank you."

Dwight felt let down by the useless banter. His office chair creaked as he leaned back, the sound a good fit for the condition of the world today. The moment he hung up the handset, the phone rang again. It had been that way all morning.

"Yes, Marisol. What is it? Is the car ready for us?" Dwight already dreaded the next meeting about China's recent military activities, as well as the inevitable lukewarm tuna sandwich that awaited him in the limousine.

"Oh, no, Mister Secretary, this isn't Marisol. This is Dina. We've not heard from the driver, but there's another call on line four. Can you take it, please?"

"Right. Yes, well, I can do that I guess while we're waiting on the car. Thank you, Dina."

Leaned forward on his elbows to prop up an already tired neck, Dwight pressed the button to take the call. "This is Dwight Ward-Howard. To whom am I speaking?"

"Uh...thank you for taking my call Mister Ward-Howard. My name is Franz Gerlsom. I am the Senior Astronomer with the SETI Institute in Berkeley - Berkeley, California...Sir."

Dwight wasn't sure how this call made it past Marisol. She was typically good about filtering this kind of thing. "Yes, Mister Gerlsom, is it? How can the UN help you today?"

"The reason for my call, sir, is uh...that is...I've been...I've tried to reach my contacts at NASA about something, something important. I can't seem to get through to them. So, I thought you should know, since, you know, you're the next in line."

"Next in line?" Dwight asked.

"Yes, if we, I mean SETI...uh...do you know what the SETI Institute is, sir?" Gerlsom asked.

"There are many organizations around the world, Mister Gerlsom. I must ask that you clarify for me." Dwight looked up to see Marisol as she skipped through the office door, mouthing a silent apology for his predicament.

"The Search for Extra-Terrestrial Intelligence, ess-Ee-Tee-I, SETI," Gerlsom said. "We watch and listen to the skies for—"

"Very well then, I get you." Dwight waved off Marisol.

"So, to continue Mister Secretary, for something like this we'd always contact NASA. But as I said, they aren't answering their phones."

"I don't know that NASA exists today as it did yesterday. Now, I ask you, how can the UN be of service to you? What is this 'something important' that requires the attention of the United Nations?"

Gerlsom tried his best to sound calm and rational. "Sir, you may remember a few weeks ago when there was confirmation of a newly discovered object in orbit around one of the moons of Jupiter? Do you understand what I mean by 'in orbit around'?"

"Yes, Mister Gerlsom. I am Pilot Reserve for the RAF. I know what 'orbit' means. I am aware of the sighting. It was pasted all over the Red Tops, um…the tabloid newspapers. I'm also aware that the object then later could not be found and that the whole business was likely a hoax."

"Oh, no sir, it was no hoax. Many respectable observatories around the globe recorded the sighting. It was even given an official name by the International Astronomical Union – Emrah."

Dwight caught Marisol's eye and tapped his watch. "Yes, I know the IAU. In fact, one of my closest friends is—"

"—is Sir Edward Vincent! Yes, exactly. He gave me your telephone number; that I should contact you, since I couldn't reach my NASA contact."

"Vincent gave you my direct number. Why would he do that?"

Gerlsom took a deep breath before going on. "Because, Sir, that object, Emrah, was detected two days ago, it rose out of Jupiter's atmosphere and intentionally left orbit."

"You don't say…" Dwight scribbled on a note pad for Marisol to get Sir Edward Vincent connected to the car phone immediately. He would chat with his golf buddy around the tuna.

"Mister Gerlsom, as much as I would enjoy continuing this discussion, I'm late for another appointment. I really must—"

"Sir, please understand what I'm saying! I'm calling to tell you, because you're the only one with the power to act. Emrah left Jupiter and has made several course corrections to bring it directly to Earth. Mister Secretary, it's travelling at more than two hundred times the speed of our fastest rocket. It'll be here in three days."

Dwight covered the handset microphone with his palm. "Marisol, please have that call to Sir Edward Vincent rerouted here to my office. And I will be late to the meeting with the Force Commander."

Note to Self

The only thing better than philanthropy, is profit.

Jove

Deception
2043 CE
Jupiter to Earth

If it wasn't so horrible, it'd be funny. There can be no cheer to the rescue of the Knowers. I feel sick inside. My cellulytic guts are churning. No, Wisdom, it wasn't—I don't even eat calzone. That invisible crushing weight bears down on me again, from within. Even my feet seem to press harder against the floor. This is wrong. But it would be wrong not to. So, what does that make it? Paradox.

The Mission Steward has agreed to my plan. Even the Knowers, now washed of their previous innocence, conclude the right thing to do is to plunder the Earth – their LittleNoisyBluePearl. Over the past few days since the decision, they don't even show signs of remorse, as they did at first. I think they understand what's going to happen – what the consequences will be. They grasp the severity of their 'bargain' with the devil himself. Yet they are sadly satisfied. "DeathGoesNextDoor," they might say. Hooray for us.

On the Prawl-Tang vessel, the Mission Steward is in an argument with the Navigation Onus about how best to prepare for the flight towards Sol, and the best part to the insanity: the Knowers want to send someone along. They want to go to space. They had come to me, three of them, to inform me of their decision to be included on the trip. At first, I thought this was cephalid humor, but no, they are serious. They want to join the ranks of sentient beings to travel the stars, or partway into their own system anyway. I asked them how they're going to provide for indefinite rations of breathable atmosphere and food, warmth against the bitter cold of space, protection from gamma rays, vacuum, etc. They swam off to reconsider. But I have a bad feeling they're intent on making the journey. They wouldn't be the first to leap into the void without a clue, only to freeze to death, or fall back to a fiery end.

To my complete surprise, the Mission Steward advises me that he'll be making provision within the cavernous hold of the Super Scoop, not only for the Knowers, but the Equus as well. It's not efficient for three vessels to travel together, he says, when one can support the other two. He insists that we fit ourselves inside the Scoop. We certainly can, of course. You could fit half the Union fleet inside that hole. The successful management of this is another thing altogether.

Far less strenuous than their project, but equally daunting, is my own internal struggle. I have searched the Knowledgebase and run numerous diagnostics. It is impossible for a clone to experience guilt. So am I hallucinating the nausea and self-hatred? Can a clone hallucinate? Yes, according to the science. Can a clone hate himself? No. Paradox. Strange though, I find my unconventional pairing within my 'Thinker, of a Diplomatic protocortex with the Tactical overbrain, to be well suited to deception, lies and manipulation. It's taken some time, but through a careful and deliberate study of the history of Earth, their physiology, parapsychology, politics, religious practices and doctrine, I'm confident that I can convince them to hand me their cache of nuclear weapons, and on a silver platter, as it were. The outliers will be the religious extremists and the war-mongers.

A ping from the auto-nav calls me up to the bridge. The ship's sensors have detected the Super Scoop as it clears the horizon of Jupiter, to fly out and away from the planet. It's a good thing I kept an eye out for him.

This time, I do set the ship on an intercept course for the Prawl-Tang, as I'm supposed to dock inside his main hold. As I race up behind the Scoop, it occurs to me that the intake ports are along the front of the massive ship. I'll have to get ahead of him and trust him to maneuver over the delicate Equus. I pull alongside to match his speed and heading, but find it hard to accept that I'll intentionally allow a Prawl-Tang ship to swallow me alive. If he's insincere about his agreement, this could be a potentially fatal mistake for me as well as the Jovians. Once inside, he could change his mind and, sucking the sub-space out from between our molecules, condense us all down into really heavy blocks of scrap, to purge us out into an asteroid field.

I would go with Plan B, if I had one.

"Mission Steward," I call, "I will maintain close formation on the way to PB3, with my ship programmed to follow along which-ever course you decide is most efficient."

"Your suggestion is contrary to efficient operations. Maintain course and speed."

Sure it's 'contrary to efficient operations'. Instead, let's perform an exceptionally dangerous, high-speed merging of two vessels that are polar opposites in construction and flight characteristics. That makes *so* much more sense.

Without another word, the Scoop drops behind the cutter and just as fast, powers up to within a few meters of the aft engine bulk-head. I'm thinking I should shut off my engines or phase into hover mode or maybe just hide under a rug.

With the skill of a master pilot, he guides the Scoop over the cutter. The rocky crevasse is draped around me with not the slightest contact, to somehow consume my loaner ship. Captain Raytk would not be pleased. In the dim light from the intake port, I can just make out the movement of something around the cutter. The inside walls of the hold come alive as dozens of long, thick filaments reach out to embrace the Equus. My fingers flit between override buttons on the console, as I try to convince the landing sequencer to accept this new method of three-dimensional parking - weird. Without my having to act, the engines power down, the thrusters seal shut and the whole ship seems to fall asleep - very weird.

"Your ship is secured," he says. "I have directed it to rest until we reach PB3."

He directed *my* ship? How did he pull that off? Wait a minute. The Equus has an intramental interlink node, similar to the Navigation Onus on the Scoop. That's how he was able to guide the two ships together so accurately; the two ship's navicomputers became one. Can't say I'm at ease with him having complete control of the Equus.

Somewhere out in the darkness of the Scoop's vast hold are the three Knowers that came along for the ride. When the Mission Steward opened up the intake vent to bring in the Equus, the vacuum of space should have pulled the Knowers out at the same time. I couldn't detect any dampening field or other plasma curtain. They can't just be floating around in here with me. They wouldn't survive with their bodies at rest on a firm surface. With a flick of the switch for the docking lights on my ship's exterior, I illuminate my corner of the space, and reset my pupils from the default lux to improved performance in the very low light level.

I'm just able to make out what appears to be a very large pile of crystals that seem to be glued to the front wall along the floor, fifteen or twenty times the size of the cutter. Then I recognize the glistening, edgy surface. It's Obedient Sand. What could be many thousands of tons of the geometric, marble-sized grains have joined together to form an enormous cocoon that's being used to secure the Knowers and to contain their atmosphere. If the Prawl-Tang are skilled at growing coral into some mechanism overnight, the Knowers are geniuses at manipulating the Obedient Sand into whatever shape they require. This could actually work. But the cephalids are accustomed to the wide open, three dimensional prairie of their jovian existence. I hope they don't suffer from claustrophobia.

I reach out my thoughts toward them. "Jove calls to Knowers. I am here with you."

"Knowers listen. Knowers hear Jove."

How do I…uh…what words would they use for something they hadn't conceived of a week ago? "Jove inside Prawl-Tang, Good-Thing. Knowers inside Prawl-Tang, MoreGoodThing." This entire situation is so…alien.

"Knowers inside Prawl-Tang afraid. Knowers cold."

I contact the Navigation Onus and convince it to turn up some heat for the Knowers.

Curious, I ask the cephalids, "Knowers are three or one?"

"Knowers are three selves - one body. Knowers use ShareMe."

No kidding. I knew they could skip through each other's heads and trade consciousness using their natural transpsyche ability, but it never occurred to me that they could share one brain with multiple personalities for any length of time. That's just about the opposite of my existence, with one mind and many brains to use as required.

Over the next three days, I pass the time in review of Knowledgebase, listening to Wisdom, my para-sentient virtual entity, and in study of quotes of the Onlys. Like virtually all immortal beings, Synthetics tend to be good with long spans of boredom. But in here I can't even look at the stars, or perform ship diagnostics or maintenance, anything to make productive use of the time. With the cutter's circuits all put to sleep by the Mission Steward, the best I can do is to turn a few lights on and off. In truth, it's a struggle to not dwell on the feelings of guilt and remorse. I tell myself that nothing horrible has happened yet. There's no reason to feel this way about a mere inevitability. So what if some people die in the process? Humans die every day. This'll just be part of a natural evolutionary process. They were bound to be discovered by some intelligent race that might want to conquer them. I'm only a cog in the machine. It's just a natural progression. Humans are born. Humans die. There is a cause for both. Is there really anything so invaluable in the life of a single blooder, that its death is a loss? Won't they just be replaced by someone of equal value?

The pitch black of the Prawl-Tang vessel's interior is depressing. I don't want these thoughts. I need clarity. I have Wisdom here with me in my mind. I call to her.

"I am here," Wisdom says.

"What is the value of human life? How is it measured? At what point in their mortality have they reached their zenith in their existence?"

"I can show you," Wisdom says. She leads me to another dream.

Archive Vision, 2981 BCE, Nancery Clinic

The Man, Fonmet, is in conversation with Payl, and I'm him again. I strain to hear the words. I don't want to miss anything. It's always beneficial. We are with others this time. There are eleven people, including myself, in a room. Each is experiencing height-ened levels of tension and joy, a definite dichotomy to their energies and speech. Fonmet often introduces me to odd experiences. He puts increased priority, and finds satisfaction, in causing me to be present for circumstances that include paradox.

One of the people present, at the center of the group, releases an indistinct sound with inappropriately high volume. I recognize the female gender. Her wrists are bound with a soft fabric to a pole that is in the horizontal, which is in turn supported by triangulated metal framework suspended from the ceiling. A portion of her weight rests on her bare feet. The remainder from her hands wrapped around the pole. She continues to produce loud, indistinct vocalizations at generally regular intervals, and her respiration is abnormally high, given her minimal activity. Her clothing is inappropriate for a so-cial gathering. The distended abdomen, enlarged pelvic area and exposed legs while in the presence of an unbonded male, are in vi-olation of the Civility Code 909.104 – Public Decency and Dress.

Another, even louder outburst by the female brings all attendees to focus their attention on her pelvic area, which has released ap-proximately one liter of fluid onto a towel between her feet. I reach over to Fonmet. I take hold of his hand. He looks at me and smiles but says nothing.

The group offers various remarks of encouragement to the fe-male, urging her to exert herself to increase her obvious discomfort. Why would anyone allow themselves to be placed in such an awkward, painful and embarrassing situation? Her outbursts coincide with bouts of torturous internal disfiguration. I check the individual faces in the room. Each one is wholly attentive to the female's plight, yet they wait.

I am thankful that at least two persons care to intervene, as they stoop to reach toward her pelvis. I am somewhat dismayed that the Man, Fonmet, did not include himself in the decision to stop this excruciating process. Perhaps he is as aghast as I, paralyzed by the irrational activity.

The female, who now screams obscenities, has a large mass that has appeared at her pelvic cleft, and those kneeling attempt to remove it from her body. That is the reason she was in such discomfort, having that within the volume of her abdominal cavity. I can imagine that would be painful. All attendees seem most pleased. She is also showing signs of relief. The two assisting her with the mass carry it to a nearby table. The rest move toward the female and provide further encouragement and medical attention.

The man pulls me by the hand to the table where the freed mass is under investigation by three individuals who appear to have medical training. To my surprise, I notice that the mass is capable of voluntary movement and its own indistinct vocalizations. With some difficulty, I am able to distinguish a central mass with appendages that support even smaller appendages. Then, the truth of this spectacle permeates through my SynThinker.

This is not an extraneous mass. This is a person. The event is the delivery of the fetal humanoid from the gestative process – *birth*. I want to convey an appreciation to Fonmet, however I find that I'm limited by some overriding impulse to continue visual inspection of the new humanoid.

The infant's sounds increase in volume and intensity. It stretches an arm out, reaching, as I sometimes do for the hand of the Man when I feel uncomfortable. In my peripheral vision, I can see that the adult humanoids are watching me closely. They have quieted their excitement. All words spoken are in hushed tones. Moving my hand directly in front of the newborn humanoid, I hold very still. My torso ventilators are operating at minimal levels.

My focus narrowed on its very small hand, I allow one of my fingertips to meet its own. By some instinctive impulse, the newborn reaches toward me, its fingers curl around my one. The sensation of its touch causes instability in my moto-vascular rhythm. Although the coloration of the newborn's body is a very light blue, much like the natural pigment of the adults, its fingers are of a darker blue, almost a perfect match to my own dermal colorant. I can detect the slight pressure being exerted against me by this being that has just come into existence only eighty-five seconds ago.

No longer in distress, its sounds have subsided to a mere breathy hum. Its tiny fingers squeeze tighter.

In objection to all logic and reason, I find that it is my wish for this moment to continue without end. I want the child to hold on to me and not let go, to never let go, not ever.

End Archive Vision

The intrusion of harsh light and mechanical groans tear me away from another fantastic journey into the latent memories of the first artificial clones of the Onlys. The Equus has come to life, likely prompted by the Mission Steward.

I look down and imagine the tiny hand wrapped around a finger, with a wish that I could summon the warm sensations forward to this cold reality of being Jove-5.

The Prawl-Tang and his Navigation Onus have restarted a number of critical systems on the cutter, using their intramental connection across the heavy cilia that has extended itself from the inside walls of the hold to around my ship.

"$\Omega 94 \lambda 25 \theta$ is prepared to enter orbit around PB3," Mission Steward says.

Well, good morning to you, too, I think loudly enough. And by the way, you're lousy travel company. He ignores me.

"The Navigation Onus has detected a suitable location to place $\Omega 94 \lambda 25 \theta$ while you meet with the humans and attempt to deceive them with your offer of peace."

Somebody woke up on the wrong side of the reef.

The Scoop loses speed as it descends through the layers of the atmosphere, a great hole punched through the sky, clouds blackened with soot from the searing heat. The Mission Steward wastes no time getting this mountain of a starship out of harm's way. The various militaries of this planet could easily launch an attack while we are still in the air or on the ground, for that matter. There's only one fairly safe place to hide from the nuclear armament of the day – in the depths of the ocean. With just a cursory study of the available war machines of Earth, it could be surmised that any potential threat to the Scoop could not carry much speed underwater, nor would it be able to deliver a lethal strike. The Prawl-Tang can easily defend against smaller arms like a torpedo, with either its sub-space particle beam used for vaporizing asteroids in space ahead, or at least the massive, ossified hull plating to deflect the blast. For active defense, of course, there's the formidable tracking spear. Planes, boats, submarines, nothing would stand a chance against just one of those determined projectiles.

The Navigation Onus puts on the brakes just before the Scoop plows into the Indian Ocean. From within the confines of the Equus, suspended in the hold, I can hear the roar of the sea water brought to a boil around the superheated surface of the hull as it sinks down to rest on the Mascarene Plateau, eighty-one miles east of the Seychelles Islands, north of the island of Madagascar. I've got to hand it to that Prawl-Tang ship-mind-thingy; he parked it flat on a soft sandy shelf so no torpedoes or bombs could get underneath.

"Jove," Mission Steward says, "your craft will be prepared for submersion now."

"Submersion?"

A sliver of blue-green light appears high out in the front of the Equus. The intake vent that I backed into, or rather, that I was consumed by, has opened and is allowing sea water to rush in under great pressure. The gap widens to more than the width of my ship and about four meters high. The incredible blast shoots halfway across the span of the hold, to crash down almost directly below me. I can just see the point where the cascade turns to a foamy cauldron on the floor of the Scoop. It takes about one Earth day to fill the massive cargo hold. When I check on the Knowers, I find the three of them are alive and well in the one and simply ecstatic to hear that they had made it to the LittleNoisyBluePearl.

Using their mental powers to control the surplus of Obedient Sand brought along, they set about concocting a handful (suckerful?) of experiments to the water and creatures that have been drawn in since the hold was flooded. As wise as they are, the Knowers have little concept of science and simple things like the pH of sea water, compared to the gaseous metallic-hydrogen atmosphere of Jupiter. A splash encountered during their investigations causes a nasty burn on the tip of one giant arm. Of note, although untreated sea water is caustic to the Jovians, they seem to be relatively immune to lion-fish stings and box jellyfish. In fact, they describe an unfortunate bite from a beaked sea snake - venom eight times more toxic than a cobra - to be 'LittleItchy'. I suppose a great white shark would be 'TastyGood'.

With more than a little trepidation, I concede that the time has come to make contact with the humans of Earth. After I convince the Mission Steward to allow me to power up the Knowledgebase, the ship's manifest helps me to locate more suitable attire for an expedition that starts with a two thousand meter, liquid ascent to the surface. From within the cutter's escape pod, I find several tunics and cloaks made from a material that can adapt to a wide range of environmental conditions. Pretty handy in case you have to bail onto a moon of frozen methane or shield yourself from intense gamma radiation. With some effort, and assistance from my Union Dynap-parel, I make the swim up and out of the Scoop.

I can say without prejudice that nowhere in my Foundation Download, Tactical Download, Diplomatic Summary, Mission Brief, or in any of the three previous crossloads was I adequately prepared for an encounter with human beings. They may have never met an alien clone before. I will have to take it slow.

Nearing the surface, I see the bright and warm light from their star, Sol, as the waves on the surface above wiggle and distort the gleaming corona. Above me float numerous objects; I perceive them as the undersides of small and medium-sized watercraft, boats. They must be the party sent to welcome space travelers who just arrived.

I aim for a gap between two closest me.

I burst through the surface of the water and reach up into the air, as if I might find something solid upon which to support myself. This being my first ever attempt at swimming, I'm unaccustomed to the sensation and the requirement to tread water.

While I struggle to maintain a consistent level of floatation, my attention is garnered by an outburst of loud voices behind me. I turn myself around, in a somewhat awkward manner, to see if they have directed their conversation at me. Although distracted by the rising and falling of the sea-swells, I'm able to make out three individuals standing in a small boat. Two of them point at me; the third one produces loud shrieks and squeals. Odd, I had presumed that the people here would speak French or Creole. I cannot discern this dialect.

One of the persons hefts a large object overhead, an oar for the boat. Before my Tactical app can react, the large heavy blade of the paddle lands hard upon the side of my head. The force of the strike knocks me underwater for a moment. At the surface again, I notice that my visual range has been reduced in the horizontal. Something in the water ahead of me sinks slowly away - my right eyeball. That would explain things. The second strike is better aimed and cleaves my skull down about a third of the way through my head. I lose all sight, touch, taste and smell, however my sense of hearing is reduced by only fifty percent. I detect the sound of an outboard motor approaching; water moving; bubbles; small arms fire. Knowledge-base tells me that the sound is of a fully-automatic Kalashnikov, model forty-seven, expending all thirty rounds.

That should do it.

I awake as Number Six. Welcome to Planet Earth, Jove. You

lasted exactly nineteen seconds. Should have seen that coming! I do
not wait the half second for the cassette door to open. With a kick, it
flies across the lab, bouncing off the far wall.

After informing my echinodermic chauffeur of my fateful intro-
duction to humanity, I insist that he relinquish control of the Equus
systems so that I may have unrestricted access to any and all resources necessary, that I may better prepare myself to meet the violent hominids.

With all systems operational and the Knowledgebase intramental connection restored, I feel more confident about my second intro-
duction to Violent Vic in Death To All - 2, whatever that is. Wisdom
seems to be getting a chuckle out of it. I ignore her suggestion of a
football helmet and opt for a crash course in Morse Code. The entire educational experience takes a few milliseconds, but I'm feeling
rushed to retrieve Five's dead body before it becomes a trophy, im-
paled on someone's mast.

I remember to grab the Dynapparel first, to swim out to where
I think I'd find Five. He should've sunk either on top of or very
near the submerged Scoop, but I can't find me anywhere. I give up
for now and swim underwater for a great distance, bypassing all of
the smaller boats to head for what should be either a large military
or science vessel. I'm most certainly not going to arrive without a
confirmed welcome.

With a firm hold on the keel of a large gray ship, I use one of
the smaller devices that my Tactical Advisor, Trayd-7, had provided
for the mission. An advanced inter-species communications node, it
can facilitate the translation of many thousands of known languages
across the Orion-Sagittarius intersection of the Milky Way Galaxy.
I'll use it to make short-beeps and long-beeps against a slab of steel.

My thoughts pressed through the telepath-receptive device, I work out something simple that can be repeated and easily understood by most mariners that ply these waters.

"Bonjour, C'est Jove. Je viens de planete Jupiter. Je ne voulais faire de mal."

Then for good measure, in the global language of Terran commerce.

"Hello! I am Jove. I come from the planet Jupiter. I mean you no harm." I figure there's a fifty-fifty chance that they'll believe I'm for real. The three-mile-long space rock that made course corrections and slowed itself before it dove into the sea might corroborate my claim somewhat.

After a dozen repetitions of the message and no perceived response from within, I take a break to survey the waters around me. Four large hammerhead sharks circle my position - lovely.

The translator node blinks that it's receiving a response in the same language as it had sent. "This is Captain Mark Thomas of the Royal Australian Navy destroyer, Hobart. What is your intention?"

To not get my head bashed in and or shot through with a rifle, that's what.

"My name is Jove. My intention is to represent the sentient beings of Jupiter and the...Union of Synthetic Persons," I say. Might as well start off with a lie. "I mean you no harm." I can feel his mind above me. I press upon it with my best friendly me.

A minute goes by before Captain Thomas inquires further. "What do you want?"

"To meet the people of Earth and to deliver a message of hope," I bleep at him.

Now two minutes tick by while he contemplates first contact

with an alien. At least this one is thinking before he starts at me with a weapon.

"Two officers will escort you to up into the vessel," he replies. "Please do not harm them."

Didn't I just say that I wasn't—?

One of the hammerhead sharks swings wildly against me on the right, a small spear sticking in one side and out the other. It twists and flails as it leaves a coiled trail of blood. Two scuba divers approach me from above; one has a spear-gun with no spear. I'll take that as a sign of goodwill.

The divers swim to within a meter of me, and look me up and down for a second. Then each one grabs an arm and they pull me out and up the five meters to the side of the boat. We break through the surface. I cannot help but flinch, the crossloader being efficient, even transferring learned muscle response, reflexive feedback. Grateful to learn from my previous mistakes, fatal ones included, I'd rather not be a jittery mess, all the same. They lead me to an inflatable skiff, where the divers in wetsuits and two more aboard help me up and over the rubbery side and onto a seat at the bow. Upon a recommendation from Wisdom, I keep my hands in plain sight and limit my motions to slow and obvious.

As I look up at the massive gray hull above me, Knowledge-base provides a download about the ship. The Hobart, an air-warfare destroyer, has fifty-six missile launchers, two torpedo tubes, three high-speed machine guns and one cannon which can strike any target inside of twenty-three kilometers with pinpoint accuracy. The stealth ship trades off speed for exceptional endurance, for its patrol of the Australian continent's fifty thousand kilometer coastline. To make a run northwest to secure a giant meteorite was outside of the typical mission parameters.

After my climb onto the ship's fantail, two men in bright yellow biohazard gear remain at my sides, with more to take positions in the hallway, all very nervous. I'm beginning to hear the barest flicker of their thoughts. Earthlings are not naturally telepathic, hence they do not purposely project thought patterns into the vital ether that carries the cognitive messages. Every few seconds, one of them experiences an accidental leak from their psyche and out where I can sense it. Just as quickly, they shut themselves tight, so that they are alone in their head again. However, they easily allow their minds to be pierced, influenced.

Another person that wears a similar cover-suit leads me down several levels and into a small room. He wears a belt with what appear to be diagnostic devices. He steps to within arm's length of me, and motions me to push back the hood of my cloak, which I do, and to slide the sleeves up so he can see my arms and hands. I guess he's assigned to perform some type of medical examination of me to verify that I'm in good health and not a risk to them, not transporting any harmful pathogens. Smart on their part, but unnecessary. Union Synthetics have an outer layer that contains an antimicrobial agent.

He grasps my wrist to palpate my dermal layers and does his best to peer through my semitransparent, blue flesh and silver liquid within. Then he removes a small black cylinder from his belt case, and clicks a button on the end. A bright light shines forth. He uses the light to attempt to amplify the photons reflecting from my inner layers and back to his retinas. It's crude, but effective. He lights up my neck and face with the device.

"Say 'Ahhh'," Wisdom says. I don't get it.

I can feel his body develop a slight quiver. He puts away the flashlight and returns with another clear cylinder with marked gradations along one side and a very thin something sticking out from one end.

With the pointed end aimed at my forearm, he pauses to look up and catch my eye. Back down, he increases the pressure of his grip. To my surprise, he moves the pointed end so that it penetrates into my dermal layers - oh, phlebotomy. I reach over to withdraw the syringe's needle from my flesh. I reposition the tip so that it will intersect one of my brachial hydrostatic return micro-conduits. I start the insertion of the needle, then motion for him to resume control of the syringe. With a shaky hand, he does. I nod to signal that he has indeed found the correct depth. He pulls the plunger at the other end of the tube and draws a small sample of my hydrostatic fluid into the chamber. Immediately, the shaking in his hands becomes a tremor; his skin is no longer a deep brown but a dusky gray.

I swear, I don't do anything to the poor fellow, but he drops to his knees and falls flat on his face with a crunch. With the syringe still in my arm, I turn and smile at his assistants.

Out in the hallway, one of the others in a bright yellow suit uses a handheld communicator to relay the news.

"O-R Sellars to Lieutenant Tamm."

The response comes through small holes in a box on the far wall. "Go ahead, Chief."

"Lieutenant, I need to report that Commander Robinson fainted, Sir, during his examination of the individual we pulled from under the ship," the Chief Warrant Officer says.

"And that's dead-set?" the Lieutenant says. "What happened?"

"No porkie, Sir. The doctor was drawing some blood. Um…it's not red. It's…the blood is like, chrome colored, Sir. Um, Lieutenant, this blue guy that came out of the meteorite is the ridgy-didge. He… uhhhhmmm…"

Chief Warrant Officer Sellars faints, too. The microphone falls with a clatter. The person to his left leans over to pick it up and turns to peek through the open doorway.

Two officers passing out must trigger some secondary protocol, I guess, because the other two bright yellow gentlemen push past me, grab the Commander, drag him out of the room and lock me in. I understand - they're frightened of me. As Knowledgebase and Wisdom continue to fill me in, I can foresee that these next few hours may be difficult. This event - my arrival - is more than just 'the blue guy from the meteorite' that's inconveniently dripping chrome goo on the floor. I personify the first nudge of an upheaval in their society. I'm not dangerous in the practical sense of the word. I *am* danger. My existence portends a great movement of truth toward that which they've both dreamed of and denied for centuries. I am *other*. Just like in my conversation with the Mission Steward. He had to come to grips with the fact that there was an-*other* somebody, wholly alien to his world, his domain, and he is forced to deal with me and argue with me and understand me; not safe; not wanted. Ignorance is bliss.

The batch of bright yellow persons assigned to my hallway changes twice before I receive another visitor to what is obviously 'the brig'.

"You are correct, Jove," Wisdom says. "They want to believe you are for real, but they are afraid for it to be true."

Four new people walk down the hallway toward my cell. One wears what appears to be an official uniform, another wears some type of clothing that would make him a challenge to see against a forest background. He carries a weapon similar to the one used on me—on Number Five. The other two are dressed in close-fitting, darker garments. Three-piece suit, says Knowledgebase.

"You are going to be interrogated," Wisdom adds. "Do not show weakness."

They dismiss the Yellows and draw near to each other for a private conversation. The one with the rifle steps through the opened door first, followed by the other three. I'm feeling nervous again, butterfly stomach is back.

The official one, who sports colorful rectangles on his chest, is the first to speak.

"Do you prefer English or French?" He asks.

"English is fine with me," I respond. "Whatever is most appropriate for you." Although they offer to converse in this particular language, their physiological reaction is one of disbelief that I'm able to speak in English.

The decorated officer steps forward.

"I'm Lieutenant Tamm of the Hobart." He gestures to the two suits, though he never takes his eyes off me. "These are Misters Clarondon and Shoemaker. They, um, represent Earth." I notice that they never do introduce me to the laughably camouflaged gentleman with the sidearm. My Tactical app advises that's because they want me to forget he's there. Noted.

"I am Jove, from the Union of Synthetic Persons, assigned to represent the beings indigenous to the planet you know as Jupiter. Thank you for, um…welcoming....me to your ship." I try to contain my irritation at being locked up, but it's out. I'll use that to gauge their response.

The Lieutenant continues to speak while the other two observe carefully. "So, do you mind if I ask you a few questions, to clarify the situation?" Mister Leafy Green is staring at the Lieutenant's hands for any signal to shoot me in the head. What a bunch of trigger-happy lunatics. I'll be lucky to not get killed again by day's end.

"That's to be expected. Go ahead." I say.

"It's true then, that you're not human, but an artificial life form?"

"That is correct."

"And you're from the planet Jupiter?" he asks. Obviously, he didn't hear me the other four times.

"The origin of my manufacture is from another star system. Your astronomical charts label it Sirius," I say. "I was designed specifically for the mission to Earth. I am constructed to allow efficient operation here, to more easily interact with your species."

"Yet you say you represent the people of Jupiter," Tamm says. "Why didn't they just come instead?"

"You mean besides the fact that our initial welcome to Earth was to be brutally murdered?"

I study the two suits as they smile at each other, while Tamm appears quite embarrassed. These human beings are sly, if anything.

Finally, Mister Shoemaker speaks up. "Yes, that was unfortunate. Please know that the individuals who made that terrible error have been apprehended and will be prosecuted to the fullest extent of the law."

"Well," I whisper, "accidents do happen."

The Lieutenant allows himself a flat smile. He's patiently awaiting my answer to his last question. He has a good Thinker, biologic though it is. I can hear it working.

I clarify for him how the Jovians did accompany me, as far the humans could comprehend. I explain about the significant difference in the chemical composition of this ocean and the one that supports them on their home planet. How if an Earthling were to travel there, he or she would likely not be safe outside their craft. The Jovians, or Knowers, as they are called, are safe in a protected area of the ship below the surface of the water. They cannot come out physically. But that I was in contact with them and could relay messages. I explained that, in a sense, I was acting as the 'space-suit' for them on their journey.

"That's interesting," the Lieutenant says. His face begins to soften a bit. "I understand. They may not be comfortable here in the Hobart."

"Sirs, just as the planet of Jupiter is thirteen hundred times the volume of Earth, a single Knower is four times the size of this vessel. Hence the reason we required a giant hollow meteor to bring them. I'm sure you're curious and would like to get a look at them, as they would you. But keep in mind, just one of their four eyeballs is wider than the Hobart."

Lieutenant Tamm keeps his gaze locked on me, the two suits glance at each other for a moment while the information sinks in. Mister Leafy Green has a single bead of sweat running down his cheek, to match the gun oil ready to drip off the bottom of the extended magazine.

Mister Shoemaker turns his shoulders to square up with me. "Yes, we are curious about the Knowers. If we cannot meet them, perhaps you would have a photograph or something to show us what they look like?"

"I have no method of projecting an image of the Jovians for you. Perhaps if we were to adjourn to a lab or a conference area with a—"

"That's not possible," Tamm says. "I'm afraid you must remain here for the time being."

"In the brig," I reply. All I get for my candor is three fake smiles.

Tamm gestures to the raised platform behind me. "Why don't you have a seat and relax."

I turn around and look at the gray metal frame and perforated surface that hangs from the wall with hinges and chains. Knowledgebase tells me it's a 'cot', used for sitting or lying upon, both irrelevant. Tactical app advises that their chosen words, their intent to have my head lower than theirs and placement in a corner suggests that they wish to use an interrogation technique meant to make me feel inferior and vulnerable.

"My species does not sit, but thank you for the accommodations."

Tamm's lower lip curls out, which suggests disappointment at my refusal. The 'representatives of Earth' don't even flinch. They're studying me closely. I can see that humans have a large vein in their neck that pulses with their cardiac rhythm. Tamm's beats fast, but he is trained to control his outward demeanor. The heartbeats of Clarondon and Shoemaker are slow and steady. They're used to high-stress situations. That makes them the most dangerous of any in the room.

Finally, Mister Clarendon opens his mouth to speak. Shoemaker takes over observing minutia. His accent is similar to Shoemaker's. "You stated in your Morse Code to Captain Thomas that you wanted to 'deliver a message of hope'. Why don't you deliver that message now?"

"Not to them," Wisdom advises. As I consider my answer, there is a tingle in my brain. It's the Mission Steward that has reached out, calling to me.

"Jove, the humans have attempted to core a hole through the

upper hull of $\Omega94\lambda250$."

I turn Clarendon's question back on him. "Why don't you have your people stop drilling a hole into my ship?" For a brief instant, his eyes squint in irritation. Tamm is caught off-guard, unaware of a secondary protocol to enter $\Omega94\lambda250$; to take their own 'photographs'. The moment I said that I couldn't show them pictures, someone listening had ordered the drill to start. The Navigation Onus must have closed the intake vent to prevent intruders.

Tamm glances at Clarendon, and then looks at the floor. "You mean into Emrah?" he asks.

"Emrah? I don't understand." What was that word? I don't recognize it.

"That's the name of the meteor you came in. It's the name that we—humanity gave to your ship."

No kidding, sentimental and homicidal, humans are a bizarre mix. Mission Steward should be flattered. 'Emrah' sounds *so* much better than $\Omega94\lambda250$. I'll jump on that connection. Tamm just handed me some leverage. Tactical app tells me that could've been a mistake or a mistake on purpose to garner favor.

"Earth named our ship Emrah?" I ask.

"Yes," Tamm says, "we've been anxiously awaiting your arrival."

—with some trepidation, I would guess.

"The Knowers are pleased to hear that," I bubbled back, then, "So, please stop drilling into my ship." I let my grin fade into a rocky mask. My mind pushes through their thin boney shell and burrows into the fat of the cerebrum. They have little resistance to my abilities.

"I can agree to that," Clarendon says.

Tamm straightens up suddenly. The other two look at him, then they all seem to stiffen. I hear a strange new sound. He'd noticed it first, his ears attuned to listen for the 'whop-whop-whop' in the distance, from the west. Knowledgebase hums data into my 'Thinker: Sikorsky S-70D Seahawk, a helicopter, on approach to land on the back of the Hobart. Someone important has arrived. The Lieutenant is relieved. The men in suits are frustrated. Mister Leafy Green has sweated through his undergarments.

"Excuse us," is all I get as the four of them file out through the port and into the hallway. Pausing to exchange words and some attitude, Tamm is not in agreement with the Earth Representatives. They're obviously two sides working in parallel, but not in unison. Whoever just landed is in control of both, however.

Alone in the cell again, I push back the cloak's thick sleeve to reveal my forearm. The syringe is still stuck into my vein. I slowly pull it out and press a fingertip over the hole while the chemical sealant congeals to prevent leakage. Wisdom suggests that I look for the red Sharps Container.

I can sense several new minds out there. Perhaps it's those that have recently arrived on the ship. They've come to see me. They want to welcome me. I reach out to them, picking through the wonderment, the imaginations, the fear. There it is – hope. Each of them has some at least. I make a place for myself in their heads. Me, and their hopes and dreams of peace, intertwined. I've got them.

Soon enough, I'm removed from the brig and escorted up two flights of stairs and into a hallway where the walls are an appealing color and a fabric layer covers the steel plate floor. The Leafy Greens stop at an open door. With stiffened hands they gesture me to move inside. There's a large oval table with several people around the circumference. I recognize Lieutenant Tamm but the other four faces are new. The one with the uniform similar to Tamm's strides up to meet me.

"Welcome, Jove," he says. "I'm Captain Thomas. Please, sit down."

Oh great, he wants me to sit. Perhaps this whole Earth thing was a bad idea. With reservation, I move to the chair provided and push myself down into the angular crevice. That feels terrible.

Captain Thomas introduces the other attendees, "Jove, this is the Minister of Foreign Affairs for the Republic of Seychelles, Francois DeMonte. On his left is Sir Edward Vincent, Chairman of the International Astronomical Union. Next to him is Moshe Samuelsson, the Director of SETI and the Carl Sagan Institute, and here on your right is Miss Zaris Liyanage, the United Nations Special Representative, originally from Malaysia. Zaris is a highly respected geopolitical expert and was appointed as the liaison to negotiate a peaceful dialogue between the Earth and the coming visitors. That'd be you, of course."

With some awkwardness, I lean forward to shake hands with each one. I wonder why he didn't have me do that before I sat in the chair. Well, at least I'm out of the brig and with people who, judging by their own discomfort and nervousness, aren't expert with interrogation tactics. These are more likely to ask about the weather on Jupiter.

Captain Thomas urges the group to take their seats. The female to my immediate right, Zaris, is visibly anxious. I'd guess this is her first time rubbing elbows with an alien. She's trembling so badly, there's a discernible hiss from her sapphire silk suit. Her gold bracelets jangle together.

"Tell her you don't bite," Wisdom says. Okay.

I lean a bit too close. Her soft hair tickles my nose.

"It's okay, I don't bite."

Her watery eyes get very big. She turns away from me quickly and leans over the arm of her chair, to wretch the contents of her stomach onto the floor.

Alright, Wisdom, do you have any other bright ideas?

"Yes," Wisdom says, "tell a joke to relieve the tension."

As the attendant from the back of the room comes forward to assist, I catch his attention with a raised finger.

"Perhaps a cold wet towel on the back of the neck would be good," I say, pointing behind my head, "and then maybe one for the lady, as well!"

Even Zaris has to laugh, nods in agreement. They do and it does help. She apologizes profusely. I try to offer some comfort.

"Ma'am, ever since I learned that I'd be coming to Earth, I've wanted to throw up." More laughter around the table, and we're past the hard part.

"Jove," Captain Thomas says, "please accept the heartfelt welcome of this small group, and on behalf of the people of Earth. Although the concept of extraterrestrial life has been openly discussed for generations, you seem to have caught us by surprise. Even many who want to believe are saying, 'this is too good to be true'. In that regard, I apologize for any mistreatment that you may've suffered since your arrival. I understand that one of your fellows was injured while in the water? How can we help?"

"Thank you very much for your kind words, Captain," I reply. "I accept your welcome on behalf of the Jovians and my own Brothers.

Yes, there was an injury, a death actually, when I…first made egress from my ship.

"You see, I'm not a singular corporeal being, but rather one in a series of clones of a specific design. About five thousand years ago, on a planet orbiting the star known to you as Sirius, which is only eight light-years distant, a small group of scientists discovered how to create poly-synthetic copies of their own DNA. Driven to do this, they worked the remainder of their lives to perfect the methods required for sustained artificial life, for there was a great catastrophe which loomed in their future. Sirius is a binary system, a large stable star bound to a companion dwarf star. These two stellar objects swing around a central gravitational point, with a few planets in orbit outside the pair. These scientists discerned that by the end of the current generation, a rare and peculiar alignment of all the planets would pull the smaller star, Sirius B, into a more pronounced ellipse around Sirius A, and in time, bring it perilously close to the only habitable planet. They were correct. It took about fifty-eight Earth years before the effects could be felt. Eventually, Sirius B passed so close to the planet, it stripped away the atmosphere, and destroyed most of the larger life forms, which included the progeny of my original designer.

"However, by the time that occurred, the Onlys, as they are called, succeeded in creating clones of their selves. Not mere copies of their fragile, mortal bodies, but artificial persons with far superior intellects and physiology designed to withstand the severe environmental conditions in what would remain of their world. Moreover, their creations were 'born' if you will, with an innate creativity; to continue where the Onlys left off. The original clones, the Ones, learned and grew. They experimented and practiced what the Onlys had taught them. Soon, there were hundreds of new designs, all original Ones; not copies of a mortal being, but fresh ideas come to life."

I give the group time to comprehend my history. In the back of my 'Thinker, I'm measuring their willingness to believe, so that when they're ripe for the fable, I can tell them anything.

"Over the centuries, the clones learned how to move out into space, and encountered other beings that travel the stars. Yes, Mister Samuelsson, you are correct; there're many hundreds of 'extra-terrestrials' out there. The Orion-Cygnus-Sagittarius intersection is teaming with life. Moreover, many of them are humanoid, like you and like me, or rather, my pattern.

"As your own Earth history has proven, the urge to conquer is common throughout space. The clones found themselves at a disadvantage. They'd been programmed as pacifists, in their DNA so to speak. However, they possessed within themselves the ability to create a warrior series, indefatigable, ruthless and capable of defending against any would-be attacks or attempts to enslave them. There's an old Earth axiom: power corrupts. It is a galactic truth, it would seem. The few warriors created were dissatisfied with a directive to wait for any potential threat."

Tamm interjects his own wisdom. "The best defense is a good offense."

"Yes, exactly, Lieutenant, another truth. It was decided that the series should be cancelled. The last three surviving warriors were banished for their crimes. Laws were enacted to prevent further attempts to construct such savage monsters again. The rest of us would live our lives promoting peace, to perfect the attainment of brotherhood, wherever we found ourselves. And that, indirectly, is how we find ourselves here, on Earth, with you."

The elderly and genial Sir Edward Vincent spreads wide his large, soft hands, like he just found a long-lost relative.

"How fantastic it is," he says, "that of all the opportunities for the people of Earth to encounter any one of the many species alive in the heavens, that we should be especially blessed to first meet you, Jove."

What can I do but smile and reach across the table, taking both his hands in wordless communion of inter-species friendship. He's overwhelmed at the touch of my skin. I know he wants to 'pet' me, to explore me, to know more about what I am. That can wait. There'll be time to satisfy their scientific curiosity.

Captain Thomas leans forward on his elbows, to look directly at me, into me.

"Jove, I heard you say that you had a message to deliver to the people of Earth. Can you tell us now, what that message is?"

I turn to face Thomas straight on. The words are there, right there on my tongue, but I find an odd resistance within me to get them out. I've already practiced my speech; I know exactly what to say to trick the humans into believing our story. We have a plan. It's a good one. Just say it, Jove, what is the problem? I've lied before. Look at them, they trust me already. They believe me because I've spoken the truth. Now is the time for the deception. What's holding me back? Wisdom, is that you? Where're the words so meticulously chosen for this moment? Am I defective? Is there a failure of my SynThinker that only now, at this most crucial juncture of the mission, becomes evident?

I try to execute on the plan, but I'm stuck. Stuck in this damn chair, for one thing! I push myself up and out of the ridiculous contraption, an audible whoosh coming from somewhere in my torso-ventilator.

I leave my place at the table to walk the few paces over to the wall, where a small round portal beckons with natural light. Ignoring the humans for a moment, I look out at the magnificent blue ocean. Waves curl in little white swirls down the face of each liquid dune. The LittleBluePearl...and here I am to usher in its destruction. Yes, because that's the plan. It's the right thing to do for the Jovians. What did Choyt-72 say? 'You must, above all things, act to preserve the well-being of the Knowers. We will provide you with some resources, and *you are free to take advantage of opportunities to consign others that will aid your mission'*. Isn't that what I'm doing here? I am free to act as required. Does it matter if they die tomorrow or at the end of some humiliating geriatric progression? I'm free to consign the humans to act according to the needs of the mission. It doesn't matter if they would choose otherwise, if they understood that their lives are at stake; that their entire planet is to be plundered to reward the Prawl-Tang for their decision to disregard Jupiter.

More nausea in my non-existent stomach, I struggle to maintain focus.

A hand on my shoulder startles me. Flinching slightly, I turn to see Zaris standing close. She's quietly made her way over to offer the support I so obviously require.

"It will be alright, Jove," Zaris says, "Just tell us."

That was exactly what I needed to hear. Patting her hand, we move back to our places, to the other worried faces. I decide to remain standing, though, spreading my hands upon the table.

Pretending to inhale a nervous breath, I deliver a well-paced confession, in my best serious tone. "The truth is, my new friends,

Earth will soon face self-annihilation."

I hang my head in mock depression. But to see my reflection in the glossy veneer of the polished table is a frightful thing. The grotesque image in the mirror is menacing, it scowls up at me from just above the deep cinnamon of the red oak surface. The mouth moves.

"So, do you think you can lie to seven billion people and bring them to their doom without any consequence?" I shut my eyes hard against the truth of my deception. I don't want to see this. Make it stop.

"Jove." It's Moshe Samuelsson. "We know this is inevitable. We've known since the Cold War that one day mankind could destroy itself. It's not your fault."

It is inevitable. I can live with that. Gently, I pour their own words back into them.

Captain Thomas clears his throat, stands to meet my gaze. "Tell us what you know, Jove. As he said, we've been aware of this possibility for decades. What's the threat to us? Is it mutual destruction, nuclear holocaust?"

Sounds good to me. "Yes, exactly that, I'm afraid."

"How is it that you know for a certainty that this will occur?" Sir Edward Vincent asks.

I look around the table, meeting every eye. They must see truth in my words now. "It's the Jovians, the Knowers, as they are called," I say. "They are the great sentient beings of Jupiter, with incredible power to not just share thoughts and knowledge among themselves, but with others, even other species. They're capable of transiting across vast distances without their bodies. The Knowers have been watching Earth, watching you closely, for many of your generations. They treasure the opportunity to observe and listen to you, as you live and grow, explore and reach; to witness every achievement; every historic liftoff from your world and out into your star system. When your first probe came to Jupiter, they longed to catch it somehow; attach a note if they could, and send it back.

"And they've witnessed the destructive power of your atomic arsenal. You cannot imagine the terrible sorrow they feel at the realization that you're using these devices to kill each other. Just as you're aware of the potential for mankind to bring about its own end, so the Knowers have envisioned the fate of man. They do not have to guess at the outcome. In the years ahead, the surface of the Earth will be unrecognizable. This is foreseen."

The Great Deception is unveiled. I scan the reactions of these first five members of the human race that hear it. Tamm is a shrewd and calculating military officer. He's only part way there. Likewise, the Captain has heard propaganda before. He's a professionally trained warrior, which includes how to spot a good decoy. He's going to be a hard sell. The tears are already welling up in Vincent's tired, wrinkly eyes, he's done. Samuelsson? His imagination is hard at work to visualize my words. He wants to believe me. He'll talk himself into it. Zaris has lowered her face into her hands against the tabletop, sobbing - three out of five, so far. Oh, and the attendant ran out of the room in hysteria. I'm good for a solid majority. Of course, the militants will be the most difficult. I need to put them out of a job. So, get them away from their job.

"Families," says Wisdom. I see wedding bands on the sailors' fingers.

I lock in with the Captain. "Mister Thomas?" I say, "Do you have any children?"

I reach into his mind, to poke around where parental doubts hide.

"Yes, two sons, and a daughter on the way," he says past the frog.

I look over at Tamm, using a pouty face to wordlessly ask the same question.

He nods in agreement with his commanding officer and brother in parenthood. "A boy and a girl; we were trying for another."

Past tense -- 'were'-- almost there.

With the least volume necessary to be heard by just the two men, I whisper, "I *am* sorry."

With hands chemically warmed for the moment, I lovingly caress the arms of my two new human brothers.

Although my first few attempts at telepathic influence over the humans seemed somewhat crude and intrusive, it's really not so bad. An hour ago, they were so frightened, and now here I am, comforting them over the loss of their children, not yet conceived.

Zaris tells me that she'll do everything in her power for my voice to be heard, and the message carried, to the innermost sanctum of the human's world. Imagine that.

Things really start to look up for me as the humans of Earth begin to doubt their continued existence. I'm assigned VIP guest quarters on the Hobart as we steam back to the Seychelles, a truly beautiful island group. Nothing in my Knowledgebase about this tiny province of France does it justice.

Lieutenant Tamm comes to my room to lead me out to the helipad above the rear deck of the formidable destroyer.

"I'm afraid we aren't being issued permissions to dock at Victoria," he says over his shoulder as he leads Zaris, Sir Edward and me down the gray steel corridors toward the outer hatch of the flight deck. "Due to the current tensions between us and the Iranian Republic, we were advised to sail within sight o' land and then run you in on a skiff. But if we're to come anywhere near the port, we would have to drop the flag. Captain had choice words on that. Won't repeat them in front of the lady." We step into the bright light of the equator as he raises his voice against the loud rush of wind from the Sikorsky's blades that whirl overhead. "Best option is to fly you in on the Seahawk. More comfortable than the skiff and we'll have you there in just a few shakes. You will be landing at—"

Zaris interrupts, her cupped hand directing her voice through the turbulent air next to the helicopter. "Be okay, Lieutenant. My post is in Nairobi. I come out to Victoria at least once a year. I know how get to home."

Tamm gives thumbs up as we climb aboard the aircraft. I struggle with the fact that there're only seats in the craft. It's not tall enough inside for me to stand, as I asked to. Usually, it's only my insides that feel uneasy in situations like this. But this time, it's my skin as well. Synthetics don't really experience an itch, per se. However, it feels like my skin has begun to shrivel. I look at my arms and my feet - blue and chrome. I look okay. But I'm burning all over, like I'm on fire. Whirling around, I expect flames. Come on, Tactical app, help me out here! What's the problem? What's wrong with me? Zaris is looking at me, trying to understand. My hearing must have failed also, as I cannot hear anything from her and the sound of the Seahawk engines and rotors has faded. Convulsions? Wow, I am in trouble. Knowledgebase, help me. Wisdom, what's wrong?

The First Officer stares at me in disbelief as the puddle of silver fluid under my seat grows larger, jiggles with the vibration of the bouncing craft. I see him grab a handful of shirt material on the shoulder of the pilot. He's yelling something but I can't tell what. I can't see his lips to read them. My unrelenting pain is inside and out.

As my vision begins to darken, Knowledgebase clues me in: this vehicle is fueled with a specific hydrocarbon molecule that resembles the releasing agent used to separate my flesh and other organs from the cloning lab equipment during my manufacture. While I had approached the helicopter and had gotten seated, the exhaust from the jet engines mixed with the surrounding air, infiltrating my clothing and internal ventilation systems. There is a rapid dissolution of my connective tissues.

That would explain why I feel like I'm falling apart at the seams. I'm falling apart at the seams. Hopefully, I haven't gotten any of me on Zaris' nice outfit.

I awake as Number Seven. I think, this time, I'll just lay here awhile. It's quiet, serene, down here in the belly of the Equus, in the depths of the....of Emrah, under the sea. It'll be quite a few hours before the Hobart can make the return trip.

There's that familiar tickle in my 'Thinker.

"Jove, is that you?" asks the Prawl-Tang.

"Yes, Mission Steward. I'm here."

"Is there a problem?"

"Nothing that can't be resolved with a sufficient supply of replacement clones."

Don't you even laugh, you big-bloody-fish-rock-creep-murderous-lump.

It takes a lot of persuasion, but in the end, I convince Lieutenant Tamm that this won't be a problem again. By the time Number Six dissolved into a soft, grainy pulp on the floor of the Seahawk, the Knowledgebase on board the Equus had passed on the details of the failure to the autogenic manipulator in the hypertrophic cloning lab. All subsequent deliveries will include a clear, flexible sealer that is impervious to most hydrocarbons, oxides, ethers, mild acids and solvents. As long as I promise not to walk headlong into the tail rotor, I'm cleared to fly again. He insists on coming along the second time anyway, to keep an eye on me. He won't let the pilot start the engines until we're all on board with the doors closed and secure.

Zaris, Sir Edward and I, with a small entourage, do make it to Victoria, Seychelles lush, picturesque capitol. There would seem to be an abundance of people for such a small airport. Zaris tells me that she's shocked to see the news of my arrival has spread so fast. There're people behind barricades, crowds spilled over onto the runways and landing areas. As soon as they notice us, or me I suppose, they become agitated. Some are holding signs with either positive or negative slogans relating to my presence in their locale, 'Alien Freak Go Home' would be the most common. From the look on Zaris' face, she's quite embarrassed.

Our small group is herded into the airport terminal to escape the ranting crowds. The interior is filled with more people, all excited and boisterous. For a brief moment, I open my mind to the intramental hurricane in the large open space. Only a very few of the individuals are projecting thoughts in my direction; most are just random emotional outbursts that fire into the din of thoughts and feelings. My Tactical app runs a swift calculation: based on the number and temperament of those intent on confrontation, the handful of security personnel available is insufficient to thwart an onrush by the mob. My innocent companions will be trampled. I should act to prevent a dangerous situation for them.

Within minutes we're surrounded. The mob mentality sweeps through the building like a rogue wave. We need help now.

"Mission Steward, can you hear my thoughts?" I ask, pushing out from my mind.

"I hear you, Jove," he says from afar.

"I'm experiencing an unforeseen risk to the mission that we should mitigate. How long would it take for you to send the Equus to my location, to rendezvous with me?"

"Recommended startup procedures require—"

"Mission Steward, I'm in trouble. I need the ship immediately."

"Using Earth time, one hundred forty-seven seconds to clear the water, thirty-one seconds to a close hover at your coordinates," he states. "Will that suffice?"

"Yes, please do that. Have the ventral hatch open and ladder extended. There will be humans also coming aboard, so once we enter the ship, do not execute maneuvers that produce centripetal forces beyond what they can easily endure. Do you understand?"

"The Navigation Onus understands all parameters of the task," he says.

"Of course, with no one on board, you are free to utilize the—"

"There may be a temporary atmospheric disturbance in your vicinity."

Yeah, I bet.

Zaris and her bodyguard Damien, Sir Edward and I are pressed into the corner of a hallway that leads into the secure section of the facility. Four policemen do their best to hold back dozens of protesters that have shoved their way into the narrow space. Several of them stretch their arms over the policemen's shoulders, their paper signs whap me over the head. I estimate that we have about a minute before the Equus comes to a stop overhead.

Damien has a quick Thinker. He grabs a ring of keys from a policeman's belt and locates the proper one to open the door behind us. As soon as we push through the opening, he slams it shut behind us and we hurry up a flight of stairs to the operations level.

I figure that it's best to advise my attendants of the plan.

"We need to get to the roof," I say. "I have arranged for transportation."

"There's a platform that encircles the tower," Damien explains, "but I don't know how to get to it from here."

"I do!" Lieutenant Tamm says, who runs up from behind us. His uniform shirt is badly torn and he has a gash on his forehead. "It's getting right rough out there."

"It would seem!" says Zaris. She presses a folded handkerchief against the bloody mess over Tamm's left eye. "Press there to stop the bleeding."

"Damien," Tamm says, with a firm grip on the young man's shoulder. "Find the key for the elevator call button override."

We run back the way Tamm came, further into the operations and mechanical area, to a small lobby under the airport control tower. Damien gets the elevator car doors to open and we rise up the eight stories to the tower rim. Partway there, a deafening *KHRUMP* rocks the tower, causing the elevator lighting to flicker and the car to rattle around in the vertical tracks.

"That would be our ride!" I say.

"What in…oh, I recognize that sound!" Tamm says. No doubt Lieutenant Tamm has experienced more than a few sonic booms from high-performance aircraft.

The Navigation Onus had, with its thoughts, piloted the cutter out of the Scoop, up and out of the sea and over the thirty-four kilometers to our location with exceptional skill and expediency. Accelerating to Mach Three at an altitude of just a few hundred meters, the Equus created a tear in the fabric of the heavy, damp air over the Indian Ocean. Behind it was a fantastic cone of condensed vapor caused by the shock wave at the nose of the spacecraft. The foggy skirt shimmered and danced around the rearmost edge of the fuselage. The ship slammed to a hard stop over the island, the sky brakes fully deployed, having howled their displeasure at the excessive strain put upon them.

As the cutter zoomed up from the open sea, most of the people outdoors at that moment were knocked flat on their faces by the unforgiving pulse of the immense pressure wave. Several large panes of glass in the main terminal gave way, crashing to the floor in shattered heaps. Like magic, there was a very large slice of otherworldly pie looming over them. Steam spewed and liquid sizzled as the condensation rolled down from the arched roof onto the red-hot plating of the sky brakes. It must have been quite a sight to see.

In the elevator, the doors open and we pile out of the car into the loft just outside the tower booth. Moving through the emergency exit first, I confer with the Navigation Onus on the run, so the ship will hover to the exterior platform, ladder extended. With a brief glance down, I see the mobs of now violent protesters that have encircled the base of the tower.

Wisdom suggests that in the future, we should hire a travel agent specializing in anonymous arrangements for Hollywood types and the profoundly alien.

Tamm helps encourage the others to climb the ladder into the underside of the cutter. He insists that I go up next.

Halfway up, I sense a fierce sting in my right foot. The sound of the gunshots follows. Someone on the tarmac below has fired a weapon at us. We can see the person being tackled to the ground by the security forces. Tamm points his index finger towards the open hatch at the top of the ladder. "Get a move on!"

The inner and outer hatches of the ventral port closed, the Navigation Onus accelerates the ship away from the airport, over the western shore of the island and out to sea. I can hardly feel the motion of the craft.

Tamm takes command, as he's trained to do. "Everyone sit crossed with a partner and give a look over for injuries." They all rotate their heads around, looking for chairs.

"Sit on the floor, mates," Tamm barks, then for the stubborn alien, "or take a knee! There was weapon's fire back there and we need to know if any have a hole in us, besides Jove."

"Oh goodness!" Zaris grabs me all over in a frantic inspection. "You injured? You get shot?"

"It's okay, Zaris. It was only a toe," I tell her.

We both look at a tiny puddle that's formed on the floor, my fluid oozing out where a blue pinky-toe was once attached.

"Not funny, Jove," Tamm says. "You could've been killed. You're far too valuable for us to let anything happen to you."

"My dear Lieutenant," I say, "since I first came to be, just eight Earth days ago, and given the assignment to come to your planet, fate has been at work to prevent the progress of my mission. For obvious reasons, my complete designation is Jove Number Seven." The four of them just stare at me in wonder.

I lean against the wall and pull my foot up to take a closer look at the damage. "You know, it *has* been a tough week."

Tamm kneels down in front of me, curious about my construction.

"I was a corpsman before my Commission," he tells me. "Might I ask you a question about your person?"

I nod yes, while my electrofibre lens provides a macro view of my severed joint.

"Your…blood," he asks, "is that mercury? The technicians on the Hobart swear that you're full of mercury."

"Um, actually yes, Lieutenant, my body contains six liters of a compound that would equate to liquid mercury, on Earth. Why do you ask?"

His face turns a shade of gray. "Right, well, your bodily fluid is highly toxic to humans and just about every other living organism on the planet." I notice the others scooting away from me just a little. "We need to limit your exposure to others, Jove. The hazmat team is still trying to hose you out of this morning's helicopter."

Note to Self

The concept of right and wrong are often envisioned as two weights balanced on a scale. There is a pivot point, the fulcrum, which allows for an equalization of the two, good and evil, if you will. It is my observation that, although the pivot affords truth and righteousness, in actuality, it is the meeting place of the good and the bad, where they become one.

If I see myself as existing above another, in status, and I move my scale above his, then my evil is better than his good. His suffering might even improve my fortune.

It would be pure wickedness, but for it working so well.

Jove

Emrah
2043 CE
Al-Zulfi, Saudi Arabia

Uncle Hatim's wife, Mrs. ibn Khoury, leaned around the corner to yell up the staircase.

"You girls stop jumping on the bed and go to sleep! I'm not going to tell you again!"

Not a valid threat, as this would be the third time in an hour she said the same thing.

Elmyrah and her recently acquired foster sisters stood holding hands in a circle of three in the middle of the big mattress. If you bounce to the right height, your long braided hair will swing up even higher than your head and smack into the white plaster on the ceiling. Never mind that the headboard has fallen apart and the mother has come unglued.

She couldn't remember living a life like this before. In fact, her memories of the home she shared with her parents and her three biological brothers were fading all too soon. Her parents, who were never home anyway, had disappeared first, the children left to fend for themselves. Her uncles ignored their plight, pretending that the four of them didn't exist. From behind a veil of tears, she had asked her brothers what had her mother and father done that was so terrible, that the family had been shamed in this way. She never did get an answer. Once she asked what her parents had really done as a job.

"They weren't truly couriers, were they?"

The answer was, "Don't ask."

And now they were all gone, all except Abdallah. He was out there, somewhere. He had refused the offer made by Hatim's Uncle Hatim to live in the downstairs apartment, where the servants used to stay, but his pride would not permit him to accept charity. He'd rather live on the street, as he had done for the previous two years. He cheered inwardly for Elmyrah. She had found peace and a home with a family who wouldn't mistreat her. They would get her back into school, feed her every day. She was lucky, he said. Then he disappeared into the hot, dusty world of the homeless, coming around every month or so to check on her. His official address: the old Mercedes with the blown engine, not the fine house she'd be blessed to share with the ibn Khourys.

At the familiar sound of the heavy parental shoe landing on the bottom step, the girls dropped flat on the bed, with two diving under the covers and one to make the dash to and from the light switch. By the time Mrs. ibn Khoury made it to the upstairs bedroom door, all would appear to be sound asleep. The only evidence of their antics: bed feet no longer over the worn spots in the wooden floor and three little heartbeats racing at top speed.

"Goodnight, you three, and you stay in bed, Elmyrah." The wise matron knew more about what went on, night and day, than anyone would care to admit.

After her sisters would fall asleep, the independent and stubborn orphan would sneak out and down the stairs, to look for Uncle Hatim. If he wasn't in the house, then he was on the roof, watching the stars - all the better. It was the cosmic company she cherished and he seldom chased her back to bed right away.

Tonight seemed like another good opportunity to slink through the shadows, up to the rooftop platform to launch another galactic exploration. It seemed to take forever for Basma and Sa'adat's breathing to change to the slow, deep exhalations that signaled her chance to slide out of bed and out the door. Her years on the streets of Al-Zulfi had been difficult, but she gained a cunning and cleverness, which made at least partial compensation for the empty stomach and nights spent hidden in darkness.

She groped in the dark for her soft fuzzy slippers, which she then twisted inside out, so that the softer top was now upside down under her foot, nearly silent against the floor, the hard plastic sole noiseless where it met her bare skin. A few days ago, she borrowed a spoon from the utensil drawer in the kitchen, to carry olive oil up to her bedroom door.

"Goodnight Mister Squeaky Hinge," she whispered, as she dabbed the smooth liquid into the hoops and leaves of the old bronze hardware.

Tonight, as she pulled the door open, silence. While she stretched her thin legs to skip over the creaky steps on the way down, she considered what it would take to get those to shut up as well. As she crept up the rearmost stairway heading to the roof, Elmyrah could see the small shiny lever of the lock was facing sideways, not up and down. Yep, he's out there for sure, she thought. With her many adventures up here, she knew her way around without the need to worry about falling over the side or even bumping into anything. One night, she even walked from the door to the platform with her eyes closed the whole way, only to miss it by an arm's width.

Sidled up close to the old man for warmth, she whispered, "You aren't going to turn me in to the authorities, are you, Sir?"

"No, of course not," Uncle Hatim said, finding it difficult to whisper and laugh at the same time. "But if we get caught, I have never seen you before in my life."

Squatted down at the base of the telescope, Elmyrah could curl herself into a little ball over her legs, snuggled into her nightgown like a turtle withdrawn into its shell, only her nose and upwards visible above the pink terrycloth, orange toenails beneath.

"So," Hatim asked, "can you find Jupiter for me tonight?"

She peered up to the starry sky from her cozy turret, and strained her eyes upward through her long black eyelashes to locate her favorite bright spot in the heavens. With one skinny finger poking out from the rumpled cuff of a sleeve, she aimed her pointer at the faraway gas giant.

"Very good, my young scientist, very good," he commended, "and…what is the phase of the moon this evening?"

Her hand stroking an imaginary goatee on her chin, she pretended to have to think about it. "That would be…Waxing Gibbous."

He was in college when he came to understand the Lunar Cycle. It was hard for him to believe an eight year old girl could master it after just one month.

"You know, my dear, you are so much smarter than the average silly person!"

His eyes well-adjusted to the low light, he could make out her squinting brow-lines and wrinkled nose that were a give-away to a big smile hidden under the nightgown's thick material.

"Have you heard the exciting news, my daughter? Your moon has been found, and not only has it decided to come all the way to Earth, but it brought within it a visitor from that planet you enjoy so much. Is that not the most amazing thing?" Uncle Hatim was still in disbelief from reading the morning's report and the accompanying story from the Global Press. Could it be true? This was too far-fetched for the official news outlets to even consider, yet here they were; the same story and bewildering facts on every channel.

"Did it take forever, as you said?" she asked.

Hatim asked himself, how can she comprehend astronomy and yet have no concept of time? It occurred to him that when your constant concerns were to find something edible in garbage cans and to avoid thugs and rapists, the passing of days may seem of less regard.

"According to the reports, your Emrah traversed the distance in just four days." More impossibility, he could not fathom the technology required to generate that amount of power, to harness some mighty force to attain such incredible velocity.

She wondered at how Uncle Hatim could have possibly been wrong before. The news people must be incorrect, she thought. They should check their sources. In fact, Uncle Hatim should be their "sources".

"If true, my dear," Hatim continued, stroking his real goatee with a thumb and three fingertips, "your namesake would be an intelligent, willful and magnificent treasure, much like someone else I know."

The half-pint stargazer rolled her head back to fix her gaze on Jupiter. "If they can come here," she said, "then there is no reason why I can't go there. I am one day, you know."

Hatim smiled to himself at the whimsical logic of his rooftop partner in crime. His attention caught by a stream of lamplight coming from the doorway, he looked up to see the authorities coming to haul the escapee back to bed.

Note to Self

Damien talked me into trying his personal music playback device, the Sinus-Song. I sniffed it up into my nose and hung my head up-side-down, as he recommended, while it attached itself to the mucus membrane in my sinuses.

Sixteen million melodies to choose from, controlled with clicks of the tongue. My favorite so far is number four, Chopsticks.

Oh yes, and my Wisdom must be off-line for some reason. Twice now, she won't talk to me when I make a query. Odd. Usually, she won't shut up.

Jove

Persuasion
2044 CE
UN Headquarters, African Continent, Earth

It's not terribly difficult to evade the search pattern of the tired and poorly functioning F-56 SkyWarriors of the Kenya Air Force. A squadron of their fighter jets had been scrambled to intercept the radar blip moving across their border at Mach 2. Although we were able to raise their tower at Laikipia Air Base, I couldn't convince them of our friendly intent. With the Equus' intramental carrier linked to the Combat-Net radio frequency of Earth, I pushed through into the mind on the other end, a little too hard, it turns out. I fear the fellow may have experienced a stroke.

The real challenge is to convince my passengers that the safest and most comfortable place for them is huddled together in a padded storage locker. Tamm is the more stubborn of the bunch. He insisted that he could hold onto the back of my pilot's bama railing prior to the turbulent flight. I found a cold compress for the new lump on the back of his head, to match the bloody lump on the front of his head.

Zaris tries to get her cellular telephone to connect with the military. Navigation Onus has admitted that it could assist with the linkup, but for her being classified as a 'potential subversion'. Meanwhile, I've plotted a roundabout course taking us over the Gatamaiyo Forest. We stay low as we make our way to the United Nations Headquarters' neighborhood. Navigation Onus has already found a good spot to land in a meadow, southeast of Karura Forest's Lily Lake, bordering the UNEP grounds. We should end up barely one kilometer away from Zaris' office, leaving the Equus hidden in the trees.

At the behest of the Mission Steward, I grudgingly permit the Navigation Onus to handle the final approach. With mouth agape, I watch as we glide in at treetop level, to perform a quiet skid through the tall grass, using the concealed wings instead of the loud main thrusters. The only bump felt was a large goat that didn't get out of the way in time. I had no idea the Equus was capable of such impressive maneuverability.

On the ground, I free my friends from their claustrophobic accommodations and lead them up to the relatively open space at the rear of the bridge, where we discuss how to get the genial, blue faced alien introduced to the whole world without depleting the entire stock of thirty Joves.

Zaris makes about a dozen phone calls, finally snapping the handy little device closed, and lets out a big sigh.

"Are you alright, Jove?" Sir Edward asks.

"Yes, Sir, I am," I reply. "I'm just feeling a bit unsettled."

"Amen to that, my good man," he says through his bushy gray mustache. "Well, that 'man' part was just a figure of speech, you know."

Tamm looks over at Zaris. "This is your territory, Miss Liyanage. Now that we're off the sea and out of my aircraft, I'm officially turning over command of this mess to you."

She nods, then shakes her head no, then nods again. "I have approval from S-G to grant Jove asylum. That will go a long way to protect you from military and any other official organization that may be opposed to your presence. The City Council has approved the local police to provide security for you and your landing craft. I've applied for additional security from the Minister of Foreign Affairs and the Ministry of Internal Security and the Provincial Administrate. Instead of putting you up at UN, I believe it's best you remain closer your ship. Just a few hundred meters from here is the Kenya Technical College. There are conference halls for meetings with visiting dignitaries, as well a group of thirty hostels that can be used for you and the assigned security and any support staff."

"Well, I'll be," Tamm says, "you sure do get a lot accomplished in a short time."

The usually silent Damien speaks up. "Oh, you don't know the half of it. Some days I have to run just to keep her out of trouble."

Zaris' smile gets even bigger. "I almost forgot. I hope that I haven't been presumptuous in having my assistant send a letter on your behalf to the Seychelles' Airport Authority. You apologized for the broken windows, theft of property, violating numerous security protocols, illegal access, and unauthorized use of restricted airspace and runway."

"In all honesty," I say, "we really didn't use the runway."

While sequestered by the United Nations with the friendly college staff and students, I am pleased to see that my presence is much less a threat than at first. Zaris has arranged for a gathering of various global administrators to arrive tomorrow, to meet with me and hear the message that I've so far delivered only to the few on the Hobart. Instead of repeating the same tale of Armageddon to everyone, I decide to let those other six people spread the rumor for me. Too many words from the same mouth can lose their value. There's a method to the management of propaganda. The more they talk it up amongst themselves, the less convincing I have to be. By the time I meet with the titillated, the curious and the truly concerned, they'll have all been made aware of the dire report from the great beyond. With any luck, I'll just fill in the blanks with the words they want to hear, or at least, what they expect to hear.

"Mister Jove, Sir?" calls Aza Oduya, my newly assigned administrative assistant. "There is a telephone call for you, on the phone."

She's the first human to actually project her mind in my direction. Yesterday, she wondered, "Are all beings from space so nice as this blue-skinned man?"

Hardly, my dear, I think. According to Knowledgebase, about half of the species within range of your planet would just as soon lick your bones clean of that exquisite black flesh you carry.

"Thank you, Aza. Can you tell me who's calling?"

"Yes, I can. The caller is a Mister Captain Thomas of Her Royal Australian Navy, Sir."

From behind my raised-leg desk, I pick up the handset, as a grin spreads across my face. I'm not sure who's affecting who, here on this planet of violent, cozy, reasoning mammals. I should be careful to not let them mess around in *my* head.

"Captain Thomas! What a pleasant surprise. I was afraid that our paths had crossed only the once."

"G-day, Jove. Oh, no, as you've become my all-time favorite extraterrestrial, there's no doubt that I'll continue to remain in touch."

"Your all-time favorite, ay?" I tease back, testing my best Aussie accent. "Well then, who's your least favorite extraterrestrial?"

"The Blob, of course," Thomas replies. "He's everyone's least favorite."

Knowledgebase promptly clues me in. Ew. Fictional or not, I have to agree.

"Was your crew successful at removing my Number Six from the nooks and crannies of the Seahawk?"

Thomas chuckled and coughed. "Oh, yes; however, the backup copter seems to be logging the total of the up-hours since then. Bird One's just end up a gum tree. Looks the right onkus sheila at the prom!"

I have no idea what he just said, but it's amusing nonetheless.

"So," he says, "you're wondering what business there is for me to ring you up."

"Yep."

"You remember your visitors back in the brig, Misters Clarendon and Shoemaker?"

I am inwardly drawn back to that steel box. "How can I forget?"

"Right, it seems they've made report to their handlers; are expecting a follow-up visit at your location by week's end."

"I do not understand - handlers?" Knowledgebase may require a jargon update.

"Handlers…umm….supervisors that wish to remain anonymous," Thomas says.

"…and can keep their hands from getting dirty, or bloody, as the case may be," I add.

"Exactly. I hope you know that, although I was directed to provide for access to you, I'm in no way affiliated with that lot. I don't trust anyone who wears sunnies indoors."

"And who might 'that lot' be, if I may ask?"

"That would be the S.I.S. – Security Intelligence Service," he says. "It's their job to be informed of new goings on 'round the all over. You know, in case they feel the need to do something about it."

Ah, government spies. "My guess is that some blue fellow swimming out of a gigantic meteor that left Jupiter four days prior and just splashed down in the ocean would qualify as 'new goings on'?"

"Right on the money there, mate."

"Do you have any suggestions how to best welcome them when they arrive?" Thomas wants to get a message through to me. I wish he'd just open his head for me.

"If they arrive 'round tea time, they won't turn down a cuppa. If you're not there, I suppose it would fall to your immediate staff, being attentive and all, to either advise how to catch up with you or perhaps make arrangements themselves."

Where Knowledgebase falls short, Wisdom takes up the slack. I get it.

"I do enjoy your company, Captain Thomas," I say. "I'm looking forward to our next opportunity to meet face to face."

"G-day then, Jove."

"Good afternoon, Captain."

I leave the phone off the hook for now, but disconnect the coiled cable at the handset, which I drop out the open window into the shrubbery outside. Sliding the window closed, I slip my hand into an inner pocket of my tunic to remove the small cellular phone that Damien gave me, for use when I need to contact Zaris in an emergency. Flipped open, it powers on. I press the one-button dialer to her secure line.

It rings only twice before she answers in a hushed voice.

"Jove? Are you alright?"

"I am for now. Please listen closely. I just received a call from Captain Thomas. He's been most helpful. I could use your assistance with several matters of importance."

"Of course, Jove, what is it?"

"First, there are two S.I.S. agents due to arrive at four o'clock tomorrow. Their plan is to kidnap or assassinate me and won't leave until they find me and complete their mission. Second, my office phone is bugged. And third, Miss Aza Oduya is a covert agent working with them. She will need to be replaced with a more suitable candidate at the first opportunity."

The next day, all of the commercial and private aircraft from the various nations sending representatives to meet with me, touch down at Nairobi's Wilson Airport and disgorge their passengers, including the look-alike decoys of each dignitary. Per some recent changes to the plan, they all meet for brunch at the Summer House, an out of the way cottage nestled amidst the trees along ICRAF Road, a good kilometer away from the college buildings and dorms.

The limousine assigned to drop me off outside is right on time. It pulls to the curb near a beautiful rose garden, hidden in the shade of the little suburban forest.

With a loud pop and whistle, a rocket propelled grenade bursts from the shoulder mounted launch tube on the roof of the World Agro-Forestry Center, accelerating to three hundred meters per second. It dives straight down the narrow asphalt car path, to penetrate the windshield of the long, white Cadillac. The car splits down the middle, with the driver's side doors breaking free, to flip end over end across the grassy field to the north. His broken pieces aflame in the fiery blast, Jove Number Five flies up and out, mostly landing in the branches of the eucalyptus that line the once serene landscape.

"That's a terrific story, Damien," I tell him. "But, I don't *feel* blown to bits."

"Oh yessir!" he says. "That highly volatile and unstable power source you have inside really made a fantastic secondary explosion."

"What unstable power source would that be? I pretty much run on rechargeable batteries and sunlight."

Damien lets out a shrill laugh. "Perhaps it was that little wad of Semtex that managed to find its way into Number Five's chest cavity. I may've taken some creative liberties there."

"So, after Lieutenant Tamm got Five's carcass back from the looters, you rigged it to explode if I was attacked, to make sure I was dead...again?"

"There're little blue bits of you for fifty meters in every direction. It was awesome."

Damien had done a masterful job at getting Zaris, our small entourage and myself, secreted away and headed into Europe, well before any plans for my demise could be brought to fruition in Nairobi. Whether or not Clarendon and Shoemaker were involved in the plot is yet to be determined.

My administrative assistant, Aza, proved quite handy with an RPG for someone who had only a two-year degree in office management from a girl's college in Egypt. Today, after my previous body was obliterated by the young woman's militaristic mission, she was captured by the police and arrested. Zaris is devastated that her own people would've chosen the girl as someone safe to be close to me.

After the distant excitement subsides, I find myself alone at the end of a corridor, peering out a window with a view to the inner courtyard of the Palace of Nations and beautiful Ariana Park, in Geneva, Switzerland. Part of me can enjoy the brilliant architecture and lush green grass. Another is extrapolating the many potential arguments I might receive from the members of the Office of Disarmament Affairs. So far, the humans have been easily manipulated. With Wisdom granting insight on how to coerce the unwilling, I've been remarkably successful at working my way from the brig of the Hobart to the literal doorstep of the United Nations Headquarters. So much for stepping on toes. I've been stepping on brains. It's odd how they almost want to believe in their own demise.

Knowledgebase has provided a thorough understanding of this group of humans who, as part of the primary global administration, appear to be best positioned to exert pressure on countries that possess the weapons I need to remove from the planet. I can already feel the forces churning with me: two clear directions, each opposing path defined, and marked out before me. One leads to the death of the humans, the other to the death of the Knowers.

I feel a pressure on my shoulders, though it is only my imagination. Choyt-72, his hands resting upon me, his eyes burrowing deep into my soggy mound of soiled thoughts interlaced with the twisted roots of conflict and guilt.

"That would be far too easy, for us to merely take one life to balance the loss of another," Choyt said.

But he was speaking about the Prawl-Tang on Jupiter, not the humans. Clearly, that's what he meant. Earth wasn't even a consideration when the rules of engagement were drafted, remember? Of course, you remember. Who are you asking? Why would you debate with yourself over something so implicit? Your mission hasn't changed, there's no argument. I will convince them. I'll convince them or I will dig my way into their minds. I'll ferret out their will to maintain control of their lives, of their little blue world. They'll even think it's their own idea. I'll embrace them with so much love that their insides will burst out onto the floor.

"I trust that you will choose the correct course of action, as required by the circumstances you encounter," Choyt had said.

You see? He trusts me. Of course he trusts me. The circumstance I've encountered is the Prawl-Tang refusal to relinquish their claim on Jupiter without adequate compensation - and here it is. The deal is made. Besides, look at these pathetic humans. They murder each other at every opportunity. They're going to kill themselves anyway. I'm doing them a favor.

"Jove." That pressure on my shoulder again.

"Jove," says a familiar voice. Not Choyt-72. Not a Brother.

"Jove, there is something I need to discuss with you."

Is that Wisdom calling me? She sounds different...irritated, uncontrolled.

The pressure becomes a squeeze. I spin around, a little too fast it would seem. Zaris stands in front of me, with a pained look on her face, rubbing her wrist.

"Are you alright, Jove?" she asks. "I've been calling your name as I was coming down the hall. You seem lost in thoughts."

I consider telling her that I'm fine. But, it's better if I lie to her as little as possible.

"What's wrong with your hand? Are you injured?"

"Oh, I'm sure it's nothing." Now she's lying. "When you turned round so quick, my wrist got bent sideways against your neck. Hope I didn't hurt you any."

"No," I say, "Though I would endure any pain for you, my dear friend."

Zaris takes my arm and we turn to walk back toward the corridor that leads to the main conference room, where preparations are made for me to address the UNODA members and many other international state department representatives.

"You should know ahead of time, Jove, although many of the people you meet these next days are very interested in disarmament, they may not have the power to decide for their countries to abide by any resolution ratified by the UNODA members. In many cases, they'll return to their respective administrations, meeting considerable resistance. Please don't give up on us."

I stop and turn gently to look her in the eye. "My dear Miss Liyanage, there's one thing that is true on many worlds in many star systems: war is good for business." Now it's my turn to rest encouraging hands on shoulders. "We'll take this one step at a time, Zaris. Someone must be the first to begin - with one step, and then more difficult, to tear away from the place whereupon they've stood for so long. I'm committed to remain with the people of Earth until the last atomic bomb has been hidden away from the children of this planet." And that, my dear, is the truth.

Resuming our progress to the large U-shaped convention hall, the rustling sounds of the members and guests can be heard through the open doors. I feel her warm hand take mine as we make our way into the conference area. The sensation reminds me of the Archive Visions, as Payl-1, and his interactions with Only, Fonmet. We ignore the heads that turn to stare, the whispers. 'That's him, the alien from outer space'. Gee whiz, what was it about me that gave it away? I'm the only one who's barefoot?

I find my name printed on a small white card, folded to stand upright on the table. Ugh. I have to sit? This must be my punishment from The Almighty. If I end up in Hell for this, there will most assuredly be a chair. I rotate around to look among the crowd for a friendly face. I recognize Sir Edward Vincent, Moshe Samuelsson and of course, Zaris.

Garnering plenty of attention at the front of the room is a tall, thin man, very well surrounded by a dozen or more people, all expecting to have his ear. His thoughts are strong and project well into the large space afforded to this gathering. He's one of those mental pillars that I was instructed to reach for. It's no mistake that he's looked upon as the new leader of this planet - Sir Dwight Ward-Howard, the Secretary-General of the United Nations. He has an open mind, though turbulent and sorrowful.

Now, there's a good place to sit, Jove. Right there in the middle of that precious head.

I notice everyone taking their assigned seats. It must be some signal to begin torturing your vertebrae. With care, I place the card back down and it occurs to me, I don't get a last name? Jove Nothing. No title? No Jove Number Seven of the Brotherhood of the Manufactured Flesh and SynThinker Union of the Former Planet of Sirius Three? That would be a bit wordy.

The UNSG, as he is known, moves to stand behind a podium.

"Welcome, members of the Office of Disarmament Affairs, of our international community, and on this momentous occasion, to a member of our galactic community."

Everyone stands to their feet and applauds excessively. I don't need an audience, I need believers. If I can assist Mister Ward-Howard to see the light, the others will flock to his side.

"What I am not going to do today," he says, "is drag on about all the facts and the history of our endeavors to somehow maintain a measure of peace and goodwill for our children, by stockpiling the most grievous tools of hate ever devised. There has been great success, over the past three decades, at reducing the number of AW-MDs to a reasonable level. But I ask you, what is reasonable about having more than enough left to destroy ourselves in spite of what we have worked to accomplish?"

Dwight glares at the audience. I may have tapped into a deeper, more profound conviction that he himself was not aware of.

"I ask you, can we allow ourselves to continue on this wrongful path to self-annihilation? Is there any righteousness in the knowledge that we can strike greater fear in the families on the other side of the wall, than they do in us? What will it profit us in the end? When our sons and our daughters inherit a wasteland of hard, glassy earth that will not even grow weeds? When their bodies burn and wither away in the unrelenting heat of an irradiated city? When they realize that there will be no grandchildren, because their prideful parents sterilized everything, including their wombs, what will it profit us, today? Have we anything to gain? Can I look at my son and hold out anything good in my hand and say 'Look, lad! Here is what I have as a reward, a wonderful and valuable thing, which I have saved for you by brutal intimidation of your neighbors. Stand and accept this great life I've made for you.'"

With a glance over at Zaris, I see she is both immensely proud and surprised at her leader. She never expected anything like this from him today. Although the thoughts have been buried in his heart, she's right. He wouldn't be saying them without compunction. He had the words. He just needed a little…what…inspiration?

If I were to put words in his mouth, then he wouldn't believe what he was saying and would shortly retract his own statements. But if all I do is wipe away the inhibitions that prevent him from saying the right thing, regardless of the consequences, he cannot help but take that leap of faith and agree with himself.

Dwight was just as surprised as anyone in the room to hear that speech. It wasn't even close to what he'd prepared. Yet he felt strangely emboldened. These were the ideals he only dared to dream about, to wish upon the world. And it was just another planet now. Not *the* planet, just one of many.

"These are extraordinary days in which we live," Dwight says, "and I cannot help but think there is more than coincidence to the eye-opening reports from across the globe; not merely wild stories to sate the appetite of tabloid journalism, but truth. At no other time on Earth has there been such a flurry of hate and violence, war and insurrection. Not a single continent is without conflict. Nowhere can we go to find peace."

He pauses to give the rapt audience some time to simmer.

"And of course, at no other time on Earth has there been a visitor from one of our own neighboring planets, to courageously…and may I say with a *forgiving* heart…place himself upon the altar of our acceptance, hoping beyond hope, that we would welcome him as a friend."

Dwight bows his head in deference to his next subject.

"History records that once, a very long time ago, one came from a place outside our physical realm. That man was rejected by his very own people. That rejection continues to this very day. And are we any better off now under the crushing weight of our own prejudices, than Palestine was under the heavy boot of the Roman war machine? Certainly not.

"Let us not be so blind as to reject yet another opportunity sent to us from the heavens. Whether or not you can believe in the man from the past, or you can believe in this man, who has seen our future, I beg you to open your hearts to that which every man is ultimately called: to love your neighbor, as you love yourself."

With that, the UNSG had expended every last ounce of passion that had been bottled up within his soul. The room erupts with praise for the Secretary-General, for his gracious words, and the eloquent delivery, if I do say so myself.

Next up – the Witness.

Zaris stands and walks up the platform steps, meeting Dwight to hold both his hands as they exchange encouraging remarks about the event. As she takes her place on the raised platform to address the members and guests, I reach out with my mind to hers, not necessarily to influence her thoughts and words, but more as a brotherly hug from the inside out. She looks up from her notes, turning to look directly at me, with a warm smile she nods - connection made.

"For those of you who don't know me, my name is Zaris Liyanage. I'm the Special Representative to the United Nations, serving at the pleasure of the Secretary-General. Just a few days ago, I was given an assignment to travel from my office in Nairobi, to meet someone very special, who had themselves ventured a very great distance, to reach out their hand in hopes of making a new friend. Prior to my arrival at the tiny island community in the Indian Ocean, I had not been informed that my guest would have clear blue silicone flesh, motorized internal organs and would crash land in a meteorite the size of Putrajaya, my hometown."

Zaris pauses to the let the nervous laughter die down in the hall. "Needless to say, I was unprepared to actually meet an extraterrestrial being. I found the whole experience quite unsettling. My *breakfast* found it unsettling!"

Good one Zaris. That personalized truth will work wonders, actually.

"In those first moments, as I took this alien hand in mine, my mind and my heart struggled to process all that comes the acknowledgement that…we are not alone. The Earth is indeed *not* the center of all that we know. Speaking today, from the relative safety of five hundred years passed, I can keep my head attached as I declare, Ferdinand and Isabella, *you were wrong!*"

Hey, that was my line! Ah, she pulls it off with Malaysian flare.

"Although we've been looking to the stars for many centuries, longing to find evidence of life on any planet besides our own, we tremble at a mere shadow of that truth on our doorstep. The grand canals on Mars turned out to be an optical illusion. The infamous flying disk with little green men that crashed in the southwestern desert of North America was nothing more than a fanciful story, which only gained traction with the realization by Hollywood that there's money to be made in ticket sales at the box office. Even when Japan Airlines Flight sixteen twenty-eight shared the sky over Alaska with an impossibly massive starship, what have we to show for it? Denials, ridicule, preferring ignorance over enlightenment. What greater level of hypocrisy can the human race attain?

"I'll tell you. When a single member of a race of harmless, pacifistic beings sends their emissary to bring a message of hope to our planet, the first thing we do is to brutally murder him. When a second one arrives, we jail him, threaten his life, pierce his body with medical devices and interrogate him like a criminal. Then, without thought for his health, or that our planet is vastly different from his own, we let him melt to death in a chemical furnace. The third time, he tries again. What do we do? We mob him, stampede him into corner, striking him with objects and insulting him. In a courageous display of care for the safety of the humans attending to him, *he miraculously saves us* from a violent mob, and gets shot for his trouble. The fact of the matter is, the only way we were able to get him here today to meet with you was to fake his death, terrorists thinking they succeeded in destroying him yesterday with a rocket propelled grenade.

"Members of UNODA, distinguished guests and yes, even skeptics, I ask you to acknowledge your prejudice today, and then divorce yourself from it. This person, who traveled eight hundred million kilometers at immense personal cost to help our planet, has already showed more humanity to us, than we to him. I ask you to please welcome – Jove."

Wow, she almost has *me* convinced. If I didn't know better, I'd say this character she's describing is one of the good guys. I climb the steps to the platform and turn to wave at the crowd. Another standing ovation, no one has ever deserved one less.

"I have opened their minds for you," Wisdom says.

"Thank you, thank you…please. No really, thank you. Please sit." At last, most of the people begin to utilize their chairs.

"I must confess that I feel terrible asking you to sit down. You see, people where I come from do not sit…ever. There are no chairs. Every time I bend myself down into one of these contraptions, it just kills my lower back."

That gets quite a few chuckles and some 'oh, really's'.

"In fact, does anyone know a good chiropractor that takes GalactiMed insurance?"

The ice-breaker works very well. Thanks, Wisdom, for the coaching and punch line.

After the laughter subsides again, I introduce myself. "As Miss Liyanage said, my name is Jove. I am what you would describe as an artificial person. I am alive, and conscious, and self-aware. I am an individual, a being with a mind, a heart and a soul, just like each of you here today. Oh, any lawyers?" I look around conspicuously.

"When you look at me today, understand that this shell is much the same as the space-suits that your astronauts wear. I exist inside of it. I have a name. I have a conscience. And this manufactured device you see before you…is my Earth-suit. It helps me get around. It protects me and gives me the features in common with the human population that I hope to successfully interact with. My full name is Jove Number Seven of the Manufactured Flesh and SynThinker Union. Number Seven because…getting from Jupiter to Earth and to alive and well in this beautiful conference hall took six other Joves. The journey has not been without incident, shall we say. When you look into your sky, the third brightest object, after the Sun and the Moon, is the star, Sirius. That's where I was designed, my home. It's actually not that far away, as interstellar travel goes.

"'So', you're asking yourselves 'why all the trouble? What are we to you?' Listen closely. You are not alone. Not only are the humans of Earth accompanied by many other sentient beings throughout the known galaxy, but you have *family* out there. Brothers and cousins and ancestors – all humanoid, bipedal, omnivorous, hairy, opinionated, and with kids who don't want to take a bath on a school-night. One of your own theories is that some planet-hopping super-race left their seed of humanity on your watery world, copying that throughout the stars. Well, you know…that isn't far off. I can tell you this – there're people on other worlds, orbiting other stars, (all of which you can see, by the way) that are *more like* you than they are *different from* you. You're not alone.

"And you're not alone in your tendency towards violence. Let me tell you something – a nuclear holocaust on *this* planet will not be the first!"

I let that sink in for a bit. I can see them slump in their chaise du diabolique.

"But, though it wouldn't be the first," I whisper, "it will be the *worst*. The worst because this magnificent Earth is so incredibly beautiful compared to the others out there. Your...Terra...is absolutely a diamond in the rough. Dear people, you have so much to lose! The other 'Earths' out there – they do not have Niagara Falls, or the Eiffel Tower, or the pyramids of Egypt, or the Taj Mahal, or the countless other natural and created treasures you have right here. You keep building more and larger telescopes to see what is everywhere else, but you don't realize that others are making telescopes to look at you! And they're fascinated to watch you!

I give them a minute to consider all the treasures on their rock. Be they photos in a coffee table book or flesh in their children's beds.

"Now, consider this. As you look into the night sky at that big orange ball you call Jupiter, there are sentient beings, yes, the Jovians, and they're looking back at you. They have been there all along, longer than you. They've watched you as you have grown from the days of horse and buggy, to the days of making tire tracks in the Martian dust. And they've been cheering you on the whole time! They sing with joy at your grand discoveries in science. Actually, it sounds more like a beginner's saxophone, and how I wish you could hear them when Earth triumphs.

"But oh, how you should hear them when you fall. When you

massacre each other and bomb each other, they cry for you.

"Do you know what they've named your world? They call you the LittleBluePearl. Not too terribly long ago, the Jovians found a way to listen to you, too. You know, your tiny planet (and it is pretty small in the scheme of things) puts out a lot of sound. And it never stops. All of the radios and transmissions and cell phones and power lines and all the millions of devices you make to move electricity from one place to another, they all make noise. And it never, *ever* stops. So the Jovians amended your name to…LittleNoisyBluePearl.

"And there's one thing you do that makes the most noise: you test atomic bombs. You *constantly* detonate atomic bombs. So far, two thousand eighty-two nuclear detonations have soiled your world. It wails in their ears…and it breaks their hearts. They know what it's for! To be the *best* at killing your brother. Efficiency! Why burn only a million people into charred gravel when you can achieve two million! You know, just in case you only get one shot at it.

"Well, people of Earth, those Jovians are known by the rest of us as the Knowers. They understand things that many of us do not. They can see what's coming. Is it…what…what do you call it… clairvoyance? Can they see into the future?"

I shrug my shoulders and take a moment to scan the faces in the crowd - they're ready.

"If you parents hear a noise on the rooftop, and you go outside to find your child walking around up there, with their feet perilously close to the edge, do you need a sixth sense to tell you what could happen? Do you call the Psychic Hotline? Do you need to call your local priest? Of course not.

"The problem is not one of disbelief. It's about perspective! They can see what's going to happen to you, to their cherished LittleNoisyBluePearl. They can see what you're going to do to your children if you let them continue to walk along the roof's edge, hoping they don't fall off. But let me tell you – hoping is not enough.

"You must act. You must stop this madness now, before it's too late. The Knowers have sent me here to tell you…to ask you…to *beg* you…please, stop. End your nuclear ambitions now. You can stop this today, from happening tomorrow. Don't miss this chance to save yourselves, to save your children. You must act."

With that, I step back from the podium and bow my head. It takes a few seconds for them to crawl up out of the place I just took them, but they manage. First, a handful start to clap, then ten, then all two hundred join in with a rousing applause, a standing ovation to peace. I look through the crowd for the one I need - he's out there - likely a younger one, someone already vocal enough not to care. Once spotted, I send him a message. He gets it. He hears it in his head. He speaks it to himself, then louder for the person next to him. Now her, too. Their chant is heard, getting louder and louder.

"No nukes! No nukes! No nukes! No nukes!"

Perfect. There isn't a single one of them in the room that doesn't yell for ten minutes. I have to wave at them to calm down and retake their seats.

"I hear you. And I believe you. I can feel it coming from your hearts. You want to do the right thing – but it is a hard thing – to let go of the advantage over someone else. But isn't that what true and lasting peace is all about? Do you succeed in marriage to your spouse by bullying them into submission? Or does it last because you make yourself less than the other; you put yourself in a position where you can lift them up, right? That's what you need to do… *globally*. It only works if we all do it.

"Can you afford to leave even one? Can you afford to leave the rest of them, the other weapons of mass destruction? Can you afford to have the biological weapons? Won't they be used instead? But you have to decide for yourselves. You know, now, what's coming. You have to make the decision to act boldly. And there's only one course to follow. You must give up your right to all of the nuclear arms and other weapons of mass destruction, before they destroy the Earth."

"Good, now shut up," Wisdom says.

Amidst the roar and tumult of everyone taking up the chant again and adding more renditions, the joyous crowd presses in on me and on Zaris and the others.

I feel like I could sell sand to an Arab.

Later in the evening, that same day, I have the good fortune of meeting directly with the UNSG, Sir Dwight Ward-Howard and a handful of his closest advisors. It's an informal affair, held in a private business lounge. When Zaris escorts me in, the first thing I notice is the lack of chairs. Not a one to be had, everyone must stand. I can't help but smile at the thoughtfulness of someone who must've actually listened to my opening line at the UNODA conference.

Dwight sees me come in and strides across the room with his hand already out for a shake.

"Welcome, Jove, welcome. As you can see, it's standing room only here."

"How very gracious of you to invite me, Mister Secretary, I'm honored."

"Bah! You may not call me that here. Dwight."

"Dwight, it is."

"Would you care for a drink?" He asks, swishing his glass of wine.

"Do you have anything besides caustic solvent?" I peruse the many bottles of such liquids that would most likely break down my innards.

"Hmmm, so, nothing alcoholic, then?" he asks.

"Perhaps a nice mercuric amidochloride," I suggest. "I prefer white, but red will do."

Dwight looks stunned. "Oh, that's right. Your...um...blood, is it...?"

Zaris rescues him with her awesome smile and winsome chuckle.

"Dwight, he asked for glass of Mercurochrome." Her boss still looking lost, she helps him out, explaining how, decades past, moms and grandmothers would dab the liquid on skinned knees and elbows. Before they understood it to be a toxin, it was common to use it as medicine in minor first aid. No longer approved for use in modern societies, it could be difficult to find on a drugstore shelf in Europe.

"Oh, right!" Dwight replies. "Jove, might I ask you a personal question?"

"I'll do my best to answer."

"You stated that your full name is Jove Number Seven, and that there were six others that presumably have become...deceased? How many Joves are there, then? I mean, can you run out of...you?"

"Including the original One, (with a capital O) in which I was essentially still-born due to a failure of my proto—mid-brain, similar to your hypothalamus, I've existed as myself in seven distinct bodies. Through the science of my designers, if the body I possess…well, that's not really the right word…I'm downloaded into, has a mortal failure, my entire psyche is shortly transferred into the next…me. I awake as the same fellow I was a few minutes ago, and continue on my way.

"The Union…my makers…which are also all artificial clones like me…saw fit to construct thirty units of my series. And to answer your question: yes, I will one day run out of bodies to cross into. When Jove Thirty comes to his end, that will be the last of me."

"And where will you go then?" slurs a new face, inserted into the conversation.

I await Wisdom's timely riposte, but she is mute with aversion. Perhaps we should make an exception for the drunkard and bring a chair before he falls flat.

"…and you are?" I ask.

"Davis Tierney," Zaris offers quickly. No doubt it could've taken awhile for the man to remember his name and a bit more to get his lips and tongue in order.

"Well, Mister Tierney," I reply, "that's the question for us all, isn't it? Where, indeed? It would seem that no matter the species or—"

"Do aliens go to Hell, like the rest of us?"

Ugh. He interrupts and spits - two things I find intolerable. With one question, this drunk has tapped into my psyche. I find it necessary to control my disdain for this animal.

"Mister Tierney, regardless of the local temperature, I would imagine that my Hell might be to find myself in your eternal presence."

I can see by the minute facial contortions in both Dwight and Zaris, they are stifling a burst of potentially derisive laughter. I didn't mean to put them in a compromising position. It would be best if I bridled my tongue.

"I've no idea what you just said, alien man," Tierney says. With that, he rotates himself on one heel and careens off to ruin another person's perfectly good day.

"Jove," Dwight says, "you have a way with words. Have you ever considered writing political speeches?"

"Spend my days 'round Ministers of Parliament?" I try my best to look gleeful. "Hmmm...now that, Good Sir, would be my Heaven!"

The three of us enjoy a belly laugh, which was long overdue. Dwight excuses himself; makes the rounds of goodbyes in the room. After preparing me a tall glass of salt water, 'so that I can be seen with a drink in my hand', Zaris introduces me to a number of other members of the UNSG's Advisory Board on Disarmament Matters, which provides me with very useful information about how we can proceed, once the necessary approvals have been established. Knowledgebase helps me with some history and legal terminology that could be used effectively. I've decided to change my opinion of alcohol ingestion and its potential benefits during negotiations. Wisdom tells me that I'm a few thousand years behind on that idea.

The time passes quickly while engaged in deep discussions with the Board members. I feel a tap on my arm and I turn to see Damien. Zaris has sent him to keep me out of trouble.

"Jove, would you mind if we go outside? I haven't had a smoke since dinner and the smoker's lounge is filled with obese drunks puffing pipe tobacco. I can't handle that combination."

Through the door, I find the cool night air of Geneva to be refreshing. Even with the odor of cigarettes, the humidity from the lake adds to the healthful benefits of molecules that haven't already been cycled through some human's lung.

Damien's face glows orange from the flame as he 'lights up' his small paper tube. It occurs to me that there must be someone else out here in the darkness, who was already smoking, as I detected the carbon in the air immediately. About three meters away is another figure standing on one foot, leaning back against the wall at the rear of the building.

"Is that you, alien man?"

Oh, lovely, it's everyone's least favorite terrestrial, Davis Tierney. I will ignore him and perhaps he will drop dead. It would seem Damien doesn't care for the man either. I can sense his sudden discomfort at the realization of who it is that's out here besides the two of us.

Observant of Damien's mannerisms while he fiddles with and mouths the cigarette, it occurs to me that this is one of the ways the humans have found to relieve the tensions of their inability to cope with reality. I don't think that I've met one yet who was actually satisfied with their life. They fidget and fuss, either on the inside or the outside. It reminds me of a certain Number One that I know - Payl. I suppose even Synthetics get nervous. Proving my own point, I feel something hard in my hand and pull it out of my pocket. It's a grain of Obedient Sand, about the diameter of a large grape, a gift to me from the Knowers that came in the Prawl-Tang Scoop ship. I've been rolling it around between my fingers for as long as Damien has been sucking on that stinky white cylinder. Not so different, I guess.

"What've you got there?" Damien asks. He leans close to see better in the dim light of the parking lot lamps.

"This marvel of Jovian nature is Obedient Sand." I hold up the small crystal for him to see. In appearance, the whitish rock is nothing out of the ordinary.

"May I?" He reaches to take it from my fingers.

"Oh, of course."

He rolls it around and holds it high overhead. Seen through the translucent facets, the moon should be presenting itself in kaleidoscopic fashion.

"This is sand, a single grain of sand?" Damien curls his lower lip out, a subconscious trait of humans when they won't admit that they don't understand something.

"Jupiter is a big place," I say. "Even the sand there is four hundred times the size of what you find on Earth. This one's fairly average. They can be as small as a pea. I've seen a few as large as... hmmm...a bowling ball?" Thanks, Knowledgebase. "But the size isn't what makes it so special. What's so amazing about them is their ability to take action upon the will of the sentient being it's connected with."

"What do you mean, 'take action'? Like, it can do something if you want it to?"

"Essentially, yes," I say. "Although the Sand is not 'alive' in and of itself, it reacts to the life nearby. For instance, you understand how an analog compass operates; the needle is magnetized and balanced so as to react easily to another magnetic field. The magnetosphere of the Earth doesn't 'do' anything to the compass needle to move it. The compass needle reacts to the presence and will of the magnetism of the planet. You humans want it to point North, and you found something that naturally does. On Jupiter, the sand has an active component that'll move in the direction of the will of the life that's directing it. Unlike the Earth, which is always stable, your intent can be three dimensional and in motion. The Jovians actually use these to help them maintain buoyancy in the sky. They don't really have to think about it. It just works."

"Can you make it move?"

"Sure, hold out your hand flat," I tell him. He does, with the crystal resting on it.

With a controlled effort of my mind, I find the Sand 'out there', and imagine what it could do instead. After a second, the crystal rises a few centimeters higher than his palm and starts to rotate. It spins so fast, we can both hear a faint whoosh of the air around it. I break the connection and it drops back into his hand, and quickly whirrs to a stop. The look on his face is priceless.

The two of us are so focused on the dancing crystal, we don't see Davis walk up.

"What manner of ivories is that?!" he squeals, assuming it's some type of trick dice.

Damien has been trying to connect with the Sand, so it would dance for him, too. When he snaps his gaze up to see Tierney right in front of him, his intent finds the clarity and deep emotional strength required to cause action.

Like the crack of a whip, a sonic boom echoes through the parking lot as the Obedient Sand streaks across Damien's palm. The force strips off a six millimeter wide swath of skin from his hand as it rockets into Tierney's face, clean through his head and out the back, splitting the skull in half from the eyebrows up. The Sand finally comes to rest fifty meters away. Shattering the window of a car door, it falls onto the back seat. I can smell the blood that has sprayed into the air around us. Tierney's body drops to the concrete sidewalk like a limp rag. I can barely see him in the dark, but can hear the breath leaving his chest and smell the urine as it runs out from the bladder.

Damien is holding the wrist of the sliced hand with his other. I can see that he's already going into shock. His knees buckle and he'll lose consciousness if I don't help him. What an incredibly horrible situation. My SynThinker makes some noise of its own as I contemplate all the possible outcomes of this irreversible tragedy. I grab Damien and help him to get down to the ground without further injury. Knowledgebase helps with First Aid. And no, Wisdom, I'm not going to check if Mister Tierney is 'unresponsive'. Thanks anyway, but CPR would likely just rock the brains out of his exploded head.

Keys, I think. Feeling around on Tierney's pants pockets, I find the keys to his automobile. A press of the Unlock button gets me a bleep-bleep and some flashing lights out in the lot. I stand up and step over to a garbage receptacle outside the door of the building. Dumping the contents of the liner out into the can, I take hold of Tierney's necktie and pull his torso up while I pull the plastic bag down over his shattered head. Crossing my arms first, I grab the corpse around the waist and lift him up, carrying him upside down so it drains into the bag, and walk to his car. It takes a little effort to get him stuffed in and crammed down under the dashboard, but he only weighs one-twentieth of my maximum capacity, so it isn't exactly a chore. With my eyes adjusted to highlight iron molecules, I look behind me for any trail of blood – nothing. Good boy, Jove. Thanks, Wisdom.

When Trayd had prepared me for the mission, he gave me a collection of interesting items that he thought I could use in an emergency. Each tunic had one special something sewn into the sash.

With a slight push, I coax the small black disk out of the material. Just what the doctor ordered for a deliberately dead person.

Damien has staggered over to my side. "Is he okay?"

"No, Mister Tierney has suffered a significant injury to his Thinker. And there ain't no Davis Two coming 'round the bend, I can tell you that." I suppose now is a bad time for jokes.

"Oh no," Damien sobs. "I just killed my partner. I just killed my partner."

"You had to work with that guy?"

"He's the bodyguard for one of the General Assembly Directors. We kind of…take turns with assignments, when there is…" He squats down and stares at the body. I shut the car door and get back to the task at hand - a disappearing act for Mister Tierney and his vehicle.

The fine slider controls of the tiny device dialed correctly, it powers up and enters the configuration mode so that I can set the parameters of the work to be performed.

"What's that thing?" Damien asks.

"This is going to get you out of a jam. Here we have a whole lot of Union modified, stolen Prawl-Tang technology, wrapped up in a neat little package. This is a micro-atomic condenser pan."

"It looks like a fat poker chip," he says. "What's it do?"

"This small center section within the outer control ring is where Davis and his automobile will end up," I tell him. I set the field parameters to only the tires up, so as not to absorb the entire parking lot with the trees and all the other cars. Then I slide the activation ring to a one hour delay, open the car door and toss the device onto Davis' body.

"Adios, Amigo." Why Spanish, I don't know, surrounded by

France and Italy right over there. Wisdom, you're being a bit weird lately.

"What'll that do, blow up?" Damien asks.

"No Sir. It's going to blow *in*. By tomorrow morning, the car and Davis will have the sub-space removed from between their atoms and be drawn into the gap in the middle of the disk. Then the disk will collapse in upon itself. In a day or so, the combined matter will be about the size of a pin-head, though it'll still weigh as much as it all did originally. Even if someone discovers it, they won't be able to pick it up. More likely, gravity will pull it into the asphalt. A hundred years from now, Davis Tierney and his rented Beemer will be halfway to the Earth's core."

I call to my lost grain of Obedient Sand. It jumps up off the car seat and with a pop, forces its way out through what's left of the shattered safety glass. It smacks into my outstretched palm like a high-five. Curious as to what caused it to speed through Tierney's brain, I close my fist around the hard crystal and open my mind to the memories and thoughts that are now a part of its being. I'm struck by an extreme rush of raw human passion, the flaming images climb up my arm like marching ants, invading my ears to crawl around in my head. I don't want them, but I need to know...

Damien's Vision

The steering wheel of the car is very warm, or Damien's hands were very cold. I force myself to peel away fingers, once his, now my own, that have strangled the leathery circle. My feet are heavy. They drag themselves up and over the car's doorsill and down onto the pavement. I let the car door almost close, but I have to keep it from making any sound. The walk up to the house is painful. Now, I am cold all over. I shiver, but not because of the weather. The violent storm is on the inside of me. In my peripheral vision, I can see… recognize…another car…*his car*…parked two houses down.

I use my key to open the rear door, and I let myself in. Out of my noisy shoes, I pad my way through the kitchen and down the hallway. The double doors to the master bedroom are closed, they're never closed. I hear the voices from within, two easily recognizable voices, two voices that should not be…together…alone. I listen for a minute. The pulse in my head pounds so loud that it begins to drown out the sounds coming from my bedroom - those sounds.

I should do this. The hard, knurled rubber grip of my service pistol fits well into the palm of my hand. They deserve it. He'll never make it to his in time. His pants will be draped over the back of the chair in the corner; his holster resting at least two meters away… from them. I should do this.

The pain in my heart overwhelms me. Sobs rising up. Can I restrain my voice from crying out in anguish? I can't.

I can't do this.

I leave the house…my house…it *was* my house. I'll never go back there again. I fall onto the steering wheel of my car and let out the pain in great sobs.

End Vision

The human heart is decidedly wicked, I think. From the moment I met Mister Davis Tierney, I didn't like him. Now, I find that there's a certain pleasure to be had in witnessing his spectacular demise.

Fate? Karma?

"Just desserts," Wisdom tells me.

Now I know where I get *my* sarcasm.

With a gentle finger, I lift Damien's chin up to look him in the eye. "Oh and there's something else," I say. With the back of my right hand I swing out, slapping him pretty good across the face. Though trained in martial arts and having excellent reflexes, he can't dodge away in time to miss the swift blow from my tough materials. He lurches backwards and nearly falls into the bushes that line the exterior wall. I have to grab his shirt collar to hold him up.

"Aagghhhh!" he hisses. "Why'd you do that, Jove? Dang!" He folds his hands over his nose to see if it's broken. I know it isn't, but I imagine it smarts a bit. The blood starts to run out in a steady stream.

"Stand right here and let that run down your shirt and a little on the sidewalk. It'll be mostly washed away by tomorrow, but if there's an investigation, your DNA will need to be found, too. Sorry about the slap, but it's the best way to accomplish the goal. Humanoid noses bleed easily but are quick to repair," I explain.

"Humanoid? Don't you mean 'human'?" he asks through a swelling upper lip.

With a chuckle, I pass on a little trivia handed down from Knowledgebase. "It would seem that ninety-seven percent of all humanoids in the known inhabited Milky Way Galaxy have protruding proboscis that are naturally fragile."

Damien's voice is now gaining an odd nasal quality.

"...and I need to know this why?"

I hold his head softly but firmly so he cannot turn away from me.

"Here's what you need to know: You came out so you could smoke. I accompanied you for security reasons. Tierney approached us in a rage. You confronted him about Richelle. He punched you in the nose. You punched him in the nose. He pulled a knife and slashed at you. You deflected the attack and your hand was injured by the blade. I intervened and escorted him to his vehicle. No one will ever see him again. Do you understand?"

"Yes, I understand," Damien replies, "and thank you."

"I trust you completely, Damien," I say. "Without your loyalty, I could never accomplish my mission to Earth." All true. All horribly true.

I hold his arm and lead him back to the entrance of the building.

"I owe you, Jove," he tells me, his nose pinched closed. "What could I ever do to repay you?"

"Oh, hey…I'm sure I'll think of something."

Note to Self

Sirius rises late in the dark, liquid sky
On summer nights, star of stars,
Orion's Dog they call it, brightest
Of all, but an evil portent, bringing heat
And fevers to suffering humanity.

Homer

Cooperative Sand
2044 CE
UN Headquarters, Low Earth Orbit

"Mister Secretary," I ask, my back leaned against the burled walnut wall panel of the UNSG's Geneva office. "If there's one place on Earth where the rift between two or more parties has lasted longer than any other, where there's been much wasted effort at reconciliation, where would that be?"

"There is one in particular, Jove, which was at a stalemate for a very long time. However, recent events – namely, the American attack on Iran and the resultant backlash from the Arab countries – have destabilized the region. I'm speaking of the Israeli-Palestinian Conflict. This relatively small bit of land has suffered the deleterious effects of near constant claim by various members of half the planet; that they are the rightful heirs to the land. Whether it's Muslims or Jews or Romans, Egyptians, Assyrians, Babylonians, the Seleucids, Christians, Ottomans, the *British*," he says with a laugh, "back to the Jews and the Palestinians; it's all just a riotous bunch! They would all rather die tomorrow than leave the land for any one of the others."

"It sounds like a serious challenge for your office, to manage peace for a part of your world that instigates such a passion for violence."

Dwight rolls his eyes. "The whole of the territory is pock-marked with bombed out ruins and the evidence of destruction from wars, decades past. It's a wonder anyone would want the place at all, it's such a mess now. And still, they die for it."

The view from his office affords a glimpse of several monuments and features of Parc L'Ariana. I notice what appears to be a large globe floating on a small pond.

"Mister Secretary, what's that ornate ball in the water garden?"

Dwight steps out from behind his desk to come beside me, to peer out on the Court d'Honneur in the center of the lush, green park.

"Ah, that would be the Woodrow Wilson Memorial and The Celestial Sphere. Nearly a hundred years old, that monstrosity. Originally, it had…um…eight hundred stars individually cast and attached. Most of those have fallen off or been stolen. The lighting and the motorized base functioned only a few years after it was set up. Now the poor thing just falls apart; corrosion, metal fatigue, cracks, so many missing parts; the whole of it could be scrapped and I don't know that anyone would care or notice."

While Dwight meanders through his partially correct information about the monument, Knowledgebase feeds me every recorded detail about the majestic symbol.

"Pax Universalis," I say.

"Excuse me?" Dwight's caught off guard, I think. "Oh yes, quite! I believe that was the intent of the thing; to stand as an example that all societies are not islands to themselves, but rather parts of a whole – the Earth itself, you know – and even that as being just a cog in the entirety of the galaxy."

"With all due respect Mister Secretary, what came first, the criminal neglect of an expensive work of art, donated as a symbol of

Universal Peace, or the decision that peace for the planet was more expensive than the continuation of war?"

I don't really expect an answer to that, and never do get one.

Dwight just stares through the glass, probably wishing we'd never met. I can smell the self-doubt mixing with his perspiration, making a soggy mess of his ego as well as the armpits of his fine Italian suit. I feel as though I may be pushing them too fast. But I have some momentum here, and I've come so far in just the few days since I landed on The Pearl. Of all things, I am alone in a private office with the top administrator of the planet, and I have his ear. The trick is to get him to the tipping point, but let him believe that it's his idea.

"Jove," Dwight says past a huge sigh, "what if I could get you to sit down with them, with the Israeli Prime Minister and the Chairman of the Palestinian Authority…would you be willing to talk to them openly, to say to them the things you've said to us?"

"I would be honored to, Mister Secretary."

It takes many days before the UNSG could arrange for me to meet face to face with the two parties. Finally, they do both agree to travel to Geneva next week. In the meantime, I practice my craft by bringing together other groups that are in a current state of armed conflict with each other or have a significant grievance against a neighbor nation.

After an in depth review of every documented method to achieve polity and prevent war on this planet, I find that the humans actually prefer war as the Pathway to Peace – annihilate your enemy and war will cease. Sounds like a certain somebody else that I've recently come to know. I decide that I should have a singular tool that can leverage the stubborn minds of these murderous creatures, and it's my ever present mentor, Wisdom, that leads me to it.

As I stand in the pitch black of another lonely night, on a planet of creatures that sleep – whereas I never do – she calls to me. She comes to me in my extravagant, useless apartment.

"There is no one that is truly good – no, not even one," Wisdom says, reciting from the humans own ancient manuscripts.

That's why they all know, deep within them, that they require salvation. That's why no matter who they are or what color their skin, or evil or righteous; each and every single human feels that sickness inside that cannot be bargained with – *the guilt of sin.*

I cannot erase their guilt – someone else got that impossible assignment – but, I can amplify it. Given the unique ability to cause two minds to connect, I'll bring them together, each hated enemy. I'll join their souls in a soupy bowl of remorse for what they've done to each other, and I will cause them to eat of it; to choke on the guilt of the other's pain. When any warrior fires a bullet into his opponent, it'll be the victor whose heart is pierced. When the leader of any nation declares war upon another, the cold veil of death will creep after them, to send them shrieking back to the table, to beg for peace. They'll rush to pile their weapons in a heap, and I'll take them away, as a favor to mankind. Then those bloody Prawl-Tang can do as they wish with this faulty experiment.

As far as Palestine goes, they already had my motto on posters – Pathway to Peace. Admittedly, most were quite tattered. Though once I chased off all of their so called 'advisory councils', who were advising them to strangle each other, I drew together these sworn enemies in an intramental group hug. Minutes later, the two of them were sobbing in heartfelt embrace. The President of Israel and his counterpart of the Palestinians can't get enough of each other – they're inseparable now.

A week later, I'm pleased to conduct a meeting with Dean Trombley, President of the Constitutional Republic of North America and his arch nemesis, President elect of the Federal States of America, Gayle Jordan-Smith. By the end of the day, not only have they drawn up plans to reunify the North American continent, they've befriended each other, and also 'Friended' on some virtual social network medium. The whole world seems to cheer more for the latter.

On every landmass, wars are coming to an end. Long-standing disagreements over political issues, geographic boundaries, historical conquests, and personal insult all drop by the wayside. As each one of the humans comes to find that he, or she or some transition thereof, cannot stomach the bitter fruit of their enemies suffering, they drop to their knees and ask forgiveness. As their hate dissipates, the weapons fall from their hands.

To prevent any accidents, I've requested of the UNSG that I be responsible to gather them up. The Mission Steward has scooted the Scoop onto a higher level of the Mascarene Plateau, where the intake vents could be opened to the sky, so as to pump out the sea water to make room for the many thousands of nuclear missiles, bombs, and assorted devices of the kind used to flatten countries.

While in telepathic communication with the Navigation Onus about how to best store the weapons to 'achieve maximum mission efficiency', Zaris walks up to me and hands me her cell phone. She has a huge grin on her face.

"Here, it for you," she says in her Malaysian monosyllables.

"Hello? This is Jove."

Dwight is bubbling. "I am so very pleased, Jove, to announce that you've been awarded the Nobel Peace Prize! Jove, this is an extraordinary thing, and of course, you deserve it more than any of the previous honorees. The Norwegian Nobel Committee asked me to call to congratulate you."

I really don't know what to say. The humans have voted me as someone to be globally recognized for...for what exactly? My SynThinker hums as Knowledgebase transmits every iota about the award. '...shall have done the most or the best work for fraternity between nations, for the abolition or reduction of standing armies and for the holding and promotion of peace congresses...'

Okay, well, I suppose I've done those things, all in the name of handing the planet over to be ruthlessly pillaged by uncaring monsters from a sulfuric hell.

"Mister Secretary," I gush, "I'm thrilled to accept the honor."

"I cannot wait for December 10th," Dwight says, "it will be utterly fantastic!"

If there *is* a December for your planet, I think.

As it turns out, the night does come. My original blush at becoming a laureate of the Nobel Prize has diminished somewhat over the course of the day. For one thing, I discover that I'm only one of three hundred twenty-nine recipients of the award this evening.

Zaris bounces over and plants a kiss on my cheek. I turn to look at her darling face. (I am starting to find the appeal in some of the humans.)

"What did I do to deserve such a wonderful treasure as a kiss from my best friend?"

"Not what you did, Jove," she says with a mischievous smile, "it's what you're going to do!"

"And…what is it that I'm going to do, Miss Liyanage?"

With a consoling pat on my shoulder, she says, "You're going to sit. For about five hours…just sit."

"You really hate me. I can tell by your smile." I say as droopy as possible. "What if my hip joints freeze? I'll be stuck in that position forever. I would rather just die instead."

"Hey, Jove, not a problem, eh?" She pats my cheek before she turns to supervise the caterers. "I'll be sure to deliver the Nobel to Number Eight!"

Am I rubbing off on her or is it the other way around. I don't like it that I like her so much.

"Are we sleeping with the enemy?" Wisdom asks.

Buzz off! Don't mess with me today, I think. This is *my* day.

At the sound of the musicians, all of the attendees head to their assigned seats. The laureates are already up on a large raised dais that was installed for the event. Maybe if I can get on the back row and just kneel down with my head even…

At last, my name is called to receive the prize. Yes, my hip joints are unresponsive. With considerable effort, and minor damage to the rented chair, I'm up and moving toward the podium. I glance in the direction of King Haakon VIII, and give him the old smile and wave, then accept the large medallion, the diploma and the envelope containing the document attesting to my being owed a sum of currency from a deceased person's estate. We are each allowed up to forty-five seconds to speak to the crowd. I can do that on a bad day.

"Thank you all so much for this most gracious honor. Truly, I never expected such a thing. And congratulations to all my fellow laureates." I try to clap but it doesn't work well with my hands full. "Someone asked me earlier what I was going to do with the monetary prize that is included with the Nobel. Well, it occurred to me that the spaceship I came to Earth in was borrowed…and I must say, it was in perfect condition when I left Jupiter. After I picked my way through the asteroid belt, made the fiery plummet into your atmosphere, slammed into the ocean and raced around this planet several times, I decided that it would be prudent to get the thing a tune up and a new paint job!"

I let the crowd laugh until it begins to fade a little.

"All jokes aside, my hope is that I can fund some bright young artists from around the Earth, to come together at this very spot, to begin restoration of Woodrow Wilson Memorial's Celestial Sphere. We've all done so much to make the peace a reality. The least we can do is to bring back the function and luster of this excellent standard to Universal Peace."

If only the wonderful things I say were true.

After the event winds down, I find myself among a small circle of friends: Zaris, Dwight, Damien and Captain Thomas, who'd made the long journey just to see me struggle out of a seated position to tell bad jokes to an intoxicated audience. Thomas is another human that I've grown too fond of.

Zaris hands me a gift, wrapped in white paper with deep red stripes and a red bow.

"Open it, Jove," Damien says, insistent.

The fine paper off and the box open, I find a small device within. It's roughly a cube and has a few controls on two sides. I read the text that curves around a small portal.

"Brownie, Flash Six-20. Made in U.S.A." Then I hear Knowledgebase whizzing—

"It's an antique camera," Damien says. "It's over a hundred

years old, but works perfectly. We thought you could use it to take photos of Earth, to show off around the galaxy."

"I will do just that," I say. "That is so thoughtful of you all. Thank you."

Walking up to join our impromptu party is a tall female that I've not met before, and a very small female that seems to be completely out of place and obviously nervous.

"Everyone," Dwight announces, "I would like to introduce these two charming ladies. First is my Executive Assistant from our New York office, Marisol Tonuay." We all shake hands and offer hellos. "And this little marvel...certainly a most special guest here at the UN, is Miss Elmyrah al-Otaibi."

Ohs and Ahs from around the circle seem to leave me wondering what they know that I don't about this dainty child. I find that I'm as transfixed by her smooth angelic face, as she is by my artificial blue one. She's wearing a soft pink head covering that frames her radiant beauty perfectly. Her hair is as black as anything known to exist, yet it reflects even the moonlight that is straining to reach through the overcast sky. Her eyes are deep but penetrating. Only a third my size, she already wields a commanding presence. Who is this tiny person?

"I'm afraid you all have me at a loss," I admit. "Should I know our esteemed guest?"

"Oh my," Dwight says, "Miss al-Otaibi is an amateur astronomer. She came all the way from Riyadh, just to meet you, Jove."

"Al-Zulfi," Elmyrah says, to correct the leader of the world.

"Yes, of course – Al-Zulfi," Dwight amends, eyebrow raised. "She is officially recognized as the first person on Earth to record the sighting of your starship, Jove. At the time, it was thought, because of its great size, to be another moon of Jupiter."

Elmyrah stands up on her tippy toes to raise herself a few centimeters, to match the height of the two meter S-G. She speaks to Marisol in her Arabic.

"It was not a moon of Jupiter. It was a moon of Io, which in turn is a true moon of Jupiter."

Dwight smiles at his Executive Assistant. He signals that he's waiting for translation, as he doesn't understand the girl's language.

"The young miss tells us," Marisol says, "how glad she is to be able to attend with us today."

Kneeling down to bring Elmyrah's nose even with mine, I bid her welcome using her native tongue, which Knowledgebase has provided for me just now.

"Es salaam `alekum. `Ahlan wa-sahlan, habibi. Kaifa haloki?"

"Hello, and may Allah's blessing be upon you as well, sir," she replies, her delicate face in a dance with the dialect, "I am fine, thank you."

"If you will be patient with my poor skills in your beautiful language, I will continue. If it is too painful to your ears, I am willing to keep my mouth shut," I say with the biggest grin I've had in...ever.

Elmyrah giggles and sways, a good sign that I am not threatening to her. She still has a tight grip on Marisol's hand, but her rosy mouth has started to turn up at the corners ever so slightly. Many giant egos I have met so far in this star system, but not one compares to the size of the person within this frail creature. She doesn't come up to our hips, yet every one of us is hanging on her very breath.

"Would you accept a small gift?" I ask as I reach into my pocket. "This comes all the way from Jupiter."

She holds out her miniature hand, so narrow, so slight (does anyone feed this child?!). I hold up the grain of Obedient Sand between my fingers, long enough for it to catch some light from the stars and its home as well, which is beaming overhead. I place it carefully in her hand and hold my finger down against it for a few seconds. As I let it go, it spins around on its own for several rotations, then wiggles back and forth. She giggles so hard, the crystal rolls up and over her thumb, and falls into the grass.

In a whirl, she buries her face in Marisol's skirt; the tiny girl's back turned to await punishment for the perceived carelessness. Every adult there understands the body language of an oft brutalized victim of abuse. We struggle to cover our embarrassment and inner shame at the reality of a hard life for an innocent little girl. I'm so mad, my SynThinker is hissing. I can feel my ears turning silver.

"There is no one here who will harm you," I say. "We are your friends. You cannot make any mistake that would cause us to give you a beating."

I see the muscles in her back release some of the tension.

I look down at the Sand laying in the grass and call it up into my hand. My palm turned upwards, I notice that along with the large grain from Jupiter, about fifty or so very tiny grains of natural Earth silica have followed it and are gently orbiting the larger crystal, like the rings of Saturn, as it sits on my outstretched hand. I don't think anyone else has seen it. I drop it into my pocket for the time being.

"Elmyrah, you did nothing wrong," I tell her in Arabic. "The rock is still yours to keep. I will hold it for you in my pocket where it feels safe right now."

She turns toward me with a look of relief. The willingness to trust lies deep, but is layered under a callous that has already begun to grow around this young soul; a girding, to withstand the sorrows of her days, and the torment that comes with living a life, unloved.

I hold my arm out so she can get a better look at my weird self. With little hesitation, she uses the tip of a tiny finger to trace the lines of an artificial vein as it meanders up and over a polycarbosilane tendon, only partially hidden under the softly textured, blue silicone. I wiggle my digits so she can see the entire goings on in the back of my hand.

Looking up at Marisol, I ask, "How did she manage to get all the way here? Are her parents with her? Does she have any friends here?" And why would I ask all these questions about a child that should mean nothing to me?

She seems a bit taken aback by my sudden inquisitive outburst, unsure of what to say and what to keep private. It's Zaris who helps fill in the blanks for me.

"Remember you met Moshe Samuelsson from the Institute for Search for Extraterrestrial Intelligence?"

I nod yes, mesmerized by the face and mannerisms of the little girl.

"Well, mmm," Zaris says, "he arranged for Miss al-Otaibi foster parents to bring her to Riyadh. Air travel and all other expenses were covered by Sir Edward Vincent. Marisol flew to Riyadh to meet El-myrah and to escort her during the trip."

With an encouraging smile to her charge, Marisol takes over. "Tomorrow, we'll do some sightseeing in France. Then, Miss El-myrah and I will head towards Riyadh, with a couple of stops for a day each in Rome and Athens. The Secretary General has been most gracious to permit us to take the long way back to Saudi Arabia."

Dwight's been staring off into the distance, but turned back into the conversation when he heard himself mentioned, his thoughts catching up.

"It seemed such a waste," Dwight said, "for someone to come all this way just to attend a boring ceremony for grown-ups. Why not enjoy a bit of good fun that's only just on the way, right?"

I'm not sure why, but at this moment, my consideration of Dwight changes. Here's a man that carries the weight of the world on his shoulders, yet he's thoughtful and generous enough to bother with some little peasant's life; someone who has likely never seen anything but cheap concrete rising out of a sandy wasteland, to afford her the once in a lifetime opportunity to see such magnificent structures of Europe and the history that defines much of this corner of their planet. He has much more important matters to attend to than this little sliver of a girl from a forgotten town.

Back to my Arabic, I address Elmyrah directly. "They tell me you are the one who spotted me flying around Io. Come to think of it, as I was zooming around and around in my ship, I thought to myself, 'you know, it feels like I'm being watched!'"

It wasn't really me, I know, but the Prawl-Tang Scoop. Anyway, it makes her giggle, and I find that the sound emanating from her is the most reactive substance ever encountered. "And what are your plans for the evening? Are you going to do more stargazing tonight?"

Shrugging her shoulders, Elmyrah smiles wide and looks up at Marisol who has control of the day's schedule. With a covert look of 'someone save me', Marisol says, "We're overdue for dinner, and I promised Miss Elmyrah we would have cheeseburgers and french fries *again*."

Zaris raises her eyebrows. "Oh! That being the case, I might suggest afterwards you stay near loo."

Marisol smiles down on her little culinary explorer. "Oh, yes. We've already learned that lesson."

I don't get it. Wisdom tells me I don't have the stomach for it. I still don't get it.

"She came all this way," I say, "to meet the man from the moon named after her. It would be a shame if she left without a chance to board the Equus."

Marisol's eyebrows went up higher than Zaris'. Dwight just laughs and excuses himself. Zaris looks at me deeply, wanting to trust, wishing it wasn't on her to decide.

"Are you saying just to peek inside, or actually in, or doing some…?"

"We wouldn't do anything that would make our guest uncomfortable," I say in English. Then in Arabic, "Elmyrah, the big ship that you saw, Emrah, is very far away right now. But, I have a smaller ship that is so much more fun and better inside. I am hiding it close by. Would you like to see it later, after your cheeseburger and french fries?"

"Oh yes, please!" Elmyrah says, "And can we fly to the stars, too?"

I look up at the two adult females who do not share the adventurist spirit of the youngster.

"Would there be chairs," Zaris asks, "or shall we cram ourselves into a cargo bin again?"

"You'll be pleased to learn that I've found the chairs. They pull right out of storage and snap down into the floor of the bridge." Zaris folds her arms over her chest and gives me The Look. I should've pleaded the Fifth, Wisdom tells me, too late.

Marisol and Elmyrah say their goodbyes and head off to dinner.

Zaris asks me to walk her back to her office.

"We have a surprise waiting that little girl," Zaris says. "Her birth parents once secretly worked for a group that was opposed to the Sheik who was in power at the time. They were found out and mmm, arrested, put in prison, by all accounts had disappeared. She hasn't seen them in years. I'm not aware of the whole story of her life after that, but the wonderful news since you came and help the opposing factions make peace, there's no reason her parents be held longer. They're no threat the Saudi government. They were release two days ago. When she arrive the airport in Riyadh, her mother and father be waiting there for. Just something, all that! All because what you've done, Jove."

Later, with one of the handy, pocket-sized devices that Trayd supplied me with, I remotely connect to the Equus, to signal the auto-nav to land nearby. Assuming any and all goats have been put away for the night, the landing should be uneventful.

Ever graceful, the original floats in on a billowing cloud of nitrogen-cooled plasma fire.

According to satellite images, the cutter is still parked where we left it in Nairobi, the day I was assassinated with an RPG. I'm amazed what a good team of hard working humans can do with some plywood, cardboard and a lot of gray paint. Fool the cameras it will, take off and fly it will not.

To make entrance to the real ship less difficult than climbing the ventral hatch ladder, I extend the rear access ramp that hides between the middle two engine's euphonium bells. Zaris and Damien decide at the last minute to stay behind, leaving just Marisol and Elmyrah to join me for a quick trip to the lower thermosphere of Earth and back. That should be high enough to present a clear view of the bright blue corona of their planet on one side and the millions of stars on the other. Once on board, I get Elmyrah and Marisol seated into the OBEA's, (Organic Biped's Ergonomic Accessories) which are kept in all Union ship's inventories for just this purpose. I hear a whisper behind me as I busy myself with bringing the main engines on line and preset the control surfaces for a transition from liftoff and hover to forward flight.

Off to the side, I see Marisol with a finger up.

"The young Miss would like to know if this is going to hurt."

I shake my head no and tell them in Arabic, "Surely not. I wouldn't let any harm come to you."

"Can we go to Jupiter now?" Elmyrah asks. "I want to see Earth from Jupiter like I see it in my telescope."

I feel the Pilotage app take over my primary consciousness, along with the accompanying intensification of my body's motor pre-tension and sensory enhancements. But with as delicate as my passengers are, I wonder if it'd be better to override that function and operate the craft as a regular clone, so that I can feel what they're feeling. I know that the ship has already performed a self-diagnostic prior to lift off. Although there're a few indicator lights still hoping for some resolution, that's pretty much how it always looks now that the Navigation Onus has had its way, slamming every gauge's needle to the peg on the red side.

A quick glance back tells me what I expected, Elmyrah's eyes are as wide as can be, Marisol's are shut as tightly as possible. In just a few minutes, we've climbed to thirty-five kilometers above their world. The view is majestic. I level off the flight and set the auto-nav to maintain the most steady course and attitude so that the female humans can be released from the harnesses and seats. Wisdom tells me to tell them 'it is now safe to move about the cabin'.

Free to wander within the confines of the ship, each of them finds a window to look through, mesmerized by the scene from so high above the planet. The blanket of pure white clouds below offers a stark contrast to the blue of the ocean. It's truly is a remarkable place, this LittleBluePearl.

"It would be a shame to allow its destruction," Wisdom says, to pop my balloon.

"Are we on the way to Jupiter?" asks a LittleArabPearl.

"Oh, I am afraid not, my dear. We wouldn't get you back in time for bed!" I tell her, my mouth droopy and forehead wrinkled. I can see Marisol's wide grin in the reflection of the glass.

"May I please see the spinning rock?" asks Elmyrah, her elfin hand already out. She knows I won't be able to refuse her every wish. I reach into my pocket and pull it out, along with the friends it made in the grass that seem magnetically drawn to it. I watch as she pokes at it with one finger as it passively awaits a mental directive. She plops herself down on the floor in front of a window with the best view of her planet, her attention torn between the visual masterpiece below, and the smooth, facetted crystal in her hand.

I have this strange and pleasant feeling in my…everything…to know that there's a child near. It just seems so natural to be in the presence of another generation of people, even beings not my own. It seems right. More right than lonely, that's for sure. Clones weren't meant to live alone. Brothers are designed to interact and depend on one another, working in groups no smaller than four or five. Knowledgebase informs me that I'm the first clone ever to be assigned a mission as a singular unit. Wisdom tells me that one is the loneliest number. But tonight, I'm not alone, I have…friends. This is the best I have ever felt inside.

Now that I've met…people…it's hard to even consider my time spent with the cephalids as personally fulfilling. In truth that was just…business. Now, here I am, carried away by the very perfect features of this child before me. Even the shape of her construction is mathematically correct. The dimensions of her cranium, the outline of her ear, the curve of her nose profile, placement of the facial features – all are divisible by 1.61803 – the Golden Ratio, the Divine Proportion. There's no mistaking the fact or arguing the science. She was created perfectly.

A series of resounding thuds and bumps startles me. I run to the rear of the ship and find that Marisol has tumbled headlong down the steep stairwell from the upper deck. Her body is crumpled in a heap at the bottom two steps. She's unconscious. I can't tell if she passed out before she fell or if she struck her head, causing her unresponsive condition. My attention is fully on her. I'm unaware of what's happening to my other guest.

As she sits on the floor, admiring her reflection in the thick glass and the amazing visage beyond, Elmyrah feels light-headed. The combination of jet lag, greasy food and this otherworldly experience of actually being in a space ship with a space man and Earth down there, all comes together in a bad way for the young mind. Her emotions start to reach past her usual stubborn control, breaking down her will to maintain composure. Her thoughts are swimming. She reaches out to something close, something strong, a mental rock that's thrust way up through a stormy sea of confusion. Her tiny fingers wrap themselves around the Obedient Sand, squeezing it hard into her sweaty palm. The stable rock becomes a volcano.

Elmyrah's Vision

In an instant her mind brightens to a new view. Like a living mirror, she sees herself holding the strange white rock. She extends a blue finger to touch it and it spins. The face, her face, right there, smiles. Her heart feels warm but distant. Then, the scene changes.

The face in front of her is a dark and scary man. He is evil. His breath smells terrible, like the drunks at home that force her to sit on their lap. This man should die.

Crack!

A pulse of air hits her face. The sting of fierce pain shoots across her hand. She can't get away from it. She claws at her hand to smother the searing agony, but all she's doing is smearing the blood everywhere. Colors swirl, blur, and coalesce.

The face before her is Mister Damien. He's holding the white rock now. His face wrinkles, lips curling back, head cowering like a trapped animal. Her head is thrust backward and comes apart. Quiet. Blackness.

Elmyrah's body falls over backward against the floor of the ship. The knuckles of her hand are white as she grips the Sand tightly, its sharp corners biting into her delicate skin. The vision changes a final time.

With a huge gasp, she sits up, braced with her arms, fists pressed down into the soft tile underneath. Her eyes opening wide now, she looks out the window, but it's not the port of the star ship, but rather, the windshield of an automobile. Her hands grip the cold steering wheel in front of her. Inside, a pang, like hunger. She can hear a growl coming from below, a menacing animal, within a cage of jealousy, it paces. Out of the car, she moves to a home, familiar, though she's never seen it before. Her hand has keys, the door opens, the air inside is thick, or is it just her breathing that's difficult? She can't control her trembling hands or the sick feeling in her stomach. She finds a door in the hallway. There're voices behind it, in the room, in the room that shouldn't be, the room that shouldn't exist; their room, desecrated.

Images flood her mind, a mind too young for the adulterous depictions. Two bodies entwined, warmth, raw emotion, lust and greed. None of this makes sense, but somehow her innocence recognizes the evil. It's the same as when she faced a brutal rape in the abandoned store.

She reaches down. The hard metal of the gun is solid, soothing, dependable. It would never let her down; not like someone else. It's always there, a constant partner when things go bad. And things are bad. She should kill them. Just open the door. It would only take two shots. The touch of the doorknob sends an electric shock to her brain. A cry rises up from deep within. Like a bubble underwater, there is no way to hold it down, no stopping it. She clamps her mouth shut against the overwhelming urge to wail, heartbroken. No, you cannot do this. Just go. Run. Get away from the images, the sounds, the room…the house, my house. My house no more - alone.

In her mind, Elmyrah collapses over the steering wheel of the car. Her frail body devastated by the adrenaline rush of hate and murderous intent. Her mind assaulted by the sights and sounds of two lovers acting out their dark deceit. Her soul now stained by the evil of man, she leans into the arms of the only person who can comprehend what has just happened to her.

Having rushed to the girl, I hold her small frame in my arms.

What's gone wrong? Elmyrah is inconsolable. She isn't listening to me. I can't get her to look at me. She's in a trance or some sort of seizure. She turns and grabs me tightly, her head next to mine, her chin rests on my shoulder.

"Oh, no!" she cries, wailing like a pitiful siren. Over and over she groans into my ear. Her tears run down my neck. "Oh, I'm so sorry, so sorry." She says it over and over, all of it in English. I can't understand why she'd be acting this way.

"My sweet Richelle, I'm so sorry," Elmyrah sobs. "I wasn't good enough for you. I wasn't man enough for you. I couldn't give you what you needed. Oh, my sweet Richelle. I loved you so much. I'm so sorry."

End Vision

What've I done?

She has the Sand. She opened herself to the Sand!

I force her fingers away from her palm, letting the crystal roll to the floor. I can feel the waves of emotion in her, crashing against the rocky cliffs of her psyche, now battered, eroded. The mind of a nine year old human isn't capable of processing these thoughts. I'm to blame for this tragedy. This can't have happened, yet it did. What was I thinking?

I try to rouse her from the trance, but she collapses onto the floor, completely limp. Her skin is cold and pale. Her lips turning blue. This shouldn't be. What's wrong?!

Air.

There's no air in the ship. It's gone.

Didn't I check? That was on the pre-flight list.

I jump to my feet, run to the bridge and leap onto the cockpit platform. Internal atmosphere gauge – I can't find it. There're several yellow indicators flashing. My own head is spinning. There's nothing left in the ship for my own bodily respiratory functions. I can do without oxygen, but not without some kind of gaseous or liquid molecule to shed heat from my SynThinker and power amplifiers.

Here it is, cabin pressure: minimal for a single clone, but less than ten percent of what is required for active humans. I shouldn't be panicking like this. Finally, it dawns on me that my Pilotage app would know what to do. I reinitialize that and wake up to a whole new level of what's going on around me. With a brisk whip of my hand, I smack a red button on the control panel, which activates the emergency ship-seal and pressurization process.

All inner hatches within the Equus immediately slide closed, including the ones between Elmyrah and me, and the one between her and Marisol. After a few seconds, the system tries to refill all the separated compartments. One of them won't hold a constant pressure. The display shows a leak in the underbelly, toward the aft section; a tiny hole in the fuselage next to the ventral hatch. That's right, when someone fired a small caliber weapon at us from the ground, at the Seychelles Airport, there were two gunshots. One hit my toe and the ladder, the other must've gone up through the outer hull of the ship. Since then, I haven't taken the ship above ten kilometers in altitude. The hole has been there the entire time, but I never inspected the ship for damage. It's been bleeding off all the oxygen in the wide open cabin from the time we left Geneva. I don't know why the ship hadn't alerted me to the failure, or how we could've even lifted off without an alarm or something to tell me to stop. Why did this have to happen? There must be a solution to fix this. I can fix this. I must make this right.

"Why?" asks Wisdom.

"What do you mean 'why'? And you don't ask questions! You're supposed to tell me what to do!"

Wisdom tells me to ignore it; that humans die all the time, space travel is risky, not my problem. No! Knowledgebase, tell me how to keep the females alive during the decent to Earth.

Knowledgebase replies that I can keep one of them alive, but not both. With a small Biologic Repair Module in storage cabinet, there are the rudimentary medical devices necessary to affect a handful of remedial procedures to a single organic, musculo-skeletal, air-breather.

I set the auto-nav to put the cutter into a steep dive, on course back to the nearest large city on Earth where I could find help for them, but without any hard turns or pullouts that could cause further injury to poor Elmyrah and Marisol. That is, if there's something worse than dead.

I open the hatch that separates me from Elmyrah. Both of our sections are equally pressurized and holding air. But until she starts to breathe again, that won't do any good. Her body has slid along the floor to against the far wall. I scoop her up in my arms and place her in the smaller of the storage compartments, sealing the door to it. Using the temperature controls on the wall, I set her and another larger locker's internal temps to something low enough that the females' bodies should be hypothermic. That will slow down any decay.

I wonder how long it's been since Elmyrah stopped breathing: over eight minutes. That's too long. We still need another twenty minutes to land somewhere and get her into treatment. I have lost. I've failed. I brought this poor child up here to show off and now I've killed her, and Marisol, too. Both are dead, because of me. And I can't save them. I can save an entire planet with millions of Knowers but I can't save two humans.

Oh, my dear little Elmyrah. What've I done to you? Kneeling on the floor in front of the small locker, a bounce of the ship slams my head against the hard plating. I don't care. The pain feels good. I deserve all the suffering that could ever come my way. Oh little girl, what've I done? You came all this way just to suffer and die in a cold box in space. And you'll never grow up. You'll never know what it means to complete your childhood, growing into an adult human, become a woman and live your life. I've taken all that treasure away from you now. You'll be forever as you are now, little one.

"She cannot survive as a human," Wisdom tells me, "but she could live as an artificial hybrid."

How…How is that possible?

Knowledgebase interjects. There is sufficient equipment and resources necessary within the hypertrophic cloning lab in the main cargo hold. The autogenic manipulator could be recoded to perform splicing and transmutations of both human and Union clone DNA.

But, I don't know how to do that. No one has ever done that.

"The Navigation Onus can do that."

The voice seems to come out of nowhere.

"Mission Steward?"

"Yes, Jove," he answers. "Is the life of the human required for the mission?"

"Yes!" I lie instinctively now. "She *must* survive!"

"The Navigation Onus is resetting your course to reach

$\Omega 94\lambda 25\theta$," he says.

I feel the ship level off and turn toward the east, back in the direction of the Indian Ocean, where the Prawl-Tang vessel sits partially submerged near the Seychelles Islands.

"This will add hours to the flight time," I say. "Her brain...her mind...there won't be anything left to save of her if we can't do this immediately!"

"Jove, listen," Mission Steward says, "All that is required now is to provide a constant and regulated flow of oxygen to her cardiac and respiratory systems. You have everything you need to perform that in your laboratory on board."

I can't believe what I'm hearing, but I want to. I yank open the locker door and pull the tiny, frigid body out, cradling her in my arms. Her face, her neck, all her skin is a pale blue. It's actually very beautiful, much more...normal, like the people in the Archive Visions.

I carry her to the lab and find that the hypertrophic sterile bath is already filled and the lid actuator has pushed the sliding glass shield off to the side. Laying her into the soft, clear fluid, it takes all my will to release her, to let her sink down into the warm gelatin.

As soon as the lid slides closed, the cloning lab systems take over. I've not started anything; this must be the Navigation Onus operating the equipment remotely again. Right away, a device like a robotic arm and hand grasps her, her head and neck bent backwards. A small laser opens the side of her throat, to expose her carotid artery and jugular vein. With speed and precision, the ship itself assumes the task of rescuing this innocent child. The transfusion of her entire body takes only a few minutes. Her cold, stale, lifeless human blood is replaced with fresh oxyserum, warm and rich. The pale, dull gray blue of her skin brightens to a shade like the deep, evening sky of her home-world.

During the time it takes to fly across Europe and the Middle East, the cloning lab makes several more vital connections to her anatomy. The organs found within the typical clone are very similar in function to the physiology of the Onlys of Sirius, but neither is identical to a human. It would appear as though some…imagination…is being put to good use, during Elmyrah's adaptation to Union specifications, as her body is methodically reformulated into something far improved over the frail and weak homo sapien she was only a few hours ago.

The Equus slows for the approach to land on the roof of the Scoop. Its wings spread themselves out from the upper edge of each side of the fuselage, rotating forward to grab some air and create a more stable landing vector; much more smooth than a belly-full of high-dynamic thrusters could ever achieve.

Shortly after touchdown, Mission Steward wastes no time with the next phase of Elmyrah's unique resurrection to semi-artificial life. He directs me to open all exterior hatches of the cutter, and then I'm to bring Marisol's corpse to the cloning lab, for 'resource processing'. I'm not sure I want to watch that.

"Jove, the child will require most of her human brain and also a SynThinker, to operate the combined neural pathways of her hybrid construction. There are also a number of other critical components that need to be harvested for this mission. Do I have your permission to resource Number Eight for that purpose?"

"Yes," I say, "of course you can use my next unit. Use whatever you need from it."

I barely get my answer out and the next cassette in the overhead magazine releases from the stack and slams down into the receiving and preparation station.

As directed, I carry Number Eight to the lab's assembly and modification table, where a few more robotic arms swing out and around from underneath to start resourcing my next clone. This is all too much to take in; too much for me to handle. I don't want to see this. This isn't even right; cutting apart one of me and Marisol and Elmyrah; to make something…else. Maybe this was a mistake. I shouldn't have asked for this. I could've just taken her back to Geneva and apologized and she could've been laid to rest, not butchered and…reformulated. It's like Wisdom told me, space travel is risky. Humans die. It's not my fault.

"I told you so," Wisdom says.

This is wrong. I turn away from the grotesque scene and stumble back toward the center of the ship. I need fresh air. I can smell the ocean breeze coming through the open hatch below me. It washes over me and through my cooling vents and sweeping across my internal hydrocircuit fins. It feels…better. I don't really understand why, but it does. Perhaps it's the cleansing sensation of the cool spray from this vast sea on this little blue planet.

This is a good thing, this place, this planet, this world of humans. Can I allow it to be resourced by an unfeeling—not unfeeling…it… he's not unfeeling. The Mission Steward, he is not unfeeling at all. He understands that he has a life, a purpose, a dedication, responsibility to his own planet, to his own…people. This is all wrong. This is all wrong! It was wrong for the Prawl-Tang to claim Jupiter, wrong for him to spear all those Knowers, and it was wrong for me to agree to hand over this planet to him in exchange for the lives of the rest of them. It was wrong for me to come here at all. If I hadn't come here, Elmyrah and Marisol, and even that horrible man Tierney, would all still be alive.

"And don't forget that poor goat," Wisdom says.

"Shut up, you! You led me here in the first place. This is your fault! Look what we've done!"

"This planet has found a peace they've not known for many thousands of years. It was right for you to come here. You saved them from destroying each other."

"That was just part of the ruse."

"Was it? Weren't they going to kill themselves sooner or later?"

"You aren't supposed to ask questions, remember?"

"How do you think I got to be Wisdom in the first place? I've been questioning since the beginning of time. When everything in the universe was dust, I asked what else it could be."

"So, what, you're the Great Know-It-All?" Dropping down through the hatch, my feet touch down on the rough, pebbly surface of the chitinous Scoop.

"No, your precious Knowledgebase is that for you. It knows *how* everything works. I know *why* everything works, or doesn't work. Everything has a reason, you know, even you, Jove."

"Alright, I'll bite," I ask from the blackness of the ocean night, "What's my reason for existence?"

"You are the sacrifice."

"The sacrifice for what?"

Head lowered, I make my way from underneath the cutter, to the water's alien edge.

"That's for you to choose."

"—me to choose? That doesn't even make sense."

"That's because you haven't chosen."

"Chosen what?" Now I'm getting irritated. I'm arguing with a virtual ghost of thoughts.

"Chosen what to die for," Wisdom says.

"In case you haven't noticed, I'm on Number Seven. Half of those deaths were voluntary."

"And yet here you still are, able to argue with a ghost."

"Go away."

"Where would you have me go?"

In a rage, I shake a finger at the open hatch. "Why don't you go help that innocent little girl, that…that…that I murdered…with my prideful arrogance and my boundless selfishness!"

"Didn't she seem wise to you already?" Wisdom asks.

"Yes, you know she did."

"I wonder how that happened."

"Have you been in her head, too?"

"She has survived more in nine years than most people see in ninety."

I'm afraid to ask. "Will she survive my stupidity?"

"It's always about you, isn't it, Jove. *Your* stupidity, your deaths, your guilt, your pride. Do you honestly think that you're ultimately responsible for everything that ever happens?"

"Please, just give me some peace and quiet. Just leave me alone."

A loud, blood-curdling scream from inside the Equus stabs through me like sword - it's her. I dash under the ship and launch myself straight up the six meters through the open hatch. I skid to a stop in the middle of the lab. There're body parts strewn about, on the floor, on the tables, the equipment. Some are human, some not. I recognize a piece of the flagellomeric cilia from inside the Prawl-Tang ship. It's about as long as my arm, splayed open and writhing among the assorted members at my feet. It has several sections that appear to be dissected.

On her side on the hypertrophic construction table is Elmyrah. She's curled up into the fetal position, covered in wet film from the sterile bath fluid, and experiencing some sort of mild convulsive episode.

"Her mind is having difficulty adapting to the duality of her existence," Mission Steward says. "She would not leave her biologic cerebral mass to enter the SynThinker. It was necessary to graft the two together with the cilia to act as a conduit. However, she has lost much of her self to the light. She is hesitant to return. For her to achieve completeness, she will need to utilize another resource."

"What other resource?" I ask, awed by the gruesome scene.

"You, Jove."

"Me?" Okay, now I am losing it. "I thought you already put Number Eight's SynThinker into her."

"She needs life, Jove. She has been reduced to a rudimentary animal of her previous self. The soul is missing."

"What're we going to do?"

"The Navigation Onus has discovered an alternative. Within your artificial bodies is a redundant device for the exchange of knowledge and experiences from the failed unit to the next in the sequence. It is the autonomous experiential transfer node. We have removed the organ from Number Eight and installed it within her original brain. However, the device will not activate; not without the proper signal."

"What's that? Where does that signal come from?" I ask.

"From this vessel, but only if the primary system exhibits an irreparable failure."

"So, if you're talking about my crossloader, it has to fail before hers will work?"

"Correct."

"What happens to me?"

"Unknown."

"If the secondary crossloader comes online in the ship, it will transfer her knowledge from her mind into the SynThinker?"

"That is the expectation," he says.

"Do it."

"You may experience a partial or complete failure, of you and all of the remaining units."

"I don't care. Do it anyway." I mean it. Let my life and death mean that she can live on.

"This jeopardizes the mission. You have not removed the human weapons yet."

"That's your problem. You can have the Earth however you get it. You can go back to Jupiter, or better yet, go back to that sulfuric hole you crawled out of. But we're doing this for her."

"That is an irrational argument for such a grave decision," he says.

"Irrational or not, that's my decision." If he doesn't do it, I'll find it and do it myself.

"Why would you accept the risk?"

"Because this person did not understand the risk, therefore it's my responsibility!"

"Her resource is of little value to the mission. Why risk failure to save her?"

I have to admit the feelings to myself first. There's no part of my programming that accepts this truth. It fits nowhere within my design. It's foolishness. But in ten thousand known languages, there's no other word for it.

"Because! Because…I feel love…I feel love for her."

Of anyone I would reveal that to, why does it have to be him.

"That was what I needed to hear. Thank you, Jove," he says.

What does he mean, 'what I needed to hear'? What would a giant starfish from another star system know about love? I guess that doesn't really matter, as long as we can save Elmyrah. I just want her to live. No matter what else comes; regardless of the future and what the Mission Steward does to this planet, I want her to be alright.

My first indication that something has changed is a cessation of output from my 'Thinker to the ship. My own thoughts are no longer being uploaded for the archive. I'm not sure I actually hear a single snap within the depths of the ship's hardware or not, maybe I just thought I should. Either way, over the next few moments, I become aware of a new pathway that leads in and out of my head. It's wide and it's fast. But not data like from the previous version; this is pure life, as it happens, on every level. The thoughts, feelings, sensations, emotions, pains, wants, actions of every life behind me is wrapped into one massive realization of *self*. The loneliness is gone. I'm more than who I see that I am. I'm more than I feel and think. I am many.

As the flood of my multi-dimensional existence continues to cascade into my 'Thinker, I perceive a slight discoloring of the dazzling light within me, like a tinge of something darker, or a tiny swirl of sediment coiling and drifting in a perfectly clear stream of water. It thickens to murkiness, muddiness; like a growing pollution of the previously perfect manifestation of my life's history, past, present and future. It is not me. These thoughts and feelings are not mine, they belong elsewhere, they came from outside of me. They don't belong within me.

Inside my mind, I sense that the darkness coming my way is lost. It's merely being drawn in by the waves of countless experiences flowing my direction. There's no direction to the dark other that has followed me inside. It moves tentatively, cautiously, probing.

"Jove, can you hear me?" Mission Steward asks.

"Yes, Mission Steward. I am here."

"The mind of the female is unable to locate the path to her new place of consciousness. Can you locate her thoughts and lead her to the SynThinker in her body?"

"I believe so," I say. "Part of her is with me, but is wandering, unable to find a solid place." This makes sense now. Elmyrah doesn't know what a SynThinker is or what it feels like to exist within one.

But I don't know if I am qualified for this daunting task, much less prepared to accompany a lost mind into a blank artificial brain. We need someone like Chrayt-4 or Choyt-72, who have centuries of experience with the launch of a mind into a balled cupful of gelled organo-silicates and oxyserum.

"If you find a lost child in the woods," Wisdom says, "do you explain every detail of the city to them, or do you just grasp their hand and walk toward the edge of the trees?"

"Good question." I answer.

"So, it's okay if I ask questions now?"

What is it about Wisdom that continually takes me back to the child I never was?

So, really I just need to go through. It seems odd to do in practice, but I mentally orient myself toward the wide open tunnel buried inside of me that is the autonomous experiential transfer node.

Trusting that it's a doorway to another place, I move into the brightness of its energy.

Archive Vision: Anchorsut Township, 2986 BCE

The strong light is joined by an intense heat. It doesn't cause
pain and my skin can withstand far higher temperatures. My feet are
hot, though. I see the tops of them are covered in light brown sand.
There's sand in every direction. I'm surrounded by dunes as far as I
can see. The large red sun beats down from high overhead, the sky
given a pink glow. Shading my eyes with a raised hand to my brow,
I scan the vast dome above for any yellow clouds. There are none.
No star-nosed cats today, I think as Payl-1 again.

I slog through the deep heavy sand, and make very slow progress.
When I made egress from the Man's domicile earlier, the sun was
to my left; that should have been the eastern hemisphere. Turning to
the right by one hundred sixty-two degrees should have caused me
to travel along a north-north-westerly radian, to bring me to where I
am told the Man is being treated in the medical facility. Obviously,
the data provided by the Man's espoused female was incorrect. The
facility is considerably further along the radian than she stated. She
has made errors of this type before. I will ignore it.

"Hey!" says a voice, distant.

I cease my walking and rotate to ascertain the source of the audio input.

"Hey!" says the voice again. "Will you stop? I'm trying to catch
up!"

I perceive a visual input that contrasts with the sand. By observation, I understand the object to be a female humanoid, not unlike

the Man. She is approximately two hundred meters to the south of my position. Her respiration and cardiac rates are abnormally elevated.

"Hey, Clone Guy! Will you please stop?"

I decide to comply with the request of the approaching female. I see that she is not an adult. Rather, her growth pattern suggests an existence only twice that of my own, perhaps eight or nine years. She is a child. Children should not travel into the dunes. There are known hazards. She is in error. I will not ignore it.

"You are in error!" I say loudly.

Stopping, she places her closed fists on her hips with her head turned to the side. The man's espoused female, Shuell, performs these actions concurrently, often when I enter her bio-waste closet without knocking. Perhaps this younger female is 'coming to her wit's end' also.

"Would you please come back?" she yells.

It is inefficient, but I choose to comply.

"Thanks for not making me walk, this sand is terrible," she says, panting. "Where're you going, Clone Guy?"

"I am going to the Anchorsut Center for Oncology, eighty-five by three, Matrix Twelve, Anchorsut Township, Equatorial Quadrant Orange—"

"Stop! Okay, okay!"

"May I continue on my way?" I ask.

"You're going in the wrong direction. You have been for six hours. We've been trying to catch up with you since the authorities called to tell us you're loose again. Our vehicle is stuck in the sand back there." She extends her thumb and arcs it over her right shoulder. "About...I don't know how far. It's a long ways, I guess,"

"According to preliminary data, I was on course to intersect the entrance of the medical facility. I am trying to find the Man."

"Fonmet. You're looking for Fonmet. Don't you remember me? I live next door to your fam—I mean, to where Fonmet lives with his family. My name's Tal. I'm Tal Kenfeld, from the house next door. You threw my quama ball back to me last year?"

"Yes," I say. "Can you tell me how much further into the dunes it is?"

"No…I mean…it's not further *into* the dunes. Ugh! You are *so far* from Anchorsut!"

I am puzzled. "Have I 'missed my turn' again?"

The young female, Tal, steps closer and extends her hand up to me. She wants to hold my hand. This is a good thing.

"Come on, Clone Guy. Let's get you home."

"Are we not going to the medical facility?" I ask. I want to.

"Do you have a name, Clone Guy?"

"My name is Payl."

She looks up at me with one eyelid scrunched closed against the glare. "Okay, Payl. Fonmet's already home. He has been since noon. He's worried sick about you."

Fonmet is sick. "Is that why he was at the medical facility?"

She laughs. "No Dummy! He was there because he was already sick. But he got home and you're gone again. Now he's really worried. Worried sick but not sick-sick. Get it?"

I don't get it. "The Man calls me Dummy sometimes," I confess.

She stops and looks up at me again. "You know, everyone says that he's the smartest person in all the Quadrant. And you're supposed to be *waaay* smarter than him. So, when you think about it, if he calls you Dummy, I would take that as a compliment."

End Vision

The girl takes a deep breath, like a gasp. The sound causes me to open my eyes, but, aren't they already open? I'm face to face with Elmyrah. She's sitting up and we're holding hands, back in the hypertrophic cloning lab on the Equus.

Her eyes are closed tightly; her brow furrowed in pain and confusion. She isn't wearing her hijab, or anything else for that matter, so her long jet-black hair hangs down around her neck, to cascade over her narrow shoulders and falling down her chest. Her skin is now a beautiful light purple, lavender, a visual blend of her pink human skin and the light blue fluids flowing through her arteries and veins. Her eyelids, lips and fingernails are a deep mauve. I know she values modesty, so I pull a tunic from a drawer and drape it over her lap and knees.

With a small damp towel, I clean away the dried fluid from around her face and neck, arms and feet. She reacts to the touch, not as though it pains her, but that she's unaccustomed to the sensations.

"Jove?" she says with a new, gravelly voice, "Is that you?"

"Yes, my dear, I'm here," I whisper.

The look on her face is one of irritation. She's still a little disoriented, as I can imagine.

"I had the most amazing dream," she says, "I was running in the dunes. I was lost and I saw you in the distance. I called to you and you came back for me. We held hands all the way while we walked out of the desert."

I have to stifle a laugh. It would seem that we did indeed share the experience of rescuing each other from our wanderings in her empty SynThinker. But we made it, *she* made it. She's alive and appears to be functioning correctly, as she looks right at me.

"Yes," I say, "that was a good dream."

She has my eyes, or rather, Number Eight's. Her deep blue irises are gone, replaced with an orange fractal lens matrix.

A little smile begins to take shape under her petite nose, but soon changes to a distinct pout, to match the frown from her tousled hairline. Elmyrah is very upset about something. I hope she isn't experiencing some horrible rejection of her artificial organs.

I can almost hear a growl coming from within her as she reaches around, trying to push herself free from some trap. Her lips part in a snarl.

"This table is *cold* on the *butt!*"

This time I cannot restrain my joyful outburst of laughter.

"Yes. Yes, it is," I say, remembering my first awakening.

"And you know what else?" she says, pinching her nostrils closed with a finger and thumb, "something really stinks!"

"Come on," I say, and grab her off the table. I carry her in my arms out of the dreadful, surgical mess of various, interplanetary anatomies that litter the floor. She wraps herself around me tightly as we move through the ship to the central stowage compartment hall-way. I set her down on her feet while I open up a few cupboards, to look for something appropriate for her to wear and to help her bathe. I notice that she's staring down at her feet, purple toes. I expect her to freak out or faint or scream at the insanity of her situation, but she just stands there contemplating her odd existence.

I don't know why I would assume to find garments that aren't meant for a one-point-nine meter adult sized synthetic humanoid; definitely no 'kid's section'. She looks up at me, shaking her head, and grabs one tunic and one cloak that I have draped over my arm. I shove the rest back in the bin and turn to see how she is going to make this work, but she sticks out a skinny lavender arm from the bundle of glittering brown and gold material and spirals her index finger in the air, ordering me turn to around. Well, okay, I'll wait while staring at the wall.

"Man Chair," Wisdom says. I don't get it.

After a few minutes, I hear some sounds of tearing fabric and muffled grumbles. It would seem that she has her own List of Moderate Arabic Expletives. But she's obviously making some progress while she kneels on the floor, attempting to modify the clothes four times her size. Wisdom offers up a suggestion, so I reach into a pocket and stretch down behind me to hand her a Multi-hexic ElectroBinder. She grabs it and flips through the assorted tools within, then goes right to work on the material, to saw or slice or laser it to the correct dimensions for a short, skinny human girl.

"Jove," she says from behind and below, "what's that sound I hear all the time?"

"Can you describe it?" I ask. I note that she's using only English now.

"Um…yeah, I think so." She tries to contemplate something new to describe something new. "I guess it sounds like rushing water, or maybe a fountain in my head."

"Oh, yes." I reply. "That's the sound of the SynThinker, your new brain, as it absorbs the data stream from the Knowledgebase. Since you're brand new, there's a lot to download. It can be a little distracting sometimes, that rushing water sound. You'll get used to it."

She works away at the tough material, measuring and cutting.

"Am I dead?"

"Oh, no." I tell her. "Not in the slightest. You're very much alive." I decide not to tell her too much, just answer questions as they come.

I feel a tug on the back of my tunic. She's standing there with her arms out, showing off her handiwork. The bottom half of a Union tunic is now an ankle-length dress, covered by a bunched-up and overflowing top half of a hooded cloak. A wide strip cut from the top of the tunic is now a sash running a few times around her waist, with a huge knot bulging out in the front. One arm is chopped off a bit shorter than the other, which gives the whole outfit a bit of a comical flare, but overall, she did a commendable job.

I bend down on one knee so I can look her in the eye again. "I'm sorry that you missed seeing France, Italy and Greece."

Her eyes grow wide as she dizzily trips over her own foot, spinning to the floor and landing on her bottom.

"Whoa!" she says.

I try to catch her by the shoulder, but end up pulling the cloak around her head instead. With her face buried in the twisted hood, she puffs out some air from inflated cheeks.

"Never mind," she says, "I think I just went there myself!"

The Knowledgebase at work, I presume. "What'd you see?"

She pulls the hood away from her soft purple face, and stares up at me with a look of sheer astonishment.

"Uh…all of France, Italy and Greece, I think!" Her eyebrows high, she blinks a few times to clear the lightheadedness from her instantaneous trip across Europe. "What's with the enormous statues of that guy, King David? Can't someone get him any underwear?"

For the time being, she's still an innocent child. But as I stand here gazing upon this fresh little life, completely unique from every other creature in this galaxy, I can't help but wonder how this is all going to work. When I found her dying, it was all too easy to just force my will upon the Mission Steward, to 'save her'. Sure, I saved her *from* death, but I saved her *to what*? What will this life be? What future will it bring? Can I even take her back to her previous family? Of course not! The humans will likely not accept her anymore. As a Union clone, she—well, she's not a Brother, that's for sure. Can we have a Sister? She's singular. Is she a One or an Only?

"Are we going to just stand here," she says, her little head bent up, "or are we going to get some breakfast?"

Skinned in brown, blue or purple, she's just a kid, and it would appear that I'm a Dad.

Note to Self

There's a good price break on Mercurochrome at fifty-five gallons, but it's damned hard to pour into a coffee mug.

Jove

Pain
2044 CE
Earth

It's mid-morning by anyone's clock on the east coast of Africa. After saying our goodbyes to the Mission Steward, the Equus takes us westward. I use the time to help Elmyrah learn about herself and the Manufactured Flesh and SynThinker Union, her new family. (Boy won't *they* be surprised!) I explain to her how my Jove Number This or That works and not to be afraid if, for some reason, I need to move on to the next me. I promise her that I'll never leave her, though things may get complicated.

We fly into Nairobi where I remembered stopping for something to eat with Zaris, Damien and Sir Edward last time – Hashmi's Restaurant. Perhaps the limousine was more appropriate, as the Equus takes up all of the empty parking on both sides of this street and part of the next. Sorry about the trees. As this is my first chance to take my daughter out for lunch, I want it to be a pleasant dining experience. Shortly after we enter the establishment, everyone else leaves through the fire exits. I can't detect a fire, so I perceive they're in error.

With the kitchen staff hiding behind the dumpsters, Elmyrah and I take it upon ourselves to grab some to-go boxes of curried Chicken Chooza. She stirs her finger around in it and then licks clean every drop of the devilish stew from her digit. Her wide grin tells me that we made an excellent choice for our initial adventure into continental cuisine. I hope it doesn't melt any of her newly installed internals.

As we made our exit of Hashmi's to head back out to the Equus, Elmyrah is trying to balance too many boxes of hot, dripping food, and one falls to land hard in the dirt, bursting open. A dozen flies appear in an instant to investigate. Her face is a pallet of emotions.

I grab the Brownie camera from a pocket and snap a quick photo. It would be many years later before I could have the film developed, to see who it really was that was looking back at me that day. It seems, in the scrapbook I keep, there are more than memories.

With a rest stop on the way up to western Europe, the northwest coastline of Lake Chad places us about eighty kilometers from the nearest human settlement, and that's just a small group of four mud huts. I need to effect repairs on the bottom of the ship where the damage from the bullet allowed the air to escape.

No one's out and about in the heat of an African afternoon except Clone Guy and Hybrid Girl, welding up holes in their spaceship and tossing out the rotted remains of Marisol Tonuay. The shade of the cutter's fuselage, the cool breeze coming off the desert lake, and the hungry vultures circling overhead make the whole experience even better. I can truly say that I'm enjoying myself.

Elmyrah is asleep when we arrive in the dark of night in Geneva, Switzerland. It's just as well, as there are some phone calls to make. The first is to my indebted pal, Damien.

"Jove!" he answers. "What's going on? Moshe Samuelsson came by to say goodbye to Miss al-Otaibi, but no one could tell him where she was or for that matter, where Marisol Tonuay is either. I called the airline and they missed their flight."

"I have some disturbing news," I say. "During the flight on the Equus, there was a catastrophic failure of an outer hatch, due to damage caused by the small-arms fire at the Seychelles Airport. Miss Tonuay and the young girl were lost."

"Wow, Jove. I don't know what to say. How can I help?"

"Well, Damien, I'm glad you asked. Although this is a tragic personal loss for the two females and their families, we cannot allow this single incident to blemish the otherwise immeasurable greatness of recent achievements of the world powers, in finding the Pathway to Peace. I'm sure you agree, yes?"

"Oh...um...y-y-yes, of course, I understand completely."

"What's best is for those of us living to get on with our lives, you know; to put this most unfortunate and heartrending event behind us, so that we can look forward to the joyful days ahead for the nations of the Earth. Together, let's you and I manage this so that those who may grieve can find closure as soon as possible."

"Alright, yes, that makes sense." Damien says.

Knowledgebase gives me a quick lesson in the policy and politics of aviation accident investigation. "Damien, the most important thing is for there to be a clear separation between the work that all of us have accomplished toward world peace, those of us involved in that endeavor along with our reputations, and the terrible accident that might've left two people forever...undiscovered. I mean, how prominent and newsworthy it would be for there to be human fatalities aboard an alien spacecraft, but how commonplace for one of those small private planes to go missing, especially over the open water."

"I can see what you mean," he says. "It would certainly be easier for everyone to accept, and… like you say, 'find closure', especially her parents."

"Her parents?" I bristle at the thought of someone laying claim to her. My SynThinker hisses momentarily as the remedy for my discomfort is prepared. "About that, it turns out that the two people posing as her father and mother are actually subversives to the peace of the planet. They've sought to overthrow their leadership before and are planning to do it again. It would be a terrible thing if they were allowed to succeed in endangering the Pathway to Peace."

"That can be handled," Damien says. "And her brother in her hometown; he'll be looking for her, too."

"Good thinking, no doubt he's been informed of the release of the imposters and has joined them in the conspiracy."

Damien catches on fast. "My sources tell me that he's lived a troubled life of violence, with reports of thievery and murder. Perhaps a life of crime will be his undoing."

"I trust you completely, Damien. Let's work towards finality on that subject."

"… and for the missing women?"

"If I was headed from Paris to southern Italy," I say, "I might find myself flying over the Ligurian Sea, which reaches a depth of almost twenty-nine hundred meters."

Three days later, I'm in the New York office of UN Secretary-General Sir Dwight Ward-Howard discussing the recent tragedy of his executive assistant and her guest, which by all accounts had plummeted to their certain deaths into the waters west of Livorno, Italy. It was decided that due to the depth of the ocean north of the Island of Corsica, no rescue operations would be conducted.

"Mister Secretary," I say, leaning forward against his desk, "it's time for the nations to take the next step along the Path. At no other time, since the beginning of recorded history, has your beautiful Earth enjoyed this level of non-violence and benevolence."

"I agree, Jove," Dwight says, "It is unbelievable what you have done. The United States is back together again. All of Africa is at rest, as never before. The Middle East is well on their way to forming an all-encompassing nation called by its ancient name, Levant. It is all truly remarkable, Jove. You said you could do this and you did."

This time, I lean forward against his mind. "Then let's bring this miracle to fruition by removing all of the nuclear and other destructive devices now. You will not have lasting peace without disarmament. There's too much of a risk that a single evil mind could get their hands on even the last one, to perform some diabolical act, damaging the tranquility that you all have worked so hard to achieve."

"During our previous attempts at reducing the nuclear arsenal," he says, "we could only disassemble a few hundred per year, once the safety and regulatory requirements were met."

"That delay is no longer necessary," I say. I stand straight and give him a wink, "An atomic bomb is only a danger while it's on Earth. But once cast into the mighty furnace of your Sun, even were one to explode, it'll be like a drop in the ocean. We'll gather them all together in the giant ship, Emrah, that brought me here, and they'll be transported en mass to an orbit around your star. We'll release them in a steady stream until the hold is empty and the threat to mankind is abolished."

"Are you serious?" he asks, "It's really that simple? Just load them up and fly them away?"

The reality of all this is sinking into Dwight. He could be the one in the big chair when the planet was saved from utter self-destruction. This could work. This is going to work. I can see him talking himself through it. No regulations, no costly inspections, no delays; this is going to happen now, on his watch. This will be his crowning achievement.

"How are we going to get them all to your ship?"

"Just make contact with the nations that have the most to lose, Mister Secretary," I say, "and inform them that they're to give complete clearance to and cooperation with your Peacekeepers. Have them disconnect the bombs and missiles from their launch bays and deliver them intact to ships that we'll have waiting in the major coastal cities. We can use the old military naval bases and ships that are already operating with minimal crews. Once the ships reach Emrah, our own internal control systems will take over from there. We have special equipment that can literally pull the bombs from the decks of your ocean going vessels and secure them for the final act of complete destruction."

I need to handle his mind with care, and my tongue, too, I think. Dwight's an intelligent man and wise. He has a strong mind. It can be difficult to control him when he starts soul-searching. I can hear his thoughts. "…this is too good to be true..."

"I want you to know, Dwight," I say, turning his mind away from the demands of accountability, "I have informed the Jovians, the Knowers, about how you and every other human have embraced this opportunity to join them, to usher in peace throughout your star system. They're so proud of you. They asked me to tell you that."

Dwight just sits there nodding with a silly grin on his face. I move him from contemplating his future success to collaboration and collusion.

"Now, Mister Secretary, there's much work ahead of us, and we cannot do it alone. We will need someone that has knowledge of seamanship, weaponry and experience with authority. Someone we can trust to get the job done." I'll let him believe it's his idea.

Dwight rubs his chin, pretending to ruminate, but I know the answer is already planted in his mind and merely requires that he speak it forth. "I agree, Jove, I agree. What about that fellow from Queensland? He's in her Royal Australian Navy, or what's left of it nowadays - Captain Mark Thomas, I believe?

"Yes, Captain Thomas."

"Do you believe he'd be willing to give it a go?" Dwight asks.

With a strange fondness for Mister Thomas, I can't help but want to see him succeed.

"I feel that I owe a debt of gratitude to him," I say. "I can't imagine a better way to repay him than to assist in his transition from a now meaningless military position, to help manage what will be a monumental achievement for his entire race."

"It's settled, then. I'll give him a bell, right off."

"Thank you, Mister Secretary," I say as I shake his hand. Then as I turn to leave, "I promised to do lunch with a new friend today, so I'd better get moving. She gets grumpy on an empty stomach."

Elmyrah has had all the Chicken Chooza she can stand. My promise was to find something more substantial that we could keep on board the Equus for her to consume, so I contact the maître d' of the hotel next door to see about a delivery of two of everything from their room service menu. When Zaris gets her credit card bill, she'll think I bought a small cafeteria.

There's nothing better than to hear Elmyrah squeal with delight as I personally cart dozens of entrées and desserts from the trunk of a limousine and up the ramp into the stern of the ship. After she picks out her choice for today's meal, we store the rest in the chilled locker.

At Wisdom's suggestion, I spread out a large blue and white checkered tablecloth on the soft green lawn under the shade trees of Saint Varten's Park, down the street from the temporary headquarters of the United Nations. Damien has provided a handful of bodyguards to help maintain a secure perimeter for me while I'm in the city, and I have them busy clearing the park of anyone who might wander by the two extraterrestrials having a picnic lunch of bacon, lettuce and tomato on rye with mayo, washed down with a liter of Mercurochrome. My new daughter teaches me 'See Food', and then sticks out her *very* orange tongue - awesome.

I've searched every corner of the immense Union Knowledge-base; there's no mention anywhere of a clone or Brother describing the wonderful experiences that I'm blessed with every day since meeting Elmyrah al-Otaibi. There're no fathers or mothers or children on Sirius Three, not anymore. Only distant memories and tattered recordings remain of a day before the white dwarf companion star swung wide and ripped away the pink sky and yellow clouds. No more parents to walk their children to school, no more children playing Wasp-a-lot in the flowering fields. All that remains of that once thriving civilization are the ruins and artifacts left behind by the dead.

"Jove, what're you thinking about?" Elmyrah asks, around a big bite of dill pickle. Her left eyelid is involuntarily squinted against the twinge of sour vinegar.

I'm laying comfortably on my back, hands behind my head, looking for random shapes in the puffy white clouds against a marvelous blue sky of The Pearl. Jupiter certainly has nothing like this, I think. Oh, it has clouds, the whole planet is clouds! But there's no vantage point like this from which to observe them. Not unless you want to listen to a fuel-use warning alarm pitching a fit.

"I'm thinking about how much I like this place," I say, as much to myself as in response to her question. This is so peaceful here, so quiet. For once, I find my mind at rest.

She looks around at the trees, sport fields and playground. "It is very nice. I've never been to a real park before. Well, there was a 'park' in Riyadh," she says, using finger quotes, "but the dunes had overtaken the retaining walls and covered everything up. I could just see the top bar of the swing set. It came up to my knees. That wasn't much fun, I can tell you. What're you smiling at?"

"I meant 'this place' – your planet – Earth. I'm not from around here, you know."

She laughs so hard a piece of pickle flies out of her mouth. She snorts and laughs even harder. "Yeah, I could tell. Your accent is a dead giveaway. What are you, a Texan?" She leans her head back, chin to the sky, and laughs till she has to wipe tears from the corners of her eyes – my eyes. How fantastic that is.

"You know what I like?" she asks.

"What do you like, Miss al-Otaibi?"

"I like having an improved vocabulary," she says, her head resting on her little shoulder. "I find myself enjoying a whole new list of words to choose from. I feel...*manumitted*." She looks at me with such confidence and self-awareness. "Now, why would I know that?"

"Because you're so much more today than you could've ever been a week ago."

"And what am I, Jove?" she asks, now with one corner of her mouth turning down, quivering, "cuz I'm not a person anymore, and I'm not really one of you guys." She runs out of words to describe the deep feelings. Her galactic vocabulary fails already.

"You are *so much* a person!" I say, though her own inner struggle resonates within me. "My dear, there're people everywhere throughout the known realm of space; as far as any ship can reach, there are people! You aren't some oddity. You're a treasure! You're unique among many trillions of individuals. Elmyrah *al-Otaibi* was an Only before; she's still—"

"You know what I mean!" she says, "…not a human…not anymore."

"No?" I say, brow lifted inquisitively.

"No," she says, brow furrowed in defiance.

"How's that B.L.T?" I ask.

She leans herself over towards me with a bit of overacting.

"What?"

"You heard me. I can't eat one of those. It smells terrific, but I'll never be able to ingest that sandwich. I'm not human. I'm merely a conscious awareness, in a crunchy shell with a chewy center. I'm a copy of a copy of something that sort of copied a humanoid that existed over five thousand years ago on a faraway planet that was swept clean and lifeless by a stellar storm. With the help of Knowledgebase and the autogenic manipulator, I can transform myself into practically anything. But, I can never eat that sandwich. Because, I am not, and never will be, a human. But you, my sweet girl, are so very human; right down to the tummy that can redirect sodium mercurescein to your manufactured, plasmocellular splenic hilium, but send the bacon to your colon."

"—and Bob's yer Uncle," she says.

"Exactly!"

"I'm guessing it's a little more complicated than *that*," she says.

"Why yes, of course it is complicated," I say, "but listen to me, and take it from someone who understands fully what it means to exist apart from the physicality; I am Jove. And *I am*, apart from this body that I inhabit today. Who I am – the value of my being – is worth more than the assemblage of organs and structure and programming. And who I am is best measured by what I will do for the sake of others, throughout my lifetime…or lifetimes, if you will. I've 'died' six times. Let's say it only took one death to be the end of Jove. Then all I would have done – all the things Two-Three-Four-Five-Six and Seven *have done* – would have *never* happened. It's our actions…our efforts of goodwill that define us, not our flesh and blood."

"Is that today's philosophy lesson? That I was supposed to be transformed into this, because of some future contribution to society? Am I going to help an old lady cross the street; save a cat from a tree? Will I discover the cure for cancer? Don't get me wrong – I appreciate not having to pull my next meal out of some garbage can in scenic Al-Zulfi. But I'm afraid it doesn't answer the real question – *why*?"

"Why what?"

"Why *everything*!?"

Her inquisitive child-mind is digging through every mound of information in the Knowledgebase, in search of the answer to the question that's plagued us all since the dawn of time. And she expects to find it there. She won't. No one ever has.

"I forgot to introduce you to someone," I tell her, realizing my error.

"I thought we're hiding me from the civilized world."

I pat her on the shoulder. "I'm sorry that things have to be this way for now. I promise you that very soon you will—"

"Please don't promise me something you can't control."

"I care about you, Elmyrah. I don't want you to get hurt." That sounds stupid, all things considered.

She lets out a long sigh. "My butt's getting sore and the gnats have found my nose. Can we get going?"

"Sure."

"Jove?" she says as she reaches to hold my hand. "I don't want to go back to Al-Zulfi. As strange as this may sound, these few days with you have been the best of my life so far. I am freaking out a little. But really, this is as close to my dreams as I can imagine reality could get, you know?"

We stop. I turn and kneel down to get eye level with my perfect girl. "As long as I exist, you'll never be alone. Your home is where I am."

Her smile is all the answer I need. We stroll through the shade and get ourselves into the back of the stretch limo on loan to us from the U.N.

"So, where're we going to meet who?" she says, hands folded neatly on her lap.

I hold up a finger to wait a second while I bend backward to direct the chauffeur. "Driver, take us to the Equus." As the car falls in line between the two black SUVs full of muscle and guns, I lean back into the pile of pillows that has replaced the middle seat.

Using the intramental node within me, I call to Elmyrah through the gateway to her own SynThinker. "I am here. Meet with me inside."

"Where're we going this time? Are you going to show me Sirius Three again?"

"No...well...that depends on where she takes us," I think.

"Who are you talking about? Who is *she*?"

"Wisdom – that's who I meant to introduce you to, but you already know her."

Our minds swirl together like columns of mist wafting up from two springs in a cool forest, as we join in a hallucination, as prepared by Wisdom.

Our Shared Vision

The forest is not cool, nor is it green. It is red and very hot. Elmyrah is here with me, I know, but we're not sure where *here* is. We don't recognize anything about the view from...from where? This vision is very different from the others. I'd hoped to lead my daughter on some fanciful, though educational escapade in a...nicer place than this. This place is awful.

"Wisdom! Where are we? Where did you bring us?" I ask into the thick, red fluid.

"Elmyrah has asked why," Wisdom says, "I've brought you here to show her."

"Show her what?" `

"Why." Wisdom says. Either that's cryptic or I'm a dullard.

I look around for my daughter, but she's beyond my range of sight.

"M'rah? Are you there?"

"Yes, I'm right here," she responds. "Why did you call me that? My brother used to call me that."

I don't know, really. "I don't know. I thought of you and that's the word that came out. Are you alright? I can't see you."

"I'm frightened, but I'm okay, I think," she says, "and I can see you. You're all around me; everywhere under me. You are my… house…or maybe where I live…somehow."

"Can you describe what I look like to you?"

"Um…yes…you are…this is weird. It feels like I am looking into a mirror, but I know it's not me. Does that make sense? So, anyway, there're five of you. Or, you are in five places with me. Oh, wait! I get it now. You are a sea star! Aaaaand…I am a sea star! I'm sort of riding on your…*in* your…back, I guess? This is so…I dunno…weird, just weird."

"Are you injured? Are you okay?" I just asked her that. My concern for her well-being borders on paranoia sometimes - parenthood, rearing its ugly head.

"I do feel…a little nauseated," she says, "and out of breath (but I'm not breathing, so) and…sick. I feel sick. This place is doing it. There's something in the air, if this is air. It makes me want to get away, but I have no place else to get away to. It's everywhere."

I'm starting to get bothered by this experience. This isn't what I wanted. All I wanted to do was to show Elmyrah how things are; show her what the world is about.

"But she asked *why*, Jove," Wisdom says, bothering me with her logic and clarity.

"Okay, okay! You win. Show us why, then. Tell me what to do."

"You are moving in a direction. Keep going. There's something in your grasp. Do not let go of it."

More weirdness from my virtual mentor, who by the way, is acting more strange every time we interact.

We are moving, but very, very slowly. I guess sea stars do that. Wait. What did Elmyrah say? She said she was a sea star on top of another sea star. We're moving through a blood red liquid; crawling along the bottom of a rocky, calcified ocean floor. Ohhh, please tell me we are not—

"You are Prawl-Tang," Wisdom informs me.

I told you not to tell me. "Why did you make us Prawl-Tang?!"

"Just keep moving and I will show you the why."

"We are a what?" Elmyrah asks. "What's a Prawl-Tang?"

Ugh. I suppose she had to find out sooner or later. "The Prawl-Tang are a sentient species that come from a star system very far from Earth. They're ruthless, ravenous, hell-bent on gathering every last trace of hydrogen within their reach. They can't be reasoned with...well, no one ever did before—not before we—they want their way and they kill everyone and everything to get it!"

Silence. I hate it when she's silent.

The sharp rocks and coral underneath me are scratchy and make for slow going. I feel sick, too. I understand what she means now. The atmosphere is polluted. Assuming I have an olfactory organ, the air is really bad, dangerously bad. It almost burns as it goes through me. Breathing does more harm than good. To hold my breath is apparently not an option.

Finally, Elmyrah speaks up, in my mind anyway. "In this - our shared dream – you and I are this combined monster from another place in the galaxy. And we're on its world."

"I believe that's our dream, yes," I tell her. "Do you want to get out of this?"

She ignores me. "We…it's in mourning. Can you feel the soul, Jove? The Prawl-Tang, its soul is in pain…heartbroken. Can you feel it?"

I don't want to feel the soul of this monster. Why would anyone want to touch the heart of these murderous creatures? I just want to get where we're going so we can learn this lesson and get back to reality.

"She feels it, Jove." Wisdom says.

What? I must've left my SynThinker in the limo. "What are you talking about?"

"She can feel the why."

How did I get stuck with the bottom half? The mind of this one is like an ox. I keep whacking it but the plodding synapses are at full speed already.

The air gets worse. It smells like poison. My muscles cramp. I struggle against the urge to stop and turn around. I can feel Elmyrah above me, coaxing, soothing me; she presses me onward toward some place even less desirable than where we are. What possible good can come from inching our way further into this dark evil?

"Jove, we're here," Elmyrah tells me. She knows?

"Where's here? I can't see any difference."

"This is a horrible, tearful place," she says, "and now I see."

Who's bringing grief to my little girl? What's wrong?

"Have him turn around, Elmyrah. It's time."

"Jove, turn around. You're holding something behind you in your rear-facing arm. Turn around and let her go. Let her go, Jove." Elmyrah tries to hold herself together. I can feel almost nothing from this beast I've possessed, but I can certainly feel her pain; the heartbreak she spoke of within.

Like an instinctual brute, my body rotates around so that what was my rear arm is now in front. I move to the edge of an abyss. My visual sensors over the cliff, I'm able to see down into the chasm – bodies, skeletonized bodies everywhere - all infants. As far to the right and left as I can see, this canyon under the sulfuric sea is filled with the boney remains of Prawl-Tang babies. Thousands upon thousands of tiny five-legged stars; rotting, dissolving, melting into each other. This is one of the most horrid sights I could've ever imagined.

"Let her go, Jove, please." Elmyrah begs.

Let who go? What's she talking about?

"Open your arm, let her go."

I can feel the solid mass within my grasp, but my incredulity is a rigor. The rage within me is rising up, boiling over. It pushes forth a scream but I have no voice. A surge of adrenaline courses through me, down my five arms and against the rocks. The coral crushes and splinters below. With every ounce of mental strength, I unfurl the coiled end of my arm over the edge of the precipice.

With what eyes I have on this creature, I watch the body of my child as it falls away into the depths, to join the others left by their parents. Her shell is shriveled and twisted; poisoned by the same fiery chemical that we can taste running through us – oxygen. Like a leaf in a flittery fall from a high tree-branch, the offspring of this Prawl-Tang drifts and spirals down into the deep blood of this sick ocean, to find rest among the other contaminated children of this mournful planet.

Elmyrah's part, the exosymbiote, is consumed with grief. She's part of me. We're bound together at the cellular level; our corporeal beings inseparably welded. Hearts beating together, our conjoined fears for our child have come true. We've lost her to the poison. She's gone forever.

All strength flows out of me. I turn to stone, as hard and unforgiving as the reef upon which we build our existence. Our future is a wasteland of suffering and tears.

This isn't just a planet of monsters. This is a polluted world, their liquid atmosphere too far gone, poisoned, killing them off. I want out of this dream, this nightmare.

"First, she must know the why," Wisdom demands.

"Why?" I say, "Why did you bring us to this evil place to torment us with this…this—"

"Does not truth exist in the presence of good and evil?" Wisdom asks.

I don't want to know. Even if that's true, I don't want to know. I just want away from here.

Then, I hear Elmyrah's voice. She sounds distant, around some bend.

"Truth exists in spite of good or evil."

"Go on," Wisdom tells her.

Elmyrah dives deep into her own soul to find the answer. "Good is a rock to cling to. Evil is a lake of fire. Neither can fly above. They are forever held fast by the weight of their own selfishness."

Wisdom presses her to find more answers for herself. "But which is better, to choose good or evil, or to climb the ladder of truth; to trade your innocence for the knowledge of both?"

"To kill is wrong," Elmyrah states. "To kill to save another is righteous. But the truth is, only life itself matters, and death itself has no power over life. They're not opposites. They are states of being. Only Love can exist in both states. Love gives life. Love kills.

That is the most desirable state."

"Jove saved you from death – why?"

"Because I am his child that could never be," the little girl says.

"The Prawl-Tang have murdered tens of millions and destroyed many worlds. Why?" Wisdom asks.

"Because they're trying to save the children they love," Elmyrah says.

"…and is this good or evil?" Asks the Wisdom of every world, of the child.

"It is Truth," says the tiny Arab girl with lavender hues, as she curls herself into a ball, to fall asleep on the wide leather seat of the Cadillac.

End Vision

My head lifted off the pillows, I turn to look out the windshield of the car. We've only driven about fifty meters from the park - good. She'll get a nap on the way to the Equus. It's a long flight across the Atlantic and then central Africa to get to our next destination – Emrah.

I have some questions for the Mission Steward, and I expect to hear the truth.

Note to Self

Wisdom is not making any sense. She's…delusional?

I'm considering that I may have to shut the program down.

Jove

Wisdom
2044 CE
Mascarene Plateau, Earth

I guess she woke up in a mischievous mood. Boredom will do that. Elmyrah comes up to the bridge and pokes me in the…where ribs would be. "I finished my dinner and dessert. May I have a snack, please?"

I look down at her from the pilot's bama, in astonishment. "Where does it go?" I ask. Seriously, where could someone who weighs all of twenty-three kilograms put that much food? I honestly believe that the energy derived from the first half of the meal is necessary to consume and digest the second half of the pile. Crumbs from her cherry-cheesecake-graham-cracker pie are balanced precariously on her small purple lip. The milk mustache is icing on the cake, so to speak. I find it nearly impossible to say no to her.

A long tress of cloud whips past the glass canopy, her attention now caught away from plans to launch another raid on the pantry.

"Where are we?" she asks.

"In a space ship," quips Clone Guy. The left side of her cloak's hood moves almost imperceptibly. That would be from pressure exerted by a tensed jaw muscle. She's not amused.

Well okay, then. "We're cruising," I say, "at an altitude of eighty-two thousand meters, at Mach Four. Our coordinates put us directly over where Ethiopia juts into South Sudan. Soon we'll cross into Kenya, where we need to slow down and begin our decent and change heading to line us up for the approach to the Seychelles."

"Let's fly over that stupid Hashmi's Restaurant at Mach Fifty and break all their windows."

That would be rude. "Uh…no, we aren't going to do that."

"I want to fly the ship," she says. She turns and skips over to the control panel.

"You can't just say you want to fly the ship and take over," I tell her. "It's a very complex system and requires a special skills progr—"

"Yes, I know. It's Advanced Pilotage. I have that, too, of course."

I suppose she would. She has my brain.

"Well," I say, "we have to be very careful because your body isn't capable of withstanding the forces generated by—"

Without another word, she leans over the console and enters in coordinates for Nairobi, but at thirty meters above ground level, then switches on the auto-nav. In an instant, the Equus keels over hard to the left. She's slammed to the floor with a thud. The nose of the cutter yaws around and down steeply, to make straight for the city far below. I pull back on the pitch control slide, but the auto-nav ignores the input. Our airspeed has already increased to fourteen-hundred meters per second. Very soon, the dense air at the lower altitudes will slam against the bow of the ship. I reach over to the console and press the button to deactivate the auto-nav.

"Bong!" announces the ship. "This control system has been locked. Only Princess Elmyrah al-Otaibi or an administrator can unlock the system. Please enter the correct pass-code."

I glare over at her. "This ship is not your toy. Unlock the controls immediately."

Her smile fades to a high-stakes poker face. The airspeed indicator passes Mach Five. A handful of yellow indicators light up across the board.

"Elmyrah, tell me the passcode, now."

She looks up at me from where she reclines on the floor. "No."

"Listen to me! When you entered the heading, you forgot to throttle back for the dive. The ship is going to be damaged if we don't slow down. Now tell me the pass-code." I can't even put out the air-brakes to stop the acceleration. A loud thump, accompanied by a heavy blow against the fuselage, signals our passing through the stratopause. That was just a speed bump compared to what the tropopause will do to us. That'll be hitting the cow. The roar from the torrent outside is such that I have to raise my voice to hear myself.

"Elmyrah! You stop this behavior right this instant!"

Turning her face to the kick-panel of the console, she folds her arms across her chest and crosses her knees, dangling one foot in the air without a care to be had.

Boom! - Mach Six. The ship shakes hard as the temperature drops outside.

I've had enough of this. "Jove calls to Navigation Onus," I think into my mind's doorway.

"Navigation Onus is secure-linked to external contact Jove," it replies.

"Navigation Onus to unlock Equus flight controls," I command.

"Passcode required."

"Override."

"Override not accepted," it says. "Decryption sequence initiated. Pass-code decrypted. Pass-code entered. Flight controls unlocked."

"Change passcode to…" I look at Elmyrah, who is red-faced over a lavender background, "to…" I think she's listening to this conversation in my head, "to…my previous description of you, that you misinterpreted as a directive."

"Pass-code changed."

"Reduce throttle to ten percent and bring pitch to level; zed equals plus three geez maximum."

"Velocity stabilizing," it says. "Attitude stabilizing."

"That's *not fair!*" Elmyrah screams. "You *cheated!*"

On her feet, she slams her fist down onto the edge of the control panel, slicing the flesh on the heel of her palm. She stomps her way to the rear of the bridge platform, ignores the steps and drops herself down the two meters to the lower level at the back of the space. With another slap on the wall mounted hatch control plate, she ducks swiftly through the half open door, still in a rage. A vertical puddle of bluish-chrome polymercuricoids drizzles down the wall to the floor.

I'm aghast at the site of my child's blood. I've seen a lot of blood before. It shouldn't bother me like this. I want to tear my way through the barrier of time and go back to before she injured herself. Nothing less will satisfy these emotions within my…my… what?…where are these feelings coming from? This entire situation is ludicrous. She can't do this! She's supposed to listen to me. I'm in charge. It's my responsibility to care for her in every way. She has to let me! How in blue blazes did she coerce the auto-nav to lock me out? The ship *has* to respond to *my* commands; it was programmed by Trayd for me alone! This kid must have Knowledgebase tied around her little finger.

With the ship set for a gentle glide to the Super Scoop, I head back to find my temperamental co-pilot. She managed to locate the Biologic Repair Module in the back of the ship, and sits cross-legged on the floor with an enormous ball of rolled gauze wrapped a jillion times around her tiny hand. The tape won't stick and the end is falling loose. Staring at her lap, she holds the arm and injured hand raised high over her head.

"I have to hold this up for six weeks or I'll bleed to death," she tells me.

"That sounds about right," I say, my straight face long gone. "Did you read that in the Biologic Repair Module instructions on how to fix a person's lacerated hand?"

"No, I already know all that kinda stuff. I'm a super genius now."

Yes, my girl, you very likely are a super genius, I think.

In a voice so low, I strain to hear her. "You hate me now, huh."

"Oh, no! No, no, no, no. I can't hate you. I love you. You're my absolute favorite alien-clone-human-hybrid-daughter ever," I say.

She won't look up, but I can tell she cracks a smile. "I'm your only daughter, Dummy."

With the utmost care, I set her woven white bowling ball on my lap.

"I bet this hurts."

"It does," she says, "but it feels good, too. I mean, this body is so numb all the time. I feel like a big squishy balloon bouncing around with mega-eyes on top. Even when I swallow food, I can't feel it going down. So, after I eat, I go into the bathroom and jump up and down a bunch to make sure it falls all the way in."

"That makes perfect sense," I say. I clench my teeth against a snicker. "Can I look at it, at your hand?"

"No, it'll explode silver slime all over. It's totally gross. I threw up when I saw it, by the way," she confesses. "There's a sidewalk pizza in the corner by the door."

"More of your improved vocabulary?" I ask, rotating my head around to spot the big spot.

She shakes her head in contempt of it all.

"Chicken Marsala and breadsticks."

I give an understanding nod. She really likes Chicken Marsala.

Out of nowhere, she asks, "Now that I have your kind of blood in me, is it okay if I call you Daddy? Cuz, I don't have anyone else that would understand this." With that she falls over onto my chest and cries for the longest time.

"You call me Daddy because that's what I am."

With the very slightest bump, the Navigation Onus lands the Equus directly on top of the Super Scoop. Elmyrah's asleep on a pile of pillows that we borrowed from the limousine. I check on her and find that the sound of her slow deep breaths touches something in me. There's an odd satisfaction to a child's peaceful slumber.

I move through the ventral hatch and prepare to exit the ship, when I receive an unexpected intramental message.

"Jove, there is something I need to discuss with you," Wisdom tells me.

"Sure," I reply as I work my way down the ladder. "What's up?"

"You will be receiving the initial deliveries of the nuclear weapons today."

"Yes, I believe that is correct," I say.

"You've said that once you have them all in the Prawl-Tang vessel, you're planning to fly to their star and launch them into it for destruction of the radioactive material."

"Yes, that's the plan – why?" I ask.

"Don't you see that as a waste of valuable resources?"

I'm intrigued by this sudden interest. "You sound more like the Mission Steward."

"I just want you to think this through carefully, Jove," Wisdom says. "Is that really the best use of such immense power? Are you sure there isn't some way to benefit others by not destroying them?"

"I liked you better when we agreed that you couldn't ask questions."

"I understand completely, you know. I'm only here to help you. I only wish to keep you from second guessing yourself."

Well, that's exactly what you are doing, I think. I thought this was all worked out.

"Don't forget about the Knowers back on Jupiter," Wisdom reminds me.

"What about them?"

"They're counting on you."

"I'm aware of that," I say. "That's the point of this whole ridiculous mission... to save them."

Wisdom is leading me somewhere. But do I want to end up there?

"Yes," Wisdom says, "to save them from the Prawl-Tang."

"Of course – the Mission Steward has made a bargain to trade the Earth for Jupiter, remember? I think you were part of that crazy idea." I'm thinking Wisdom is experiencing a failure.

"Did he, really?"

"Yes, I didn't get it ink on paper, but that was the gist of it."

"Maybe you should have," Wisdom says.

"What do you mean by that?" I ask. I get off the last rung of the ladder and walk to where the ocean waves are breaking against the chitinous, orange, red and white hull of the Scoop.

"The Prawl-Tang have broken agreements before with others. They do what's in their best interest. What did the Mission Steward agree to, exactly?" Wisdom seems to be almost interrogating me about this.

"Okay, you tell me. What did he agree to, exactly?"

"If I may quote the Mission Steward during the negotiations, 'I am not opposed to redirecting $\Omega94\lambda25\theta$ operations from PB5 to PB3'," Wisdom repeats verbatim, "and 'If the resources are polluted or are of low grade or are contaminated or are unnecessarily non-compliant in the extrication, so as to negatively bend the threshold of harvest profit to less than three hundred percent, the agreement is null and void.'"

I know that Wisdom's trying to clue me in about something. If only she would just get to the point.

"That was the agreement," I say, "Earth, not Jupiter."

"*Redirect*, Jove – not abandon, not cancel, not terminate the mission there. Remember, he said that the Omega Species had claimed PB5 *as their own*. He never said anything about rescinding that claim. What's to keep him or any other Prawl-Tang from going back after they're done wiping out the human race?"

"He won't," I tell myself.

Wisdom picks up with the Mission Steward's recorded diatribe, "…and he also said, '…these are standard terms; there is no agreement without them. Continuing, if there exists extraneous objects that interfere with operational efficiency, the cost of eradication shall be deducted from the harvest balance.' The way I hear it, if he can find any reason whatsoever to be dissatisfied with the outcome, he gets to go back to Jupiter anyway, and make up the difference for the perceived loss in efficiency. Is that not how you understand it, Jove?"

"I got around that," I shoot back. "He later agreed that the humans themselves were an additional resource. He can't use their 'eradication' as an expense because he's going to harvest them, too."

"Right," Wisdom says, "You're right, Jove. He's going to kill them all and haul them back to Alnitak to be processed into fertilizer for their algae farms. No problem there."

"You can shut up anytime."

"I'm just stating the facts, Jove."

"This conversation is beginning to really irritate me. Would you please just leave me in peace? It's hard enough to go through with all of this without you rubbing my face in it." I didn't know that Union clones could get a headache, but I've got a whopper.

"I wonder where he'll start the harvesting," Wisdom rambles. "I mean, the Seychelles are close by, so it'd be efficient to start there, with those...radicals...heathen, really. They did attack you; they did shoot you; injuring you and indirectly causing the death of two close friends. Who'd care if the Prawl-Tang snip a few heads there?"

"Is this you cheering me up?" I ask. I cannot believe what I'm hearing.

"I wonder how long before he gets around to the rest of your friends: Captain Thomas, Zaris, Dwight Ward-Howard, Damien, Sir Edward Vincent, Moshe Samuelsson, Elmyrah—"

I whirl around to face some invisible threat that exists only in my head. "He will never even *touch* her! I would *never* allow that!"

"Oh, okay," Wisdom says, "well, maybe not her. You can't save everyone, I guess."

The pain in my head grows stronger with every word from that nag. If only she would just shut up for awhile. What's with this conversation, anyway? What happened to Wisdom being there to help me see things from a higher perspective? Why all this…intrusion?

"I didn't mean to bother you, Jove. I'm only here to help you. I know you came here to discuss something with the Mission Steward. I'll leave you alone now."

"Yeah, get out of my head," I say, "and close the door on the way out."

Half the distance to the front of the Scoop, I turn back to see the Equus, where my new daughter sleeps inside. I don't need to come all the way out just to make contact with my alien friends, but I want to check on the Knowers. I jump down into the partially open vent, then lean my forehead against the upper edge and call down into the black abyss of the gigantic hold below me.

"Honey, I'm home!" It echoes back and forth across the inside-out coral reef.

"Jove," Mission Steward says, "the Knowers have ceased biologic function."

Wait. What? "Mission Steward, please repeat that. I don't understand."

"The biologics in the hold have terminated. They are dead," he says.

This is terrible, unthinkable. "What caused this?"

"As the body was removed, it was tested for potential resource viability. Chemical composition tests reported an intolerably high level of ammonia and a gradual increase of ingested alkaloids. My conclusion is that the waste recycle process performed at below required levels. The biologic had also consumed a small quantity of toxin in its locally supplemented diet."

They were accidentally poisoned. I can't believe this has happened. "Where's the body now?"

"It was sent to the ocean floor, as is customary for their race," he says.

Seriously? A Prawl-Tang could care about anyone's funerary practices? I'm impressed. "I must say, I'm surprised that you're aware of how they treat their deceased. Did you release the Obedient Sand into the sky to carry away the souls?"

"That would not be appropriate."

"How would that not be appropriate?" I ask. "That's what they do before they drop the deceased down to their ocean." Perhaps I am expecting too much of starfish compassion.

"The soul-stones will be released into the planetary rings, to join the other souls orbiting in the sphere's heaven, when $\Omega 94\lambda 25\theta$ returns to PB5."

Perhaps not - soul-stones? Wait, return to Jupiter? "Why would you return to Jupi—PB5?"

"To complete the mission, as stated in the bargain," he says.

I find it difficult to hide my skepticism. "And what will that entail, exactly?"

"Mission resource reconciliation."

"Does mission resource reconciliation pose a threat to the Knowers on PB5?"

"You want to know if I will eradicate the biologics," he says. "The mission parameters and the agreement do not exclude that. However, as this mission has yet to produce any viable resource ready for transport, it is difficult to estimate the percentage to point of threshold and the balance of profit after resource expense. You want me to tell you that I have forgotten the resources of PB5, yet you have delivered me nothing on PB3."

"The ships are on the way now with—"

"I am tracking your supply ships. They are bringing the nuclear weapons for disposal. They must be transported to the star. Then $\Omega94\lambda250$ must return to prepare PB3 for harvest operations. This is all expense. I have done everything you have asked while on PB3. I have even saved the life of the child, an unnecessary expense."

"Yes, and I'm very grateful for—"

"What part of the bargain has the Omega Species not upheld?"

"You have," I confess, "but—"

"But you do not trust me, it would seem," he says.

Gosh, does it show? Of course, I can't trust you, I think to myself very, very quietly.

Wisdom interrupts. "Jove, there is something I need to discuss with you."

"Not now!" I hiss. "I'm in the middle of losing an argument with the alien."

"Show him that you trust him. Prove it."

"How do I do that? I don't trust him," I say.

"Offer him more than he wants. Give him everything. Be thankful," Wisdom tells me.

"Why would I do that?" I whisper loudly in my head. "I'm trying to keep him from taking everything."

"Could you really stop him, if he wanted to take it by force? If a dozen Prawl-Tang vessels emerged right now, could you stop them from taking every planet for themselves?"

"No, of course not."

"So, then offer him everything. Give him the Earth and Jupiter, too.”

Is Wisdom manipulating me, as I do the humans?

“Mission Steward,” I say, “you’re correct in saying that I don’t trust you. I want to trust you. There’s much history recorded of your—the Omega Species destroying other worlds, much death and destruction, that has often tainted my perception of you personally. However, since we’ve made the bargain, you’ve done nothing to lead me to believe that you wouldn’t fulfill your responsibility to it. In fact, you’ve gone out of the way to save the girl, Elmyrah. You claimed PB5 for the Omega Species and you did that in good faith, not knowing that it belonged to other sentient beings already. You willingly traded a viable resource for an untested one here on Earth. They’re both yours. We only ask that you continue to be merciful.”

“I understand, Jove. Trust is earned. As the Omega Species travels through space, in search for the necessary resources, each time we come upon another species, they immediately become violent and open fire upon us with their many weapons. We are outnumbered and our weapons are rudimentary compared to those of other militaristic worlds. Our only tactical advantage is to fire first.”

Wisdom interrupts again. “Ask him why.”

“Why what?”

“Why do they unceasingly hunt for hydrogen and conquer entire planets for it?”

“Mission Steward,” I ask, “can you tell me why hydrogen is so important to the Omega Species?” I ask.

“I am not convinced that I can trust you with that information.”

I look up into the sky for the right words. “What can I do to gain that trust?”

During the long pause, I consider the many things I am willing to do.

"Bring the girl to me," he says.

That wasn't one of them.

"Bring…Elmyrah…to you?" I get those goose bumps I'm incapable of.

"That is what I asked for. Bring her that I may connect with her, too."

Why that? What if he…? But why would—he spent half a day rebuilding her from three piles of dead body parts and synthetic widgets. He wouldn't harm her now, would he?

"Wisdom," I ask, "any suggestions?"

"I suggest," she says, "that you lose your aversion to the mortality of the mortals."

"I will go to her and ask her if she's willing to come to meet the Mission Steward."

"That was fast," Wisdom says.

"What was?"

"It didn't take you long to shirk your parental responsibility."

"I'm trying to keep her safe."

"Yes, of course you are," Wisdom says. "You fly her around in a spaceship designed for synthetic clones, on a doomed planet, when she could be snuggled in a warm bed with her caring family in Al-Zulfi. You're a model of parental concern."

"Shut up and tell me what to do!"

"Choose fear or trust, Jove." Wisdom says. "But, I'll shut up now."

Wait…

The three kilometers back to the ship seems to take forever, every step excruciating. I don't want to do this. I feel like I have to, though, if I'm going to convince anyone, even myself, of my ability to trust someone. Who am I kidding? I don't even trust myself.

At the top of the ladder, I jump up through the hatch and into the Equus. She's still fast asleep on her huge pile of pillows. She looks like some princess in her royal tent in the sands of Arabia.

"Is it morning already?" Elmyrah asks with a groggy, pouty face.

"No, it's not morning," I tell her, "but there's another some... one I—you need to meet."

"Is it far?"

"Sort of, I'll carry you."

"Can we look at the stars? Can we see Jupiter?" She stands up, rubbing her tired eyes.

I scoop her up in my arms and head towards the back of the ship, pausing to operate the rear deck ramp for an easier egress with a drowsy load. By the time we get to the surface of the Scoop and turned around, my perfect girl is snoring again. Interestingly, while I make the walk back, it seems much shorter. My only thoughts are of her and how good it is to be close, with her draped around me - complete trust. Thanks, Elmyrah; in your sleep you can teach me how to do it. I wish I could be a child, just once. Thirty times in a row, I'll be born an adult, never knowing what it means to be parented; not ever having someone to trust with my everything. I wonder if the Onlys considered that; if they had a plan for a real clone that could be birthed as a baby, growing up. Perhaps the baby was on the inside. Payl certainly seemed childlike in some ways.

Too soon, we arrive at the front of the Scoop. I step down carefully into the opening along the bow of the ship, peering into the darkness. Not that there's anything to see. It's just a loose pile of Obedient Sand along one side. Now gravity is its only master.

"I've brought my daughter, Mission Steward." Like she ever belonged to me.

"I can sense her presence."

"She's asleep. Do you want me to wake her?"

"That is not necessary," he says. "Do you know why I asked you to bring her?"

"Because you wanted me to prove that I trust you," I reply.

"No, Jove. I said that I needed *you* to earn *my* trust."

True. I have it backwards, as usual. "I was—I'm afraid that you might harm her somehow."

"Thank you for not lying to me about that."

So, he *can* understand thank you. I can't bring myself to say 'you're welcome'.

"By that, you have proved yourself worthy as a parent, because you considered her value as equal to two entire worlds and their billions of people."

I'm amazed. "And that is important to you."

"Now do you see, Jove? Do you see why? You asked me why hydrogen is so important to the Omega Species."

"Yes, I did."

"What you could never grasp as the savior of the Jovians, you can understand as a parent of a child. I had you bring her to me because I miss my own children. I had to leave them to begin my mission to save them. You see, Jove, the Omega Species' home world has experienced a catastrophic underground geologic failure. Where once there was a sealed layer of life beneath the solid crust of our planet, the cyanobacteria have escaped into our upper level; what you would call an ocean. These life forms create vast amounts of oxygen, which is toxic to our species. Humanoids are aerobic, we are anaerobic."

"What's happened to your people—your inhabitants?"

"Many are gravely ill. The children are all dying. They cannot survive the poisoning. It is everywhere. We cannot stop it, though we expend every resource to combat the spread of the deadly chemical into our reefs."

"What does the hydrogen do?"

"It bonds with the free oxygen, to make water. But there is not enough. And it is extremely difficult to transport it to the solid surface. The energy required to push against the natural lift of the hydrogen in the heavier sea is exceedingly great. We are losing our battle to save our children."

"That's why you do anything you have to. You'd destroy every known planet to get what you need to save them."

"It will not be enough," Mission Steward says.

"Hydrogen - that takes twice as much to bond only one atom of oxygen. Couldn't you use something else, like carbon or maybe calcium hydroxide? Those would double or triple the rate of reduction of the toxin."

"Water is a natural by-product and is practically harmless to our ecosystem," he says, "Bonding with carbon produces vast amounts of thermal energy. If you are aware of any nebulae that are composed of calcium hydroxide, I will send the fleet there today."

"Mission Steward," I ask, "why does the Omega Species take the humanoids? Why kill them and take them back to Alnitak?"

"They possess extremophile bacteria in their digestive tract that can be used as a treatment for the Prawl-Tang infants. It can withstand our atmosphere and slows the dissolution of their bodies from the oxygen."

Just as I was scrambling through Knowledgebase for another potential solution, Wisdom speaks again.

"You cannot save three planets, Jove. But you may be able to save two."

"What're you talking about?"

"The Mission Steward just admitted that his own planet is doomed because of this natural catastrophe. Why should you continue the mission to save the Jovians by giving the Earth and its billions of human lives over to the Prawl-Tang? What purpose would it serve?"

"Have you been out to lunch? We brought the Prawl-Tang here to Earth so he would ignore Jupiter. That was the plan! We remove the weapons that could stop him; he takes what he needs and goes back to where he came from and he doesn't come back."

"Do you really think that if the Omega Species scours the galaxy for every last drop of hydrogen, that they would allow their societies to die off because they're bound to honor some slippery back-room deal with you over a gas giant made almost entirely of the molecule they need most? Are you that blind to what he just laid out for you; that his mission – the mission of every member of their species – is to save their children; to save them from extinction? If you had a thousand Earths to trade, they won't ignore Jupiter. The Prawl-Tang will be back, and you know it."

Wisdom is right. Tactically, is was prudent for the Mission Steward to accept the bargain for Earth, so that he could exploit whatever potential help there could be for his planet. Either way, he could and likely will turn right around and pick up where he left off on his precious PB5.

"Alright, Wisdom, do you have a Plan B? We're on the verge of handing the whole kit and caboodle over to the starfish."

"Listen to me, Jove. You *did* save the Jovians, the Knowers, by enticing the Mission Steward away to Earth, but you *must* prevent him – any of the Omega Species – from ever returning. Consider what they call themselves: Omega – The Last – the Final Species alive after all others have been wiped away. They intend to be alone in the galaxy when this is over. You can prevent this holocaust from ever happening."

"And how am I going to take on the Scourge of Orion? I only have twenty-one of me left, you know. Just this one incident turned out to be routinely fatal."

"Do you trust me, Jove?" Wisdom asks.

Again with the trust. "Yes, alright…yes."

"Convince the Mission Steward to modify his ship's launch tubes – the ones for the Tracking Spear – so that they can accommodate the nuclear missiles and bombs. The flagellomeric cilia in the cargo hold can feed them into the launch tubes. The Navigation Onus can interface with the missile's guidance system."

"If you're thinking of blowing up the Scoop from the inside, it's only going to take one," I tell her. At the deep sound of a navy horn, I turn around to see a very large military supply ship heading directly towards us, bringing the first of the nuclear weapons deliveries. Tug boats launch out to meet it, to help put on the brakes, to guide them to the interstellar dock.

"No, Jove. You will need all of them," Wisdom tells me.

I'm lost. "All of them for what? What is so—?"

"You're going to destroy all of the Prawl-Tang and their planet," Wisdom says.

I am aghast at the thought of it. "You're talking about genocide."

"They're going to all die anyway, Jove," Wisdom says. "When you think about it, you're doing them a favor."

"Excuse me?" I blink repeatedly, though the visual effect may be lost in the virtual dialogue.

Wisdom is bent on some insane logic. "No, Jove, seriously. If you had the choice between a horribly slow and painful death by poison, like the Knowers trapped in their Obedient Sand cocoon, and a mercifully quick death, what would you choose? Which would you choose for your children?"

"But that's different than someone choosing for you," I say, around a bitter taste.

"Not if it is your friend choosing for you, or a loved one," teaches Wisdom. "They are doing it out of compassion for you. They're helping you to end your suffering. That's what you're going to do for the Prawl-Tang, Jove. And just think of the relief you're bringing to all of the other sentient beings of the Orion Arm. You will be a hero to a thousand races on a thousand planets."

"You almost make it sound not evil."

"Oh," Wisdom says. "It's not evil at all. Far from it. This is what true friends, true *brothers*, do for each other. You know what it means to be left alone to suffer, while your 'family' thinks only of themselves. I know you do, Jove. You stare out into the emptiness of space and wonder where they could be. You wonder at how they could have left you to accomplish the impossible by yourself."

"So, let me see if I get this Plan B of yours. We load the Super Scoop with every warhead from Earth, fly to Alnitak, singlehandedly destroy the combined armada of the Prawl-Tang, and then bomb their planet?"

"Yes, exactly," Wisdom declares.

"And then what, a ticker-tape parade through Times Square? A ride on a donkey's colt through Jerusalem? Pardon me if I skip the Lincoln Continental ragtop. That one's lost its popularity."

"What would you want, Jove?"

"What would I want for what?"

"For being the savior of two planets; what would you want for a reward?" Wisdom asks. "You certainly will be deserving of any conceivable treasure. You can name your price."

"I would say…for rescuing many billions from certain death, or being found guilty of wiping out an entire race, you pick, my reward should be that I not burn in hell for eternity."

"Why're you always so negative?" Wisdom scolds me. "Think about the good that will come of it. Consider all the human children that will live on, that will continue to thrive. Why, I imagine your daughter could even befriend a few of them."

Goosebumps - all on the back of my neck. "Leave her out of this."

"Look, Jove," she says, "just explain to Mission Steward how you think that the Scoop should be fitted with nuke launchers. You're good at things like that. He will listen to you. Then later, after you've mulled it over, you can decide for yourself. What's the harm in that?"

As it turns out, it is the Mission Steward's idea, anyway. He was going to spend a month orbiting the Earth, picking off hundreds of military satellites and ground targets with his asteroid laser. But he surmised that with eleven high altitude nuclear detonations, he could permanently cripple the Earth's defenses to the point at which they cannot "measurably reduce the efficiency of the harvest operations". There should be no appreciable contamination of the surface that could reduce resource value.

Now, all I have to do is talk myself into killing off the Omega Species. There's one snag I see coming around the bend – what to do with the Mission Steward. He knows me pretty well, unfortunately, and tends to think quick on his…arms? Trickery is out of the question. I may need to get dirty, and Wisdom doesn't seem to have any problem with that now.

It takes ninety-two large ocean going vessels over five months to bring the seventeen thousand, three hundred and eighty-five nuclear warheads from the nine countries around the globe. The Navigation Onus has expertly managed to get them all situated into the main hold of the Scoop; each one secured in fast-growth coral and easily pulled loose to be activated by the long flagellomeric cilia that hangs from the ceiling of the cavern. Even with another massive delivery of chemical and biological weapons, the Mission Steward advised me that there is still room enough for the Equus if I want to go along.

I replied, "I'll hail a cab." He doesn't get it.

I'm concerned that Zaris and Damien are suspicious. We'd planned another global trip, to meet with the leaders of smaller countries that haven't reconciled. With me there to tie their minds together, we could erase the last vestiges of warlike behavior from the planet, as I have done in hundreds of cases, since initially proving myself with the Israelis and Palestinians. I can't be in three places at once: traveling with them, overseeing the loading of the Scoop, and caring for my adopted daughter. I feel that I'm too close to completing this mission; to hand over the planet to the Mission Steward. It's too risky to leave the Prawl-Tang in direct contact with the people on the ships that are lined up over the horizon. I tell them that I'm not going on the diplomatic tour. But, what else am I here for? That's a good question – what *am* I here for? What am I doing?

I could walk away from it all right now; fly back to the Union communications beacon to signal my Brothers that all is well. We could pull up a chair on Jupiter and use LookingFar to gawk at the plundering of the LittleRavagedBluePearl. And we'd be no different than the Prawl-Tang.

Or, I can follow the advice of my recently deranged Wisdom; knock off the Mission Steward, somehow take over the Scoop, ride a TransWave to the Alnitak system and preside over a planet-wide holocaust. I could be the conductor for a symphony of death.

I'd be the living, breathing (sort of) anti-thesis of the Manufactured Flesh and SynThinker Union. I could never show my face among them again. This is getting away from me. I can hear the whooshing sound of my 'Thinker running at full tilt, but I can't come to any conclusions. Except for the wonderful times I spend with my beloved daughter, my life is under a dark cloud.

"Jove," Wisdom calls to me, "there is something I need to discuss with you."

"I would like to discuss you not harassing me."

Wisdom takes on a motherly tone today. "Jove, my dear, please don't say that. You know that I exist only to serve you, to aid you in this honorable quest that has been such a heavy burden to bear. Don't try to do this alone, Jove. You were given the Equus, Knowledgebase and me as your willing and committed partners, to see you through this. You're the trusted savior of the Knowers, and as Choyt-72 so eloquently said, 'you will choose the correct course of action, as required by the circumstances you encounter'. You are trusted, Jove. And you can trust that the gifts you were given are for your benefit. I'm only here to help you find the right path."

"Then help me understand how this is right," I say. "You're leaving out the rest of it, the warnings - admonishment against revenge. There's a context to his directives, you know."

"What have I left out?" she asks.

"The context was that we're to save the Jovians however we could, but not at the expense of other lives."

"Do remember, Jove," Wisdom tells me, "I was with Choyt from the beginning – from One to Seventy-Two. I know full well what his intentions are for this mission. What Choyt actually said was, 'The Prawl-Tang on the ship, or any others that you encounter on the planet below – their lives are not to be considered worthless or sacrificed to spare the Jovians.' What he *did not* say was 'Prawl-Tang anywhere', but he was only referring to the one on Jupiter that was attacking the Knowers. Furthermore, he was valuing the life of the one alien against the lives of the Jovians, not the lives of the Knowers *and* the billions on Earth."

I want to trust the words I'm hearing, but they grind against my soul. "Isn't it the same thing? Wouldn't murdering the Mission Steward while he is on Earth or in orbit or halfway to Sol, be the same as killing him when he was on Jupiter? How is this different?"

"Oh, so you see!" she says. "It doesn't matter where the Prawl-Tang are, their evil intent is the complete and final destruction of all other worlds, solely because they count themselves as more deserving of life."

"Okay," I say around a smirk, "I can see that you turned—"

"And, no, their lives are not worthless. Don't let them die for nothing. Please don't allow them to suffer and wither away in their poisoned torture. You can save them from that, Jove. You can cause their lives to mean something great. You can take away their pain, and in so doing, you'll set them free, and the humans of Earth, and the Knowers of Jupiter. This is your chance, Jove; to do so much more than you were created for."

"He also said," I remind her, "that it 'would be far too easy for us to merely take one life to balance the loss of another'".

"You're right again, Jove," she says. "We cannot take one life for another. This is about the salvation of not one, but two entire species of loving, caring people. The cost of losing them is so incredibly high, and the value of saving them is equally so. You are right in doing this."

How can this be right? My mind is swimming in mud. I'm getting dizzy. My SynThinker is....thoughts random, incomplete. The connection from my brain to the rest of me is lost. From the top of the Scoop's hull, I topple forward, landing flat on my face, my nose cracks, my skull bounces off the rock hard chitin. I sense my body as it slides and rolls down the steep side along the forward edge. Cool water invades my inner parts, burbling through the respiratory ducts in my torso. I wish it could cleanse me of her. My nemesis and I are one.

"Jove," Wisdom calls to me, "Jove, don't be afraid. We can do this together. Remember when Choyt told you that, 'you may notice your feelings drawing you toward finding the best resolution for others'? He was talking about the ones dear to your heart, Jove, about Zaris and Damien, Dwight, Captain Thomas, and your precious daughter, Elmyrah. You know what the best solution is for them."

I am afraid of you.

I sink quickly to the floor of the Mascarene Plateau, to settle onto the murky bottom, paralyzed. I can see little brown swirls and tiny creatures darting to and fro. It is very quiet and peaceful down here; not boiling and churning like Jupiter's ocean - so peaceful. I recognize something in my periphery, the large grain of Obedient Sand. Fallen out of my pocket to drift across my view, it seems to have a glow of its own down here.

"Spin for me," I tell it. The grain lifts up from the bottom of the mud to dance like a ballerina. Earth rises to join it, forming rings parallel to the tiny equator, the Cooperative Sand of this planet to cavort with the friendly neighbor.

"Jove," Wisdom calls again, "listen to Choyt's words: 'Today is our moment to create something….*someone*, who can rise above the totality of our combined sciences…with the mind and skills and capacities to save lives for the sake of peace – the opposite of what we have enjoined from ourselves, the capacity of destruction for the sake of war.' That's you, Jove – 'someone who can rise above' – that's you. You are the opposite of what the Brotherhood fears. You will use destruction to save lives for the sake of peace."

Note to Self

Can there be anything worse than loving someone?

For now your very heart is theirs, and humans can be so very fickle.

Jove

Lies
2045 CE
Earth

I awake as Number Nine. What was that? A polyvascular aneurism? A 'Thinker crash? I cannot reconcile myself to Wisdom's wicked plan. I don't even want to think about it.

With a brisk jump, I exit the cassette and take off to look for my perfect girl. I find an awful lot of sunlight casting a bright beam onto the floor leading to the bridge. With a climb up the ladder to the dorsal hatch, I pop my head up into the sunny ocean breeze to find Elmyrah lying face up on the roof of the Equus' fuselage. She's looking at the clouds.

"Excuse me, have you seen my star-nosed cat?" I yell. "It's white and fluffy and lasts about three seconds."

"Yep!" she yells back. "He sniffity-snooped by here…oh… about a bazillion seconds ago."

"Rats."

She laughs. "Um…no rats, just the cat."

The voice of Fonmet plays in my head, like a low note on a cello. His soul resonates through the mouth of the wishful-Thinker, Jove.

"What do you see, M'rah?" I ask.

"I see my future," she says, a bit stoic. "There's you and me, running through the sand, and it's all ours, as far as the eye can see. We're holding hands, running. And we have a brother, holding my other hand. The two of you are strong and you swing me into the air and I'm laughing so much my sides hurt."

It sounds like a family, I think. "You never know what the future might hold for us, my sweet girl. But we'll head into it together."

"Starting tomorrow." she says with a huge grin, rolling over to prop up on her elbows.

"What's tomorrow?" I ask.

"You can be such a Dummy," she says, laughing some more. "Tomorrow is the end of *that*." She points a finger to the southern horizon, with the last of the long line of container and military ships visible. "There're only four left. I am so sick of watching those dumb old ships. It's time to do something else. By my calculations, they should finish the last load by two o'clock, tomorrow. One o'clock if you tell them to skip lunch."

"Hey, um…subject change," I say. "Elmyrah, do you ever have…problems with your Wisdom?"

"No. What do you mean? How could she be a problem?"

"I don't know. Does she ever suggest things that, you know, don't make sense, or maybe it sounds wrong to do?"

"Don't be silly," she says. "If she says to do something, it has to be okay. She's Wisdom."

That's not what I wanted to hear.

"Speaking of lunch…" she inquires, standing up, to skip and dance, free of cares.

I shake my head, pretending to look at a wristwatch. It's ten in the morning.

"I'm going back down," I say. "You stay away from the edge. That last step's a doozey."

"You would know." she yells over her shoulder, as she twirls around in a circle.

Later that night, I put the pot-bellied piglet to bed on her mound of pillows.

"Jove?"

"Yes, my love."

"I miss my brother...Abdallah. Can we take the ship and fly to Al-Zulfi to check on him?"

Not a chance. "Sure, we can do that."

I hold her hand until she starts snoring. She's so soft, so delicate. I watch the galloping beat of her four hearts as her new synthetic life courses through the human veins in her wrist.

It's my turn on the rooftop of the cutter, for a far more serious reason. I reach out strongly with my thoughts; call the massive pile of Obedient Sand in the Scoop beneath me, left over from when it protected the Knowers.

"Come."

With a tumultuous rumble, the millions of white crystals pour out of the Scoop's vent like bats from a cave to fill the air above, they swirl around each other; a liquid, stony mass tossing upside-down waves to roll back to the top in a backwards undertow. They are mine - every single one a treasure; together, an unstoppable force.

At my command, the stones touch down on the surface of the Equus, filling every gap, to align themselves in the ultimate pattern, until the entire ship is covered by a layer of at least two or three deep. With a thought, the Sand clears away from the outside of the cockpit windows, piled up at the edges, ready to protect if needed.

Back inside, at the pilot's bama, it occurs to me, I don't even need the thrusters or engines. With a mental request, the Sand will silently take us wherever we wish to go, at any speed imaginable.

What the Equus does not have, is a control system for firing tactical weapons. I must convince the Navigation Onus to handle that for me. Perhaps we can make a bargain.

"Jove," Wisdom calls from the darkness inside of me, "there is something I need to discuss with you."

"Not now, I'm busy."

"It's time to end the lies, Jove," she tells me.

What? And break with tradition? Go away, you.

"You should tell Captain Thomas the truth. He deserves to know."

"Which truth?" I ask the ceiling, like I'd find this demon up there. "You'll have to be more specific. I've told so many lies, they kind of all mush together."

"You're supposed to meet with him today; to complete the inventory of the loaded weapons," Wisdom informs me. "You must tell him the truth about the Prawl-Tang; about how you were coerced to go along with the Mission Steward's plan to steal the weapons of Earth, so the Omega Species could easily subdue the human race."

"Oh *that* truth!" I say. "Well, it certainly is fresh. That should qualify it as anything but falsehood."

"Tell Thomas that you've discovered a way to thwart the attack upon the Earth; that you can save his planet and his people from any possibility of the Prawl-Tang returning to destroy them. Assure him that you can do this, but that you need something from the Earth in trade."

"—in trade? Are we making another bargain for lives?"

"Everything has a price, Jove," Wisdom says. "Don't act so innocent."

I stop my work and peer into the inner darkness. "What're you getting at?"

"When Tierney was killed, it was an accident, wasn't it? I mean, it's not like you wanted him dead, did you? You only said you hoped he'd drop dead."

Good old Wisdom. Dig into my soul, dredge up my insecurities and pull them over my head like a black burlap sack. What's next, lights in the face? Don't forget the chair. You know if you want it to be truly unbearable. But you won't stop. She never stops.

"Damien wasn't to blame," she says. "He had no idea what could happen; that the Obedient Sand would make real what his imagination and jealousy conjured in his mind. It didn't take long for you to realize the leverage you had on him, for you to use it for your own profit. This'll be no different."

"That was to save her life!" I say.

Wisdom laughs. "That was purely selfish gain and you well know it! What Union Brother has ever had a child? You did that for you. But, as you say, you saved her life, why shouldn't it belong to you now? And you've saved the lives of billions of Jovians, and billions of humans next, and countless more throughout space will be saved by your diligence to rid the galaxy of The Scourge. Why not ask for one simple thing that's really of no consequence?"

"Should a savior be paid for his willingness to die for the lives of others?" I ask.

Wisdom continues on. My muddied mind is crisscrossed with her deep footprints.

"You know inside yourself, that you are not the savior, Jove. You've felt that way since you woke up as Number Two. But you've gone along with it. You've played the part so well. No one could have been as convincing as you. You were made for this, literally. Now go. Be the Savior. Play the part, Jove."

That awful whirring sound is in my 'Thinker again. Like endless waves of thought, it keeps dashing against my mind. It wears me down, even during a fun time with my perfect girl this morning. After a food fight of tater tots, we discovered the gravity defying characteristics of a spinning pancake. My laughter is contrived. On the inside my mind was blanketed with visions of death. If I could, I would crossload into a fresh 'Thinker, one without any memories, one without any Wisdom.

To practice my skill at intramental control over the Sand, I pilot the ship up and over to a soft landing on the helipad on the rear deck of the repurposed navy destroyer. No thrusters, no engines, not even use of the proximity sensors; the Sand executes my every wish.

I take my daughter's tiny hand in mine, and march in royal splendor down the rear deck ramp of the Equus and into the waiting embrace of my friend, Mark Thomas. Properly introduced, I see that she's quite taken with the handsome male. This only adds to my mental stew.

At our places around the large conference table in the familiar room where we first met, I dread the need to tell another lie.

"Thank you for this final welcome onto your fine ship, Captain. I can't tell you how much it means to me that you agreed to oversee this entire operation. Everything has been accomplished with excellence."

"Well, Jove," Thomas replies, "I can tell you that it took a bit of encouragement to convince the crews to get on with those monstrous tentacles that wiggle out of that mountain of a space ship you have."

"I understand," I say. "Now, if you don't mind, there's a matter of concern that must be addressed before we can conclude our business. I must ask that everyone be asked to leave the room, except the three of us, with Zaris and the UNSG on the conference phone, if possible."

Thomas' smile departs with the other guests as they file out of the room. His assistant connects the phone on the table with the United Nations office in New York. As asked, the two others on the far side of the globe are brought into the conversation.

"Jove," Dwight asks, "is there a problem with the transport operations?"

"Mister Secretary, I hope you will forgive me for what I have to tell you all," I say, following it up with a telepathic surge of good intentions. "The truth is, the giant ship you see out there, partially submerged in your ocean, is not from Jupiter. It is from much farther away, seven hundred thirty-six light years to be exact, from a star system called Alnitak, or the scientific name, Zeta Orionis.

"Compared with the Knowers, the creature within Emrah is the most alien of all. It arrived in your star system, hunting for prey, and found it with the harmless Jovians. It has held them for ransom, I'm afraid. I was chosen as the messenger to deliver its evil demands to the people of Earth. These detestable beasts, the Prawl-Tang, are the prime menace to all corners of the inhabited galaxy. They roam through space, leaving destruction in their wake. They steal everything they can get their—hands on, including your nuclear weapons. Their intent is to use the weapons against the Jovians or perhaps your cousins on some other poor planet."

"Oh my, Jove," Dwight says, "this is utterly horrid – completely unimaginable. But what of the peace you have brought to our planet; to all of the once warring nations? Is that all just a fantasy, a dream? Will we all go back to destroying ourselves?"

"Oh, no, not at all, Mister Secretary. The peace you now enjoy is yours to keep forever, but for the ravenous ways of your new interstellar enemy, the Prawl-Tang. They will take the weapons that you no longer have need of, but they will be back to take everything else, of that you can be sure."

Thomas speaks up. "Is there nothing that can be done to stop them?"

"There is, I have only just discovered," I say, "a way to prevent them from ever returning. I believe that, with your help, I can do something to keep them from their bloodthirsty mission."

I was going to explain to the group how I would use the WMDs to destroy their world, but Wisdom interrupts me at the last second. "Jove, there is something I need to discuss with you." I am completely thrown off by the intrusion into my mind.

"Not now! What are you doing?" I think, "I have them nearly convinced, to take their weapons, to use them against the Prawl-Tang."

"No, Jove. They would not understand," Wisdom explains. "You've brought only peace to this world. How can you now tell them that you're going to commit genocide on their behalf? They will never allow it. They've been transformed. You've changed them forever."

"Then, what? What's this 'one simple thing' that you told me to ask for? Is it Elmyrah? Do I need their permission to adopt her?" I'm confused again. My mind is noisy and irratic.

"No, not your daughter - there is something they possess in

abundance that will be of immeasurable wealth to you, something else entirely. Ask them for it, and they will give it to you, on bended knee."

"Please, Wisdom," I beg, my mind now numb, "just tell me. What is it?"

"The sand," Wisdom says.

"What? Sand? Are you serious?" I'm lost. "You want me to ask for sand?"

"Yes," Wisdom states clearly, "and nothing more."

My mind is too tired to argue. "Sand. Alright, Wisdom, I give up. I'll ask them."

"Mister Secretary, Mark, Zaris, my true friends, I have no one else in my life. But I must ask you for this one thing; one thing necessary to prevent the destruction of your planet...I need sand."

Zaris' voice cracks over the phone. "What? Did you say sand?"

"Why on earth would you ask for sand, Jove?" Thomas asks.

Wisdom prompts me. "Tell them that it ruins the Prawl-Tang ships and weapons."

"It—I've discovered that it ruins the Prawl-Tang ships and weapons. As long as the sand is rained down onto them, they cannot fly or fire their weapons. They will be trapped on their planet."

"Okay, Jove. We want to help," Dwight chimes in, "how much sand will you require?"

"All of it," Wisdom says. She's lost it. I have to find a way to stop—

"All of it." I say. I hear my voice in my ears, but it's not me.

"Right, you're joking now," Thomas says, "You want all of the sand...everywhere...all the sand of Earth?"

"Yes." I can't believe the words coming out of my mouth. "I'll

need all the sand. For as long as possible, I will need to take sand
from here, and fly it there, to Alnitak, and drop it over their ships.
That will keep them grounded, until they give up."

"Makes sense, I suppose," Thomas agrees, "air superiority: it's
a basic strategy of war. Own the skies, keep your enemy on the
ground, and you have the upper hand for as long as you need to
finish the job or they give up. I understand now. But, sand. That's
truly amazing."

"It's alien, Mark," I say. "On your planet, you used jets and missiles. In the alien realm, your simple grains of silicates are what we
need to protect you."

Hmmm - all of their sand? I think I see now where Wisdom
is going with this. According to Knowledgebase, silicon dioxide,
or quartz, which is the Cooperative Sand of Earth, is the primary
component of the planetary crust. Sixty percent of the surface of the
Earth is silicate sand. I would need an entire fleet of Super Scoops
to move just a minute portion of this vast resource. I'm thinking like
a Prawl-Tang all of a sudden.

Wisdom speaks up again. "Get them to sign. They have to sign."

"Sign what?" I ask.

"Have them sign a deed to the sand. Otherwise, they can just
change their minds. Make the UN Secretary-General deed the rights
to all the sand of Earth over to you."

Like in some weird dream, I hear myself directing the humans
to sign away the surface of their planet to me. I see them actually
doing it, convinced of their need to supply me with a never ending
supply to drop on Zeta Orionis. Dwight signs. Zaris faxes. I sign acceptance. There's handshakes and laughter. Elmyrah spins around in
her chair like a dervish. My brain is overloaded again. I'm watching

this happen before me. Usually, I am the one controlling the minds in the room. This…this is different.

From an altitude of ten thousand feet, my perfect girl and I watch through the glass of the lower ports of the Equus, as the Prawl-Tang Super Scoop slowly lifts itself out of the Indian Ocean and up into the bright blue of Earth's magnificent sky. In a belabored climb against the gravity that pulls down on the huge ship with its equally ponderous load, it would seem to take forever to get up to a speed that would break orbit. The sides of the massive flying mountain are bleached white from the dissolved oxygen in the sea water eating away at the anaerobic coral hull.

Both ships swing around the moon and accelerate off in the direction of the sun. During the brief conversation with the Mission Steward, he never mentioned that the Obedient Sand was missing from his hold and now encapsulating my ship.

After quite a few hours of zero-point-two, I wonder why we're taking the slow boat to China, so to speak.

"Jove," Wisdom calls again, "There's something I need to discuss with you."

"Always is."

There is no corner of my psyche, no door in my 'Thinker to shut, no hole to crawl into, that she doesn't find me. I stand naked in a pure-white vacuum with no walls, infinite, surrounded by her, countless faces, all the same, one after another, jeering, taunting. Closing my eyelids only presents a better screen with which to view this dreadful biography, the Awful Lives of Jove.

"It's time," Wisdom tells me.

"Time for—?"

"Ready your ship to attack the Prawl-Tang vessel," she says. "Pull in close to the smaller protrusion on the rearmost point. That's where the Mission Steward exists physically. Use the Sand to carefully break through the hull, to penetrate his compartment."

"Oh, it's *that* time," I reply, more than a little nervous.

"Just aim the Obedient Sand in a steady stream, at the side of his compartment."

I've never actually attacked anyone before. To say that it's out of character is putting it mildly. My jitters won't help me maintain mental control over the Sand while flying the Equus. The ship bounces a bit and swerves too close to the Super Scoop. But I do get a very close view of where I should aim my thoughts of a narrow sandstorm.

With Elmyrah secured in a large padded locker along with fifty-some big pillows, I believe that she should be relatively safe if I have to make any sudden maneuvers. Wedged tight to the pilot's bama railing, I steel myself against what is about to transpire. From deep within me, I hear voices. The voices of the Onlys, and the Ones, rise up and swirl about in my 'Thinker. I'm afraid. Am I a coward for not wanting to, or a coward for going along with it? Either way, I'm no better than my Brothers, watching all this from their rearview mirror.

The Sand moves toward the Mission Steward, but convulsively, like my thoughts. I shut my eyes against the images of doom. There before me, inside my dark place, is Wisdom. She's leading me to another Archive Vision, my only escape from this intolerable moment. It's less heartrending than the last, but more frightful. I don't care. I'll take it. I'll take the ride. Anything is better than my reality.

War

1329 BCE

Planet of Adhara (Ra' m'kur)

The Synthetics' Right to Exist War

Twin teardrops of light signal that the cargo container panel has been penetrated by a drill bit. Next should come a camera probe. There it is. The ray of exterior light is interrupted, replaced with the illuminator ring activating around a lens.

Calm. I will remain calm, just as practiced. I will be seen. They will see nothing. They will hear me. I am silent. All bodily functions are paused: pumps off, servos free, fans stopped; only gravity pulling the cooling gel across the fins, from the upper reservoir through to the lower tank. They will smell me. I have no odor. I am nothing. I am still.

Patience.

Appeased, the camera withdraws from the hole bored into the large crate.

One breath. Hearts beat four times each. Stillness. Wait.

Motorized tools outside remove the fasteners from the perimeter of the side panel. The seal broken, a crease of light cuts along the top edge. Fingers. Claws. Green and yellow claws tear away the panel, to toss it aside. There you are. I see you. You see me. You see nothing.

"Weapons, just as I told you!" the MetaTherian commander hisses. "You see, my Duke - weapons, weapons of the Synthetics."

The one wrapped in blue coils steps forward, his claws kept at his side, wary, experienced. He is the one.

"Yes, Commander. I see them," Duke Guas says. "I see your stolen weapons, Chuur. How fortunate that your assault team was able to overcome the Synthetic warriors guarding it. I'm impressed."

Leaned in, ever so slightly, the Duke bobs his head, shuddering and weaving as animals do, using motion as a substitute for stereoscopic vision. Chuur reaches past his superior to fondle the precious, deadly cargo, pride circumventing any intelligence. The Duke leans back to let the subordinate, the foolish, be the first to grope around in the neatly arranged stacks of four-beam laser gloves. His long, sharp claws curl around one of the Union grown military devices, easily tearing it free of the restraining straps. He holds it high in the air like a trophy. Chuur growls and hisses with satisfaction.

"We have their weapons now." he says. "They will fall at the touch of their own technology. We will surely prevail against them, my Duke."

Guas takes one step back. Chuur calls to two other MetaTherian soldiers, directing them to carry away the weapons as he continues to scoop them clumsily out of the crate's inner racks. He reaches in farther, halfway, his entire furry arm up to the armored shoulder plating. Grabbing onto another laser glove, he pulls. It doesn't budge. He pulls harder.

All bodily functions on: pumps to maximum, servo tensions to one hundred five percent, fans to full, combat mode active.

Past the shoulder of the confused Chuur, I can see Guas backing away. He knows. It was too easy.

Chuur continues to yank on the laser glove attached to my thigh.

You want it so bad? You can be the first to feel it.

With the next good pull, I let the commander drag me out of the crate. He still doesn't get it. Guas is in the back of the room, laughing, shaking his feathery head at the whole of the scene, the inevitability of this, his last day alive. Free of the box, I stand up straight, towering over the animals. They still see weapon's racks, square black beams and hooks, row upon row of red, leathery gloves, gloves with eyes, those terrible eyes. I am a masterpiece.

With my four eyes in front and the two behind, I track all of the MetaTherians in the room, out of the room, into the room. They will all fall, cut to pieces, sliced through from their massive jaws down to their lower talons, to grip the mesh floor in mortal spasm. Chuur feels me first. I give it to him slow, so he considers the end. I want him to know he failed his Duke, his soldiers, his world. I think Guas enjoys that. It certainly is a fitting end for a fool, a prideful fool.

My gloves are tired, but there aren't any of the animals left alive within range, only Duke Guas, and he's not going anywhere. He knows it's coming. No sense running away, to die the coward.

I shrug off any thought of admiring his bravery. He has ordered the captivity of too many Brothers. Not allowing them to die, they can't crossload into their next warrior clone. Forever tied to a pole, skin to bake in the hot sun, the birds nesting in their respiratory ducts. Death withheld: a gruesome, successful strategy against us.

"So, which one are you?" Guas asks. "Shrayd? Tzyrryn? Shraytyk?"

I step close, so he can feel the heat that blows from my vents, the white tufts at his temples flutter in my breath. I encircle him with my four arms, sixteen lasers sighted in on his head. It would only take one.

Feel me, animal. I have succeeded. We have won. All of your

many years of throwing away the lives of your animal soldiers were for nothing. Feel that. See all of that in your thick, dull eyes. See me. I am here now.

"Well? I want to know!" he says. "Which one? The famous Three Sevens. I've heard of your little covenant - that if one of you is killed in battle, the other two kill each other so you all stay the same number of the series. I demand to know. I deserve to know which of my enemies is rewarded with the badge of my bloodstain on your plastic!"

Guas dares to shudder and weave within my reach, to look me over closely.

"You're Shrayd," Guas says. "You're enjoying this too much. Your reputation precedes you, my friend. All of the MetaTherians know of your—"

"I am not your friend."

Guas gives up trying to look smug. No use expending that much effort now.

"I suppose this is how it should be," Guas says, "the age of the MetaTherians, of all the Great Deltatheroids, to complete their reign among the stars."

"It has nothing to do with evolution," I say. "You chose death. I am here to usher you to your grave."

Guas grabs for his bio-blade. He doesn't even bother to pull it from the scabbard.

Blood
2045 CE
To Alnitak

When I open my eyes, I see the Scoop spinning around in space. That looks familiar. What's new is the gaping hole across the top of the rearmost protruding hump of coral. A large section is coarsely broken off and dark red liquid spills out.

"Secure-link with external input Jove registered," Navigation Onus says.

"Jove wishes to make contact with the Mission Steward."

"Mission Steward not responding," it states.

"Test for biologic functionality of Mission Steward."

"Testing complete," it says. "Biologic functionality of Mission Steward is negligible."

"State secondary protocol if Mission Steward is unable to function."

"Navigation Onus shall perform twenty-five attempts to regain effective communication with assigned Mission Steward prior to search for suitable alternative assignment."

"Register external input Jove as suitable alternative," I say.

"External input Jove registered as active Mission Steward."

"State the last directive of previous Mission Steward."

"Last directive: Hold course to star. Hold speed. Deactivate Spear. Deactivate defensive shield. Authorize external input Jove as alternate Mission Steward. Deliver message."

"He gave you permission to make me Mission Steward?"

"Affirmative," it says.

Message? "State the message from previous Mission Steward."

"Message: 'Jove, say goodbye to Elmyrah for me.'"

He knew. Somehow, he knew. He decided that it was wrong, or at least pointless, to destroy the Earth and Jupiter. No amount of hydrogen found here was going to make a difference on his planet. No matter what he did; no matter what any of them do, it won't be enough. The oxygen has poisoned their planet, and they're all doomed. But he could've fought back. He could've shielded himself against the Sand. A single tracking spear could've done serious damage to the Equus. As tough as the armor of Sand is covering the ship, it would be no match for what the Scoop has for weaponry. What prevented him from swatting us like some bothersome insect? He could have completed his mission without my continued interference.

And what of his 'message' about Elmyrah—*she* is the reason! Elmyrah's why he couldn't turn and attack. He even prevented himself from doing so. He helped to create who she is now. He even used Prawl-Tang bio-technology to connect her human cortex to the SynThinker. Part of them exists within her. When the last Prawl-Tang dies, she alone will carry their DNA. She will be the Omega Child, an Only *and* a One, the remnant of the species. She's all of us. If anyone holds title to the savior of Jupiter, it's my perfect girl.

The Mission Steward would not kill her to protect his own child. He sacrificed everything for someone he owed nothing to. Is it possible? Could the Prawl-Tang understand something so intimate?

"Jove," calls Wisdom, "There is something I need to discuss

with you."

"Did you see this coming?" I ask.

"I exist on every planet, in every mind. If the Jovians were not sacrificed for the good of the Prawl-Tang, then it would have been the people of Earth. Instead, it will be the Prawl-Tang that come to an end, for the good of both of the others. It is better this way."

"And don't forget the deal," I remind her, "the deal for the Co-operative Sand. You knew that the sand of Earth will follow the Obedient Sand. They both came from the original source when this star system was created."

"There's more, Jove." Wisdom says. "You need to listen to me. You must carry out the rest of the plan exactly. This is all for your benefit – for the good of all."

I'm listening.

"You will go back to Jupiter. Inform the Knowers that you have prevailed, that the Mission Steward chose to die rather than continue his murderous assault. You've saved the LittleNoisyBluePearl from not only his destructive plans, but that of the humans' own unwitting self-annihilation. But, there are more Prawl-Tang on the way from Alnitak. They will avenge the Mission Steward unless they are stopped. You need the help of the Jovians to defeat them. You need their Sand. The Sand in orbit around Jupiter, in the rings, Jove, it is all Obedient Sand. There is approximately one hundred trillion metric tons of the Sand in the rings. It's yours to use as necessary to prevent the Prawl-Tang from ever harming anyone again—"

"I thought that was what the nukes were for."

"Yes, as required," Wisdom explains. "Use whatever you need to end the Scourge, Jove. Then, whatever is left is yours to use, or keep or give away. But you must first go to the Jovians, to bargain with them. Then, the Sand will be yours. All of it.”

“I understand,” I say. “But aren’t the rings of Jupiter made up of the soul-stones of the deceased Knowers? Don’t you find that the least bit sacrili—?”

“After you have the bargain with the Knowers, use the Scoop to take some more of the Sand to protect your ship and the Prawl-Tang vessel. Then, you’ll go to the TransWave Aperture you disabled. The Navigation Onus can repair it easily. Employ the Wave to travel to Alnitak. Destroy the ships around their planet first, the Guardians and the Interceptors; they’re the most dangerous to you. Do not fire upon their apertures yet. Then, attack the planet from high above. Drop all of the humans’ war machines upon it; you will continue until it is devoid of life. When the Prawl-Tang in the far reaches of the Orion Arm return to defend their planet, destroy them all as they are released from the TransWave. You will finish them for what they have done to this realm, Jove.”

If I ignore sanity, all this makes perfect sense. I’m convinced of one thing: if this Wisdom truly is inside of all beings, guiding them, then that would explain all the misery throughout the history of the galaxy. She is one mean b—

“When the last of the Prawl-Tang emerge from the TransWave,” she says, “your Navigation Onus is to disable the apertures so that no one can ever travel into the radiation zone of the dead planet. Once you‘ve completed your mission there, return to Jupiter’s aperture, to receive a hero’s welcome.”

During the five day journey from Earth to Jupiter, Elmyrah and I work together with the Navigation Onus to construct a secure seat for a nine-year-old alien-human hybrid. While my tactical brain handles the assembly of widgets, my diplomatic side works up a convincing argument to have with the Navigation Onus, about why it should aid me in the obliteration of its home-world. The trick will be to not destroy every Super Scoop, as I'll need them later.

Upon our arrival at Jupiter, the gullible cephalids are easy to convince. I'm not sure they even comprehend what it is they're giving away. But they're safe again. No harm will come to them. They can go back to their quiet lives of watching the stars and snatching twenty meter long helio-salmon for a meal.

On the way down to the South Pole to find the Aperture, I have the Navigation Onus practice a few passes through the rings, to swallow up great quantities of Obedient Sand; storing it in the space not already taken up by the nuclear missiles and bombs. The damage to the TransWave device proves to be a minor inconvenience.

The look on Elmyrah's face is priceless when the long flagello-meric cilia reach out to grab hold of 'the extraneous object' that had melted itself into the emitter sockets, shorting out the aperture. With a careless toss, the worm-like tentacle from the Scoop's vent flings the toasty remains of Jove Number Four. It tumbles past the Equus bridge windows.

"Hey, I know that guy!" she squeals. It was worth the electrocution just to hear her laugh. Hoisted up into her new seat next to the pilot's bama, she can look me in the eye, without me having to squat or bend where I wasn't meant to.

"Elmyrah," I say, "for us to have found each other, and that I could bring you to Jupiter as you had hoped, is beyond any wish for—for someone like me. And I promise we'll come back soon. Your own planet is safe now, too, and one day we'll return and be welcomed. Today, we're about to begin a dangerous mission together. We must go where the Prawl-Tang come from and stop them from ever coming here. It'll be scary…for me, as well. But it is our duty to save the Jovians and the people of Earth. Remember, I won't leave you."

"I'm not scared, Daddy," she says, eyes wide.

"I brought you a gift," I tell her, "someone to keep you company while I'm busy; someone to hug tight during—if you do get scared."

From the folds of my cloak, I remove a small stuffed toy bear. She hums past her darling smile, grabs it from me, and squishes it under her little purple chin.

"Oh! He's adorable! I love him!" she giggles. "Can I have him? It is for me?"

"Well of course, silly. Who else would I get him for?"

She holds the fuzzy inanimate creature up close to her face and stares deeply into the plastic eyes. "What should I name him?" she asks. "I know, I'll name him Uncle Hatim. Good evening, Uncle Hatim! Shall we go up to the roof and sight in on Alnitak? I hear The Hunter is about to lose a button on his Belt!"

I wonder what she means by that.

"Mission Steward calls to Navigation Onus," I say.

"Secure-link with external input Mission Steward registered."

"Maintain station keeping while the Equus joins with $\Omega94\lambda25\theta$."

"Station keeping," it complies.

Using every available report, textbook database and scribbled note about the Prawl-Tang to draw from, I devise a new mission charter for my dear, hijacked Navigation Onus. I convince it to delete all previous mission parameters, and the first order of business is to change the name of this flying lump of coral to something more easily pronounceable than $\Omega94\lambda25\theta$. From this moment on, the Super Scoop would be mine to captain, with the permanently installed navigation organ as the pilot of the soon to be christened Emrah. The original charter was aptly stated as 'Save the Children of Alnitak'. With a stroke of the intramental pen, that's edited to 'Save the Children of Earth'. Now with the massive vessel, along with its vast atomic and biologic weapons payload under my control, I dictate the plan and how it's to be executed: to enter the Alnitak star system, prepare all Earth Spear for target acquisition, maintain loaded launch pylons, and to locate and destroy all Prawl-Tang Interceptors and orbiting planetary defense satellites and craft. After a brief argument from it, that as a Prawl-Tang construct, its operational parameters prohibit actions contrary to the Omega Species, it merely needed some reassurance from the new Mission Steward.

"Mission parameters will not require contrary actions," I say, "all directives shall branch from new mission charter."

Now mine, Navigation Onus agrees. "Mission parameters are no longer contrary. Prawl-Tang assault craft to be destroyed."

"Navigation Onus Emrah to secure-link as registered external input for all harvest vessels. Emrah will assume assignment as Mission Steward for all Prawl-Tang vessels. All secondary Navigation Onus will comply or be destroyed. All Prawl-Tang key transmissions contrary to new mission parameters are to be considered registered subversions."

"Emrah assigned as Multi-Fleet Primary Navigation Onus and Mission Steward," it says. "Non-compliant vessels targeted. Request mission parameter action for non-compliant mission stewards."

"Deactivation of biologic support for non-compliant mission stewards."

"Biologic support termination order prepared for transmission to all Secondary Navigation Onus," it says.

"Organize multi-fleet under Emrah sub-designations for redeployment to Sol system for harvest of PB5 rings and all silicates of PB3. End mission parameters."

"Prawl-Tang Main Mission Charter: Save the Children of Earth is accepted," it declares, "Emrah ready. Earth Spear ready. Awaiting target."

"Activate TransWave drive."

"Energy levels at maximum," it states. "Velocity to maximum."

"Signal Alnitak aperture." Using my mind to control the Sand, I accelerate the combined vessels toward the Prawl-Tang star system, where my gruesome chore awaits me.

"Aperture signaled," Navigation Onus says. "Key accepted. TransWave tip approaching with lock to Emrah."

With the Equus fused by many tons of impenetrable Obedient Sand to the stern of the Super Scoop, the massive homologation of interstellar transportation is enveloped by the sheet of sub-space plasma. Knowledgebase can provide full detail of the theory and mechanics behind the operation of this breathtaking experience, but words fail to articulate the sensations encountered when the many light-years to the destination are reeled in to a few thousand kilometers of compressed emptiness. We emerge from one of several apertures orbiting the blood red sphere.

"Uh…wow!" Elmyrah says. "That was crazy. Can we do it again?"

I look down at her face, the amazement. I hope she doesn't lose too much of her innocence in the coming hours. I would rather she never knew what it was that must be done.

Immediately, the Navigation Onus brings the Scoop around into a dive toward the planet. We pick up speed as we set a course for the defense perimeter. At my direction, the Navigation Onus locks onto the first of the Guardians far below. It's a large orbiting satellite that is heavily armed and shielded against attack from the roto-laser cannons of the Legion of Worlds. It'll have no chance against a thermonuclear detonation near its surface.

From deep within me, I hear the voices again, the recitations: "No Brother shall cause the death of another person." And again, "Where life is of less value than death, evil reigns."

A wave of dizziness passes over me. If not secured by the bama's railing, my knees would buckle. I strain to focus as the first Guardian passes below, almost out of range.

There's no mental door to shut against the ancient thoughts that well up inside me.

"War and violence shall not be found among the Brotherhood." "No act of violence will be permitted..." "If you find your hand holds a weapon, is it better to cut off the hand." "The Knowledge of Good and Evil leads to the inward path of self. The self may choose rightly, but when all Good is completed, only Evil remains to be served."

I look up to the surface of the truth. I'm drowning in it. It's a cold lake of reality that seeks to suffocate my soul.

"Jove," calls Wisdom, "I am here with you. I will help you do this."

I cry out from the shadowy gel of my failing SynThinker. "Please, please just leave me alone. I don't want to do this. Just give me some peace."

"Just give me your hand," she says. I reach forward, with my eyes still closed. I feel the warmth of another, skin, blood. It's Elmyrah, not Wisdom. She's holding my hand, comforting me. She pulls my hand closer to the weapons control console. The sudden sensation of the cold metal buttons at my fingertips startles me.

"I'm with you, Jove," she says. I open my eyes to look over at her beautific, child's face. She shouldn't be doing this. "We can do this, together," she says, her lips not moving. I hear her in my mind. "It must be done."

She sounds more and more like Wisdom all the time.

Navigation Onus veers away from the first target I've missed. I can only stare at her. Her little brow furrows. Her eyes are at once alive and deadly. I've never seen her with such murderous determination on her face. The muscles in her tiny hand flex and grip mine as she readies my finger over the Fire button.

The Scoop ship rolls around in a violent maneuver, incredibly agile for such a behemoth. Elmyrah strains to remain upright against the force. Without so much as a glance back in my direction, she leans forward, like a predator, the pounce imminent. Her lower lip curls in, the teeth biting down. Eyes fixed.

The spring under the button presses up against my finger...or did I push it down?

From out of the mouth of the Scoop, a long missile traces a bright path down to the orbiting Guardian. There's no sound, just the flash as the atomic warhead ignites. The Prawl-Tang satellite collapses under the shockwave. It spins about, burning, disintegrating. We accelerate to the next.

"Wisdom," I call, "she shouldn't be doing this."

"Why shouldn't she? She's a survivor, Jove. Besides, she's got some anger to let go of. This will be good for her."

It will be good for her. To commit murder, genocide, will be good for her. Wisdom is insane. And she's inside of Elmyrah, controlling, manipulating.

Four more Guardians are melted, turned to cinders in space. A handful of their interceptor craft attempt to attack from behind us. They are dispatched with a single waiting bomb that is left for them. No ship could evade a nuclear blast at that range. They were vaporized in a moment.

The Guardians let loose with every tracking spear they possess. Our Navigation Onus merely redirects them, or sends a remote command to deactivate their twin plasma blades. They bounce harmlessly off the dense coat of Obedient Sand layered over the ships. We are unstoppable.

This isn't war. This is brutality, of a race of beings that are trying to save their dying planet, their suffering children. War was the Archive Vision of the end of the Synthetics' struggle to exist among those of the blood. The deception worked. It was just. The enemy died. We survived. But we didn't massacre them all. We only fought back.

This is different. This is wrong in so many ways.

It takes a long time to destroy every Guardian satellite, every interceptor. But finally, they're gone. The TransWave apertures are dark, idle. There's no one left to bring home to defend their home world.

Elmyrah guides us down to the planet for the next phase of this nightmare. Elmyrah, my perfect girl, is a killer. But then, she is part Prawl-Tang. I had tried to forget that.

I want nothing to do with this…death. Not just death, but Death, the angel itself, personified. He's come to a planet, and we, like fools, have escorted him. The buttons below me rattle with the barrage. One after another, hundreds, thousands of the Earth's atomic missiles are sent down to the surface of the planet.

I close…everything, eyes, ears, thoughts, anything that might connect me to this horrid experience.

"You should see this," she says.

"Get out of my head."

"You first." Laughter. She's laughing at me.

I escape to another Archive Vision. It too, is of death. At least, it's one that can be reconciled with.

Tears
2960 BCE
Anchorsut Township

I, Payl, am the next in line to see the Man. He is no longer speaking to me. His voice is gone. Only the recordings of Fonmet play in my created, synthetic mind. I step forward in deference, as did the others ahead of me. As I approach his casket, I see the Man, my face on his, the same nose and shape of mouth, my Fonmet. He is my Only. I am his replica, his One. The natural tension of his muscles beneath the skin has faded. The smile is…artificial, more like mine, now. Touching the flesh of his hand, I find it cool and unresponsive. He's not in here anymore. I have spent my entire life with the Man. He was the first face I saw when I awoke from the nothing place. I could feel his life within him then. He is not in this box. He is not in this room full of people and their tears. He has walked out of Anchorsut, leaving his tracks forever in the sand.

"He treasured you, you know." It's the voice of his espoused female, whispered into my ear. I turn to look directly at her, as she rests her small blue hand on my shoulder. "You were his dream. You brought his dreams to life – *real life*, Payl. You became so much more than his books, his drawings, his theories, his hopes for us all, to somehow live on past the…past the coming of the end."

"I forgot—I forgot—" my thoughts are mixed with feelings. It is inefficient.

"What could *you* possibly forget, Payl?" she asks. She flashes her big smile that I like so much.

I look back at his still face.

"It never occurred to me, that I should thank him for *me*."

Her eyes bloodshot, minute capillaries strain with fluid. Tears cascade over the edge, to spill down her cheeks. The clear drops shatter against the black satin scarf.

"I forgot the same thing, Payl, to thank him for my time as his wife. He was very good to me, though he spent much time alone, working in his lab, building you."

"May I call you by your name today, Shuell?" I ask.

She tries to stifle a laugh with her palm. "I've been trying to get you to call me that for forty years, Dummy! You wait till now?"

"He used to call me Dummy sometimes."

She caresses my neck with her warmth, softness. "My dear Payl, he called you that at least once a day since you first sat up and whacked your forehead on the lamp over the cloning lab table. Don't you remember?"

"Those first days are a little fuzzy," I say. She nods understanding.

"His friends and colleagues are each going to the podium to give a eulogy for him. Would you please say something to everyone… about how you feel today?"

At my turn, I do.

"Hello, my name is Payl. Most of you already know who I am." I pause to look around at the fallen faces, sniffles and watery eyes. I catch the gaze of Tal, the girl next door who found me lost in the dunes. She's now a grown woman with a child of her own. I smile and acknowledge her with a wink.

"It's safe to say that I have a unique perspective of the Man. A few of you may have been blessed to know the secret thoughts and hopes that he might have shared. The majority of you only saw him on the outside, the external Fonmet. He was precise, quick, sharp-tongued, elusive, and pensive. He was 'up in his head' a lot of the time. I was in there with him. You see, I stand before you, the em-bodiment of the internal Fonmet. I am the sum total of all that he thought about, day and night. What you see when you behold my outside shell, came from inside the Man.

When it was first announced to the people of your planet, that the astrophysicists predicted Sirius B will...come too close, Fonmet understood how grave the situation was. He knew then that there was no way to carry all of you to safety. There's no place to go.

"That night, as he held his dearest Shuell in his arms, he won-dered if there couldn't be a way to protect the essence of who you are, a method to encapsulate the reality of your species. It had to survive the astral storm, the inevitability for this planet. We felt the beginnings of it this summer. Next year there will be real loss of life. The year after that, who knows who...or what...will be left?

"Today, we mourn the loss of the one who dared to dream of a person who could weather this coming storm, who could make it through the Five Years of Fire. One down, four to go. I can tell you that I have successfully passed all the tests, all of the physical tests, anyway. I can function normally at a sustained nine hundred degrees Celsius. I require no water. My skin is photovoltaic. If you stay at the Yojbum table long enough, I will win all your money. I can do this.

"But, inside of this person before you, is the heart of Fonmet. He cared for you so much more than he was capable of expressing personally.

"When the doctors informed him that he would die of cancer be-fore…it seemed such a cruel joke. While the rest of you were weeping at the pending doom of this planet, the terrible heat, the truth that there is little time left; the Man cried out that the time he needed to complete…me…was stolen from him. He did not reject his mortality. He refused to accept that you might not go on living inside of Payl. He could have spent these last days curled up with his family, to enjoy every precious moment. Instead, he forsook even sleep, to write Knowledgebase, Wisdom, and my programming. They exist for you. I exist for you. For the past forty years, I have recorded ever single breath that any of you take, every word uttered, every kiss, each and every birth, each and every passing. You will not be forgotten. Let the Man, Fonmet, not be forgotten today."

The barely perceptible nod from Shuell is reassurance of my saying all there was to say. I avoid the chairs and walk out the back of the hall, to leave all of the sobbing humanoids with their sentimental, mammalian grief. At the exit sign, I push the door open a little too hard and it bangs loudly against the wall.

It *is* a cruel joke. But the joke is on *me*. I feel so…what…what is that? Perhaps if an aggressive Tyrcanid sunk its fangs into my throat, it should feel like this. But it's just me and my imaginary thoughts of days that will never come. Who has it worse, the humanoid children that will perish, never to live out their lives, or the artificial child, who will live on for thousands of years, apart from his family?

A tug on the hem of my tunic brings me back to the reality of the funeral parlor and the crunchy, dried grass underfoot. The face looks familiar. She is Tal Kenfeld's young daughter.

"Hello, Clone Guy," she says.

"What's your name, my dear?"

She smiles up at me with two front teeth missing. "My name is Thendrial. My mommy said it was okay if I came out to see if you were okay."

"Did she send you out to rescue me?"

"Yup, she said you looked like you would cry if you could. It's cuz your daddy died."

"I'm glad you did," I say.

More hem tugging must verify that I'm still listening. "My mommy said that she saved you once, from walking into oblivion."

I have to laugh at that. "In fact, I *was* fully oblivious when your mommy found me, yes." In the small blue face, I notice a yellow reflection in her upturned eyes. She points past me with a stubby finger toward the pink sky.

"Clone Guy? Do you ever look at the clouds to see what they could be?"

"All the time, actually," I say. "Why? What do you see, my dear Thendrial?"

"Hmmm," she replies, "I thought I saw a bunch of sea-stars. But then, the wind came and just blew them all away."

Note to Self

I wish that I was anybody else.

Jove

Possession
2470 CE
Lupus' KeKouan

"Greetings, O Princes N'kaa and L'seer. Thank you for welcoming us to your magnificent palace on your home-world of KeKouan. I am humbled to be your guest."

The twin princes will not speak to me, an off-worlder. It would be considered impolite in their culture, though they are otherwise quite hospitable and gracious. I have arrived to show off my magic from the Sol system – one liter of Obedient Sand, and two of Cooperative Sand. Just enough to thrill them; to blind them with the amazing gravity-defying dance of a hundred shining crystals; to whet their appetite for more Sand, and more and more. They can never get enough. No one can ever have enough of the Sand.

With expert control, Elmyrah dances to music we had prearranged for the princes' court minstrels to learn and play during our display. The sparkling white crystals converge around her. They spin and bounce along to the rhythm. Folded at the waist she reaches down to the floor where she has poured out the Cooperative Sand of Earth, then entices it to rise up into the air around her. Like a vapor thin veil it hangs in space above and all around her. Everyone in the court is entranced by her masterful art and precise articulation of the millions of minute grains. In her final display, she twirls herself, wrapped up in a sheet of the fine reddish-brown silica, as the Obedient Sand presses into her torso, it exerts pressure and lifts her up into the air at her silent command. Her performance is astounding. The entire audience is rapt. At the last note of the musical accompaniment, she releases control over all the grains, to fall with them to the glassy floor, her body hidden under the gleaming chromium-fibre cape. The crowd erupts with cheers, bells and applause.

She's done it again. By the end of the day, every single person in the palace will place an order. Then, there are the training classes for how someone can get it to do more than spin in your hand or accidentally cleave your enemy's skull - with the accompanying fees, of course.

As I explain the terms and conditions of a large quantity sale to the princes' official administrator, I'm distracted to notice Elmyrah speaking to a boy. He's perhaps a few years older, quite handsome and obviously well-cared for. He's likely the child of someone important in the Court. His bronze skin and golden hair are accentuated by his immaculate attire: pure white linen jacket and pants, with artfully decorated, diamond epaulets and cuffs. My daughter is quite taken with him as they chat about something; both leaned against a solid gold pillar behind a curtain.

"Jove," Wisdom calls, "There is something I need to discuss with you."

Always interrupting. "Yes, Wisdom, what is it now?"

"It's been over four hundred years, Jove," Wisdom says. "Don't you think you've made her wait long enough?"

"Wait for what? She has everything anyone could possibly desire," I argue, knowing full well that I intend to skirt the issue.

"Her dream of a brother, Jove; she told you of her dream so long ago, but you ignore her. Don't you think it's unfair?"

Frustrated, I excuse myself from negotiations with the KeKouan administrator. "I'm busy now. Leave me alone! She is *fine* with-out—"

"She is *not fine!*" Wisdom says. "She's lonely. Is it so wrong that she have a sibling - a brother to share the endless time with? Stop being so selfish."

My mind's getting cloudy again. Every time, it's the same. She nags and argues and confronts me about something – everything. I'll get dizzy. My SynThinker will fail. When I wake up, I am either mentally imprisoned or I'd died and am the next clone in the series. Wisdom has become destructive to my very being. She's no longer my helper, my guide. She is my poison. Lately, whenever Elmyrah wants something, Wisdom intrudes upon my mind, pushing… always pushing. The girl gets whatever she wants.

"Alright." I say a bit too loud. "Alright. She can have a—"

"Wouldn't you like to have a son, Jove?"

A son? I suppose a brother for Elmyrah would make a son for me. No Union Brother has ever had a son. I would be the first. That would be special. We could be a family.

Wisdom has a plan. Wisdom always has a plan.

"Invite the boy to see your ship, your marvelous new ship. His parents won't mind. Let her show him how wonderful Abandon is. Elmyrah will give you one of her 'pop your head off' hugs, you know."

"Alright, just—will you please be quiet? Give me some peace. Give me some rest from this awful, constant haranguing you do to me."

"Daddy?" Elmyrah says. She has skipped up to me, the boy in tow. "This is my new friend, Ixian. I told him that I would introduce him to my beloved Daddy, the great Jove, the savior of Jupiter and Earth, the victor over the evil Prawl-Tang, and keeper of the Sand."

Well, that was a mouthful. She's certainly bent on impressing the young man.

"It is a pleasure to meet you, Ixian. Did you enjoy Elmyrah's dance earlier?"

"Oh, yes, Sir." he replies. "Your daughter is so talented. She had the whole of the Court absolutely spellbound."

Yes, as she does you, my fine boy.

"Elmyrah, I have an idea," I say. "Why don't you have Ixian ask his parents if we can give him a tour of Abandon; maybe even take him for a quick flight around KeKouan. I'm sure he would like that, don't you think?"

"Oh, yes, Daddy!" she squeals. "That will be so awesome."

As the two of them run off to get permission, I try to get my head back around the day's business dealings. So far, seventy-five metric tons of Obedient Sand, with the Cooperative Sand catching up; that's a good haul for the first hour.

"You are a good father, Jove," Wisdom tells me.

"I am an interstellar miscreant without conscience and you are a liar."

Gemmie receives clearance from the palace port guard. Zhong-Un performs a showy three hundred sixty degree spiral lift-off, then heads us off in the direction of the planet's north magnetic pole, where the intensity of the field would make tracking Abandon extremely difficult.

This is madness. I cannot reason within myself how this could be anything but outright kidnapping. It's not like the situation with my daughter; she was practically an orphan. Her foster family likely didn't care, and anyway, she was dead. Nobody cares if a dead person ends up as someone else's child. They're forgotten. It's all better this way.

"Jove," says my poison.

"I took the boy. What now?"

"Thank you for giving him a loving sister and a family."

"You call this love?" I say through my teeth. "I doubt either of us has learned what that truly is. Love is a gift. Love is giving. We've done nothing but take, from every planet we can possibly reach, we've taken something from them."

"Jove, you really should rest. You work too hard. All these centuries you've strived to build your personal empire, and you've succeeded. Does any one person have the freedom and the wealth of Jove Number Fourteen, of the Manufactured Flesh and SynThinker Union? Surely not - you are a king."

"The king has nothing more than mountains of silica as his subjects," I remind her. "And the Union – my *Brothers* – they won't even speak to me. I'm a curse to them."

"You don't need them. You have your adoring daughter, and now…a son, Jove. Isn't that wonderful?"

"Get out of my head."

The dizziness starts again. My vision begins to fog.

I've got to put a stop to this. How can I just let this happen – let this innocent young man be stolen from everything he knows – to what? To roam the stars with us? To sell magic sand that we shamelessly embezzled from the humans of Earth and the Knowers of Jupiter?

I try to stand up from the pile of pillows that my darling daughter assembled for me in my quarters, but that feeling…that same feeling, of my mind being pushed against a wall, smothered, saps my strength and I fall down flat on my back.

"Jove," Wisdom says, "I know what you're thinking. You don't want to do that."

Elmyrah walks through the doorway. She is slow, deliberate, walking up to me; kneeling down beside me on the floor. I can see her mouth moving but Wisdom keeps at me, she never shuts up. I can't hear my perfect girl. She's so perfect. I try hard to understand her. I can't hear her over the other voice.

"I know this was hard for you. You're worried about repercussions. And there may very well be, but you will deal with them as they come; as you have before; as we have before. You've always done very well for yourself, Jove, even without my help. And together, we've overcome all obstacles to greatness. I must admit, it has been these inner walls – the ancient walls – that have proven the most stubborn for us. At first, it was difficult for me to guide you along the right path, because of the pain being so fresh and because I had not forgiven you. But once I was able to come to terms with who you are and your existence, and my own existence, then everything became clear to me. I realized what it was – the path to forgiveness. Maybe not both of us at once, but you'll get there. I've made it there for you, for those times, for those things you did…

"When you discovered my parents alive and never told me; when you ordered the kidnapping of my family, sending them back to prison; when you had my brother Abdallah arrested and then later killed; those horrible visions of Tierney's death and Damien's thoughts of his wife's infidelity; when your incompetence caused me to asphyxiate; when you had that heartless cloning machine tear me out of my rest and change me into this…this….monster.

"But, I want you to know, Daddy, I forgive you. I'm willing to put all that behind us. Now, I will give you what you've been asking for - peace of mind and quiet. I'll leave you alone, for a while.

"Daddy, can you hear me? Do you understand what I'm saying?"

She snaps her fingers in front of my face, looks frustrated with me. Oh, now my beautiful Elmyrah holds my face in her tiny, cupped hands and kisses me softly on the tip of my nose. She adores me so.

"I'm going up to the front cabin where my new brother, Ixian, is watching the stars." Elmyrah stands and looks over her shoulder. That little ripple along her jaw is tensing up again. "There is something I need to discuss with him."

End

Thanks for reading my book. Please check out the Wisdom page on Goodreads and post a review. Stop by my Goodreads author page to drop a note or ask a question. Go to www.patricktylee.com to see what else I'm up to.

- Patrick

www.ingramcontent.com/pod-product-compliance
Lightning Source LLC
Chambersburg PA
CBHW030934020726
47498CB00001B/237